I0758338

ISBN: 979-8-9900569-2-3

Cover art by Cecily Trout

Cover and book design by
Render design + publications
renderpublications.com

I Am Danvers

Kate Kaminski

For Betsy with all my love.
And for Mrs. D., my muse, with my deepest thanks.

PROLOGUE

At the end, it's all ashes.

I have set something in motion that cannot be stopped, and now it will all come tumbling down. I will destroy their peace, those two who have made a mockery of everything. I will raze the place where I have spent the happiest, most complete moments of my life because this house cannot contain my hatred. My bones demand retribution. Manderley must be sanctified by pure fire.

There is enough fuel in all its precious contents to accomplish my mission of complete annihilation, and each priceless, hand-bound first edition will help spread my message of purification. Old houses have faulty wiring, and a well-stocked library soaked in a cellar full of one hundred proof spirits is a goddamn conflagration.

The gray light of this dreary day falls through the library windows as I finish making my pyre. It is not a small irony that the last book to be laid is a leather-bound first edition of *Frankenstein*. Rare things don't last forever, do they, Mr. Maxim de Winter?

I've brought six bottles of his favorite single malt to get things going. Another irony. Westerfield loved Arthur Patten's finest as much as he could love anything. Always echoes from the past, fateful decisions that have caused me nothing but trouble and sorrow … as they say. Manderley will take Westerfield with it into hell. I refuse to continue to carry this house. Or him. Nothing will come between me and her again.

Everything is in readiness, except for one last task.

I go to her room. Of course I want to be close to her, touch her things and set the room to right one last time. But still, I'm surprised to see her standing behind me when I look in the mirror.

There we are. *Us* again, as we were in the beginning. I can only hold myself together by wrapping my arms around myself.

I pick up her comb to smooth my hair. *Don't. I like it that way.*

I search the table. Red Madness. Scarlet Sensation. The one I'm looking for is missing.

In the right-hand drawer, Danny.

The gleaming gold of the tube is a bullet aimed at my heart, the way the lipstick itself has conformed to the shape of her perfect lips. Paradise Peach, a shade somewhere between fresh apricot and the deep pink of the tea roses that grow in the arbor.

Kiss me.

The velvety color bestows a kiss from beyond the grave. A benediction. And a goad.

I know she isn't really here. What a cheat. Danny's face in the mirror now. Danny, all that's left. Danny's lion's heart beating in my chest. Always there, always ready when I need her to guide my hands in some terrible and necessary task.

And what about the one who shall not be named? The one who thought she could replace a goddess. Oh, she will rue and be haunted. I've made sure of that. But *he* will need a special, everlasting gift. A reminder of what he lost before he even knew he lost it.

An envelope will arrive tomorrow, general delivery, for Mr. and Mrs. Maxim de Winter. Inside, a letter written in her handwriting. Her words flowing from my pen. A confession. The story of her one and only great love, the one she waited years for, who brought her the most happiness, the one who served, worshiped at her altar, gave everything of herself, would have given her lifeblood so that she would know she was loved.

It is a reckoning and it's coming for him.

We were meant to live. She and I. Us. Entwined forever and ever.

That is not what happened. That is why we're here.

It's time, Danny.

Back downstairs, I crack open the first bottle. By the time I've opened the sixth I could get drunk on the fumes alone. When I empty that last bottle, I toss it on top and lick sticky liquor off my fingers.

I've stood at this very precipice, jumped and survived. I'll happily burn it all down for love. But I need you to know that survival isn't a guarantee of happiness, it's only a promise that you'll suffer.

I take one last look. She lounges in the doorway, a slight smile on her lips, a necklace of heavy gold encircling her lovely throat. When she lifts a hand in farewell, I turn away. Once something is set in motion, it cannot be stopped.

I strike the match.

Tumble down, you pile of rocks. Burn, my beloved. We will be together again soon.

PART ONE

HOW IT'S GOING

"Fuckin' twat!" Yuri bellows. "Fuckin' twat fuckin twat."

I want to tell him to shut up, but when you do that it sets him off and he starts shrieking, and then Mrs. Krawczyk will wake up early from her nap. I want to be anywhere else right now.

"Fuckin twat fat bastard fuckin twat shut up shut up."

Then he starts whistling. The pitch hurts my ears, but I'm afraid to go near him. And he's blocking the door. The last time I tried to get him to go sit across the room with what I thought was a gentle nudge with the feather duster, he attacked me—went for my head—and I had to go to Quick Care. The PA who glued the bloody wound Yuri had made on my scalp thought it was funny.

"Fuck you, Yuri," I say under my breath.

"Fat twat fat twat bastard!" he shrieks.

Whenever you think you've found a refuge, it almost always isn't. That's the lesson I fail to learn every time I get in over my head and have to reset. And so it is with Mrs. Krawczyk. On the one hand, we're hidden away in a staid but transitional neighborhood where most of the older folks couldn't afford someone like me to live-in. On the other hand, it's not exactly an executive-level position; in fact, it's more like paid companion who does the cleaning and simple meal preparation. But the pay isn't terrible, and there's little chance I'll accidentally run into anybody I knew from Winnetka.

For the most part, the old lady is sweet. She calls me Miss Dan, and she never complains. We get along, except for her blind spot about Yuri, who clearly hates me with an insane and focused passion. I return the sentiment. "You have to give him a chance to get to know you," Mrs. Krawczyk said when I came home with that bandage on my head. But Yuri knew me from the minute he laid his beady eyes on me. I'm Enemy Number One.

Finally, it seems Yuri has amused himself enough at my expense. He lets out four sharp chirps as he flies over to his specially made wooden perch. He gives me side eye while he settles his wings and preens his red tail feathers, fanning them out. Then he squawks and deposits an obscenely large green poop onto the fresh newspaper below.

Yuri was Mr. Krawczyk's best friend, and now the bird is Mrs. Krawczyk's responsibility and she takes her duty very seriously. She claims not to know why Yuri has such a foul mouth and a bad attitude, but I'm guessing Mr. Krawczyk was an asshole and Mr. and Mrs. quarreled a lot. Nevertheless, she's arranged for Yuri to be well cared for when she dies, since he'll likely outlive her by several years. In captivity African gray parrots can live to be sixty years old—I looked it up. It's going to be *fuckin twat* and *fat bastard* day in and day out for another thirty? That sounds like hell to me.

I roll up the shit-covered papers in Yuri's ornate oversized cage and shove them into a plastic garbage bag, spreading fresh newspaper on the bottom. Since the cage door is never closed except at night, he can come and go as he pleases, so I keep a close eye on him. We're both aware that he could decide at any minute that I don't have any business being near his cage.

"Don't look at me fuckin twat shut up fat bastard!" Yuri shrieks, bobbing his head and rocking on his perch.

I'm spreading a final layer of day-old *Chicago Sun-Times* on the bottom of the cage when my eye catches on a color photograph centered at the top of the Life and Culture section. A shot of five people standing in a group at the end of a long, white-walled gallery with paintings hung on both sides. I reach in and pull the section back out. The woman in the middle. She's tall, made taller by heels, chestnut hair pulled into a chic low chignon, wearing a form-fitting dress under an expensive-looking wool coat. Stiff-spined men in suits stand on either side of her as if guarding a precious jewel.

Cal Whitaker. Her face unchanged despite the ten years on and the style shift to "conservative chic." The text below the photo gives details about a private collection of rare Whistlers on a Midwestern tour. Schweigert Gallery, Arts District. Tomorrow, 6–8 p.m. And the show's art-loving sponsors (pictured above) will be there.

Cal is in Chicago.

Shut up fuckin twat shut up shut up shut up, Yuri shrieks.

I had looked her up after that last time I saw Ian, as one would. She hadn't been difficult to find then and she isn't now, a fact I find bitter and sweet simultaneously. Loads of photographs resulting from simple searches document the big, society wedding now almost ten years ago, and the high-society life since then. The famous couple, their London flat, the cavernous country home. Cal had moved with her husband to England following the honeymoon in Bali, had since established herself as a patron of the arts.

Following in Daddy Whitaker's footsteps, I suppose. I promised myself that was the end of it a long time ago. But Cal in Chicago? That is an irresistible temptation.

The next morning, I tell Mrs. Krawczyk I have a date for the evening, and when she assumes it's with a man, I don't correct her. She asks if I'm in the market for a boyfriend as if she's worried that I'll leave her, and I tell her it's not that kind of date.

"Well, what kind of date is it, then?" she asks, spooning pea soup into her mouth. Her red lipstick only emphasizes the deep crevices marching along her upper lip, but I give her credit for doing her hair and makeup even though she never leaves the house.

I tell her it's my cousin. That he's only in town for one night.

"Family is so important," Mrs. Krawczyk says, and from the other room Yuri shrieks, "Shut up fuckin twat fuckin fat bastard shut up!"

Mrs. Krawczyk smiles benignly and says, "Yuri's in rare form tonight, isn't he, Miss Dan? Just listen to him go!"

On the "L" I question my decision to wear Sugar's leather pants. *Wear the look, Danny, don't let it wear you.* My own words mock me.

I arrive after the first wave, so the gallery is already crowded. I stay at the edge of things because I want to see her before she sees me, but when it happens, I realize she wouldn't have noticed me even if I had walked into the room on stilts.

Cal is focused on the man who faces her. The man who looks unhappily back at her. He tries to turn away but she grabs his arm, digs her nails in. He swings around but she laughs, then says something that makes his eyes narrow. When she lets go, she pushes him with enough force to make him stumble back a step. A few people have noted this unseemly behavior. The man smiles tightly at those nosy Parkers and moves away through the crowd. Cal smirks and slinks away. I pass her, unrecognized, as she chats with a woman just outside the women's restroom.

One of the two stalls in the restroom is already occupied, and a girl stands at the sink touching up her lipstick. I catch her eye in the mirror as I pass and she smiles.

I go into the unoccupied stall and wait while the exit door opens then closes. The toilet in the stall next to me flushes. I glimpse sensible, low-heeled shoes and black slacks. The water goes on, goes off, the exit door opens, closes.

I quickly grab the roll of toilet paper from the stall I'm in and duck into the other stall just as the door opens. Heels tap across the floor. I get a whiff of her perfume, but I bend over to verify. Yes, it's her. The low-heeled Blahniks with a crystal decoration on each toe. I wait, listening to her pee, from my perch on the toilet. She whispers, "*Shit.*" Then aloud, "Hey … hello? Are you still here? The loo paper … can you help me, please?"

She speaks with a slight British accent. I spin off a big handful and hand it to her under the divider.

The diamond wedding set on her left ring finger. The husband's grandmother's diamond.

I leave the safety of the stall and go to the sink to wash my hands that aren't really dirty. I take my time. Finally, the toilet flushes. I put my head down and keep rinsing my rinsed hands. When she comes up beside me, she laughs.

"Isn't that always the way?" she says.

"What's that?" I say as she removes her rings, placing them on the counter between us.

"When you least expect it," she says. "The old crimson wave."

I watch her in the mirror while I give her a good, long look at me. *Surprise!* Slow-blinks as if she doesn't trust her eyes. "*Danny?*" Like she can't believe it, maybe isn't too happy about it. "What the hell are you doing here?"

She turns back to the sink to rinse her hands, calmly picks up her rings and slides them back onto her finger, puts a hand up to smooth a nonexistent stray hair.

I say, "Living that good-wife life, huh?"

She turns to face me. "You have no idea what you're talking about."

This act is annoying. "What's with the phony British accent?"

"Oh fuck off."

I have to laugh. "That's the Cal Whitaker I know. Do you still make your little monsters?"

She tilts her head, gives me a faint smile. "No … I gave that up." She looks away. "But I'm still a fucking mess."

I tell her the mess doesn't show, at least not on the outside.

"You left without saying goodbye," she says. "I'm not sure I can forgive you for that."

Of course we go right back to the beginning. We've been stuck there for years. It's comforting that she's been right there with me. I tell her I'm sorry. I tell her I had a good reason. She doesn't ask me what it was, and I get this frisson of joy, like maybe none of it matters anymore. We can let it go.

She takes in Sugar's leather pants. "You look different, Danny." Then she shrugs, pastes a fake smile on her face. "I don't go by Cal anymore," she says.

I tell her nobody calls me Danny but her.

She fiddles with those rings. "So why are you here? Tonight."

I could tell her the truth, but instead I say it must be a coincidence, that I spotted her earlier but I wasn't sure it was her until now.

Her upper lip curls. "It's mad that you're standing here in front of me," she says, giving me this shoulder hug and air kissing both my cheeks. She taps her phone awake and says she has to go. She's a little manic, searching in her handbag for something.

"Who's the guy?" I say. "It's not your husband."

She pauses with the mint she'd been searching for held between her fingers, then pops it into her mouth, coming close enough that I can smell the minty freshness of her breath. Her mouth is slightly open. Those vampire teeth peek out from behind her top lip.

"I want to see you again, but I can't do this right now. Get an encrypted phone number and text it to me here." Cal scribbles a string of numbers on a card and presses it into my hand. "Tomorrow."

I've told Mrs. Krawczyk that my cousin is having emotional problems so I have to meet him again. She tells me young people take themselves too seriously these days, but she doesn't complain that I'm taking another night off. She's watching *Monk* reruns, and I suppose she's got Yuri for company if she's desperate.

It's getting dark when my Uber drops me at Navy Pier. For this meeting I've chosen an all-black ensemble and I'm wearing my Blundstone boots. I want to feel powerful in this outfit, but I've got this shivery feeling in my gut. Something is going to happen with Cal tonight. Good or bad, we have met at this crossroad for a reason and I intend to go all in.

I haven't been here before, so I immediately understand why Cal has chosen it as our meeting place. It's crowded with tourists.

She is trying to blend with the milling crowds in her thousand-dollar jeans and Gucci off-the-shoulder sweater under that chic wool coat. But Cal Whitaker stands out, the way she always did no matter what she wore. Her hair looks good down. She has her hands shoved into her coat pockets.

We find a corner in a sports bar, quiet ahead of the evening drinkers. We order the same red wine.

I state the obvious. "This is strange."

And she says, "So strange."

We sip our wine, the silence between us so heavy that I get nervous. Maybe we don't have anything to say to each other after all that time apart. Finally, she says, "I forgive you. I've been thinking about it all night. I was a bit lost then, wasn't I."

It isn't a question so I don't protest. And if I could have explained fully, I would have. I tell her I'm glad. I tell her I'm sorry. Again.

"This is fate," Cal says. "Us meeting like that. I thought about you for so long, wanting to—" she stops. "And then I made myself stop doing that. There wasn't any point to it. I couldn't find you again, even if I'd wanted to. It's not like we were going to become Facebook friends." She laughs. "I did look for you on there. Do you know how many Marie Danverses there are?"

I say, *No, how many?* and she says, *Way too many, and none of them were you*, then she asks me what I've been up to and that's a pretty hot topic, so I tell her I'm a travel companion for a wealthy older lady who's in a wheelchair because of a heart condition. The old lady loves Dollywood and country music. I tell her it's fun, because it does sound like a job that would be more fun than what I'm really doing.

"It sounds … unbelievable."

I realize she's being ironic. She knows I'm lying. We both laugh.

"I'm so happy to see you, Danny," Cal says. "Really … it's like coming home. I don't ever want to go back to England."

I tell her, "You always seem to do things you don't want to do." Then she starts crying, but I know better than to try to comfort her. Cal is like me in that way. Animals like us lick their wounds in private. We scratch when people get too close.

"I'm unhappy," Cal sobs. "Terribly, horribly miserable."

Meeting Cal Whitaker again, the way that it happened, finding her ready to spill all the tea and confess her misery, it was coincidence and fate all rolled into one beautiful fantasy. The truth of either of our situations didn't matter.

Her confessions that she'd thought about me, that she'd actually looked for me, blasted whatever peace I had into ground glass. After that night Cal invaded my every thought, kept me prisoner to my phone. She texted day and night. I don't know when she slept. I sometimes fell asleep to the sound of her voice. So close. And safely far away.

I wanted to see her, obviously. Screens are unsatisfying. Words typed with clumsy intentions can be dangerous. Autocorrect is a real bitch. And to make it harder, she constantly hinted about me moving to England. What was holding me in the States? But I could too easily lose all sense of myself if I wasn't careful. She had that kind of hold on me, even if I didn't want her to.

I still had my Ten-Year Plan in place, in spite of this temporary derailment with Mrs. Krawczyk—and Yuri. I might have been stalled in a holding pattern, but I had every intention of changing that as soon as I could. I still believed in my plan. Maybe I'd finally face going to Vegas. No trouble there getting the kind of work I do.

Meanwhile, after seeing Cal again, I lost all fear of Yuri, and finally that bird stopped fucking with me. I mean, it was still *fuckin twat shut up dickhead* when he was awake, but he didn't try to kill me anymore. And Mrs. Krawczyk was as batty and agreeable as always. She decided to teach me canasta because she was tired of gin rummy, and would jokingly accuse me of cheating since I was the one who kept score. I let her win until she suggested we should play for money, then I only let her win some of the time. I don't know what other people call it, but I was happy. I thought I was safe.

Then, disaster. On a hot June day, poor Mrs. Krawczyk suffered a paralyzing stroke, and Yuri went silent. It was weird being there without her or Yuri's voice to stop me from rewinding all my mistakes, how I'd gone wrong from the moment I left Cal and the Whitakers behind.

I found Mrs. Krawczyk's will and saw where the situation was headed. It hadn't been enough time, but I didn't hold it against her. I still went to visit her in the rehab. She couldn't talk, but I saw *her* in there, behind those same filthy old spectacles. Unfortunately, she couldn't hold the cards anymore so we couldn't play canasta or gin rummy. I always felt empty and sad when I left, so after a week I stopped going.

Then one day Mrs. Krawczyk's niece Natalia showed up and went through the apartment and took notes on her iPad about her aunt's "valuables." She asked me what I was going to do about Yuri, and I told her Yuri wasn't my responsibility, and then she said she was going to let him go in the park, and I said if she did that I'd report her to the Humane Society. Natalia slammed out of there after that. And the next day a man identifying himself as Natalia's husband Phil came and told me I was fired.

I don't know what happened to Yuri. *Fuckin twat.*

3

I dream I'm there again in that miserable house. I wander from room to room where vines drape the doorways and sprout along the window edges, creeping across the floor and twining around the scarred wood of the banister. Strange, pallid flowers that don't need the light.

Those turning stairs. I have to feel my way up. The vines slither wetly below, following me. I'm afraid, but I go on … to Sugar's room, where the coverlet brushes the floor, fingers of fringe splayed. On the side table, the script left open. Raindrops cold as ice roll down my scalp, drip off the end of my nose. A gaping hole in the ceiling shows bright blue Los Angeles sky, not a cloud to be seen.

In the center of the bed a smear of red pigment undulates, a living thing. I put out a hand.

Not paint.

The dinner jacket's shredded inner lining marks a bloody wound.

The vines are busy pushing themselves up my calves, between my thighs, crawling under my clothes to reach my most private places. Hot-wired adrenaline floods my veins.

Welcome home. Where you belong.

Over the years I've learned some things about the Art that is spelled with a capital A, not the assembly line, small-a art of the sort they hang on the walls of this crap hotel. The most important thing to remember is that capital-A Art is worth what somebody is willing to pay for it, and some people will go to great lengths to own it.

Unscrupulous people have been known to sell forgeries of their Art in order to make money on it while also hoarding the real thing. A strange fetish, those subterranean locked rooms with their Warhol or their O'Keeffe or their Rembrandt. Audience of one.

The bottom line is that capital-A Art is only for the people who can afford it, the ones who need somebody like me to run things for them, make sure their flowers are fresh, their floors so clean they could eat off them, their refrigerator arranged in ordered rows. Whatever their kink, I'm their girl.

With Gregory Lahoud, a capital-A Art connoisseur, I found myself in a unique position to be helpful. A lifesaver even. Employers like Lahoud, the ones so busy they delegate unusual power to their staff, those employers are rare finds. Most of the time they are distrustful control freaks. By comparison Lahoud was a pussycat.

We were discussing his wardrobe for an upcoming business trip to Singapore. The weather there was expected to be hot and humid. (I had checked.) And, since he'd be going in and out of air-conditioning, I was reminding him we needed to pack transitional layers.

He slammed the *Phoenix Fine Art* magazine onto the coffee table with a sigh of disgust. "Whatever you think, Danvers," he said. "I trust you."

I asked if everything was all right.

Lahoud stared at me with tragic eyes. Had he gotten bad news about the family he rarely mentioned or saw?

"Gabriela Ogosto is having a show at Ataazaz. Downtown," he said. "While I'm in Singapore."

Now I understood. Gabriela Ogosto was a young Brazilian painter, an art sensation bursting onto the scene with large moody landscapes and vibrant street scenes, scooped up by an impressive roster of international museums. All the paintings were large-scale. All selling in the neighborhood of fifty thousand and up. Affordable. For now.

Lahoud was obsessed with Ogosto and hot to collect her, but she hadn't shown in the States. And now she would be right here in Phoenix and he had to miss it. He was emotional, like his best friend had died and he was obliged to miss the funeral.

I saw an opening and I took it. I told him I'd be more than happy to meet with the gallerist as his authorized representative. I guaranteed him a red dot.

"You?" He was surprised but he was also intrigued. Lahoud really wanted an Ogosto, and he was the type of person who generally got what he wanted. And he'd said it himself. He trusted me.

I made it sound as effortless as I assumed it would be. Galleries wanted to sell paintings. He wanted to buy. So before the show opened I'd arrange a meeting and get photos and a price list. He'd choose the one he wanted, and I'd arrange an immediate bank transfer. The painting would be marked sold in the catalogue, and I'd make sure it was hanging on the wall waiting for him when he returned.

He didn't think about it for more than a couple of seconds. "Okay, that's a good idea, Danvers. I like your thinking." He could already see an Ogosto adorning the living room wall. He smoothed his already-smooth hair and stood up. "I have to take a shower."

Fast-forward two weeks and now I need out of Phoenix. My recurring nightmares are back. Yesterday I could have sworn I saw somebody on the street that I knew a long time ago. But it wasn't him, because he's dead.

Plus, there is the possibility that Angela could still decide to sic the police on me for a frivolous misdemeanor fraud charge, even though Lahoud had gotten his Ogosto and the finder's fee refunded. Angela hated my guts, and my lizard brain told me she would come after me if I didn't do what she wanted.

I should have known when she jumped on the proposal without asking any questions. I may have been too distracted by her red hair and the tattoos to question it. These kinds of relationships usually took time to mature. People had to get used to the idea first. They think they could never do something like that, so it isn't a split-second decision. You had to bring them along slowly.

Angela and I had enjoyed a cordial, private walkthrough before I contacted Lahoud, during which I had outlined how she and I could scrape some cream off the top for ourselves without anybody knowing. I made sure to emphasize that nobody would be hurt. Lahoud would be out some money, but he would be happy to pay the price I was suggesting. He wanted that Ogosto that badly. And in a year, who knew what he could get for it at auction if he decided to sell? When I texted Lahoud photos (it was 9 a.m. in Singapore) he quickly chose *Jogando em um sonho* (Playing in a Dream), listed at $58,000.

I could see Angela's mind working on the scheme, trying to see where it could go wrong. But I was confident and patient and I could feel her bending toward my idea.

"And he won't ever find out we pushed the price to seventy-eight?" she said. I reassured her. How would he ever know, if you aren't telling and I'm not telling?

"So I put it in the book as sold privately with no price listed," Angela's eyes sparkled (I thought with greed). "Did I get it all straight, Marie?"

I suggested that she could pass at least some of the bonus to the artist if she liked.

And Angela had said, "Why would I do that?"

My stomach lurches at the memory. Fucking red hair. What a liar. The shitty motel coffee wants to come back up, so I go hang over the toilet bowl for a while. I hate puking, so I'm glad when it stays down. I notice the maids aren't cleaning under the rim, but I'm in no position to complain about standards being relaxed.

I supervised the hanging of *Jogando em um sonho* the day it arrived. For an artist who painted large-scale, this one was relatively small, a six-foot-square oil of two dark-skinned children kneeling on the street playing some kind of game with what look like rocks, the crowd around them bright dashes of movement. The artist had created a stillness surrounding the two kids, a beautiful, private world within the chaos of the street. I have to admit it was stunning. I was sure Lahoud was going to be grateful. I considered the possibility he might give me a raise or appoint me to look after all of his art dealings going forward.

I called Angela when the hangers left, but according to her assistant she was on another line. "She'll call you back," the girl told me and disconnected. I waited for two hours, three, four. She finally called just before five. I didn't have a clue anything was wrong. I was thinking maybe she would suggest we celebrate our windfall with a cocktail. But Angela said I needed to meet her at the gallery because it was *closed*. The way she said the word *closed* suggested to me that she was *open*. I dressed carefully.

An unfamiliar man sat on a folding chair just inside the locked door when I arrived. I tapped lightly on the glass to get his attention and he let me in. No smile. Bulge of handgun under his jacket. I told him I was there for a private meeting with Angela. I could feel his eyes on my back as I walked away. Yet, even then, I didn't suspect any trouble.

Angela was sitting at her desk when I walked in, busy with her cellphone. I sat down and asked if she wanted to see a shot of the Ogosto on the wall. She looked up, dead-eyeing me.

The thing is, at that point I still didn't have a clue. I mean, I felt the chill and I was surprised by the armed guard, but I wasn't thinking all-out disaster. I asked her what was wrong and it was like I unleashed the beast.

"I'll make this brief," Angela said, "and if you try to make a scene, I will have my friend out there escort you out."

I wasn't getting the money, fine … but the main thing was to keep myself from bolting out of there like I wanted to. Angela's *friend* was waiting in the lobby, and I wasn't sure what that meant. Would he stop me from leaving at gunpoint?

And the hits kept coming. Angela had talked to Lahoud. And naturally she had been videotaping our encounters. Look. Over there on the shelf. Smile for the blinking red light.

I warned her to be careful about insane accusations. Then she gave me the ultimatum. If I left Arizona, she would keep the police out of it. Like a tin-star sheriff in a western. Kicking me out of the state probably wasn't even legal.

I hate people like you, she said. *You're a leech.*

Arizona is a crappy place to live anyway. Not enough water.

4

For two days I stayed in my room, hung the Do Not Disturb card and ate hours of junk cable television and vending machine food. I reviewed all the should-haves and the what-ifs, but it always ended in the same result. My embarrassing defeat.

You may feel exhausted, anxious, lonely says the commercial, *but don't worry, take this pill and change your brain chemistry from sad to glad.* In my experience, all those drugs ever did was turn you into a compliant alien, but you were still an alien. No drug can change that.

On day three I made myself shower and initiate whatever this latest reset is going to be. But see? That's how luck can turn. I'd been bracing myself to endure worst-case scenarios: landing in Las Vegas and dealing with that mess. As far as I knew, Patty was still playing the slots hoping for a windfall that would never come and working as a barback lackey at the Excalibur. Luckily, I doubted my dad or any of my numerous stepdads were still on the scene. So Vegas might not be ideal, but if I had to I'd roll the dice on running into Patty. I have to go where the money is. What were the chances of that happening anyway?

What I didn't expect was the solution to my problem coming through my English friend. That was a surprise I never anticipated. So lucky me. I'll be arriving in merry old England in two days. I'll see *Cal* in two days. Forty-eight little hours between me and my destiny.

Some people want it all when they should be satisfied with the perfectly reasonable portion of luck they're allotted. When I think back, I may have, on occasion, mistaken good luck for bad and vice versa. I may have created my own kind of up-is-down and down-is-up world. I may have even acted in haste or hesitated and lost a golden opportunity. But now is the time to purge it all.

The trash bag holds things I once called treasure. If the last page of a screenplay is missing, that means there's no ending, doesn't it? Or maybe it means the ending was a dumb idea. Or take the neatly folded rectangles of silky lining: aren't they a trophy (of a bloodless death), a version of a deer head on the wall (and far less barbaric)?

A recriminatory letter is a stupid thing to keep. We say things, in the heat of anger. We might mean it at the time, but later we might regret being so final, cutting off all contact so cruelly.

But now I can stop carrying these worthless tokens. I can stop seeing a certain person's nasty face on some random stranger when I least expect it.

I reach for the leather pants, lay them across my lap, touch the faded bloodstain on the waistband. Sugar in those ridiculous Spanx, a Barbie doll, smooth and sexless.

Those pants had had a starring role one humid summer night in Chicago. A liaison with yet another unhappily married woman. Me sweating like a beast, both of us trying to take the damn pants off, her hands sliding down my legs to peel them off, only making me hotter.

The commercial ends. It's the last five minutes of *Murder, She Wrote*. I raise my glass to Jessica Fletcher. She's about to crack the case of the mayor's missing wife. At this point I'm assuming the mayor has killed his wife and buried her in their herb garden, his wife's pride and joy, but sometimes this show surprises me.

Maybe I could wear the pants one more time and then drop them in a trash can somewhere along Airport Boulevard. It's possible that clothing retains the memory of its wearer, and even holding them brings Sugar back, her flesh pressing hot against me. I can't imagine anybody else having them. Maybe I should mail them back to her, no return address. I try and fail to imagine what her face would look like when she opens the package.

I put the pants on the "maybe" pile and open my treasure box. On top is the heavy gold necklace nestled inside its blue velvet bag. This one is for my English friend. A gift for rescuing me. She will wear it and, when she does, she'll always think of me.

Oh, there it is. Sugar's phone number. The page torn from *People* fucking magazine, October 2019, stolen from my dentist's office. *Yes, You Can Actually Text These Celebs Right Now (& We Have Their Numbers!)* The inset text over a photograph of Sugar, with the red in her hair dialed up to eleven, says, *I love hearing from fans!* I could hardly be mistaken for a fan, but I could call her right now. If I wanted to.

Blame the bourbon for even *thinking* such a thing. The number won't work. It's a tease. A scam. And even if it is her number, she won't pick up. Sugar doesn't answer her own phone.

The impulse to do the very thing I shouldn't is always strongest at times like this. I can show a stubborn streak. I believe the shrinks refer to it as oppositional defiant.

It isn't her number, idiot. She won't answer.

So I punch in the numbers. It rings. Twice. Three times. Then … breathless pause … a man's voice, suspicious, sleepy: "Who's this?"

5

London, England

Mrs. de Winter has sent her chauffeur and her Mercedes to fetch me at Gatwick. The chauffeur is named Oscar. I don't think the Mercedes has a name, but if it did it would be Black Beauty.

Oscar is a good-looking, polite young man with immaculate grooming. He tells me Mrs. de Winter herself has planned the route from London to Cornwall, insisting I be given a driving tour of western England through every last one of the innumerable quaint hamlets, past Roman arches older than time, with a stop at Stonehenge to walk with the Druids.

Soon enough you'll be trapped here with the rest of us. You might as well get a feel for the country lifestyle.

My employers had no idea how eager I was to be trapped in the country with them. I welcomed days of monotonous sameness. Routine was exactly what I needed.

"The villages all look interchangeable," I say to the back of Oscar's head. "Shops, pubs, and cobblestones."

"Don't say that out loud on the high street, ma'am," Oscar chuckles. "And especially don't say that in a *pub*. Every village likes to think they have the corner on charm."

So far, Oscar has revealed that he is malleable and prone to gossip even without pressing too hard. He's also half-French, which accounts for the dropped *h*'s and emphatic *t*'s when he speaks. He is eager as a puppy to impress me.

Somewhere near a town called Bristol, Oscar says we're "almost there." I wish that meant something to me. I'm impatient to put my feet on solid ground, and I've had enough of look-alike villages. We are making a final stop for petrol and so Oscar can get another cup of tea, a beverage I haven't quite learned to love yet.

I have a walkabout while Oscar is occupied. Across the way is a curious, crumbling stone building perching at the top of a steep hill. It looks precariously balanced at the lip of a protruding ledge, its edges crumbled, nibbled away by relentless rain.

What are you trying to tell me, Danny?

Before I cross the road, I remember to first look right instead of left. The hill is steeper than it looks, and I have to pick my way through a tumble of moss-covered bricks from the building's collapsed chimney to get to the top. To be able to look inside the ruin, I put my head through what was once a window opening. Inside, crossed and blackened timbers slowly disintegrate into charcoal on a floor composed mainly of stone rubble.

On my way back to the car, I look up to wave at Oscar that I'm coming, and that's when I slip on wet rock and go down, right on my ass. It's a nasty jolt, but luckily my spine is cushioned by a thick coat and thicker moss. I'm up before Oscar can even get across the road. I wave away his concern, but it's an unnerving reminder. Gravity always prevails.

Back on the road, Oscar is solicitous—perhaps worried that I'll say he didn't look after me properly—but I do not enjoy people making a fuss, so I distract him by asking how he likes working for the de Winters and he tells me he likes it very much and that Mr. de Winter is a "good bloke."

The omission of any mention of Mrs. de Winter is an itch I have to scratch, so I ask him what he thinks of her, and he says she's *fine* and that he really only interacts with her when he takes her to London *to shop*. The way he says it sets off a jangling alarm of something left unsaid. So I tell him shopping isn't such a terrible vice, unless you're spending money you don't have. And … he clears his throat, glances at me in the rearview, and drops the bombshell.

"A few times, I picked her up at the Franklin," Oscar says. "The Franklin *Hotel,*" with another meaningful glance. "I don't like to gossip," he says.

I let the silence lengthen because he absolutely *does* like to gossip and I want him to know I'm ready for more.

"They argue," he says at last. Then, a little defensive. "It's no secret. Shelley—she's the day girl—she heard them rowing over some party or gala that they were invited to attend. Mrs. de Winter didn't want to go because— *she* said—all his friends are *boring and old and gross.* And then *he* said she probably thought the same about him. And she said, 'Yes, I do.'"

Oscar certainly has a good memory for juicy dialogue exchanges.

He shoots me this worried look. "You'll keep this between us, won't you, Mrs. Danvers?"

I tell him that he can always trust my discretion and that he should just call me Danvers.

Don't be fooled. Your secrets are not safe with us. Even nice young men like Oscar can't resist the temptation to share your deepest, darkest. That's tradition, part of the give-and-take among the upstairs and the downstairs. Everybody loves a scandalous story, and secrets are currency, sometimes literally. On the other hand, if we don't know you—*really* know you—how else can we serve your most intimate needs? You're in a bind. To trust or not to trust. Allowing us in is the risk you have to take, and the best of us will guard your secrets like our own. We'll keep it only in the family. Just us. I'm assuming you can guess which type I am.

Lulled by the motion of the car, the ambient music Oscar has selected, and the soft whoosh of the Mercedes's wheels, I close my eyes.

Yellow fence post teeth yellow dress. Say it, Danny. Say what you want. If you say it, we'll let you live …

"Ma'am?"

I sit bolt upright, heart pounding. What a horrible nightmare. Always Westerfield and his too-close-together eyes, his crooked, oversized teeth ready to take a bite of my flesh.

Oscar apologizes for waking me up and points ahead as the road begins to climb. "It's Manderley."

And then … I see it.

I'm here.

Finally.

Forget Sugar. Forget Westerfield. Ian is nothing more than vapor, only a sometimes fond memory. Like Danny herself.

I am Danvers now.

This is the future.

The stone manor house looms at the crest of the hill. Ancient and magnificent set in its wind-scoured, alien landscape. As the car picks up speed on the steep incline, the sun dips shyly behind the massive structure. It seems that Manderley eclipses even the brightest star. My heart knocks in anticipation. I can't take my eyes off of it.

And a voice whispers, *She's waiting for you, just like that other time. Remember?*

PART TWO

HOW IT STARTED

1

New York City: Ten Years Ago

"Blanton's? You sure?" Suze asked, her gravity-defying mohawk waving. "That's twenty bucks a shot, hon."

I laid two twenties on the bar, then added two more. "Make it a double, please."

Muttering about me robbing a bank, she moved off to pour my order.

Easy money was what my manager, Mike, had called it. But I had learned that his compliments about my work ethic and diligence weren't sincere, because he never offered those encouragements unless he needed me to do something he wasn't willing to do himself. And I generally obliged by extracting favors in exchange: particular shifts, unearned days off, and once, when my apartment was being fumigated (again), he let me stay in the presidential suite if I promised to make it look like I'd never been there. But what he wanted me to do tonight was definitely not part of my or anybody's job description at the Tower Arms.

"There was an incident and it needs to be cleaned up," Mike had said. And I'd laughed because I thought *how gross can it be.*

I noticed, then, the unnaturally stretched eyes like he was seeing something he couldn't unsee, the way his fingers trembled when he lighted his cigarette. Mike was a red-faced, beefy Irish guy, but his color was alarmingly gray.

"You're the only one I can trust with this, Marie," he said.

The alley was deserted, but he kept looking over his shoulder. I said I could fix the situation, whatever it was, for five thousand. I thought that amount was a reach, but when he didn't hesitate I knew I should have asked for more. He made me promise to keep my mouth shut, that it was required unless I wanted legal trouble. "And if you get caught, Marie, you go down by yourself," he'd said. "I'll make sure of that."

Suze dropped off my drink, started to turn away, then leaned her elbows on the bar top. "Are you okay?" Her cigarette-roughened voice held actual concern.

I assured her I was fine and she moved off to wait on other customers. I took a swallow of the bourbon, held it while I breathed the amber fumes. Head-clearing, rough-edge-smoothing bourbon. The five thousand had been a lifeline. That morning I had less than ten dollars in my bank account with payday still four days away. But I wasn't sure if bourbon was powerful enough to erase the images … or the smell. I took another sip, held it.

"Cheers," Suze was back, watching me with this seen-it-all expression. "You look like you really need that."

I held up my glass in a salute. What would she think if she knew what I'd spent the last five hours doing?

"It was a day," I said.

"I've had a few of those myself," Suze said.

I doubted that. I thought about the look on Mike's face when he handed me that stack of bills. Like he saw me in a new light. I was now *that girl*. Clean up on aisle five! Get Danny, she'll do it! Every time a well-known hotel guest "accidentally" stabbed their date and didn't want the police or the press to find out about it, Mike would call me. We were in it together now. And my new status would require renegotiating my "per incident" rates.

I felt rather than saw somebody slide onto the stool next to me. I swiveled my head and the man said, "Hi, Marie. Fancy meeting you here. What're you drinking?"

Ian St. Martin flashed his flashiest smile at Suze and ordered two more.

I asked him what he thought he was doing in a lesbian bar, which made him laugh. He told me he was collecting diverse experiences and said I looked lost, that I shouldn't have that worried crease between my eyebrows, the one that shows when I frown. He said I should ditch the polyester blazer because it didn't fit me properly. Ian wasn't shy about sharing his opinions. I already knew that.

I had first met Ian St. Martin the previous Wednesday at BUS, an art gallery in Chelsea. I was following some random redhead I'd noticed on the street. I only wanted to see where she was going. But the gallery event was an invitation-only thing, and I got into a tussle with The Gatekeeper, some woman—you know the type, the kind who wants to keep you out and only let the special ones in.

Ian St. Martin came to my rescue, so to speak. He even made The Gatekeeper apologize. "Next time offer a hundred," he told me later. He said I needed to understand the price of admission and be "in it to win it." I soon forgot about the redhead, and Ian and I got to talking while we looked at these photographs that were not at all anything special.

He was fine featured, older—maybe forty, but he could have been fifty. The creases at the corners of his eyes only made him more attractive. He was lean gold and wiry glitter with dark-wash denim eyes rimmed by the kind of eyelashes sometimes wasted on beautiful men.

In the beginning it was the usual chit-chat leading with mutual what-do-you-do's. Ian was something called an art advisor, and he'd come to this show because the photographer on display was about to "break." His job was to look for *new blood* and let his wealthy friends in on the secret while the artist's prices were still affordable. The smile, the obvious false modesty when he said he was *merely a facilitator.* I only half-believed most of what he said, but he had clearly zeroed right in on the dead-end nature of my situation. *You work at the Tower Arms? How awful.*

Before I'd had a chance to rebut his assessment and defend my career choices, he ran into somebody he knew, so he got carried off while I wound up going home alone after all, and having to walk an extra couple of miles because of that redhead.

It bothered me, him telling me I was lost. This bar was my turf, not his. He didn't know me, but he acted like he could see inside my head. I wanted to shock him, tell him I had just cleaned up a crime scene. I wanted him to know he shouldn't underestimate me. Besides, what was he doing here?

Suze delivered our drinks and wandered off again. I told him I never expected to see him again and asked if he was stalking me.

Ian laughed. "Sometimes you want to drink in peace and not have every guy in the place hitting on you," he said.

Which wasn't an answer, but I said there were worse problems in the world than being the prettiest in the room. He told me I was funny. But I wasn't sure if he meant funny-strange or funny-good.

He waved a finger toward my Tower Arms blazer logo. "I went into two other bars within a block radius of your delightful place of employment. One was scary. The other was expensive. This was the lesbian bar."

I told him I wasn't lost, but maybe he was.

"Did I hurt your feelings, Marie? I didn't mean to."

I shrugged and sipped my Blanton's. Why did I care about this guy's opinion? I didn't want to.

"I like your hair that way. You're not hiding behind that … *mop.*"

Somehow I wasn't insulted about the whole *mop* comment because the way he said it, I knew he was interested in me, and that puffed me up in spite of myself. I told him my hair wasn't his business, but there wasn't any sting in my tone. He sniffed the air in front of my face and asked me why I smelled like a swimming pool. "Are you a lifeguard?"

"Obviously not." Now that he mentioned it, I might as well have been sipping bleach. I put my drink down.

"You must see some weird shit," he said.

Like waging a pitched battle against a troublesome stain. But I wasn't telling. I took Mike at his word when he said I was the one they would blame if I didn't keep my mouth shut.

I asked Ian if he was trying to make friends with me or make me walk out, and he was amused. "I was just as lost when I was your age," he said. "It's nothing to be ashamed of. You can't quite reach the kind of life you really want. Not without some help. Believe me, if I hadn't taken advantage of exactly this kind of coincidence when I was your age? I'd probably be dead by now. Or I'd be working the makeup counter at Saks and living in some dreary coffin of an apartment." He contemplated the bourbon. "Where'd you learn to like this stuff? It doesn't match your ..." He drew an outline around me with an extended finger, "... vibe."

I don't know what made me do it, but I told him how Patty used to put it in my bottle to keep me quiet. That it was the only thing that worked to shut me up. Apparently, I'd been a nuisance from the start.

"But that's not ..." He stared into my eyes. "People don't really do that," he said.

I assured him that people really *do* do that. People leave a dog tied outside a busy cafe or in the park so that they can feel okay about abandoning it. People like to tell themselves that some nice person is going to come along and rescue the poor mutt. It's the same with children nobody wants. I can still easily recall when I realized Patty wasn't coming back for me. First, shock. Then fear. But fear is not going to save you. Only rage will do that.

Ian was silent for a minute. "The only good families are the chosen ones. They're the ones that save us," he said.

I had this image of him throwing me a life preserver as I slowly sank below the surface of the sea.

"I have a feeling about you," Ian said. "And I'm never wrong about these things." His words were like a warm hand cradling my cold heart. I said, "My friends call me Danny," and he smiled.

"Somebody saw something in me when I needed it most, and I see something in you," he said. "You want to ditch that hideous blazer, Danny? Go into private service. Get cozy with some high-net-worth individuals who know how to treat their staff. That's where the real opportunities are."

I had no idea how I was going to "get cozy" with those kinds of people and I said so.

"But see? That's where I come in." Ian smiled and leaned in, like he had a delicious secret to share. "I have connections in that world." He leaned back. "In my line of work, those kinds of people are my clients. Many of them are old friends. And I also know many desperate and starving artists who want to be introduced to those people. Now, I can't tell you her name for obvious reasons, but one of those desperate, starving artists wasn't on anybody's radar until I put her there, and now her work sells in seven figures." He signaled Suze for a second round and I hadn't finished my first, so I hurriedly swallowed what was left (since he was paying).

Ian said, "I might be persuaded to help you get connected too."

I said being an artist and being a housekeeper in a shit hotel aren't even close to the same thing, and he held up a finger. "Exactly!" He seemed so excited for me. "Housekeepers have much greater access and many more interesting opportunities. Housekeepers get the keys that unlock all the doors. Wouldn't that be nice for a change?"

I thought about that for a minute. I asked him what exactly I'd have to do to persuade him to help me. I was not unfamiliar with creeps, and I still hadn't one hundred percent decided whether Ian was a creep or a savior. Maybe suspicion had crept into my tone because he didn't answer. Instead, he carelessly dropped a black credit card on the bar. "Unfortunately," he said, "I have to leave now."

I'd blown it. Even if I wanted to find out more of what the man had in mind, I had just put an end to it. I was wondering if I should apologize when he said, "Don't worry. I really do have to go, but you have to decide if you're committed." He gave me a frank look. "I don't want to waste my time. Or yours."

I looked down at the credit card he'd laid on the bar. The name on the card was Stephen something. Not Ian St. Martin. When I looked up he was grinning.

"It's no fun if there's no risk, Danny." He handed me his business card. "Don't wait too long to call. I have a short attention span."

2

It was one of those kinds of encounters that replays. You meet somebody by mere chance, and they work their way into your brain until they're all you think about. That night and the whole next day, it was Ian St. Martin and his pretty face, his silky voice. I kept pulling that business card out of my pocket. Heavy stock in a creamy white, the name and phone number engraved in blue-purple ink. The area code was 310. California, I had looked it up. I called him as soon as I clocked off and he said he'd been expecting my call. He offered to take me to dinner after my shift.

Over plates of enchiladas and street corn at the only restaurant that served after eleven, Ian wanted to know what was important to me, what made me happy, where I saw myself at this time next year. I wanted to impress him with my seriousness so I mostly told him the truth. That I only had myself and I took care of me first. I said the world was full of assholes who try to hurt you, even break you. But what made me happy was knowing I'd done something perfectly because perfection was always my primary goal. I took pride in my work. And I said I was hoping that next year I'd be doing something completely new, that I was sick and tired of the grind. I told him I wanted that high-net-worth life he'd been talking about, and I was ready to commit to whatever he suggested.

So after dinner we went to his for a nightcap to seal the deal. I was eager to see his place, and it was exactly like I had imagined it. The apartment itself was huge, high ceilinged, the furnishings a flawless blend of industrial and 1950s Scandinavian that Ikea could only dream of. He settled me on the sectional couch, then brought out a brandy snifter and two paper-thin crystal goblets. I mimicked the way he warmed the golden liquid with the palm of his hand.

Fueled by the alcohol, I told him about Ginny, my first girlfriend, and her evil little brother, Mason. About my stint in juvenile detention. About Beth, another ex, who got me my first real job and taught me that pleasure through placement could keep you sane in an insane world, how she broke my heart by getting married to some dude from New Jersey. I told him I was lonely sometimes and that I was glad I'd followed that girl to BUS because otherwise I wouldn't have met him.

I basked in the warmth of his interest.

Ian's story was a modern-day fairy tale. He was the black sheep of one of those very high-net-worth families I was hoping to snuggle with. His name wasn't originally Ian St. Martin, but he wouldn't tell me his real name because it was dead to him—and "to protect the innocent," he joked. He had let go of a fortune, though not by choice. The family had kicked him when he was down, and he had finally gotten the message. He told me we had more in common than I could ever imagine.

"And this place …," he waved at the room, "and the brandy you're drinking, everything you see, I don't pay for any of it. I'm dreadful with money. I have no self-control, you see."

I asked him who the hell paid for it, then. *Was he some kind of gigolo?* And he laughed and said, "Now you're getting it." But his benefactor lived far away, so their relationship was not only transactional, it was also long-distance, an arrangement that suited them both. Oh, and the relationship was also *open*. Don't ask, don't tell was the only rule.

The way he was looking at me, I thought I knew what he was suggesting. I didn't want to make it awkward, so I told him flat out *I'm not doing that.* And he laughed and said I had a dirty mind, that he had no intention of trying to fuck me. At least not yet. I think he must have been amused by my vehemence and, considering what came later, confident I'd eventually come around.

He poured us a fourth, middle-of-the-night shot and told me what he really wanted from me was authenticity. A friend. Somebody he could rely on. Somebody with the same goals. We both needed *security*. We needed to stop letting other people drive the car and call the shots. The life we deserved could be whatever we wanted, once we had squirreled enough money away. I hated to remind him that he'd already confessed to being incapable of handling money.

And I—Marie Danvers—was going to make his life interesting again. It's hard to describe how deeply these kinds of pronouncements settled into my consciousness. Ian went to my head faster than the brandy. He would pay his own good fortune forward, and fortune would come back to him tenfold when I became the success he foresaw. I'd heard people talk about mentors. Now I had one, and I could feel my life expanding. I breathed hope.

Until he pointed it out, I'd had no idea I didn't belong at the Tower Arms. I had considered myself lucky. It was steady employment, and though it barely kept me afloat in an expensive city I'd dreamed of moving up in the hierarchy, maybe someday getting into management. But no, I was destined for bigger, better things. My employer was the lucky one, to have somebody like *me*. I deserved much more than the Tower Arms could ever offer.

By the time the sun came up, we had mapped out my escape route. With Ian's help and connections, I would land a position as a highly compensated domestic facilitator. (He liked that description better than "housekeeper.") My obsessive attention to detail would be seen as a strength, my discretion and ability to fade into the background would prove my trustworthiness. I would be given ultimate access. And my new best friend would be right there with me, all the way.

You aren't a criminal if there isn't a victim. If there isn't a victim nobody gets hurt. Hurt is only a relative term anyway. Does it hurt to lose a five-dollar bill if it's your last five dollars? Yes. But what if you're a billionaire? What if you're so greedy that you not only want your own cake, you want everybody else's cake as well, thank you very much.

But we weren't talking about cake, were we?

Ian's schemes were uncomplicated if you looked at them in a certain way. You borrowed the original, you copied it, you returned the copy and kept the original, nobody the wiser. Or you took a hefty finder's fee for putting together coalitions of private "collectors." The kind who couldn't show their faces in auction houses for fear of Interpol showing up and sending them to the Hague to be prosecuted for war crimes. Just as an example. There were a multitude of ways to make bank in the art racket, and Ian said if we worked together, me on the inside, him on the outside, there was no limit to what we could accomplish. I liked that idea. And once we got started, even he had to admit I learned fast.

3

"You look just like Victor in that suit!" Ian shouted from the bathroom.

"Victor? Ow …" Blood oozed from the tip of my forefinger. *Oh yeah, Victor.* Ian was obsessed with the movie *Victor/Victoria.* It starred Mary Poppins and some old guy I'd never heard of that Ian cackled was mostly famous for hawking beef. Ian had made me watch the movie with him, and I hadn't had the heart to tell him it was boring and kind of retrograde in its gender politics.

I licked the drop of blood off the tip of my index finger, then laid the sewing needle aside and tied off the last stitch of the hem of Ian's spangled minidress.

We were going as Victor and Victoria tonight. Of course. The pinstriped suit I was wearing was Prada (from the 2018 collection). Ian had pulled it from the depths of his closet where he'd banished it because his benefactor told him he looked like a gangster in it, and not in a good way. I was playing Anastasia, an art expert from Canada. Ian was Carter Ridgeway, my client and business associate. I hadn't had to do much tailoring to get the suit to fit me. Ian and I had similar builds, tall and narrow through the hips. Ian liked to remind me that when he'd first seen me at BUS, he'd thought I was a boy, joking that he'd only been mildly disappointed I turned out to be a girl.

Ian emerged from the bathroom in six-inch Jimmy Choos and a thong, his makeup and raven-dark pageboy wig perfect, washboard abs and narrow chest shaved free of hair.

I told him he looked very pretty and handed him the sequined minidress. He pulled it over his head and struck a pose.

"Too long?" I asked. The dress barely covered the front or back of him.

He snorted, "You know I love your hair like that, *Victor.*"

Our Uber driver was a sullen, middle-aged woman with questionable taste in music. All the way to the ass end of Long Island, our silence was accompanied by a soundtrack of Blake Shelton and Toby Keith. I was trying not to be nervous, but I knew tonight was a test.

Scooter's summer cottage turned out to be an oversized, self-consciously grand modernist box with brutally trimmed rows of pointy evergreen topiary. Scooter was tall and willowy with acne scars on his cheeks that he hid behind the curtain of an acid green, to-the-waist Cher wig. He was dressed in a floor-sweeping caftan and was touchy-feely with Ian and cool toward Anastasia, which was fine by me. I wasn't here to make friends.

The gathered guests seemed to have known "Carter" for years. I carefully followed Ian's conversations with Scooter and other people he introduced me to in case it was important, but I kept getting mixed up about who was who. It was a lot of Tippy and Bunny and Chip and Babs and Arch.

At some point I lost Ian and wound up cornered by a woman named Melanie who was built like a bodybuilder, narrow waisted with spectacular breasts.

"You like those, do you?" she said to me.

I dragged my eyes away from her chest.

"That's Stevie," Melanie said, nudging the waif with hunched shoulders standing next to her, dressed in a wilted, grubby Glenda the Good Witch gown. "Stevie's my wife."

Stevie had smeared mascara under her eyes and down her cheeks to make it look as if she'd been crying for days, and her black lipstick was painted outside the lines of her lips. Sad Goth Witch? If that was your cup of tea, Stevie was your girl.

"Stevie doesn't have much to say, do you, baby?" Melanie said, with a hint of malice.

Stevie looked away.

Then Melanie started crowding me, asking me what I had on underneath my suit jacket, so I distracted her wandering hands by taking them in mine and admiring her elaborate, gem-encrusted manicure. Once I got her talking about her nail artist I excused myself to fetch another glass of champagne. When I glanced over my shoulder they were both staring at me from across the room, so I gave them a toothy smile and stayed right where I was.

Having obtained the champagne, I settled into a corner far from Melanie and Stevie to observe and listen. I was waiting for a sign. Anastasia was here for a specific purpose, but Ian had been cagey about details. I only knew he'd had me studying auction catalogs for a reason, and tonight I was going to find out why.

Across the room, Ian was entertaining a group of people, making them laugh and keeping them hanging on his every word. He had that ability even with strangers. People always wanted a piece of Ian's attention. I noticed that his gaze kept straying toward Scooter and a stone-faced woman with icy blue eyes huddled together on the sofa, deep in what looked like an argument, only with smiles. Ian finally cut away from the group and came over to my corner. Bringing his lips right against my ear, he breathed, "It's time, Anastasia." His whisper triggered a full body shiver. I was excited to prove I had the chops for whatever was coming.

When he ambled out of the room, I waited a minute then followed him to the powder room. While he repaired his makeup Ian explained that I was going to be shown a painting and I was to estimate low six figures. I needed to make it casual because it was an ambitious price for this particular work, and Scooter had to buy what we were selling. Ian put his lipstick away and turned to me. "The most important thing is we take the painting with us."

I asked him how that was supposed to happen, and he said, "Improvise, Danny. That's part of the game."

Then he turned me around and pushed me out the door where Scooter and the blue-eyed woman were waiting for us.

Scooter slyly asked us what we'd been doing in there, and Ian simpered a little and put his arm around my waist, pulling me to him. The blue-eyed woman looked completely bored with all of us.

Scooter wagged his head at me. "I hear you want to see my Krasner."

The blue-eyed woman looked at Scooter and said, "Who the fuck is *she* anyway? What are her goddamn credentials?"

Scooter gave me a shamefaced smile. "This is my wife, Tippy."

I told him, smiling, that we'd met earlier, but Tippy wouldn't look at or acknowledge me. She was too busy murdering her husband with a focused glare that animated her face in a strangely attractive way.

"Why should we trust her?" Tippy snapped. "We don't know anything about her."

Ian tried to step in to save the situation, and that's how I knew they had history because Tippy turned on him, calling him a crook and a liar, insults he accepted stoically. Then Scooter stepped in and was sharp with Tippy and she stalked away, throwing a "Fuck you, Scooter" over her shoulder and a shouted "And fuck you too, Carter!"

"It was Daddy's painting but Mommy got it in the divorce," Scooter explained.

"I know Tippy's a bit bearish," Ian said in his silkiest voice, "but it is *yours*, isn't it, Scooter?" Driving the wedge deeper, he added, "Don't let her old grudge color your decision to sell. I would never steer you wrong. You're my oldest friend."

The things I still didn't know about Ian St. Martin could have filled several volumes.

We stood at the foot of a boat-sized bed staring at a small painting framed in simple black metal. The Krasner. An abstracted female body rendered in bright colors against a stark white ground. So this was why Ian had had me in those catalogs. I had seen nothing like this though. And when I caught Ian's eye, I knew he'd planned this challenge precisely to see if I could handle it.

Scooter squeezed Ian's arm and leaned into him. To me, Scooter said, "I told Tip that Carter had gotten us somebody neutral to take a look, and that's why you're here. My wife … she isn't the most trusting person. But your credentials speak for themselves. You'll have to tell me what it was like to sit on the board at the Vancouver at such a young age."

Ian smiled at me with genuine amusement. "I hope you don't mind that I told Scooter about that."

So I said *of course, it was fine* and my time there had been amazing. A real learning experience. I asked Scooter if he'd ever been to the museum and he said no, but he hoped I'd give him a private tour someday. I said it would be my pleasure.

I walked up to look more closely at the Krasner, letting the silence lengthen. I wasn't sure how I felt about the piece. It seemed insane that this rather unassuming painting could be worth that much, and I hoped I could spin Ian's proposed price with authority.

When I turned back to Scooter and Ian, I said the painting was an extremely rare offering and that I believed low six figures was not a stretch. Not at all.

Scooter's breath hissed. Ian watched me with this half-smile tugging at his mouth.

Then I dropped the bombshell that I would have to consult with my team of experts who focused exclusively on midcentury American modern. And in order to do that, I needed to take the painting with me.

"Just to dot the *i*'s and cross the *t*'s, eh?" I looked at Ian and I thought he was going to burst out laughing that I threw in that "eh."

"Take it with you?" Scooter's will seemed to waver. "To Canada?"

Ian slung his arm around Scooter's shoulders and laughed. "She'll bring it back, won't you, Ana?"

And before Scooter could change his mind, we were standing at the front door saying goodbye with the painting tucked safely inside a padded portfolio, Scooter waving us off and telling us to take care of his baby.

In the car, Ian cradled the Krasner on his lap. He was triumphant. He squeezed my hand and whispered, "You were *great* tonight."

And I whispered back, "I was better than great."

4

It was drizzling, and my hair was now a frizzy mess. It was one of those humid New York City days in spring when everything stinks of garbage and urine. I prayed I wouldn't sweat through my suit jacket. Ian said this was *the one*, the position that was mine to lose.

The Whitakers were ideal. Old money (him, a plastic surgeon) had married New Money (her, a former 1980s "it girl" and model). Three homes: one in Brooklyn, one in the Hamptons, one in a village in England where Mrs. Whitaker had family. She was well-known for her good works, he for his professionally curated modern art collection. And there was a daughter still living at home, a debutante who was engaged to be married. The Whitakers had a checkered history with housekeepers and were known to be particular and somewhat paranoid. Applicants were screened carefully.

Ian was giddy. I was cautiously optimistic. After my performance with Scooter and Tippy, Ian had gone to work through every back channel he had to find me the right situation. He had even consulted his benefactor, whose name (and gender) he stubbornly—frustratingly—refused to reveal. The benefactor had celebrities in their contacts list. But we had to be careful because the benefactor was also a jealous person. We could not have the benefactor find out that we'd crossed every sort of line by now. We were friends first, but with Ian sex had become inevitable. I found it all surprisingly vanilla, but he seemed to enjoy it. Still, there were rules we followed. I was never again allowed to spend the night after that one time, early on. I was forbidden to answer his house phone. Ian even bribed the doormen to keep my name off the digital visitors' list. Whatever you called what we were to each other, it had to remain a secret.

And then the benefactor hit gold with their suggestion of Charles and Jennifer Whitaker. The couple were personal friends of theirs, and the Whitakers were looking for somebody who could handle the pressures their kind of lifestyle brought to bear on staff. The benefactor agreed to provide me with a glowing reference. So Ian had polished up my resume with a bunch of lies about my experience, including that I once worked for some minor Bulgarian royal in exile (a person that didn't exist). And I would dress to impress in the Prada suit.

If the Scooter affair was a test, this interview was the final exam. Everything had to go my way. I had to say the right things and be formidable. I had to be everything my resume said about me. I had to be just what the Whitakers ordered.

But getting this job was going to be for *me*, not Ian, even if that wasn't what he believed. And it wasn't for his benefactor either. I might have to pretend I was part of the team, but becoming executive housekeeper to the esteemed Dr. and Mrs. Whitaker with their three homes and their art collection was the first step in my own secret Five Year Plan, the details of which I wasn't about to share with anyone.

The Whitakers' Brooklyn house was one of those classic brownstones, warm and intimidating at the same time. It probably had twelve-foot ceilings to keep cobweb-free and lots of window glass to keep sparkling. All in a day's work for Marie Danvers. I rang the bell and waited.

When the door opened, the girl that stood there was not what I was expecting. Calista Whitaker, debutante daughter of my potential employers, was an outsized goddess. Dressed all in black, jeans skin-tight, BLINK 182 T-shirt with the sleeves cut off. Her eyebrows were dark dashes when she frowned at me, her mouth set in a grim line. She radiated suspicion and suppressed anger.

I held out my hand. "I'm Marie Danvers," I said. "I'm here to interview for the housekeeper—"

Ignoring my outstretched hand, she threw her head back and yelled, "Mo*ther*! Your new *spy* is here." She glared at me. "Come in … if you dare."

I took a steadying breath and stepped inside, offering my best hotel smile. "You're Calista."

"*Cal,*" she snapped. "*Not* Calista."

I held out my hand again. "It's nice to meet you." My useless appendage dangled in mid-air while she glared at it. Eventually I let it fall back to my side.

I glanced at my watch. Yep, still early. Deep breath. Stay on track. Don't let this rich girl rattle you.

"MOTHER!"

Her voice carried impressively.

"How did you know my name?" she said. "That's weird."

I told her the internet was a fountain of useless information, and she said, "Ha ha." I stopped myself from glancing at my watch. Where was dear mother?

"I'm getting my nose pierced," she said.

I told her that sounded painful.

"Yeah, so? Isn't that the point? Mommy's against it. Because of the wedding. How old are you?"

Her mind seemed to race from topic to topic. I told her I was twenty-eight, and she said I looked too young for the job. I observed that she seemed too young to be wearing that square-cut diamond dragging on her left ring finger.

She hooked her hands in the pockets of her jeans. "I'm twenty-two and I'm getting married," she said, looking down her nose at me. "How come the internet didn't tell you *that?*"

I had to bow my head to hide a smile. Her short nails showed a dark line, as if she'd been digging in the dirt with her bare hands.

When I looked up she was watching me like she knew what I was thinking about her and that ring. She had pointed canine teeth that gave her a feral look. She would have been well cast as a vampire downtown girl.

The sound of approaching footsteps made both of us freeze. "Here comes the dragon mother," she whispered. "We'll talk later. I'll find you."

I wasn't sure if that was a promise or a threat, but she was halfway out the door when her mother appeared. "Where are you going, Calista?"

The girl's shoulders slumped and she pushed the door closed more forcefully than she needed to.

Jennifer Whitaker winced. She was smaller overall than her daughter, painfully thin in that New York socialite kind of way. Spotless white linen dress, toned fat-free arms, tan but not too tan. She smiled coolly at each of us in turn. First Calista. Then me.

"Miss Danvers, is it?" She glanced at her wristwatch, diamonds flashing on her slender wrist. In contrast to her daughter, she had perfectly manicured nails. "Oh, but … you're early, aren't you." She said it like an accusation.

I babbled idiotically about the rain and not wanting to be late. *Yours to lose, Danny. Don't fuck it up.*

Mrs. Whitaker nodded dismissively. "Stop fidgeting, Calista. You're not a child. Please, Miss Danvers, go through. My office is the first door on the left. That way …" She waved a vague hand. "I'll be right with you and we can talk."

Cal Whitaker's raised voice followed me: "I know, Mother!" And then louder, "Stop harassing me!" The door slammed.

The interior design of the house was excessive, overwrought. Paintings were stacked from eye to ceiling level, covering every wall. I saw a Miró and a small watercolor study of a flower signed by O'Keeffe. I'm sure there were other valuable paintings on the wall, but the overall effect of the art juxtaposed with the decor was overwhelming, and nothing else stood out to me. The Whitakers' aggressive mix of modern and antique wound up seeming idiosyncratic and regrettably ostentatious. Too many extravagant fresh floral arrangements. Too many cluttered end tables holding collections of glass and silver and small statuary, including a stunning little bronze that looked like a genuine Henry Moore.

There would be plenty of dust gathering to keep me busy when I got the job.

I found the office. A large glass-top desk was adorned with a sleek silver laptop that sat closed in the center. Nothing else. No pen. No paper. By the window two leather wing chairs sat opposite a sofa with assertive pillow coverage, an inlaid coffee table separating the seating. An unmarked green folder was placed square in the middle of the table. Across one of the sofa pillows was embroidered the word *BOSS*, a jarringly Christmas Tree Shops note in a custom-designed interior ready for its centerfold close-ups.

I chose one of the leather chairs even though that left me with my back to the door. When I checked my watch, that was another ten minutes gone. Was Mrs. Whitaker pulling some kind of power play? If so, that was somewhat more comforting than imagining she'd already decided against me due to my early arrival.

I stood when the door opened. "Oh good," Mrs. Whitaker said, closing the door behind her. She glided across the thick rug on soft-soled Italian loafers to perch on the couch opposite me, folding her hands on her pristine lap. She reminded me of this skinny Siamese cat who napped on the counter at my corner bodega. Predatory but also fragile.

I told her the house was lovely. Always good to start with a compliment.

"Oh … yes." She was distracted by something. Her shitty relationship with her daughter no doubt.

"I'm sorry," she said. "I should offer you something, shouldn't I? Soft drink?" Without waiting for my answer, she stood and went over to a flat-fronted armoire that, when she opened the doors, turned out to be a fully stocked liquor cabinet with a fold-down wooden counter and recessed lights.

"How about a Diet Coke?" She peered into the mini-fridge, came out with a can in her hand. "Or you probably don't need to watch your weight, do you? A young woman like you. You're wiry, aren't you? You look quite strong."

As if I were a racehorse. I decided this was a plus on the scorecard.

I thanked her, declining the soft drink. She popped the Diet Coke and poured it into a crystal wine glass over two round ice balls and handed me a bottle of water. "Now then, Miss Danvers—"

I told her to call me Marie.

Mrs. Whitaker's smile was brittle. "Marie, I know you've been vetted, and even I must admit your references are sterling, but this isn't just a formality, you know. You need to be a good fit for us. For *all* of us. That includes Calista. She can be very … difficult. Honesty, integrity, hard work … so many young people these days don't know the first thing about any of that."

No comment.

Mrs. Whitaker's eyes met mine as if I had suddenly come into focus. "Prewedding jitters. That's what I keep telling her. Of course, she doesn't listen to me. Never has." She was bitter about that. She picked up the green folder lying on the table in front of her.

I asked her if she had any questions about my resume or references.

"You've run households much larger than ours," she said, pulling out my resume. "You might be bored here."

I told her I sincerely doubted that. I said there was always something to do if you wanted a house to run smoothly.

"Our last housekeeper …" She made a face. "To be frank, she was a problem. Let's not get into *that*. All water under the bridge." She took a breath. "And Kara—the girl who comes in twice a week—she's hopeless, needs *constant* supervision. She and Calista don't get along. And then there's Jerry." She sighed. "He fixes things. But he's old, and I don't know how long we're going to want him climbing ladders. My husband is worried he would sue us if he fell."

I decided to jump into the break. "You don't know me very well, Mrs. Whitaker … not yet. But I want you to know that if you decide I *am* the right fit for your family, I guarantee that your home will be as clean—and run as efficiently—as a Swiss hotel." Then I tied it in a bow by telling her I would love to help her love her home again.

End scene.

She cleared her throat. "I'd expect you to dress suitably. Not like that." She waved vaguely at my outfit. "Plain black or navy pants. Or a skirt? Maybe a nice blue shirt with a collar? For the top. Like a uniform, but chic. How do you feel about wearing an apron? I think it looks professional, don't you?"

Like her daughter, every thought expressed aloud. My smile expressed my willingness to wear whatever the fuck she wanted me to.

She squinted at me, suddenly suspicious. "Are you … you aren't married, are you? Or maybe you have a boyfriend?"

She had to know she should not be asking those questions, so I let the silence get awkward before letting her off the hook. No, I was not married, and no, I didn't have a boyfriend. What would she think about my friends-with-benefits relationship with Ian? I had to suppress a smile thinking about that.

Mrs. Whitaker then wanted to know when I could start. Since I had no intention of giving the Tower Arms two days', much less two weeks', notice if she hired me, I said I could start immediately.

Now she looked a bit uneasy, like she was fighting some internal war. "My husband, he usually insists on a background check, but ..." And here she glanced down at the resume again, "but you come highly recommended, so I'm not sure it's necessary." Then Mrs. Whitaker leaned forward. "You'll have to sign a strict confidentiality agreement. We insist on it."

She was in a hurry so I told her, of course I understood how important privacy is to my employers. It is vital to trust somebody who would be living with them like family.

"Like family," she repeated. "I should hope not."

5

The door to the office flew open, and Cal gripped the edge of the door with exaggerated theatricality. "Mommy! David wants to talk to you. He's on the house phone."

Mrs. Whitaker gave an ecstatic gasp, told me to wait, and practically ran out the door. Cal smirked at me. "How's it going?" she said.

I told her it was going fine. I asked who David was, and she sneered. David was her *wedding planner*.

"I hate him, so of course Mommy loooooves him. You'd think *she* was the one getting married. Whenever he's in the room, she goes into heat."

I kept my expression neutral. This girl was capital-T trouble. Something about her reminded me of me.

"I want to show you something," she said.

I asked her what she wanted to show me, but she just turned and walked out of the room, so I followed her.

The little house at the bottom of the garden was almost hidden by an overgrown shrub just beginning to show signs of sprouting green.

"She doesn't want my mess in *her* house," Cal said.

Inside was a workspace, the petite kitchen island cluttered with odd materials and jumbled, lethal-looking tools, piles of newspapers and tangles of wire. Dried brown clay splattered the counter's stone surface. Something large, draped in wet cloth, was set onto a wooden pedestal. The rest of the room was taken up with shelving holding clay pieces in various stages of doneness, some fully fired, some awaiting firing.

I looked at her. "You're a potter?"

She scoffed. "No, I'm not a *potter*. I'm a *sculptor*." She poured herself a glass of wine. "You can't have any, right?" She laughed. "You have to be a good girl and impress the dragon mother."

I asked her again what she wanted to show me, and she waved her arm at the shelves across from her workbench crowded with what I can only describe as demonic creatures. Many had two heads, all were nudes with oddly shaped limbs, agonized expressions, mouths gaping, showing rows of sharp teeth. Twisted steel wire for pubic hair. Gaping vaginas and misshapen penises with oversized scrotums.

I picked up a raku creature, turning it in my hands. Two bulbous heads stuck with strands of metallic hair sat on thick, wrinkled necks, snake-like tongues lolling from slits where eyes should be, rows of teeth inside yawning mouths. Grotesque but well carved. Cal Whitaker had ability.

She asked me what I thought of it, and I said it reminded me of this photo I'd once seen of an ovarian cyst that had hair and teeth growing out of it. I said the piece was compelling. You couldn't look away. The figure was tragedy and comedy all in one.

"Are you for real?" she said. I wasn't sure if being "real" was a good thing or a bad thing in this situation, but I didn't get a chance to ask because we both got distracted by the ding of a text notification coming from Cal's pocket. She pried out her phone, frowned at the display then slid the phone back into her pocket. "Fuck him," she said.

I asked her who "him" was and she said *him*.

"I need money," she said.

I didn't know what to say to that. She was zipping along and I was trying to catch up.

"Six hundred dollars," she said. "I know where to borrow the money, but I need somebody to go get it for me. Somebody neutral. Somebody like you."

This was finally getting interesting. I asked her what she needed the money for.

She ignored that. "It'd be *really* nice of you," she said. "And I *promise* you won't get caught. Please, Maria, if you do this for me, you'll be saving my life ... *please*."

The way she emphasized particular words made me think she was a liar. I didn't correct her about my name.

She said that she needed to repay a debt, made some vague reference to the purchase of party favors for the wedding. Party favors I assumed were drugs or something else illegal, or else why wouldn't she just put it on a credit card. I told her it was a big ask of somebody she'd just met, somebody who was interviewing to become a trusted employee of her parents.

She got this cheeky grin on her face, those pointy teeth gripping her bottom lip. "It's strangers on a train," she said. "You know ... the movie? You do my crime, I'll do yours?"

I said I was familiar. It's a movie every gay film fan has studied. The way the two men flirt in that opening scene unmistakably a rainbow wink at the audience. I didn't point out that the crime in that movie was murder, but I did point out that she had said she was only "borrowing" the money, so was it really a crime? Furthermore, if it was only six hundred she needed, why not ask her mother or father? Then I asked the most important question: Are you pregnant?

She got pissed off at all my questions—didn't I trust her?—and drank the whole glass of wine in one go, muttering that she should have known I was the goody-two-shoes type. Also, how dare I imply that she was stupid enough to get pregnant.

I wasn't fooled. Her manipulations were transparent. Immature. But honestly, that's what made me want to hear her plan. So I asked her to outline the scheme, stipulating that I wasn't agreeing to anything.

Simon was the Whitakers' neighbor who lived two doors down and across the street. Her parents knew Simon because he was a chef at their favorite downtown restaurant. What they didn't know is that he was also a real party boy. Simon kept cash around for drugs *and stuff.* In a specific drawer. In his kitchen. She knew this because she'd been over there a few times. I got the impression she'd done more than party with Simon, but I didn't hold that against her.

I was going to tell her no. Politely. I even considered making an offer to loan her the money and have her be in my debt. But then it occurred to me I should ask how she planned to pay me back if I did her crime. What was I getting out of this deal? And she said, "You want this job, don't you? I'll make sure you get it."

I might be able to imagine doing a lot of things that could be considered criminal. I wanted the job. I wanted it in a way I had never wanted anything. And I wanted Cal Whitaker to admire my nerve by agreeing to break into Simon's house to "borrow" his hard-earned cash. But that didn't mean I had any intention of doing what she was asking.

When I told Ian the story he was skeptical that she had that level of sway over her mother's decision vis-a-vis my employment, but I convinced him to loan me the money. We were hedging bets. Six hundred really wasn't that much, and besides, I had made the right impression on Mrs. Whitaker. The only reason she hadn't offered me the job then and there was because she'd been distracted by David the Wedding Planner.

So Ian agreed it was worth a shot, and I met Cal Whitaker for the handoff the next day at a midtown coffee shop. She was already there when I arrived, sitting in a booth at the back. Even by New York City standards, she was Technicolor and everybody else sepia-toned. I waited till she noticed me, her eyes lighting up when I finger waved.

I sat down and slid the envelope across the table. She looked inside, smiled a little, then tucked the envelope into a bubblegum-pink handbag that was French or Italian, maybe even a Birkin. She could have easily consigned it and gotten way more than six hundred bucks for it.

Cal said she'd heard I was starting on Monday. Again with the smirk and the peek of pointy vampire teeth.

I said *yes, I am* and *thank you for putting in a good word for me*. She laughed and said, "I told Mommy I thought you were awful. She loves you now."

6

"You're wanted," Jerry said.

The guy looked pale and sweaty, and I knew he had a heart condition so I asked if he was okay, but he shrugged. He held hedge clippers, and a tarp was tucked under his arm. I jokingly asked if he was doing the landscaping now, and he sighed heavily, said it sure looked that way, didn't it. The boss wanted the mock orange trimmed back so that Jerry could apply a fresh coat of paint to the little house's exterior. And of course she wanted it done *now*, not tomorrow.

Mrs. W. had been haranguing Cal for a couple of weeks that *the bride* needed to clear out all of her *crap* and stop wasting time on those disgusting *things* she called sculptures. Besides, they needed the little house for catering for the outdoor events, and all that *shit* had to go. Preferably into the trash. Cal blithely ignored her mother. I had peeked in recently, and the disorder and clutter were unchanged.

Jerry ran callused fingers through the sparse gray hairs clinging to his scalp and shook his head. "This wedding … the boss has lost her damn mind, Marie. And you can tell her I said it." He grimaced. "No, don't tell her that. I need this job."

He had just come from a closed-door consult with Mrs. W. about various fixes to be done before the wedding. Several events were to be hosted by the parents of the bride, and there was a lot to do to prepare for the onslaught of wedding-related gatherings.

Most of Jerry's tasks were uncomplicated, touch-up painting here and there, putting together the catering tables, supervising the placement and raising of the big white tent, hanging fairy lights in the trees and shrubbery. But the old fellow often seemed in over his head, and he was slow. I assumed the Whitakers liked him because he was inexpensive and because they could exploit his amiable nature.

"That *David* person is running this show, I'll tell you that," Jerry said. "He's got us all running ragged." He peered at me. "How are you holding up?"

I told him I was fine and, in truth, keeping chaos to a minimum was me in my element. Methodically knocking things off my to-do list helps me sleep at night. And David and his agenda didn't dictate my day-to-day, even if tasks did flow from him through the boss and inevitably on to me.

"I'm going to have to get my nephew to help me with this punch list," Jerry grumbled on his way out. "Good luck to you … she's on a tear. As in, she's ready to tear you a new one."

After he went out, I knocked on the boss's office door but got no response. It was dead quiet in there. So I carried on tackling the day's tasks, and an hour later I was upstairs putting away laundry and checking in on Kara's bathroom-cleaning skills.

Kara was in her forties, stocky and strong, two assets for a maid in such a big house, but the woman was also prone to daydreaming. Plus her eyesight was terrible but she refused to wear glasses, so she often missed fine details. But Kara had a discernible work ethic and was never late, so I wasn't going to rock the boat. Everyone deserved a chance to improve. As for her ongoing feud with Cal, that seemed rooted in Kara's envy colliding with Cal's mean-girl impulses.

I found Kara on her hands and knees, drying the just-washed floor in Mrs. Whitaker's bath with an old towel. "Almost done," she said and sniffed loudly.

Kara had nasal issues. Allergies, she claimed. When I had asked early on what she was allergic to, she said *other people*. I appreciated that she wasn't particularly talkative.

She glanced at me over her shoulder. "Did you hear the latest thing?"

"Do I want to?" I asked. The latest thing would be related to some detail of the coming nuptials. Cal and her mother had been raging, especially the last couple of days. They were like feral cats, drawing blood to protect their respective territories. More than once, one or the other was left sobbing and screaming obscenities. The essence of the conflict was that Cal hated all of the fuss and wanted nothing to do with David or the planning of the wedding because, she insisted, none of it was what she wanted anyway.

Kara had a breathless interest in the infighting. She sniffed and wrinkled her nose like it was itching her. "Calista is back on the whole nose ring thing." She wadded up the towel in her hands and stood, stretching her back. "The boss should just let her do it." Kara glanced at me. *Sniff.* "But Calista won't do it anyway because she's all talk and no action."

I wasn't so sure. I said Cal's decisions were none of *our* business, which only added fuel to Kara's inner gossip.

"She's so spoiled, it's disgusting," Kara said. "She's a brat who doesn't even know how lucky she is. But I heard the boss say if she did that, Cal would be throwing away her future, that she'd be disfiguring herself and no decent man would want her. And get this …" She craned her neck to see into the bedroom beyond as if Mrs. W. might be lurking there, eavesdropping on us. Kara lowered her voice, "She also said … if Calista *fucks this up*, they're going to commit her to some fancy funny farm upstate. Can you believe that? Threatening to put your kid in the loony bin because they got their nose pierced? That's cold." *Sniff.* "Sure did knock that one down a peg, though. After that I didn't hear a peep out of her." She sighed. *Sniff.* "Where to next, boss?"

I gave Kara the rest of the afternoon off.

All afternoon I had this feeling like a storm was coming. The house was so quiet. Mrs. W. and Cal were still in her office, door closed. Jerry had finished his landscaping task and he'd left early so he could pick up the paint for the little house project. I didn't have much to do, so I called Ian, but he wasn't home (or wasn't picking up) so I took a coffee break and sat outside staring down the length of the yard at the newly shaped mock orange. The sweet scent of its flowers wafted on the breeze.

My phone vibrated and I saw there was somebody at the door cam. A man, but I couldn't see his face because he'd turned his back. I assumed it was some kind of delivery, but when I went into the front hall, David the wedding planner was facing the camera, one hand holding a bulging briefcase.

I opened the door and he stepped in, pirouetting to face me. "Are they in her office?"

I said to my knowledge they were, and he said, "Oh, good. That will give you and I some time to have a little chat." He put down his briefcase and walked into the living room. I trailed after him. What could he possibly want from me?

David sat down on the couch and crossed his legs, patting the spot next to him. I sat.

"How are you today, Marie?" he asked. "Is all this wedding *drama* getting to you yet?"

I told him I was fine, thanks.

"Ian said you were as cool as they come." He radiated sly cheerfulness. My mouth was suddenly too dry, and I was having trouble swallowing. My thoughts tripped over each other. *Ian said. Ian and David know each other. Ian sent David to the Whitakers.* Of course he had. Ian and David were working together.

David patted my leg. "So, listen … there's been a teensy change of plan."

7

Cal lay on the couch with her feet up, staring at the ceiling. She didn't glance my way or acknowledge me when I walked in. Her suppressed fury was palpable. Mrs. W. was at her desk, her silver computer open before her. She looked up. Controlled as ever. Kara wasn't wrong about her. Iced Diet Coke flowed through her veins.

"Marie, I'm putting *you* in charge," Mrs. W. said, glancing at David behind me.

"Ma'am?"

"Calista ..." Mrs. W. began. "Calista, my charming daughter, the flesh of my very own loins, is incapable of *civility*, or *gratitude*, so David and I *quit*." She gave me a tight smile, no teeth showing and held out her hand to David, who went to grasp it, their fingers intertwining. He stood behind her, his other hand protectively on her bony shoulder. They stared at me.

"We're pausing," David said. Benign smile in Cal's direction. "For now."

I was to be David's surrogate, tasked with escorting Cal to her wedding dress fittings, the catering tastings, and keeping to-do lists current. I was even supposed to make sure she picked the right kind of goddamn cake, since she was not to be trusted to make decisions like an adult.

"Do you hear that, darling daughter?" David's gentle, approving nod from above. "The housekeeper is there to make sure you don't fuck this up even more than you already have."

I thought that was the end, but there was an encore. "Remember what I told you about repercussions if you get that ring in your nose like a goddamn cow."

Cal got up in one smooth move and glared at all of us. "So on trend, *Jenn*," she said, and gave her mother the finger. Mrs. W. gave it right back, but it looked to me like she wanted to cry. She made a shooing motion at me and said in a dead voice, "Just ... go."

I felt David's eyes watching me as we left. When I was pulling the door closed he gave me a furtive wink.

Cal had not spoken a word since we'd left Mrs. W. sitting there at her beautiful glass desk looking like she'd aged ten years in ten minutes, with that ghoul David smiling like he'd eaten the dog. We waited in silence in the front hall for the Uber that was to carry us to the fitting appointment. Then we sat silent through the entire ride from Brooklyn into Manhattan, listening to the driver's easy-listening Pandora station. Not a word was spoken until the car stopped in front of Bergdorf's.

Cal didn't immediately move to get out of the car, so I waited. She stared out the window, this bleak smile on her face. "I wasn't really going to do it," she said. "Fuck all of them. Let's get this over with."

When we went inside, they put us in a private room, mirrors all around, walls and surfaces in muted mauves and pinks to give a glow to the cheeks. Cal sat down on the edge of the fitting platform. Her knee jittered while she picked at her filthy fingernails.

I took a seat on a sleek two-seater settee. A side table held a plate of waxy petits fours and a split of cheap champagne with two flutes.

The door opened and a woman who could have been either thirty or fifty came in. She was immaculately groomed and as sleek as the settee.

"Calista," she said warmly. "I just spoke with your mother. I'm so thrilled with your selection. It's perfect for you."

"I didn't *select* it," Cal snapped. "*She* did."

The woman turned to me, clasping her hands with excitement. "You must be the maid of honor."

"She's the *maid*," Cal said and threw me a dirty look. "Hadley's late."

The woman figured out that Cal wasn't playing the Happy Bride game and withdrew. We listened to each other breathe for a few minutes.

"Hadley and I go way back. My first friend." Cal looked up. "She's shallow and stupid. You'll love her."

I told her that wasn't a very nice thing to say about a friend, and she snorted and called me goody-two-shoes, her favorite insult for me. I imagine there were lots of other things she could have called me, so it was kind of sweet that she chose that one.

We lapsed back into silence. She picked at her nails, flicking bits of dirt onto the carpet. So far she had resisted her mother's insistence that she get nail extensions for the wedding events. According to Mrs. W., Cal was disrespecting her husband-to-be's granny or mother or whoever had supplied that magnificent, *heritage* rock with the shameful condition of her hands and nails. I was surprised when some of Mrs. W.'s barbs hit home. Cal had recently taken to picking at the skin around the nails, leaving her fingertips sore and bloody where she'd ripped away pieces of flesh and dropped the shreds wherever she was. Those small bits of DNA marking the trail of her discontent.

Hadley arrived in a swirl of cigarette funk mixed with an overwhelming, overly sweet perfume. She could have been Mrs. W.'s double. Or what Mrs. W. looked like before she (apparently) gave up the cigs and took up Diet Coke. But despite Hadley's frail appearance, she had a knowing quality that withstood Cal's withering looks in her direction. I was impressed.

"Where have you been?" Cal said. No hello. No hug.

Hadley laughed and looked at me. "I'm always late," she said, clearly proud of herself. "Who are you?"

Cal said, "That's Marie. Mommy's spy."

I shook my head and put on a smile for Hadley. "Not a spy." I told her I was the Whitakers' housekeeper and it was nice to meet her.

Hadley said, "So … where's the fucking dress?"

The dress was a knockout. Slinky, body conscious, and beaded, with an extravagant sweep of hem and train. It already fit Cal well, but a seamstress came in and fussed over the bodice to make sure it was glove-fit. Then she pinned the hem so when the bride was dancing in her glass slippers she wouldn't trip and fall flat on her face.

Meanwhile, Hadley kept up a running commentary on the proceedings, narrating and filming what was happening with her phone camera, a memorized script about how Calista was deliriously happy, looked so hot in that dress—"Don't worry! I'll put a blur on it so he won't see it. He follows you, right?"—and, of course, how Calista was the luckiest girl there ever was. A bride-to-be. Cal wore a sour smirk on her face the whole time.

When the seamstress was finished, Hadley downed the last of the complimentary champagne and said she needed a smoke, so I stood up to leave and wait outside, but Cal ordered me to stay. When we were alone, she said, "Do you envy me?"

I told her no. She asked me why, so I told her because she didn't seem happy.

"I'm happy," she said with a scowl that took over her whole face. "Why wouldn't I be happy?"

She couldn't get out of that dress and back into her street clothes fast enough. I asked if I should go ahead and order the car, and she told me she was doing downtown Happy Hour with Hadley. When I pointed out that Happy Hour was at least two hours in the future she said, "You're lucky, Marie. You can be who you are."

I told her *my friends call me Danny.*

8

Love. People throw that word around but mostly they don't mean it. Not at all. My philosophy is words are meaningless, because it's not about what you say. It's about what you do with feelings that are far more complex than mere love.

The cake tasting. Let's start there. Or better, let's start with Ian. Because it always came back to the source.

I arrived that Sunday (my day off, Ian's and my weekly rendezvous) to find David ensconced in Ian's living room. Ian was out. Somewhere. Ian had not wanted to see me. Ian had asked David—*David*—to have a frank conversation with me about Calista Whitaker and her high-strung mommy.

Basically, I wasn't sticking to the script. And what was worse, Jenn suspected that I was secretly aiding and abetting Calista's rebellion. And now Ian—*Ian*—suspected I was catching feelings for the girl.

I said that was bullshit, and I got up to leave in the middle of David telling me how I needed to get Calista on board with him again. *You have to get her to like me.* Well, that was not going to happen and I said that, right before I slammed the door in his face.

Then Monday was the cake tasting. Hadley would be meeting us there. I think Mrs. W. had enlisted Hadley as a backup keeper for Cal. But Mrs. W. hadn't accounted for Hadley's laissez-faire approach to her maid of honor duties. She texted while we were on the way there that she couldn't make it, so it wound up being me and Cal and a woman named Chloe in the tasting room that the bakery had set-dressed as a chic living room.

But before that, even. Rewind to earlier. Cal had not appeared yet that morning, so Mrs. W. wanted me to *get that girl moving.* Mrs. W. was one of those people who can't stand it if other people are idle. She could be sitting around all day, but if she came in the kitchen and found me sitting, she inevitably asked me if I needed something to do.

I had been in Cal Whitaker's bedroom many times, but usually when she wasn't in there. I knocked and knocked and then I tried the door. It was unlocked. She was sitting on top of the bed with her tablet propped on raised knees.

I asked her why she didn't answer when I knocked, and she said it was because she didn't want to. Then she told me to have a seat. If I wanted. *Take a load off, Danny.* Since the only place to sit was on her bed, I stayed by the door. I gently reminded her that we had an appointment in ninety minutes. When she ignored me I admit I got a little sharp. I asked her what was so interesting on her tablet. "I'm watching a porn video," she said. "I'll just be another minute." So I said *let me see,* and she closed the cover immediately and set the tablet aside. "I didn't say you could come into my room," she said.

I told her she had thirty minutes to get ready. I wanted to tell her she was out of her league where I was concerned, that I took my job seriously. I wanted to tell her she didn't have to play games. Not with me. I saw who she was. I understood her dilemma. And when the right time came, I'd do it. I'd tell her what I really thought about her giving in to somebody or other's expectations. Her life was her own, not her mother's. The thought of being that blunt with Cal was a little scary, but we had kinship, had built a patchwork trust. It wasn't perfect yet, but it was a start. Cal Whitaker wanted to break away, but she lacked the courage and needed my support. Once she saw the light I could imagine a day when I would tell her who I really was. She would be impressed, seeing me as transgressive rather than criminal.

For now she still believed I was her mother's spy, so a denial would be unsatisfactory for both of us. I would have to prove my allegiance over time. At the same time I needed Mrs. W. and David (and Ian) to think I was doing what they wanted me to do. But playing both sides comes naturally when you've spent your whole life appeasing somebody or other's unreasonable demands.

When we got to the bakery, it was the royal treatment for the wedding of the year. At least that's what Chloe called it, with cheerful dollar signs in her eyes.

Chloe was an interesting girl. Doe eyes behind absurd fake lashes, a perfectly lipsticked pout. Wide-leg, herringbone-patterned pants and an elegant white blouse from some downtown label I recognized. Probably my age or maybe a bit older. She referred to her wife whenever she could while shooting me these sly, flirty glances.

My wife and I went to Paris for our *honeymoon. My wife and I both love chocolate, but for our wedding cake, we ended up with a lemon sponge with fresh raspberries and marzipan Italian buttercream. So delish. My wife and I are taking a drive upstate this weekend.* I never learned the wife's name. Chloe never mentioned it.

At one point Cal excused herself to go to the bathroom, announcing to Chloe's obvious chagrin that she was bleeding like a stuck pig and she didn't want to ruin her white pants, for fuck's sake. Chloe let out a big sigh when the door closed behind Cal. She turned to me.

"I'm sorry … is it me, or is that girl a mess on wheels?"

I told her Ms. Whitaker was the nervous sort.

"I shouldn't be surprised that she's so rude," Chloe went on. "Her mother is the same way. She wants a whole lot and she wants it wholesale." She laughed at her own little joke. "What about you, Marie? Are you married?"

I think the look of horror on my face was a definitive enough answer because she laughed. "Oh, are you one of those?"

I asked her, one of what? And she said, *marriage-phobic.* I said I didn't know that was a thing, and she sighed. "It's a trend," she said. People were skipping big weddings now. I suppose she was worried she'd be out of business if the market for elaborate and ridiculously expensive wedding cakes disappeared.

Chloe leaned in, put her hand on my knee, "Want to go out for a drink some time?"

I was startled and it took me a second to recover. I said, wouldn't her *wife* mind? And she said, "I think she'd like you."

When I looked up Cal was standing in the doorway. Chloe smiled and pulled her hand away. "Ready to taste some yummy cakes?" she chirped.

While she was preparing the samples, Cal came back and sat down next to me. She asked me if what she'd walked in on was what she thought it was. I said, what do you think it was? And she said, Chloe wants to date you? I laughed and said what Chloe *and* her wife wanted was a threesome.

Cal thought about that for a minute, then she just said, "Cool." Chloe came back with samples and left us to it, but not without putting a warm hand on my back as she was leaving, telling us to *enjoy.*

Cal said, "Wow, she's really into you."

There were four cakes to try, and we dug into the first two. Cal rejected both. She hated cherries (the Black Forest), and the almond gateau tasted "fake." She forked a bite of the next cake, vanilla with chocolate-hazelnut French buttercream. She held it up then turned to me. "Try it," she said, and brought the forkful of cake toward my lips. Cal Whitaker was looking into my eyes, my stomach was doing flip-flops, but I obediently opened my mouth like a baby bird waiting to be fed. My lips closed around the fork and she pulled it away in one languid motion.

The cake melted in my mouth. I swallowed—strangely breathless—and she asked me if I liked it. I told her yes, it's delicious, and she leaned forward and with her grimy thumb wiped away a speck of something on my lower lip. When she pulled her thumb from her mouth it glistened with her saliva. She showed me her vampire teeth and asked if we really needed to try the last cake. I told her that was her call.

Cal said, "I'm glad it's you, Danny. You're a *real* friend."

9

We were supposed to be picking up the fiancé's K-1 visa from Taft and Biddle, the family law firm whose office was located on 52nd near Sixth Avenue, but the Uber was headed in the opposite direction, so naturally I asked where we were going, and Cal said, "You'll see." That was just how she was.

Fifteen minutes later the car dropped us in front of a row of funky storefronts. A barber. A secondhand consignment shop. And ... a piercing studio.

I asked her what she thought she was doing, because I knew immediately why she'd brought us there, and I admit I might have adopted a tone of disapproval that, given the circumstances, she took the wrong way. She accused me of being the dragon's apprentice. Worse than David. A snake who pretended to be harmless.

I let her rant, and pretty soon she gave up on the accusations and apologized. She hadn't meant any of it. I was the only one who "got" her, didn't I know that? I was the only one she trusted to be holding her hand while she got her septum pierced. And by the way, the appointment was in fifteen minutes and she needed a coffee because she'd taken Molly before we left and it was hitting her ... *hard.* Then she hugged me and hooked her chin over my right shoulder and said she didn't want to imagine a world without me in it because I was her best and only real friend. "I love you," she said.

I told her she shouldn't say things she didn't mean, and she said, "I do mean it!"

I steered her toward the coffee shop a couple of doors down, and we went inside and got coffees. She kept touching things. And me. Sliding her arm around my waist. She wouldn't sit across from me, had to sit right up on me on the banquette. People were staring. I did my best at ignoring them and focused on getting the coffee into her. I was certain it would help her come down, but what did I know about Molly? I'd never tried it. I couldn't help thinking I would be blamed for whatever happened this afternoon. I had to save the situation. What would Ian do ...

When the fifteen minutes were up we trotted back over to the piercing salon and went inside. Cal gave her name at the desk, and the pink-haired receptionist said Luther was running a little late and invited us to have a seat. The soft leather couch threw us together into a cuddle puddle, and I worried what the receptionist thought of the two of us cozied up like that.

Cal held my arm and whispered, "What do you think he'll say?"

I knew who *he* was. I said "How should I know? I've never met your fiance."

And she said, "He'll hate it, of course." So I asked her why she was doing it, if it was going to be so controversial for everybody, and she didn't answer at first. She looked away, bit her lower lip with her sharp teeth. I tried to imagine how it would feel to offer my neck to those teeth.

"He'll be here in two weeks," she whispered. "*Two weeks …*" She hid her face and I thought she might be crying, but then I realized she was snickering into her shoulder, so I asked her what was so funny.

Then I said, "You shouldn't do it." *Do what, pray tell?*

I told her there were better ways to make her point, to declare her individuality. "You don't have to go through with this," I said. "And you don't have to go through with the wedding either. Not if you don't really want to."

Before Cal could respond, a heavily-tattooed man with elaborately waxed facial hair came through the door marked "Private" and walked over to shake hands with us and introduce himself. Luther was a savvy guy because he pegged Cal's condition right off. He lowered his voice and asked her if she'd taken a drug before coming in today, and she said, "only a painkiller." At which point his gaze slid toward me and I gave the slightest nod.

Luther patted Cal's hand gently and said he'd be happy to pierce her if she came back in an *unaltered* state. Then he quietly cited various laws that prohibited him from engaging in his craft with somebody on drugs. After a whispered consultation with pink-hair, he went back through the door marked "Private," and that was the end of that.

We walked to Green-Wood Cemetery where all these famous New York types are buried and walked among the mausoleums and angelic statuary. Cal's mood by this time was contemplative. She wanted to talk about Jenn and Charles. She knew they loved her, and she loved them. Truly, she did. But they didn't understand. They didn't want her to thrive doing what she loved. They didn't believe in her. They had never believed in her. And neither did *he*. He was patronizing and no fun. They all had an insane need to control her.

It was like she couldn't hear my suggestion—whether delivered obliquely or forthrightly—that she did have control over her life. She could say no. She could be something other than somebody's daughter. Or wife.

"Don't ever leave me, okay?" She gripped my arm, her nails digging into my flesh. "Danny, I can handle all of it if I know you'll be with me. Okay?"

I didn't want to believe she meant what she said. But I also wanted more than anything to believe her. Both things were true. It wasn't until she laid me down in the grass, until she pulled my shirt collar aside so she could get to my neck, put her lips and teeth against the pulsing beat of my carotid and, in true vampire fashion, left her mark on me. Then I believed.

10

Ian and I had met at our usual coffee shop, a hole-in-the-wall around the corner from his apartment. The coffee was weak, but the baristas were indifferent to us lingering as long as we wanted over our Styrofoam cups. Ian always left good tips. He said it helped people remember you *and* forget you, whichever was needed.

My mind was only half-engaged while Ian told me the details of the imminent visit of his benefactor, coming east to conduct important business related to the Whitaker project. As a matter of fact, he intended to introduce us (finally) so we could all get to know each other better.

"What is wrong with you?" Ian said. "Are you even listening to anything I'm telling you?"

He was annoyed that I had lost the thread, so I went on the offensive and accused him of fobbing me off on David, of all people. And furthermore, there was no way I could make Cal Whitaker like the man, since I didn't like him either. Anyway, what did the wedding have to do with whatever he was up to?

I remember like it was yesterday the way he looked at me when I was finished, the way he leaned back and stared into my ragged, yearning soul.

"Can I tell you a story?" he said. "I got involved with a mark. Once. Only that once though … Because you know why? It screwed the pooch on the project, and I lost money. Because I was stupid. Because I was thinking with an unreliable body part. And, Danny? We've got way too much invested in this one to let Calista fucking Whitaker get in our way. Do you understand me? Whatever entanglement you're in, untangle it and keep your head down."

I said he had no right to talk to me like that. I wasn't stupid. And I was *not* entangled. But Cal Whitaker didn't deserve the fate her parents had in mind for her. I couldn't ignore that. And I ended with: "You have no fucking idea how hard it is to work for the Whitakers."

"Are you complaining to me right now?" Ian said, his voice quiet but steely. "Are you whining about the job you were so desperate to get that you borrowed money from me to pay the girl to help you get it?" Ian looked pained. "You know how this works," he said. There was a lot at stake. For all of us.

I wanted to scream, but I swallowed the scolding like bitter medicine.

"I need you to look at me and tell me you're all the way in," Ian said. "I have to be absolutely sure that you're with us."

So I looked him in the eye and told him exactly what he wanted to hear. I believed at the time that he believed me.

Sometimes I fall apart—not to outside observers of course, but inside. And then I have to put myself back together, show whoever's looking that I'm not beaten. I'm a survivor even when I want to give up.

I got home and the house was quiet. Mrs. W. was at her mother-of-the-bride dress fitting. I'd seen the dress. It was lovely and tasteful. And white. Almost like a wedding gown. After the fitting she and David were meeting, so she wouldn't be back for hours. They drank buckets of Cristal at these meetings. David seemed to be the only one to have succeeded in prying the Diet Coke from Mrs. W.'s hand. I wondered if they were sleeping together.

I was hanging up my coat when I heard a distinct *thump*, then another and another, coming from upstairs. Cal was usually in her studio at this time of day. I stood still, visions of robbers laying waste upstairs. They would have guns or baseball bats or stun guns, and me here, with my coat in my hand and only a hanger for a weapon. Then I heard voices. Cal. And a man. Not Dr. W. Not Jerry.

A minute later the man whose voice I must have heard appeared at the head of the stairs. He was big and broad, dressed all in black, extra-tight jeans and a T-shirt that clung to rippling abs. He carried a black leather jacket in his hand. He looked down at me from the top of the stairs and said, "Oh, hello."

I said, "Who the hell are you"? And he laughed, good-natured, not at all bothered by my bitchy attitude, and jerked his thumb over his shoulder.

"I'm Simon. Cal's friend." He clattered down the stairs and stopped in front of me. He stuck out his hand. "I live across the street. You must be Danny."

I shook his hand, mine cold in his warm paw.

"Well," he said. "It's nice to finally meet you. I've heard a lot about you."

After he left I stood there for a while, indecisive. I wanted desperately to go upstairs and find out exactly what the hell was going on between her and Simon. But I could already picture her mocking response. She might pretend to be under her mother's thumb and obedient to some level of fidelity to her absent fiance, but Cal Whitaker did as she pleased, and nobody could change that, especially nobody like me.

I was having a rest in my room when I heard her come downstairs and go out the back door. Heading to her studio, no doubt. So I picked myself up and went out there. I'd spent two hours stewing, unable to let it go. I had to know. For sure. What the fuck was going on between her and six-hundred-dollar Simon?

"We party," Cal said, her tone implying I was being nosy and somewhat silly. "It's nothing serious." She looked up from using a cheese grater to add texture and dimension to some small pieces of clay. "You sleep with your *mentor*, don't you?"

She had this look on her face—a combination of amusement and surprise—that made me want to slap her. "Don't tell me you're the jealous type," she said, smiling.

The cheese grater mimicked scales when applied to the soft clay. Snakeskin. Snakes. They were everywhere. And I was the idiot for not seeing that.

"Where'd you get the money you gave me?"

It took me a second and her mouth curved into a knowing smile. I said, "I earned it."

"Why'd you do that?" She stared critically at the piece of clay.

"I wanted the job," I said.

She got up and came over to me, adjusted my apron straps, put her arms around my waist and wouldn't let me go even though I did try to pull away. "I know why you did it," Cal said. "And now we're bonded for life. You'll never get away from me."

I said in less than two weeks she was going to be a married woman living in England, and she said, "You'll come visit." I said, no, I probably wouldn't. And the pain of that truth knifed through me.

"Don't be neg, Danny," she said. "Even if I'm a million miles away, we're connected. You'll never be able to forget me. "

She reached up, pushing aside my shirt collar to expose the rainbowed bruise she'd made with her teeth, and leaned in to kiss it. Then she let me go and went back to her bench, to her cheese grater and her sculpting.

Cal had won the war of the studio. Mrs. W. and David had given up and rented an extra tent for the catering staging. That unfinished sculpture remained hidden under its cloth. Those monsters still glared at me from every surface. Nothing had to change. I simply had to stop being so neg.

11

Not the first time.

The Whitakers. It wasn't the first time I screwed up. Sometimes I think Patty was right that I came out of the womb preloaded with bad luck. How does the song go? If it wasn't for bad luck I wouldn't have any luck at all. Sounds accurate.

Or maybe it's this subconscious need to sabotage any given situation when it gets too comfortable, when you know in your gut things are about to go south so why not be the first to fuck it up? It's that same feeling right before Patty pushes you out of the car, says they'll be back in an hour. *Go on, you. We don't need the excess baggage.* Patty's whatever-he-was with his gold bottom teeth, diamonds embedded in each one. If you took a hammer to those teeth you could have gotten the hell out of Vegas.

You can learn a lot about people when all you have is time, sitting under the broiler of the sun. You can learn that people will always disappoint you, and eventually show their true colors. You can learn that smiling faces lie, that you should always be prepared to be left behind.

But who would have predicted that it would be Hadley who lit the fuse that blew it all up.

Rewind to the day I finally learned why we were all here. Me. David. Ian.

The shock of seeing Ian waltz out of Mrs. W.'s office followed by Dr. W. that morning. And I hadn't had my first cup of coffee. When he passed me in the hall he said hello, and I was only able to give a weak nod. Dr. W. didn't look at me as he passed. I don't think he knew my name even though I'd been working for him for weeks.

They stopped at the end of the hall, and Ian glanced at me over Dr. W.'s shoulder as Dr. W. gripped his hand and thanked him for his *help*. Ian murmured something I couldn't hear, and Dr. W. said, "Good, good. I'll call first thing tomorrow and we'll get this squared away." Ian patted Dr. W.'s arm and they went off into the front hall.

But that was only the first blow. The second came while Cal was getting ready for her hen party. David wanted a conference about the welcome dinner for the fiance with Cal present, and Cal, naturally, had a problem with that, insisting she had nothing to offer to that conversation. Naturally, I was tasked with getting her to agree to sit down and make decisions with them regarding decor and other things she couldn't care less about.

She was only half-dressed, and argumentative, when she opened the door. She had on a very pretty bra and a pair of jeans.

"Don't tell me," she said. "You're here to soften me up."

She was in no mood for it, but I had no choice. She had to know that. Rock meet hard place. I gently suggested that if she did participate in the discussion, at least she'd have a say in how things went. But she shot that down fairly easily by pointing out that neither the dragon nor that devil's minion David would ever allow her to really choose anything she wanted. It was only about them. Didn't I see that?

I tried distraction then. I asked her where she and Hadley and, I suppose, other young women she knew were going, and she said they were starting at the Carlyle and I said, "You're wearing jeans to the Carlyle?"

She sat down on the bed, deflated. She knew I was right. She needed to get involved if she wanted a say in the wedding plans. And she should not wear blue jeans to the Carlyle. I felt bad for her. I couldn't imagine her going through with the wedding, not after everything she'd been telling me about the fiance, but whenever I suggested she speak up, at least postpone it, she'd insist it was *the only way out*.

So what could I do? I suppose I wanted to comfort her. She was young in ways I had never been. I put my arms around her and held her for a while. She cried. I gave her a tissue I happened to have in my pocket. Then Hadley walked in.

I can picture it so clearly, as if I were a camera recording the scene. We were sitting side by side, on Cal's bed. She was cradled in my arms. I was trying to comfort her.

But that camera shot could be inflected in other ways. Hadley thought the embrace was something more than that, and her suspicion was written all over her. I let Cal go, but I had a lump of lead in my gut when she shooed us both out of there so she could change out of the jeans and into something more appropriate. She had to repair her makeup. She had to fix her hair. She would be ready in ten minutes.

Hadley didn't say anything to me until we got back downstairs. She followed me into the kitchen, her energy bristling with accusation and innuendo.

"You're getting creepy, *Danny*," Hadley said.

I told her only my friends called me Danny, but she laughed at that. I told her I didn't know what she was talking about, and did she care to be more specific about how I was "getting creepy"?

"Don't act innocent," she said. "I have eyes. You're all over her."

She said some other things about how I had it mixed up about Cal and him, the *him* who was omnipresent without actually ever needing to show his face. And Cal didn't need me making anything more complicated than it already was. I was overstepping and crossing boundaries. I needed to stay in my lane.

I've known a few girls like Hadley. Jealous and insecure. Narrow and shallow. It had nothing to do with the differences in our situations, Hadley was just mean. I hadn't picked up on it before. She'd kept her meanness well hidden, but here we were.

I told her I understood exactly where she was coming from, and she said, *where's that?* so I may have crowded her a little when I said, "You should watch your back." When she asked me to repeat myself, I was happy to do so. "You heard me," I told her.

The scared look in her eyes was comical, and I figured she had the usual thin skin of somebody who could dish it out but couldn't take it. So that was the end of it, and I was relieved she got the message without me having to take it any further.

Bad luck comes in threes, though, right?

The last time I saw Cal alone was the next morning. I'd gotten up earlier than usual, and she stumbled into the kitchen while I was having my coffee, dressed in the clothes she'd worn for the hen party and looking like she'd had a hard night of it. I didn't say anything. I made her coffee and we sat there, quiet, thinking our separate thoughts.

"I'm going to miss your coffee," she said.

I wanted so much to ask her if that was all she was going to miss. She looked so sad, fiddling with her big diamond ring.

"Hadley told me everything," Cal said, looking down into her coffee cup. I froze, but when she looked up she had this amused look on her face. "I told her she doesn't get it. You and me. Did you really tell her you were going to kick her ass if she fucked with you?" Cal sighed. "In another life ..." She left the thought unfinished.

In another life? This was the life we were both living. We were connected, remember? That's what I wanted to say. But I knew she was saying goodbye without her having to say it. Sometimes bad luck comes disguised as a brutal lesson you keep having to relearn.

12

When I landed on the pavement in front of Ian's building, ejected unceremoniously from a yellow cab that smelled of cabbage, my courage almost failed me. I had nowhere else to go, but what if he didn't take me in? I didn't have a plan B. I hadn't had time to make one.

Whenever I find myself in certain kinds of situations, my future thinking ability shuts down and it's survival moment by moment. When Dr. and Mrs. Whitaker had called me in for a "meeting" the previous evening, it was immediately clear that it was bad, but I never thought it would be *that* bad.

The looks on their faces were enough on their own to tell me I was fired, but for what cause I couldn't—or didn't want to—guess. When Mrs. W. said, "We are not bigots," I was confused. I asked her what that had to do with anything. And she said, "We understand you people have your rights, but we will not have you forcing it on our children."

If you have ever been punched in the gut, you know the feeling. The air escapes your lungs, your insides rearrange themselves, your head takes off somewhere, you're not sure where. It feels weird to be upright, because everything and everyone else are upside down and your legs and feet are not connected to the rest of your body.

I managed to ask them what they were (fucking) talking about.

"We know," Mrs. W. said, and Dr. W. turned his head away, acting like he was sickened by the sight of me.

I told them I had a right to know what the problem was. I had no idea what this was all about.

Mrs. W. said, "She's told us what's been going on between you two."

You're getting creepy, Danny.

I told them whatever she had told them, it was a lie.

Mrs. W. looked appalled. "Cal is a lot of things, Marie, but she is *not* a liar. How dare you."

That took my breath away. *Cal?* I stood up. I couldn't sit still for that. I didn't believe it. I demanded to know what Cal had said, but Mrs. W. shook her head. "You are *disgusting*," she said. "We don't owe you anything after what you've done to our daughter. After you've confused her. After you've *touched* her."

I was terminated effective immediately. I was to pack my things and be gone by the morning. I would receive no severance because I had violated my contract and their trust. As for Calista, she had gone to the Hampton house to recover from her trauma, and I was never to try to contact her again.

I entered Ian's apartment code on the callbox. Waited. Waited some more. No response. I moved away from the door and sat down on my rollie bag, praying it would support my weight.

I pictured Cal Whitaker's face when she returned home, recovered from her *trauma*, and realized I'd been in her room. I don't know what made me pick that pink handbag. I don't carry one myself, so I would never use it. But maybe that was the reason. It was useless to me, but it was something she loved. It had significance.

Of course I couldn't leave without giving her something else to remember me by. I went out to her studio. I didn't have a plan or anything. But the first thing I saw was that unfinished piece still covered on the workbench. I yanked off the cover.

Two female figures arose from a base of scraped red clay, arms and legs entwined as if they were one. The smaller figure's head was thrown back as the larger figure bent to kiss (bite) the exposed neck.

It was beautiful. Elegant. Unlike anything else I'd seen her sculpt. I wanted to smash it to bits. I spun the wooden pallet it rested on, examining it from all angles. I chose a tool made of wood, shaped like a thick pencil with a sharp point. My mark-making needed to be a shock, so I made sure to replace the cloth when I was finished.

My phone vibrated. Ian. *C'mon up.*

I had been convinced it was Hadley who had poisoned me, but Ian was blunt in his confirmation. Cal had told her mother, with David as a witness, that I had crossed the line, that she had been fooled into thinking I had nothing more than friendship in mind but then I had made inappropriate *advances*. And that I had encouraged her to break up with the fiancé. She told her parents she was afraid of me and what I might do to her if she didn't do what I wanted.

Needless to say, this all brought up a lot of bad memories. I got emotional. I broke some things and Ian looked on with something like horror. But I couldn't tell him why. I couldn't explain that ancient history to the shrinks, much less to Ian St. Martin. It wouldn't do any good anyway. It was my burden and I had to carry it by myself.

Ian was surprisingly sympathetic about the situation, even angry on my behalf. He explained that David couldn't have done anything to save me because then he would become suspect, but we all agreed that it was the Whitakers' homophobia that was disgusting, not anything I did. That said, even with David still *in*, it wasn't clear if the project would pay off in the end. I said whatever happened, I hoped it would hurt Cal in some way. Ruin her stupid wedding. I wanted her to suffer the way I was suffering.

In another surprising twist, Ian informed me that his benefactor, who had been so instrumental in getting me the position with the Whitakers, had given permission for me to stay with him until I got back on my feet. I was so grateful that I embarrassed myself—and Ian—by breaking down into tears.

But, as days turned into a couple of weeks, we could no longer blame the downturn in the economy for our poor luck finding me another position. Eventually, Ian admitted it didn't take a genius to figure out that the elite whisper brigade had done their job. As it turned out, nobody wanted a housekeeper who might be grooming their daughters and turning them queer.

The shame was unbearable. I was slipping into despair and assuming I would have to crawl back to Mike and beg for my old job back at the Tower Arms. I'd have to find a roommate situation. It wouldn't take long for any savings from the Whitakers to disappear into a black hole of rent and living expenses.

I needed reassurance from Ian, wanted him to tell me he still believed in me, but I was afraid to test that belief. As two weeks turned to three, I was sleeping less and drinking more. I felt and looked—according to Ian—like shit. I was a loser. I was living Patty's legacy in front of my own eyes. I couldn't get out of my head a scenario where Ian would apologetically have to ask me to leave.

Then everything changed. It was a coincidence worthy of a telenovela, and I had no business trusting it. An old friend of Ian's was in from the West Coast recruiting for an executive-level position in Los Angeles. Was I interested?

13

When I first came face-to-face with Dai Vernon, I was impressed by his tailoring and surprised that he was so short. He had a generous gut that strained the lower buttons of his dark blue shirt, but the windowpane-check gray suit perfectly fit his bearish physique. The pouches under his eyes were epic. His thick black hair was threaded with silver, and he had a carpet of cheek stubble. He wasn't unattractive, but he looked like he enjoyed the high life.

What could he be thinking about me and the scent of my distress and resignation?

We eyed each other. I was easily half a foot taller even in my flats.

"I like your suit," he said. "It fits you really well." Considering that his had obviously been professionally tailored, I took this as a true compliment. Prada and my needle skills to the rescue.

We introduced ourselves, and he told me to call him Vernon. Then he said, "Shall we?" and motioned me to go ahead of him. In the living room, he took the couch. I perched on Ian's favorite vintage chair. Metal and leather straps. Uncomfortable was a kind way of summarizing its merits as a chair.

"Where is Ian hiding?" Vernon laid his arm across the back of the couch.

I said Ian was in the shower and thanked him for the opportunity to interview on such short notice.

"In the shower," he repeated, smiling. "It seems we're after the same thing. Is it … Marie? Or can I call you Danvers?"

I said Danvers was fine.

Vernon said, "I need a seasoned professional. Ian says that's you."

I'd been convinced I was wasting my time, but now I realized I wanted this job, whatever it turned out to be. California. I'd be a whole country away from here. You couldn't be a gambler and not think a win was always *possible*. Even odds of crapping out were still even odds.

"Should we get started?" Vernon pulled out a little notebook and a beautiful steel pen. "What do you like about housekeeping?"

I told him I liked creating order out of chaos. People wanted to be free to live their best lives and I was there to facilitate that.

He didn't give me much feedback in his facial expressions, and I started to worry I'd taken the wrong tack, but then he broke out a smile showing even white teeth. "What do you think of that god-awful chaos you're sitting on? Be honest."

We had a laugh at Ian's expense about that chair, and Vernon invited me to sit next to him on the couch. He asked me how I'd take care of a chair like that. I told him it depended on climate. I said it was important for somebody in my position to know when to delegate a task to the experts.

He looked pleased with my answer. "My employer is an intensely private person, with extremely high standards. It can be a bit of a pressure cooker."

I told him that was my preferred environment. I liked to be busy, and multitasking was simply being efficient.

"Okay … well, this job requires a lot of flexibility," Vernon said. "You might be asked to do things outside your job description."

I didn't ask *like what?* because I didn't care. Los Angeles, California, was a mythic land to me. Everything he was implying—that the job would be demanding and exciting and unpredictable—only made me want it more. I told him I would always do whatever it took to get a job done right the first time. Winning Vernon over was suddenly my sole mission, and I didn't care that I was probably overselling myself.

"It's a hot house sometimes," he said. "The celebrity lifestyle requires a lot of coddling. But we would also need you to fit in with the other staff and be on task at all times."

I told him that was exactly the kind of position I was looking for. I thought of other staff as collaborators. We all had one job: to focus on excellence.

"Do we need to talk about your last position?" Vernon had to notice my inward cringe. "Ian mentioned it, but—" He waved his hand. "Don't worry. I know how these things happen, believe me."

I told him I hadn't "groomed" anybody. If anything, Calista Whitaker had been the one who made advances. I told him how she'd wanted me to break into somebody's house and steal money. By the end of my recitation, Cal was to blame for all of it. She was the one who deserved punishment.

Vernon listened, but in the end, he shrugged it off. *That's fine* was all he said.

Then he consulted his watch. "Are you a drinker? What about illegal substances?" He chuckled. "Do you do weed? Coke? Ex?"

I told him I didn't do any of that, but I did enjoy alcoholic beverages. On occasion. I didn't think he needed to know I'd been drinking bourbon by the liter since Cal Whitaker decided to trash my reputation and ruin my life.

"I only give a shit if it's a problem," Vernon laughed and went into the kitchen, returning with rocks glasses and a bottle. "I heard you're a bourbon girl." He held up the bottle and I nodded. He poured us two fingers each.

We clinked and drank, and he told me I was hired. If it was a surprise that it had all happened so easily, I didn't allow any subterranean suspicions to dim my joy. I loved Dai Vernon. He was a brother now. Like Ian. These two were my brothers from other mothers, giving me another chance to prove myself. I was giddy. Triumphant. In my head I told Cal Whitaker to fuck off and die. I was winning again.

Vernon said I was attractive when I smiled and then hastened to add he didn't mean that I should smile *more* or anything. Him backtracking that way was kind of funny, but also sweet. Then Ian came downstairs wearing a towel and nothing else, his spiky hair all wet, and we toasted, the best of friends, and I signed the NDA and a contract that highlighted a heart-pounding salary. And my new employer with the famous name was going to wonder how she ever lived without me.

Until Vernon and I were leaving for JFK, I didn't think I'd miss anything about New York. Not even Ian. But nostalgia hit me hard when he pulled me aside after Vernon got into the black car that would whisk us to the airport and deposit us at the first-class lounge. I deserved this happy ending, Ian said, and wished me all the luck in the world. "I hoped I could keep you here with me," he pressed his cheek against mine. "Have a great life, Danny ..."

14

From the beginning, California was a study in contrasts. Light and dark. Heat and cold. Dread of another failure and belief in a success so complete I couldn't even picture it. Even before I arrived, I promised myself I would bury my torment in the sand and the sun. I would drown the memory of Cal Whitaker in the sparkling Pacific Ocean. I would grow new, stronger roots. I would never go back to New York.

My intentions were good. Like always. And that's what matters.

So I arrived in Brentwood, an enclave within a sprawling metropolis, surrounded by a moat of privilege and wealth. It felt different from any place I'd ever been. "Welcome home to Patten House," Vernon had said. I got emotional when he said it. I think I hugged him. I was giddy and jet-lagged.

At first sight, the glass house looked as you might expect. Rooms grand in scale, enormous undraped windows to let in the continuous California sunshine. Everything was beautifully detailed and furnished and polished. The lighting scheme throughout was capable of achieving different looks and "feels" and had a twenty-page guide to show how to adjust color temperature and levels for different effects. The decor was bespoke, calculated to elicit conversation. None of this was a surprise.

But the art and photography had been curated to pull you into a narrative of lives lived under the magnifying glass of avid public interest. How you felt about that, in the end, was up to you. You might be envious. Or unsettled. Contrasts. Always contrasts.

Bebe Patten's life had been captured in dozens of photographs displayed all over the house. She wasn't pretty, but she was striking. She had strange gray eyes that could appear either silvery or black depending on how she was lighted. She often seemed to be looking beyond the lens, as if seeing something she wanted just out of reach.

I searched her name online and discovered a world of speculation about her and her famous parents. Arthur Patten was certainly beloved by a particular segment of young male filmmakers who revered his unorthodox directing techniques, methods that appeared to involve a disturbing level of mind control and manipulation. Rose Patten was most often described as delicate, sensitive, a thespian with immense talent, but a difficult person, possibly mentally ill, a living, breathing Blanche duBois. As if she had no real identity other than what was projected onto her by the press. I felt sorry for Rose. I loathed Arthur.

The pair had made eight films together. Reviews were mixed when those films were released in the 1970s and 1980s, and people still argued about their relative artistic merit and contribution to film history. But they did have their champions. I'd call some of those people fanatics. The Patten following had a whiff of cult to it.

But the internet reserved its most severe judgments for nepo baby Bebe Patten. Wayward. Spoiled. Nymphomaniac. Drug addict. Alcoholic. Vapid. Delusional. A terrible disappointment to her parents, the industry, and the profession of acting. She'd only made that one film when she was a precocious teen, playing a character named Sugar Callahan, a girl who kills her mother and a slew of other randoms while in a dissociated rage. Blah blah glamorized childhood trauma blah blah. Some people loved her performance, others called it laughable.

It's a strange thing to be placed in charge of a person's home that you've never met. You can't help but form opinions about them, but real-life context is sorely lacking. I already longed for the arrival of Miss Bebe Patten so I could see for myself who she really was.

That first week went by so fast. Vernon was a generous and lenient boss but also a stickler at enforcing what rules there were. I had to be on-call 24/7, but I could take as much time as I wanted to myself as long as the house was immaculate and well stocked with everything Miss Patten needed, even when she wasn't "at home." I was given all codes and keys, with two exceptions. Her jewelry safe combination was known only to her. And no one was allowed in Vernon's office. Always kept locked, his office was the only room in the house for which I would not be given a key. You had to wonder what he was hiding in there.

With our employer away, I could make my own schedule. But I still got up at dawn. I was so eager. I loved everything about my new life. The light. The exotic flora. The spring air that had no bite, not the way it did back home. My room was perfect. The nicest I'd ever had. My bathroom was as big as my apartment back in New York.

One of the first things I did when I unpacked was hide Cal's pink handbag in the bottom drawer of the built-in cabinet. I put it behind the wool sweaters I would probably never need again. Maybe someday I would send the stolen bag back to her, but for now I enjoyed having it, imagining her feelings when she realized I'd taken it. She would be pissed off, but would she remember its significance, the marking of that very first meeting in the coffee shop? She would never tell anyone, I knew that much. It would forever be our secret.

I tried not to think about what I'd done to her sculpture. At the time, it had seemed like sending her a message, but in retrospect I wish I'd smashed it to bits.

On Sunday, my first day off, I got up as usual, got dressed as usual, made coffee and drank it as usual. I like things "as usual." Routine is important. And I was more settled and better rested than I had been since the day I walked out of the Whitakers' Brooklyn brownstone for the last time.

I was innocently scanning the Sunday *Los Angeles Times*. I never saw it coming.

"New York Deb Marries English Lover in Wedding of the Century."

Who writes such a ridiculous headline? Cal's jealousy of doe-eyed Chloe had turned on a switch, but it was one that she could apparently turn off at will. I could practically taste that hazelnut buttercream, and it made me sick.

Oh look. A high-definition photo of the beaming newlyweds. I found it annoying that Cal looked so good in that slinky wedding dress. The fact that her vampire smile seemed genuinely happy hurt a bit, but I felt sorriest for her husband. He looked weak, and she was somebody who enjoyed leading you around by the nose. Now that she had him, he didn't have a chance.

I put my phone down, then picked it back up and dialed Ian. It rang and rang, but I got no answer. I needed to get out. I tapped my Uber app then closed it again. What I needed was fresh air.

15

Alice, lost in Hollywoodland. The grounds of Patten House were a backlot fantasy. Croquet court. Espaliered fruit trees. A French kitchen garden replete with a stone wall and greenhouse. A two-acre topiary garden. It was over-the-top and fabulous.

Yet here was an unexpected dead end. A wall of matted vines ten feet high. An optical illusion that on closer inspection revealed the outline of a gate. I reached through the foliage, pulled the latch and the gate creaked open. The sound effects department had worked overtime on that.

On the other side of the wall, a strange forest of bamboo. Filtered light stained green by rampant foliage overhead. And, emerging, I found a tattered blue circus tent. Since everything had been designed so carefully elsewhere, I half-expected animatronic clowns to appear and give me a good scare. *And here we have the Stephen King Garden …*

Ground ivy grabbed at my ankles, trying to trip me up, but that tent was a curiosity I couldn't resist. What I had thought was a wooden doorway was an illusion painted onto canvas. The actual doorway was a dark rectangle.

"Hello!"

I'm not partial to jump scares, and this one left me weak-kneed. I turned, almost afraid of what I'd find. A dark-haired woman a little older than I was, built sturdily and dressed in filthy coveralls, flapped her hand in a friendly wave and walked toward me. "You're the new girl, right?" She held out a grubby hand, the dirt jammed up under short, unpolished nails that reminded me, unpleasantly, of Cal.

"I'm Alice," she said.

I told her my name, explained I was the new housekeeper, and she said, "Don't tell me I remind you of your ex." She laughed at the absurdity of it, but she had no clue how close she was to the truth.

"I'm with the *dirt* crew," Alice said. "Me and Udo keep the topiary garden on point. Eddy does the hedge work."

I didn't know who Udo or Eddy were, but I said it was all quite … something, and she asked me if that was a compliment or an insult.

I asked her about the tent and she got animated. Did I not know about the Pattens? This was their infamous Theater of All Potential. Apparently, the official line was that the Pattens had held private performances here, back in the 1980s. Alice shrugged. "But a lot of people say they were into weird stuff," she said.

I asked her what kind of weird stuff she meant and she said, "Mind control. Rumors about TAP being some kind of sex cult, but I don't know about that. People make shit up. That's Hollywood. It's all hype. You shouldn't believe half the stuff you hear." She finally took a breath. "Do you like cats?"

I told her I was allergic and was rewarded with a look of disappointment.

I followed her inside the tent. Whether I was picking up on something truly malevolent or was being influenced by Alice's speculations wasn't clear, but the place exuded bad energy.

Alice got up on the stage and fucked around, pretending to tap dance and singing "Time Warp" from Rocky Horror, deliberately off-key. She was cute, but no Columbia. But then one of the boards, rotted no doubt by termites, cracked under her heel and pulled her boot off. She seemed deflated by that—possibly worried she'd get into trouble for damaging the stage, or maybe she was afraid of contracting tetanus.

I told her I had to get back to work, but she insisted I hadn't seen the best part: the Aerie was just steps away. Yes, it was true! The Aerie where Bebe Patten had been raised, the original family home, was located just over yonder, perched at the edge of a ravine. Walking backward away from me, she gave me a cheeky grin and said, "C'mon … you have to see this."

How could I say no to that?

We came onto the half-circle driveway through a wrought iron gate between two stone pillars. It was all theater and drama until you saw the house itself. The Aerie looked like it was about to collapse into a heap of stucco. It was beyond derelict.

Alice spun in circles ahead of me, flashing muscular calves, saying she knew a way in. That sounded dangerously like trespassing, but I followed her anyway. I was here, so why not? We got in through an unlocked basement door.

Down a short flight of gritty steps, we were below ground level in a daylight basement. A vintage refrigerator was the only identifiable thing among piles of splintered rubble, the bones of discarded furniture. The fridge had been chained except that the padlock had been left open and dangling.

I asked Alice how long the house had been like this, and she said *oh, forever*, because she'd been working at Patten House for eight years and Artie and Rose had both died in the early oh-ohs. A house left neglected deteriorates more quickly than you'd imagine.

"Miss Patten only came back here to live after they were dead, when she finished the aquarium." Alice grinned and headed toward an arched doorway enclosing a set of stairs, so I followed along. I wasn't afraid. Not exactly.

The dark stairway turned and then turned again, and I had to stop myself from clutching for the back of Alice's coveralls. Not a fan of dark, enclosed spaces. Not at all.

We came out of the stairwell into a gloomy kitchen. Dark wood floor-to-ceiling cabinetry, scarred black Formica countertop, upper cabinets with dusty small-paned glass doors and a lot of junk still piled in there.

Bebe Patten's "aquarium" was about being seen and seeing *out*. This house turned inward. It brooded.

I followed Alice into what must have been a formal dining room. A Lucite chandelier dangled at the end of its wires. Maybe it was the two of us coming in there that changed the air pressure in the room, but that chandelier started to swing ever so slightly and I had to laugh. Alice asked me what was so funny, and I said the house was the perfect setting for a horror movie.

"Except you'd never be able to get insurance," she said as if I were seriously suggesting such a thing. She turned and pointed at the far side of the room. White flowers bloomed along a living vine that seemed to grow out of the wall. The wiry branches crisscrossed the window and adjacent doorway, effectively sealing them shut. The effect was creepy. I asked her what the plant was, and she said it was called bougainvillea.

"It finds the cracks around the doors and windows and pushes its way through," Alice said. "But it weakens the integrity of the structure. When we have the Big One, this whole place is a goner." She drew her finger across her throat and laughed like a movie villain. When she came toward me I took an involuntary step back and said I really had to get back to work.

She offered to walk me back but I told her not to bother, so then she said, "Okay, whatever. I'm not stupid. I can take a hint."

I wasn't so sure about that. She was alternately flirty and testy. She could be the kind of girl you have a one-night stand with and the next thing you know, she's moving in with her cat.

16

When I was at the Tower Arms, cash flowed if you could make certain things happen, not balk about cleaning up somebody else's bloody mess. If I'd imagined that in this world it would be any different, that only proved I'd allowed myself to believe in a fairy tale. Vernon was on the take with every vendor who provided goods and services to Patten House. The depth and scope of his graft was breathtaking, and I benefited, earning upwards of half my on-the-book income in additional cash just in that first month. I stowed the rolled bills in Cal's pink handbag, an irony that wasn't lost on me.

I shouldn't have been so surprised that Vernon was in the game, but this was an extraordinarily lucrative racket. Retail was a one hundred percent markup, but bespoke was closer to a thousand, so tacking on another thirty seemed less of a gouging and more like a gentle service fee for the prestige of having Bebe Patten's business. Vernon's logic was that high-net-value people enjoyed paying more for something as long as it was "custom." Rarity was critical.

We shopped at places where you had to make an appointment, where you might be served all manner of freshly squeezed juices or specially prepared smoothies while you pondered bath towels or sheets or silver fucking candlesticks. It was excessive and, privately, I wavered between awe at the opulence and disgust at the excess.

But Vernon was good, and I decided I needed to study his techniques. He was charming but with razor-sharp edges, always ready with a snide remark. You could often find conflicting interpretations in what he said. Was it joke or insult? Few people were brave enough to react beyond nervous smiling or staring at their feet. I had the feeling they were afraid of what he'd say if they called him on his taunts, that he would show them to be neurotic or (much worse) uncool. In other words, Vernon was intimidating and I wanted to learn his secret.

I got on with Vernon, though at first he was a little cold. But I'd kept my head down and gradually he had warmed up and told me a bit about himself. He was originally from Houston, which he pronounced the seventh circle of hell. I told him I'd imagined he was Eurotrash, and he thought that was a hoot. Vernon loved my completely made-up childhood, a plot I ripped off from that movie with Tatum O'Neal when she was a little kid. He said moving around like that must have been how I acquired my *unflappability*. I had thought he might catch me in the lie, that Ian would have told him something about Patty, but Ian had apparently kept his mouth shut and so Vernon bought it. It's always a good feeling when you can fool somebody who should know better.

It turned out that Vernon had known Ian for twenty years. They'd done a few projects together but hadn't seen each other in quite some time. I got the feeling that Vernon thought Ian was the one who got away. He seemed a little bit in love with him and asked me two different times if I had slept with Ian. I lied both times and he looked relieved. I didn't want to tell him he shouldn't carry a torch for Ian St. Martin because the man was too fickle, but I did casually mention that Ian had a boyfriend … or a girlfriend, I wasn't sure which. And that they, whoever it was, paid for his apartment and his lifestyle. And that the person was very jealous. Vernon said, *is that so* as if he couldn't have cared less. But I thought he did care. Very much.

Life quickly settled into routine, but I was bored and the newspapers and gossip television shows kept showing me stories about the famous newlyweds and their honeymoon antics. Worse, even the social media algorithms conspired against me. Cal was everywhere and nowhere.

There is only so much organizing you can do before it's all organized. Eventually I ran out of things to keep my hands—and by extension, my head—busy with the mundane. I had touched everything in that ten-thousand-square-foot house and instituted small but significant changes that impressed Vernon with my efficiency, diligence, and organizational skills. But the glass house was too quiet. It held its breath in anticipation of Bebe Patten's return. So did I.

Vernon had his point of view on her. Princess (as he often called her) was cloying and dependent. But she was also affectionate and could be generous. She was self-centered and a gossip. He loved her like a little sister. They were *that close*.

I had Bebe Patten's very own hand-selected gallery of images to study and form my impressions of her. I imagined how it would be when we met. I wouldn't let her celebrity unnerve me. I would be cool and competent, retiring yet ready to offer my opinion when asked. She would be impressed by my adjustments in the home. Or maybe she wouldn't care. But that wouldn't matter, because she didn't need to know how the sausage got made, she only had to sit down and enjoy eating it.

Take Bebe Patten, age sixteen. She's the star of an experimental horror film called *All the Evil Girls*. At that point I hadn't seen it, but I could, and did, read online reviews of the film. Zero stars would have been preferable to all the one-stars that movie received on those sites where people went to voice their "unpopular" opinions. People can be spiteful and unfair when they aren't entertained in the manner they're expecting. I've found that small children can be the same way.

But the film's poster had real shock value. You couldn't look away from that snarling girl. Blood clotted on her face and in her hair, streaks of it down her neck, and in one hand she brandishes a huge meat cleaver. Lizzie Borden rip-off it might have been, but some kinder reviewers noted the authenticity of Bebe Patten's singular performance in the role of Sugar Callahan, the sheer ferocity she managed to convey.

Or consider one of few portraits with all three Pattens together. They sit on the edge of a stage, or rather *the* stage. The one in the Theater of All Potential, recognizable now that I'd seen it.

In the photo, Bebe Patten is probably a bit younger than she was in her only movie. She sits squeezed between her parents, looking off-camera, an expression of pure rage contorting her unformed adolescent features, an expression that feels like an eerie precursor to her singular performance. Rose Patten is smiling, but it's lips only. She's detached from the other two, staring bleakly into the camera lens. Arthur Patten is a big man with a thatch of dark hair that falls over his wide forehead. One beefy arm forms a chokehold around his daughter's neck. He's in the middle of saying something to whoever is off camera—the same person Bebe Patten must be looking at. He holds a cigarette in his free hand, pinkie extended. Anybody could see he must have been a real asshole.

One day I asked if I could hitch a ride with Armen the chauffeur into the city and roam around Hollywood for a while. Vernon's attitude was *whatever floats your boat.* So off we went. At my request, Armen dropped me in front of Madame Tussauds, but the line was long so I left and mingled with the freak show of humanity on the street. This was the real Hollywood, my kind of town.

I found a lesbian bar by sheer luck, and drank two shots of vodka with a girl named Kelly. She was an actress. *Aspiring.* Which meant hopeful yet insecure and working as a cater waiter. After the second shot she invited me over to her place. She wanted me to meet her dog who had been her wife in a past life. Fortunately, Armen saved me from that entanglement. He was on his way back and wanted to know where to pick me up.

Sorry, Kelly ... gotta go. Please tell your dog-wife I said hello.

17

"You think you're better than me," Becker said softly, watching me with that dead-eyed stare.

She had followed me, on the pretext of helping clear the table. But now she had me cornered me in the kitchen while Remy and Vernon lingered in the dining room. They were laughing raucously, the sound echoing in the quiet of the house.

I moved past her and deposited the dessert plates in the bottom of the sink. Then I turned and held my hands out for the plates she was carrying.

"You're not really a housekeeper, are you?" She looked very pleased with herself, as if she'd figured me out. I took the plates from her hands and told her I was, in fact, *the* housekeeper, and we were a team. I said we didn't have to be enemies, that was a choice we didn't have to make.

Becker put her hands on her hips. She had an hourglass figure and a pretty face despite the sneer. Or maybe that rictus was an attempt at a smile.

"Hope you won't take this the wrong way," she said. "But I answer to Vernon, not some stick up her ass. You feel me?"

The luncheon with Remy and Becker had started out pleasantly enough, with an elaborate five-course meal that Vernon ordered from Chin Chin. I was surprised when Armen delivered us the food but declined my invitation to stay for lunch, mumbling vaguely about errands. After he left Vernon explained that drivers don't join housekeeping staff for meals. That was the rule.

I was surprised when the two of them showed up dressed like that. Hardly professional. But I chalked it up to yet another way that California was different from New York. People here dressed more casually. Everybody showed a lot of skin.

Tasha Becker showed off a pierced navel and chin length bleached hair that she had gelled into a hard shell. Cris Remy's blue velour tracksuit had the word *JUICY* stitched across the backside. Her long dark hair was tightly braided. When I shook her hand Remy had mumbled her greeting and wouldn't look me in the eye. On the other hand Becker couldn't take her eyes off me, watching me like I was an insect she was about to dissect.

While Vernon cheerfully passed around containers of dumplings and lettuce cups, he got them talking about themselves. He'd throw me these looks as if to say, *Watch me. This is how you do it.* I should have been grateful he stepped in and got the conversation going so I could learn about Remy's acting class and Becker's rescue dogs, but I was bored by all of it. And no, I didn't want to *share my story.* Hard pass. Thanks anyway.

They were trying to make up their minds about me while Vernon pushed food on all of us. This Chinese food in California was different from what I was used to in New York, but I liked it.

When we were finished eating I cleared the plates and put the leftover food in the refrigerator while Vernon brought out a tall, multilayered cake he'd had specially made for dessert. In the center was an old-fashioned upright vacuum made of molded chocolate with a thought bubble coming out of the business end that said *VROOM VROOM.* Remy and Becker both had two pieces.

After that we took a tour of the upstairs, and I found myself alone with Becker again, in Bebe Patten's bedroom. Becker closed the door, flopping onto the edge of the big bed and crossing her legs. Her actions dared me to say it, so I asked if she realized that I would now have to straighten that.

Her pretty face reddened. She hated me.

"That bitch plays too much," Becker said. "She only gets away with it because of who she is. She's not better than me. And neither are you."

I said—mildly—that I didn't have a clue why she was so upset.

"I'm not done *talking*," she said.

I told her to keep her voice down. I wanted to warn her this could go a whole different way and she wouldn't like it if it did, but I was restrained. If this was a test, I intended to pass it.

Becker glared at me. "Watch yourself, cutie. You're in for it." When she got up she made a big show of smoothing the bed and blew me a kiss when she left.

"That went well, don't you think?" Vernon said after they'd gone.

I couldn't tell him what had happened between me and Becker without seeming like a whiny baby. *Wah, wah, the maid was mean to me. The maid semi-threatened me.* I wouldn't rat Becker out. That wasn't my style.

Vernon stood at the dishwasher watching while I loaded in glasses and cutlery. "You think you can handle those gals?" he asked. "They're blunt instruments, but they're effective."

I wanted to tell him no, I can't handle Becker. Becker is insubordinate, not to mention someone who clearly wanted to stab me in the back.

Even Remy was a potential problem, a meek follower who could be easily persuaded to cause me grief. I wanted to say we should start over and restaff both positions. But I told Vernon *sure, I can handle them, no problem,* and closed the dishwasher.

He stood there for a minute as if he knew I was holding something back, then he sighed and got busy pulling out the leftover food containers I'd put in the refrigerator, dropping them in the trash.

I asked him what he was doing, that food was still good, and he looked at me confused. "It's the rule, Danvers," and dropped the rest of the cake into the open can. *Thump.*

18

Miss P home late last night. Bring coffee 9 sharp.

Bebe Patten made a dramatic entrance into the little sitting room where I'd brought her coffee. She was every film noir femme fatale, down to the Lana Turner turban on her gingery hair. Basking in my undignified, open-mouthed awe, she said, "Oh, hello. You're the new victim," and moved into the room, depositing herself on the chaise longue. *And scene.*

I hustled to offer her coffee, holding it out to her, but she didn't take it. First, she looked me up and down. I squared my shoulders and tried to relax. I didn't know if I was meeting with her approval or not, because she kept her expression blank.

Finally, she took the coffee from my hand and said, "You're awfully tall, aren't you?"

"Just under six feet," I told her.

Her smile revealed the well-documented, and charming, gap between her two front teeth. "I need you to fit a dress for me," she said. "A particular dress. It's important that I look smashing for my audition." With a frown, "Did you make the coffee, or did Vernon?"

I had prepared the coffee and the arrangement on the tray carefully. Perfectly brewed espresso. The single waxy gardenia in a little crystal vase. Two brown sugar cubes on a tiny Limoges plate. Vernon had been very complimentary. *Good presentation, Danvers.*

I admitted that I had indeed made the coffee, and she said, "That's why it's so good, I guess," with this smile that was equal parts seduction and surprise.

It's hard to describe the effect of her charm. It was like standing in the sun.

"Should I call you Danvers?" she said. I answered that she could call me whatever she liked, and that made her laugh. I told her my friends called me Danny.

That faint smile with a peek of gap tooth. "What are you going to call *me?*" she said. "If we're already friends." I told her I would call her whatever *she* liked, and she said "Let me think about it."

The way she was holding her hand next to her lips. The red hair. So much like the figure in the painting above her head.

She looked at me over the rim of her coffee cup. "It's not a portrait," she said. "But some people might think so."

A nude woman wearing thigh-high, sheer stockings. A bright blue wig cap, a thatch of red hair between her spread legs, startling, drawing the eye. And off to the side, two other figures that seemed to be other selves. I had identified the painting right off, a midcentury surrealist woman artist, a rare breed, long dead, whose work sold in the low millions. I thought I would tell Ian about it, but we hadn't spoken since I'd left New York. I was yesterday's news, gone and forgotten.

"People say art is the best investment there is," Bebe Patten said, watching me closely. She had a way of looking at you. It penetrated you. She could flay you with the intensity of her gaze.

"Do you like art?" she asked.

I said I didn't know much about it, which seemed to please her because she said, "Me either." Her eyes brightened, tipping the irises toward silver. "If you have a nickname, I need one too."

You might think I had the answer ready, but it came out of my subconscious. I said, "What about Sugar?"

I could see I'd surprised her. "You've seen my movie?" she said.

It was obviously important that I'd seen it, so I told her I loved it. My favorite. Honestly. An amazing performance.

"Okay, okay … don't overdo it." She laughed. "So you're Danny and I'm Sugar." Then she added, "But in front of other people you should call me Miss Patten. I don't want it to look like I have a favorite."

If she was going to play favorites, I was already determined that it should be me.

She fidgeted, tightening the sash of her robe. "Has Vernon filled you in on me? I know how he operates."

I denied it, told her I was not a gossip even if he had, and she made a good show of believing me.

"Well, I confess," she said with this tinkly laugh, "I *am* a bit demanding. And I know what he says behind my back. Not everybody in this house is so discreet. This whole town is rotten with gossips." She arranged her robe over bare knees and folded her arms. "He says you're a genius with a needle and thread. Are you?"

I shrugged and acted modest, but if there's one thing I'm cocky about, it's my tailoring skills. We agreed to an after-lunch fitting. She needed the dress by the following day.

"It's a big fucking deal," she said. "I have a lot riding on this audition. You need to make Sugar look gorgeous, okay?" I told her Sugar didn't need my help with that. She seemed to appreciate that.

When I went back downstairs with the coffee tray, Mrs. Luchetti had arrived. She was short and strong-looking, with an ample bosom and thick black-rimmed glasses perched on a snub nose. A wrinkly, cartoon owl of a person. Her pristine white chef's jacket fit snugly over a pair of baggy checked pants that ended in a pair of sensible, cushioned old lady sneakers. I introduced myself as she was concocting a fruit and vegetable smoothie for Miss Patten's breakfast. We shouted over the machine noise and she was amiable enough.

Becker, also known as The Bane of My Existence, came in the kitchen door as Luchetti turned off the blender.

"She's back?" Becker said.

Luchetti and I answered yes at the same time. Then I told her she was late and I asked where Remy was, since they both lived in Torrance and usually carpooled in Remy's car.

"Cris called out," Luchetti interrupted. "I forgot to tell you."

Remy had called while I was upstairs with the boss, and Becker had had to borrow her cousin's car, which was why she'd been late. I was irritated that the old lady hadn't thought to mention all this at the top, but she was unfazed or didn't care, and she had the advantage of multiple seniorities. Luchetti calmly poured the thick green glop she'd concocted into a tall crystal glass and blinked at me through those owlish glasses.

And Becker didn't seem concerned about being late. Apparently, my predecessor, whoever they were, had not been strict on rules either.

"So you saw the boss?" Becker got herself a coffee mug. "Did you see any scars? Like … surgical scars, *you* know …" and she made a circular motion around her own face. "She must've been getting something *fixed*, else why would she be away so long?"

I told her in no uncertain terms that it was none of our business, and those were personal decisions of Miss Patten's besides.

Becker blithely ignored my outrage and walked over to the refrigerator. She swung the door open and stood there, contemplating the contents. Luchetti and I exchanged raised eyebrows and I went over and, reaching over Becker's head, closed the door firmly. She glared at me, whining that she was hungry because she'd had to skip breakfast. It was Cris's fault she was late. She had only intended to grab a yogurt. Why was that such a big deal?

"Tough luck," I told her. Luchetti's lunch would be served promptly at twelve-thirty, and with Cris out, Becker would be on dusting and vacuuming on her own. I told her to start in the foyer and she stalked off, grumbling in some language I couldn't identify. No doubt it was all about what a hard-ass bitch I was.

My authoritarian approach with the maid garnered an approving nod from Luchetti. I asked her if she'd seen Vernon. "Oh yeah," she said, "He's nursing a doozy of a hangover out by the pool."

Dressed only in a thigh-high terry robe, Vernon reclined on what was essentially a full-size, outdoor canopy bed. A bag of frozen peas perched on top of his head. He squinted up at me, then picked up his shades and racked them on his head to hold the bag of peas in place.

"I've got a rager," he said. "Princess kept me up all fucking night." I made sympathetic noises and told him that Remy had called out. "Do you want me to fire her for you?" He dropped the sunglasses onto his nose, using a forefinger to push them into place.

I said firing was unnecessary, but we should have a talk with her.

"We need to deliver a scolding," Vernon said. "Got it. Sure. What did Princess say about the audition?"

I told him she wanted me to make alterations on a dress because it was important, and he sighed. "We need to tamp down unrealistic expectations," he said.

I asked him why we would do that, and he smiled disagreeably. "Well, Danvers," with no small amount of sarcasm, "some people just get off on humiliating others. But that's Hollywood, isn't it?"

19

While I waited for The Big Fitting, I oiled my machine, inserted a fresh needle, and preloaded four bobbins with different neutral colors of thread to save time. In the larger of Bebe Patten's two dressing rooms, I took out the ironing board and iron, set them up in the corner, and dragged the fitting platform out of storage. I put it in front of the three-sided mirror so we could look at all the angles. Exciting things were happening. Bebe Patten was everything I thought she would be. I was living the dream.

When I finished my preparations, I tapped lightly on the connecting door to her bedroom and went in.

She was sitting on her bed, cordless phone to her ear, dressed in shiny leggings and an oversized flowy shirt that left one freckled shoulder bare. She winked at me. "Yeah, I know," she said, into the phone. "I'm the one that told you, remember?" She pointed at the phone with her other hand and rolled her eyes at me.

"I'm doing it," she said. "So you're too late. And you'll still get your … what? Yes, if I get it, you'll get your cut … yes, even though you—" she listened, shaking her head. "Understood. No, I said I understand! Look, work it out with SAG and earn your ten percent. I have to go." She ended the call and threw the phone aside. "Thank you for saving me from that asshole. My agent." She made a face. "They think they own you. What is it?"

I said I was ready and needed to know which dress she wanted to alter.

"You wanna know something?" she asked. "I'm really fucking nervous about this audition. I haven't read for anybody in a really long time, and this is a huge deal. Huge. So I haven't decided which dress. Verny and I had picked out something more casual, but then I thought about it and now I don't know."

The phone rang.

"Verny needs to weigh in," she said, ignoring the phone. Then she glanced at the display and her whole attitude changed, became electrified. "I have to take this, okay?" When she answered, her voice was girlish and coy. "I was just thinking about you, and here you are." She glanced over at me. "Hold on a minute," she put her hand over the mouthpiece. "Tell Verny to get up here, okay?"

I bowed my way out.

"Paul, darling. I'm so glad you called …"

Paul, darling. The unnatural way she said it sounded like a parody of a soap opera.

When I saw the dress, I was horrified. First, the color was a bang-on match of the purple bag that a certain brand of Canadian whiskey comes in. No way did I have a true match in thread. Second, it was made of silk satin. And third, elaborate hand beading covered the bodice. It was also quite narrow through the waist—I guessed a size eight, though there was no label to tell me—and the style was outdated. This dress was a hot mess, something an old woman would have worn to a party fifty years ago. And letting out that beaded bodice to fit Sugar's more curvaceous proportions would take real finesse. I might have to improvise.

I could see why Vernon was arguing so strenuously against her wearing it. But she insisted it had good karma, and when Vernon scoffed she said he wasn't being supportive and sent him away to get that thing they'd discussed the night before. All very mysterious. So many undercurrents. I felt wide awake for the first time in months. This was what I'd left everything for. To alter this ugly purple dress for Sugar Fucking Callahan. Why the fuck not?

Sugar hopped up on the tailoring platform, stripping off her hoodie and sweatpants. "What do you think?" she said. "Can you make it fit?"

I told her it would be my pleasure to alter it to fit her, and she said, "Aren't you adorable," and I said, "If you say so."

Then she held the dress up to herself and I wanted to blurt the truth. Vernon was right. The purple was not flattering. It was all kinds of wrong, in fact. But you read about actors doing weird things, like gaining a ton of weight or going undercover for a role. To Sugar, this dress was a totem.

Sugar's mood flipped when Vernon came back, clapping her hands together like a little kid. "There you are! Did you get it?"

He held up a flat pink package and strolled over, standing behind her, eyeing the reflection of her body. A serious, narrow-eyed appraisal. She held completely still, her eyes wide, apprehensive, waiting for his judgment.

Finally he smiled his approval. "You're looking good, babe," he said.

She arched her back and sucked in her gut. Then she giggled and let her belly expand. "If you think so, Verny, then I'm happy." She turned to assess her admirable backside in the boy short underpants. "I'm petrified. You'd think I was some kind of virgin." She and Vernon both laughed, and Vernon said, "No one who knows you would think that," and she said, "Why are you so mean?" But she was only kidding. I was learning that their communication style was like fighters sparring, trying to find each other's weakness but not landing any serious blows.

"You'll be great," Vernon said in a tone that I interpreted as discouraging, but Sugar didn't seem to notice. Vernon flicked me this mocking look as he handed her the package. She pulled out an oddly shaped garment resembling an unattractive, high-waisted, taupe bathing suit or a hideous pair of bike shorts so narrow they would only fit some pointy-chinned anime girl. Shapewear is what they call it, but it is basically a corset that smooths and sculpts the body.

"Oh," she said, stretching it this way and that. She made a face. "Both of you, out! I don't want an audience while I put this stupid thing on, okay? Go!"

Vernon and I retreated to the hall. "What do you really think of the dress?" he smirked. I said it was an interesting choice and he laughed because he knew I was lying. "You know who all this is for," he said. "She's in a tizzy because it's Paul Westerfield who's auditioning her."

I was surprised. I hadn't heard that name in years. Paul Westerfield had made a lot of movies in the eighties and nineties, with thin plots and derivative psychological thriller elements that audiences seemed to love and critics loved to hate.

"You know who he is?" Vernon said.

I said, "Well, he's famous, isn't he?"

"Yeah," Vernon said. "A famous hack." He said it as if he was deeply disturbed that hacks were often famous and well rewarded in the film business. "Haven't you seen the movies?"

I said only the one about the serial killing nun. I remembered what otherwise would have been immediately forgettable because it had been my first date with this girl who'd been a novitiate before she realized she was a lesbian and left the church. The girl had laughed inappropriately through the entire movie and afterward kept saying how it perfectly captured life as a nun. Her reaction unnerved me, so it was also our last date. I told Vernon that from what I remembered the movie was terrible.

"Exactly!" Vernon slapped his thigh. "Now he's supposedly going to direct this low-budget soft porn indie, make some kind of splashy Sundance comeback with a pot-of-gold A24 distribution deal at the end. Pfft. He's not talented, but she seems to think this is her big break."

His tone was sour, but also strangely desperate. Like he was trying to convince himself of something. He leaned toward me and lowered his voice to a stage whisper. "She's kidding herself. He's never gonna risk his big comeback by casting her. She's only ever made the one movie, and she was sixteen fucking years old." His breath hissed. "She's almost forty and, you know, I hate to say it, but the way she's lived? Cameras can be cruel to older women."

Thirty-eight is not that old, I told him. Not anymore. And Miss Patten didn't have a wrinkle on her.

"Botox," he said and pushed away from the wall. "You're delusional. Both of you. We'll all have to be ready to pick up the pieces when this thing goes south. I'm counting on you to be her new best friend when she needs one. You see how she is. I can't hold her up on my own."

I asked him why he was so convinced she wasn't going to get the part. I kept my voice low, hyper aware of her on the other side of the door.

"Because she'd have to carry the whole film." He said it like I was a dunce, as if it would be obvious to a child that Bebe Patten couldn't "carry" a film.

"I read Westerfield's magnum opus," he said, wincing. "When I tell you it's awful, I'm being kind. I'll tell you what: this is a total vanity project, and it's not groundbreaking either."

I gently suggested he keep his voice down, but he was on a roll so I took his arm and pulled him a little further down the hall so she wouldn't hear him trashing her movie.

"Get this," he said. "She's playing a schoolteacher by day, professional dominatrix by night. But the part is written for a much younger actress, and she spends a lot—and I mean a lot—of time half-nude or stuffed into latex. There's even a scene with full-frontal, and I doubt Bebe will be willing to get that much … removed. She's kind of a hippie down there, if you follow me. That painting upstairs. I'm sure she told you all about how people think it's a portrait. But trust me: that bush is a lot more trimmed than hers. And his dialogue has no subtlety."

I was too horrified to interrupt this stream of consciousness. Surely she would hear him. It was excruciating to listen to it. I moved even further away from the door, but he was remorseless. His voice rose. "What I'm curious about is why he's even interested in auditioning her." He looked honestly baffled. "It doesn't make any sense. Unless … like I said, he only wants to humiliate her."

He glanced at his watch and grimaced. "I wish she'd hurry up and squeeze her fat ass into that girdle. She wants me to run lines after you fit her, and Armen is driving so he'll be here. I need a cocktail, and it's not even four o'clock." He wagged his head and gave an impatient sigh. "You'll make the dress work, right?"

I said of course, but inside I was stressing about all that tricky beading. He walked back toward the dressing room. "You like movies, huh?" Then he rapped his knuckles on the door. "Are you decent yet?"

"Yeah," came her muffled voice. "Send Danvers in. You can go."

He raised his eyebrows and smirked. "I'm dismissed, I guess. Thank god."

When I went back into the dressing room, Sugar was standing on the dais, posing this way and that. The girdle had whittled her silhouette into a smooth hourglass shape from just under her bosom down to her knees. Smooth as a plastic doll.

She held up the dress. "Do you know whose dress this is?"

"Yours?"

"Yes, it's mine, silly," she said. "Mine now. It was Mummy's. She wore it when she accepted her SAG award."

I smiled helpfully at her reflection.

"She was sixty-five years old and she'd been in eighty movies, but this was the dress she wore the only time she was nominated and won. That's good luck. Verny thinks so too." She cocked her head and contemplated her reflection. "Should I listen to him? Do you think it makes me look vintage?"

I said what mattered was what she thought, and she nodded, absently plucking at the bodice. I prayed she wouldn't pop off any beads. "That's an interesting way of looking at it." She heaved a sigh. "Fuck … I can barely breathe in this thing. But it really does the trick, right?"

I stepped onto the platform, and together we coaxed the dress up over her hips. It didn't split, but it was plenty snug. We were close enough to each other that I could smell her sweat, sharp and sweet. The purple dress was a strange choice for an audition, but I hoped Vernon would be wrong. I was rooting for Sugar Callahan.

20

Picture golden hour in the hills of Los Angeles. The way the light makes anyone beautiful. This is the time of day when the sun becomes less of a bludgeon and more of a caress. Sugar's profile was bathed in gold. I could watch her as much as I wanted by pretending to look out the window on her side. It was already apparent to me that rich and famous meant something different here in California. Bebe Patten fascinated me.

She and Vernon had a shouting argument in front of me right before we were supposed to leave for the audition. When Sugar broke down in dramatic sobs, careful not to shed any actual tears, and accused Vernon of trying to ruin everything for her, Vernon backed down and they made up, all forgiven. This dynamic seemed to have its own well-worn groove. She wanted to please Vernon and have his approval. Vernon wanted to control her and make her dependent on him. The problem, as I saw it, was that she wanted this part more than she cared about winning Vernon's approval, but he didn't realize that. Or he was in denial. It was a clash waiting to happen.

I had been chosen to ride in back with Sugar, with Vernon up front with Armen. At one point she took my hand, lacing her fingers with mine, and leaned over to whisper in my ear. Are those two fucking?

Vernon had his arm draped across the back of the driver's seat, his fingertips almost touching Armen's broad shoulder.

I did one of those noncommittal headshake/shrug combinations and she whispered, All the boys love Verny, don't they?

Then she let go of my hand and leaned her head back against the seat. She was watching Vernon and Armen through half-closed eyes, almost as if she were jealous. In a low tone she said, "He doesn't know I have an advantage." Her gaze slid toward me. "I have something those other girls don't." And then she put her finger to her lips. Shhhh.

Finally, we parked in a commercial neighborhood with a mix of specialty shops with expensive, pretty things in their windows and anonymous office buildings with mirrored facades. The nine-to-fivers were gone and the shops were getting ready to close. It was quiet at almost 6 p.m.

When I figured out that Vernon wanted some alone time with Armen

I said I needed to stretch my legs, and loitered in front of the office building that had swallowed Sugar and her purple dress. I had done a spectacular job on the fit, and you couldn't even notice that there were missing beads. To take her look over the top, Sugar had applied an elaborate cat eye, with smokey purple eyeshadow on her lids and a nude lip. I told her the makeup added just the right amount of drama to her outfit. And if demented doll was the look she was going for, she had definitely succeeded.

I ducked into the shadow of the building's awning-covered vestibule and looked back at the car. Nobody saw me slip inside the building. The bland, high-rent lobby was cool and dim under subdued lighting. An old-fashioned cage-style elevator with room for two rode next to a stairway with a directory for six office suites distributed on the upper floors. A couple of insurance offices, a naturopathic practice, three single name legal firms. The top floor had only one suite without any identifier. That had to be it.

Without a plan, I took the stairs. At the top I arrived into a small carpeted lobby. I pressed my ear against the unmarked door. Nothing. I'd expected to hear Sugar reciting her monologue, of which I'd only heard snippets while she ran through it with Vernon directing her.

I stared at the doorknob, willing it to open. If they caught me skulking, I would say I was lost, just looking for a restroom. The seconds ticked by while I listened to my own breath. The decision to finally reach for the doorknob wasn't so much conscious as inevitable. Rule breaking was something I simply did. I gently pushed the door open and peered around the edge.

A narrow rectangular room with windows on all sides, the pulled shades showing bright lines of setting sun around their edges. Sugar was sitting on top of a folding table, her thighs spread to embrace a broad-backed, white-haired man who kneeled in front of her. One of the man's meaty hands bunched the purple dress in its fist. The other hand was under the skirt. Sugar stared, expressionless, at the small camera mounted to a tripod set opposite her. A red light on the camera blinked rhythmically.

The man moaned and leaned forward, pressing his face into Sugar's purple lap.

Don't breathe. I was backing out of the room when Sugar turned her head and nailed me in place. Seconds or minutes passed before she turned her head back toward the camera. I fled.

In the car on the way home, she announced triumphantly that the audition had gone perfectly, shooting me a teasing glance. From the front seat Vernon barked, "Don't get your hopes up."

In a low voice Sugar said, "Men are so moody, aren't they?"

When we got back to Patten House after a long and rather drunken supper on the patio at Chateau Marmont with Vernon and me in tow, I had to help Sugar undress since she couldn't get out of that purple dress without me. While she stripped off the girdle I fussed with the dress, putting it back onto its padded hanger and safely stowing it in her climate-controlled glass closet for vintage clothes. She watched me closely, something electric stirring the silence.

"That will need cleaning," she said. "I'm sure it stinks."

She put on the fluffy robe I offered her and went over to sit at her dressing table, watching me in the mirror. I asked if she needed anything and she said no, but when I made for the door she told me to wait.

"Did you have fun tonight?" she asked, staring into the mirror as she wiped makeup off her face. "You seem uncomfortable. Do we make you nervous?"

Not nervous, I told her. Curious, maybe.

She smiled. "I'm a little curious myself," she said. "What were you doing walking in on my audition like that?"

I turned, babbling about needing the restroom and everything being closed.

"So did you pee on the floor or what?" She turned to face me and crossed her legs, leaning an elbow on her knee to cradle her chin. "What do you think you saw?" A smile tugged at the corner of her mouth. "You think I'm sleeping with the director in order to get the part."

I told her it wasn't my place to think anything at all, and she got up and came over to me, standing a little too close. "Paul loved the dress," she said. "He knew Mummy, you know. And my father. He remembered that night, when she won." She laughed. "You might as well know. I'm fucking the old man, but it isn't what you think. We're good for each other. But of course we're keeping our relationship quiet for the good of the project."

I don't remember what I said, but it was along the lines of who she slept with being none of my business.

"I told Paul all about your many skills," she said with this playful smile.

I tried—and failed—to imagine that conversation. She didn't know all about me or my skills. What had she told him?

"Don't look so scared," she said. "Do you have dirty secrets? Did you murder somebody?" She turned and walked away from me. I followed her into her bedroom. My life is an open book, I told her. Sorry, no dirty secrets. And no murders. She dropped her robe and climbed into bed, pulling the covers up to her chin. She said, "You can go, Danny. I'm going to go to sleep now."

I picked the robe up off the floor and said good night. As I left she said, "Don't forget what I told you. Nobody else can bring what I've got. Tell Verny. He's going to regret betting against me."

21

Sugar didn't operate like other people. At first, I thought it was because she was a "celebrity." I had a lot of preconceived notions about what that word meant, most of it confirmed by everything Vernon had told me about her life before I met her, but that wasn't the whole picture. Sugar had a vulnerable side. She was lonesome. She wanted to be loved. Maybe a little too much. And when she decided on you, it was all or nothing.

I remember waking up, seeing her standing over me wearing that fluffy robe, and not being surprised at all to see her there. It seemed utterly natural for her to be in my bedroom, and I was about to ask her what she needed when she opened the robe. Underneath, a red bikini.

"We're going for a ride, Danny. Get up."

You can be taken over. You can abandon free will and place yourself in somebody else's hands. If you allow yourself to be an extension of the other, it can be paradoxically freeing … before it becomes an uncontrollable addiction.

We climbed into Cherry Baby and drove for a while. I was still in my pajamas. I didn't know where we were and I didn't care. I was with *her*, a stranger who was no stranger at all. We were already shared blood.

"Let's only tell the truth tonight," she said.

"Truth is relative," I said, obeying an automatic, internal caution light.

"The people who say that are liars," she said.

No doubt. And?

"Okay, okay … so we won't swear to the truth, but we'll be real with each other." She held out her hand. "Is that gonna work for you?"

I told her it was a deal and we shook hands.

"I'll start," she said.

I said I knew she would, and she said, "I love how you get the picture and I don't have to always explain everything."

"Don't count on that," I said. "This is all new."

"You mean … we aren't two peas in a pod already? Twinsies with two brains and one blood-stained soul?"

I told her she wouldn't want inside my brain.

"But see," she said, "when you do that … when you refuse to give me access, that just makes me wanna get in there even more. Don't you know me by now?"

I reminded her we'd only known each other a few days.

"Details," she said. "Irrelevant." *She could* know *someone in a minute. Without exchanging a single word. Was I going to try to argue with that?* I told her I wouldn't dare.

She took her right hand off the steering wheel and put it on my knee. I said, "What are you doing?" and she said, "Trying to calm you down," and I didn't know what to say to that. I thought I had been doing a good job of hiding my panic.

She said, "Here's the rule. I can touch you, but you can't touch me unless I give you permission."

I closed my eyes and focused on the warmth of her palm. Strange how her fingers were icy cold, like Cal's. Fingers seeking, wanting to hold on, squeezing so tight.

"I don't wanna know any boring stuff," Sugar said, pinching the skin on my leg as if she knew I was thinking about somebody else. It hurt, but I pretended it didn't.

"Tell me the stuff you don't want anyone to know," she said, glancing over at me. "Oh, are you afraid? Is there a reason for that?"

I said I didn't want the spotlight on me, and she said, "But that's exactly where I want you."

We arrived after a series of turns that left me lost. It was a "typical" street for the neighborhood: ultra-high hedges and big electric gates. No dwellings visible from the road. This was privacy with a capital P. Visibility was for unguarded places, lesser people. So much to protect that these folks had their own private armies of overnight security guards. Vernon said they'd set their dogs on unsuspecting rabbits. I said I didn't know LA had rabbits. Then I realized Vernon had meant that *we* were the rabbits.

"Get out," Sugar said. "We're here."

I asked her where "here" was, and she said, "I know a way in." An eerie echo of Alice's words when we trespassed on Sugar's very own childhood home.

People die in *tubs*, I told her.

People have drowned in six inches of water. That was a fact.

The pool looked impossibly large, a rectangle of black water leading into more blackness, beckoning me to slide into its unforgiving embrace. Beyond, a large house, brightly lit.

I told Sugar the word for what was wrong with me. *Aquaphobia.* She was unimpressed. I asked her, "Whose house is this?" and she said, "Nobody famous, somebody rich." Then I said, "Well, that rich somebody seems to be home. All the lights are on, and they're going to catch you," and she said, "Yeah they could catch us, but that only makes it more exciting."

She dropped her robe and dove in, came up, swam to the far side. I could make out a vague outline of her head above the shadowy water.

C'mon, Danny … it's time. Did she say that, or did I?

Maybe it was going to be alright. Maybe it *was* time. And maybe nobody was home. Maybe these were the kind of people who always left a lot of lights burning only to make us think they were home.

Sugar's voice seemed too loud. "Stop worrying," she said. "I've done this dozens of times."

She swam effortlessly back toward me, standing at the bottom of stairs that disappeared into the black water. The devil wanted me to take her hand. I said I was cold.

"The pool is heated," Sugar said, planting her hands on her hips. "Stop stalling. Get in."

Marie's afraid of the water, but nobody listened to her pleas(e). Patty laughing. Sink or swim, kiddo.

I had screamed when Frank the second dropped me into the deep end of the pool, Patty egging him on, both of them laughing at my terror. My open mouth welcomed the water into my lungs. I sank like a stone.

The witnesses all agreed it was the heroic lifeguard who saved my life. But nobody saw how I went in. Or they wouldn't say, didn't want to get involved in the mess that was Patty. But the motel lifeguard had been the one who hauled me up from the bottom, laid me on the pool deck (unconscious, I guess) and performed CPR. The bruises left by his lifesaving measures lasted for weeks. But, oh, the gush of water expelled, that sweet air inhaled. I was alive, and the sky was so blue. This boy, not much older than I was, had drawn the water from my lungs and saved me.

Of course, Patty and Frank the second had disappeared the minute I went under and all the fuss ensued. But Frank the second swore he hadn't meant any harm. They'd both assumed I would have enough sense to save myself. They'd only gone across the street for a beer. Sorry about that.

Two days later I had contracted pneumonia, and my hacking cough became annoying enough for Patty to notice. They had kept me overnight in the hospital, and I had developed deep crushes on all the nurses, even the grumpy overnight nurse with the beautiful brown eyes. My stay had cost Patty money, and that had made her furious. I was an attention-whore pain-in-the-ass.

"Come *on!*" Sugar said.

I sat down on the edge of the pool and put my feet in the water. The hems of my pajama bottoms were wet. But she hadn't lied. The water was as warm as piss.

"You're not really afraid, are you?" Sugar said. "You're pretending."

So I told her. All of it. Even the part where Patty got me discharged too soon from the hospital, only to leave me alone for two days while she and Frank the second went to Reno, chasing some private poker game. They had come back down several thousand, and we had to sneak out of that motel so we wouldn't have to pay, me hacking my lungs up while Patty threatened to gag me with her scarf.

Water lapped. Crickets chirped. The lights in the house made Sugar into a dark silhouette. When she reached for my hand, I let her lead me into the water. I shivered and my belly was doing arabesques, but she held onto me, put her arms around my waist and turned me so my back was to her. "Close your eyes," she whispered into my hair. The heat of her breath was on the back of my neck. She gave no warning when she kicked my legs out from under me, and I cried out, fell back, flailed and kicked, but she kept me afloat. "I've got you," she whispered.

A plane passed overhead. Sugar's upside-down smile. I was floating.

22.

"What is the worst thing you've ever done?"

I stumbled on a sharp stone on the pavement, wet pajamas clammy, the night air arctic against my skin. "Why are you asking me that?" My teeth chattered as I said it.

"You look like somebody with a lot of secrets," Sugar said. "It's your face. You remind me of somebody."

Cherry Baby straight ahead, a haven.

"It's a good face," Sugar said, putting her arm around my waist. "I like it."

A beach towel materialized from the backseat, and she insisted I strip before I got in the car because I was so wet and I mustn't damage the leather. We left the pajamas where I dropped them.

"Let it be a fascinating mystery to whoever finds them," Sugar said.

In the car, we blasted the heat, and I found an AM station that was playing this old-school metal so we blasted that too.

"Now you know how to swim." Sugar reached over to turn off the radio. "When you're a very old woman, somebody will ask who taught you to swim and you'll say, Sugar Callahan taught me everything I know."

I told her floating wasn't exactly swimming, and she said, "You're too literal," and slid her hand onto my thigh, hot as a branding iron against my bare flesh.

"I'm only doing what you keep inviting me to do," she said.

"Where are we going?" I said.

Her hand stayed there, fingers pressing lightly like she was playing a song, ticklish, insistent.

"Do we have to go somewhere?" she asked sweetly. "I feel pretty comfortable right here."

"Find trespassing comfortable, do you?" I stilled her hand and firmly put it back on the steering wheel.

"Don't be judgmental," Sugar laughed. "From one trespasser to another, I'd say we both find trespassing comfortable. This is just playing. Make-believe, you know?" She glanced over at me. "You have to get into the spirit of it … settle in and get comfy … learn to swim, Danny."

I said, "You're lucky."

And she said, "*You're* lucky."

When we got back, we got out a bottle of vodka. Sugar slammed a few shots and got a little noisy. I received a full rendition of the song "All That Jazz" from the musical *Chicago* accompanied by dance moves made silly because she was fairly drunk by then. Then Vernon showed up and it became a full-blown party.

We all drank too much that night, and Sugar decided she had to take pictures of me and Vernon, joking that if she ever turned up dead from an accidental fall, the police would find the photos and know who had killed her. There was no logic to it, but at the time it felt like a threat. Or a prophecy. Like she really believed we'd be capable of something like that.

Sugar also told Vernon all about where she and I had been earlier in the night, what we'd been doing, and it became obvious she'd done the trespassing swimming thing before, because he told her one of these days she was going to get caught, and she said, "If it wasn't dangerous, it wouldn't be half as fun, right Danny?" So I had to agree with her. Vernon was disgusted with both of us.

The party broke up around two. We got Sugar onto her feet but then had to half-push, half-pull her up the stairs. At the top she suddenly broke away from us, running down the hall, shedding clothes and laughing like a lunatic as she went. I picked up the clothes and Vernon hurried to catch up to her.

When I came into the bedroom Vernon calmly instructed me to pull the bed covers down. "Now get in," he said. Sugar was lolling against him, her arms slung around his neck, eyeing me. They both had the same expectant look on their faces, and I thought I'd misheard Vernon but he repeated it: "Danvers, get in the bed."

"You too, Verny," Sugar said, giving him a sloppy kiss near his mouth. "I want sanwish."

"Danvers," Vernon said, his voice stern, gently turning Sugar's face away. "Get in the fucking bed and don't be weird about it. For chrissakes, hurry up. I can't hold her up much longer." Sugar was sucking on Vernon's neck, grinding against him. His eyes pleaded with me. *Hurry.*

I kicked off my shoes and got in the bed, and then Sugar dove in and snuggled up to me. "Spoon me," Sugar demanded, reaching behind her to grab at me, so I flipped over and curled my body around her. But then there was the problem of my arms and my hands. What to do except suffer this awkward and uncomfortable position. I felt my left arm going numb.

"Vernyyyyy," Sugar crooned. "Sanwicccchhhhh …"

But Vernon wouldn't let her rush him. He methodically took off his shirt and pants and laid them neatly across the bottom of the bed. He had on silk boxers, and his body hair was like a sweater, front and back covered in thick black curls. He stood at the side of the bed. "Are you going to be a good girl?" he said to Sugar. "Don't scare Danvers, okay?"

"I'll try, Verny darling." Her tone pure innocence while grinding her ass against my crotch—and me with the pins and needles in one arm, the other obeying orders to stay put. *She can touch you, but you can't touch her.* That was the rule.

"Now get in here," Sugar said to Vernon. "I wanna run my fingers through your lovely, lovely furrrrr …"

Vernon sighed, plumped the pillows and crawled in. I tried to imagine what Cal would do if she was standing there. If she could see me/us now. I pictured her laughing. *Cringeworthy, Danny. I can't believe you let her do that to you.* And I would say, *So hypocritical, Cal. You ruined my life, and that's why I'm here.*

Sugar slung her arm across Vernon's belly. "Marshmallow sandwiccchhhh …" When she groped him, Vernon delicately removed her hand, saying, "You promised."

Our eyes met and Vernon gave me a subtle eye-roll, shook his head. I had to stifle a laugh. It was all so funny. And awful. Vernon and I had a whole conversation about the bizarre nature of whatever this was, all without saying a word, and then he whispered, "It won't be long now. She's almost there."

He was right, of course. It didn't take long at all. Soon enough, Sugar passed out.

Back downstairs, Vernon informed me that he had already deleted the photos of us from her phone. "I didn't want you to worry," Vernon said. "About the photos. I mean, next thing you know they'd be on the internet. We don't want that, do we?"

I looked up from loading the dishwasher.

"Now you see what a handful she is," he said. "Hard to really warn people without scaring them off. But you handled it well."

I asked if "sandwich" was something that happened a lot, and he said no, only when Sugar drank too much, which was why she'd gone to rehab in the first place. It was a long story involving the last housekeeper, who had not appreciated Bebe Patten's "exuberance," as he put it. Part of the settlement had included a six-week mandatory stay for Sugar at a rehab in Northern California beloved by celebrity drunks. It was where she'd met Westerfield.

Vernon looked a bit beat up about all of it, and I thought I should try to build him up a little. He was a good boss. I told him I appreciated his generosity. And I wasn't going anywhere.

"Princess likes you," he said. "It's up to you how you handle that."

Don't fuck where you sleep, Danny. "Miss Patten is a flirt," I said. "I can handle it."

He seemed disappointed. "We'll see."

Besides, I reminded him, Miss Patten was in a relationship with Mr. Westerfield.

He stared at me. "Is she now?"

"That's what she told me," I said.

Vernon shuddered. "Can you imagine getting into bed with that?" he said. "Not in my most desperate hour. He's so … sweaty. I'd bet good money that his breath stinks, but I wouldn't want to get close enough to verify." He shook his head. "Don't worry about Paul Westerfield. He won't last."

But the very next day Sugar got the call that she was being offered the role in *The Songbird and the Lioness*. And Vernon was forced to eat a triple order of crow. When we had a private moment I asked if he was okay, because he had this look in his eyes I can only describe as haunted. "We're in for it now," he told me. "This is where the rubber meets the road."

23

The longer I was at Patten House, the more convinced I became that Sugar had pure anarchy in her soul. The usual rules, the kind that keep society from collapsing, those were for other people. Her rules, capricious and arbitrary, sometimes directly contradictory, were all that mattered. Sugar was a human rollercoaster, and you'd better hang on or you were likely to crash and fall.

Cherry Baby. All winking mirror chrome and vivid red, machine as forbidden fruit. Sugar caressed the car's hood like it was a living thing, which I suppose, to her, it was. We were off on another adventure, a road movie starring Sugar Callahan, with Vernon cast as the villain who was shitting all over her dream lately, who ought to shut the fuck up and stop bad-mouthing Paul darling. I half expected to see Vernon appear to block our escape, but we rolled out of there like delinquents taking a stolen car on a joyride.

We had settled into a new routine, one that accommodated late morning until late afternoon "rehearsals" at Westerfield's Hollywood Hills home, a place once owned by some woman screenwriter famous in the 1930s. When Sugar got home, she'd take a long bath and do the guided meditation Westerfield assigned each day, and then we'd all have dinner together—me, Vernon, and Sugar—eating what Luchetti had prepared in advance and left for us to heat up. Table for three, family style.

The conversation during dinner was a monologue with only infrequent interjections from Vernon as Sugar praised Paul darling's mentoring brilliance. It was important for us to understand that he was an actor's director, not just some technician. While it was still early days in the preproduction process, they were focusing on relaxation and improving Sugar's concentration. Some of the things he had her doing sounded alarmingly like a cross between cultish grooming and hypnosis.

There were blindfolds and bondage exercises too. She had brought home a fat length of rope to show us how she was learning to tie complicated knots nobody could escape from. Vernon said it sounded more like foreplay than rehearsal, and she got defensive and called Vernon an ignoramus and a hypocrite.

"I know what you have in your bedside table, Verny," Sugar said. "Why don't you tell Danny?"

But Vernon refused to be baited. Instead he said, "But darling … the script is so frivolous. Surely you see that? You can't actually take it seriously. It's *camp*."

Sugar bristled. "What do you know about scriptwriting? You're a glorified butler." Her cheeks flushed scarlet. "Paul's been writing this story for ten years. It's his greatest life's work."

"So you've said." Vernon kept his expression neutral but his skepticism was obvious.

"It's like the most intense therapy," Sugar said. "Paul just pulls out of me feelings I didn't even know I had. I'm learning *so* much about myself …"

"Like what?" Vernon's tone was dry as a desert. He flicked me an amused glance, and Sugar shot him a dark look.

"Paul says I misbehave because I'm bored," Sugar said, "and I'm bored because I don't have a purpose. Now I've found it."

"Amazing! The end of ennui," Vernon said, putting his chin on his hand. "Do tell."

"To play this part, of course," Sugar leaned forward. "I'm learning to explore all of my suppressed feelings. I'm exposing myself. And I no longer care what other people think of me."

Vernon sat up straight with this exaggerated look of surprise. "I didn't know you cared what people thought of you!"

Sugar laughed. "Okay, Verny, okay … you're being funny. But this movie is going to put me and Paul into contention. You'll see."

Vernon smiled, examined his meticulous manicure. "In contention for what exactly?"

I stopped chewing because the grinding of my teeth sounded so loud in the sudden silence. I thought he'd gone too far and I couldn't tell from Sugar's expression what she was thinking.

"You're being so mean," she said finally. "I'm only saying this picture has the potential to be a big hit. One last hurrah for Paul, perhaps … but for me, the start of something." She put her hand over Vernon's, gripping his fingers. "Please? Be happy for me."

Vernon brought Sugar's hand to his lips. "We're all rooting for you, aren't we, Danvers?"

When we arrived at the Griffith Observatory, Sugar bypassed all the parking turnoffs and drove straight to the guarded entrance, where a burly dude with a shaved head and a long, pointy beard stepped out to let us know the visitor parking was … back there. Sugar handed him two crisp one-hundred-dollar bills, and that made everything clear for him. We got a laminated card for Cherry's dashboard printed with a large blue wheelchair symbol and the words Do Not Ticket.

We drove right up to the entrance. People were staring at the car, and us. I felt guilty, but Sugar was unfazed. She took my arm and leaned up against me. "Just ignore them. It's that *People* magazine interview. Ever since it came out I can't go anywhere. They act like I'm a *criminal* or something."

We bypassed the observatory itself—*too many gawkers*—and went up the outside stairs to the observation decks. Gesturing like she owned the view of volcanic hills, she said, "Here you go, Danny." I looked out at a layer of brownish smog hanging over the urban sprawl below.

I mean, if you've never been there, it isn't unlike being on the observation deck at the Empire State Building. Or on the 108th floor of the Strat in Vegas. You're above it all. And down there the ants scurry and toil. But let's be honest. From that distance, that HOLLYWOOD sign looks disappointingly insignificant set up on its ridge. It's the view of the city and beyond that draws the eye.

I said as much to Sugar, and she said the best way to see the sign was up close, to hike up into the hills at night, but there were mountain lions and coyotes up there. My opinion was that seeing the sign up close wouldn't be worth the risk of being mauled by a mountain lion, and Hollywood was a concept not a word on a hill. She said I was funny, and I said I was glad that I could amuse her. Neither of us were that interested in the view once we'd seen it, so we just stood there and bantered for a while, her telling me stories about what a shitshow the film business was. How it was a cesspool of ego and testosterone. How the least talented people always seemed to rise to the top. How people like her got discounted because of their name.

Naturally Paul darling and his film were *different*. The script was raw. And real. And sexy. It pushed the boundaries and was guaranteed to create a shock to the system when it came out.

I said it sounded like the kind of film her parents had made in their day. But I regretted bringing them up, because her face got sad and her eyes watered. She looked away, leaned her elbows on the railing.

"Paul's nothing like Artie," she said in this dead voice. It wasn't clear if she was telling that to me or herself.

Two teenage kids with skateboards had parked themselves against the wall opposite us. They stared rudely, so I assumed they had recognized her. In a loud voice Sugar asked them what (the fuck) they were looking at. The smaller, dark-haired kid with a backward cap said, "I know who you are," and she said, "Oh yeah?" and walked over to them, hands on her hips. "Who am I?" she said.

I stepped forward, this involuntary reaction. Sugar was a magnet for trouble—a trespasser like me—and I was ready to defend her. But her fight fizzled when the dark-haired kid said, "Don't get your panties in a twist, grandma." Then the other one, with streaky blond hair like a young Ian, called her a *nepo-baby bitch*.

So she said, "Fuck you," and they laughed at her.

It was a painful exit.

Paul Westerfield made his entrance on a Tuesday, for lunch.

Sugar stood on the dais in front of the mirror in her beige girdle and nothing else. You had to admire her lack of self-consciousness.

Vernon lounged, feet up, with his laptop open. "We're going with the red D and G bustier, the Prada leather pants, and the blue Miu Miu heels."

Another day, another bizarre outfit. Mind reader Vernon smirked, "She's playing a *part*, Danvers. She has to get into *character*."

"Come help me get into this thing." Sugar held up the bustier, and together we squeezed her into it. She had an astonishing willingness to torture her flesh for her art. I tried not to focus on what Vernon thought, watching us.

"Verny, how do I look?" she said. We both looked at him in the mirror.

"Slutty," he said. "It's in character for Crystelle. Now let's see the pants."

The pants fit her well, except at the waist because of the whittling effect of the girdle. "That doesn't look right," she said, twisting this way and that, reaching around to pull at the gaping waistband.

Vernon said, "You need to fix that, Danvers. Cinch it in a little."

I was beginning to wish I had never divulged my sewing skills, because *leather alterations?* Beyond my skill level. I had a premonition I was going to ruin those pants, but I didn't mean to stab her with the sharp tips of my scissors. It was only a small nick, but she let out a howling scream of surprised pain. Blood welled from the tiny wound, quickly staining the soft leather and the girdle underneath.

Vernon was on his feet like 911 to examine the cut. While it hadn't been my plan, the pants were ruined. Sugar kicked them off and kept twisting around to watch while Vernon dabbed at the wound with a tissue. She wouldn't look at me, and though I repeatedly apologized I was now in the doghouse.

When she went off to choose a new outfit, Vernon said, "I can't believe you did that." I said at least I didn't have to alter the pants, and he grinned, wagging his finger at me. "Mommy should've offered to kiss her booboo and make it better."

The lunch menu was raw oysters and bluefin tuna sushi—at Westerfield's request—and had been personally delivered by Vernon's regular fish vendor, a giant of a man named Gerald who liked to make suggestive comments about cannibalizing Vernon every time he delivered to the house. It was both hilarious and disturbing, but Vernon basked in Gerald's attention.

"I'd like to put you on a platter with an apple in your mouth," Gerald said, staring suggestively into Vernon's eyes. "I'd like to devour you with a side of roasted potatoes."

"My meat is beautifully marbled," Vernon said. "Would you like to see it?"

Luchetti rolled her eyes at me behind their backs.

Vernon tapped Gerald's powerful shoulder. "I'm going to walk Gerald out," he said. "Danvers, you're on door duty in case our guest arrives before I get back. Don't fuck this up, people." At the door, he gave me a pointed, amused look and added, "Try not to stab anyone else today, okay?"

Luchetti looked at me sideways, and I explained that it was a minor accident with a pair of sewing scissors. "And she didn't fire you?" she said. "I guess she likes you." She gave me a penetrating look. "Mind your *p*'s and *q*'s, Danvers."

While Remy set the table in the dining room, Becker dusted surfaces in the great room, and Vernon got his meat inspected by Gerald, I stayed at the breakfast bar and watched Luchetti fuss over the starter. Her only contribution to the lunch was a *frisee aux lardons*. She was not happy that Vernon had brought food in when she could have prepared something more elegant.

"Who eats raw oysters for lunch?" Luchetti grumbled, arranging crispy bacon bits just so on top of the frisee.

I didn't comment.

Paul Westerfield stood well over six feet and had excellent posture, a full head of more salt than pepper hair, and broad powerful shoulders. He stood at the door exuding superiority when he smiled, showing his hideously misaligned, oversized teeth.

"I'm Paul," he announced, brushing past me.

His mud-colored eyes looked closer together than in photos online, and judging by the prominent veins on his nose he was a chronic drinker. His clothes were expensive but wrinkled, and he smelled unclean: cigar smoke with a hint of the sweat that stained the underarms of his shirt when he took off the porkpie hat and started fanning himself with it. I thought about Vernon saying he was sweaty, and I couldn't stop seeing him on his knees with his head burrowed into Sugar's lap. He'd had his hand up under her skirt, but he couldn't have gotten past that girdle. I smiled to myself.

"Where am I going?" he asked. But without giving me a chance to answer, he strode off, shouting her name as he went.

I followed him into the great room, where Sugar lounged prettily on the couch, shoes discarded and feet drawn up under her. She'd changed into a ruffled black babydoll dress that puddled artfully around her bare knees.

He threw his battered leather briefcase on the floor, tossed the hat, and launched himself onto the couch.

"Paul, darling …"

"Yes, my sweetest beastie."

"I can't believe it."

"It's wonderful, isn't it?"

I hovered in the background, keeping my face blank when she looked over his shoulder. "Danny, would you please get something for Paul to drink?" She put her hand on his arm. "What do you want?"

"What do I want … hmm, what do you think I want?" And he took her face in his meaty paws and laid a long, wet kiss on her.

I waited for as long as I could stand it before giving a discreet cough. They broke apart. Westerfield laid his hand on Sugar's thigh and said, "What kind of vodka do you have?"

We had to start serving lunch even though Vernon was still absent. Apparently, his lunchtime sprint with Gerald was turning into more of a marathon. Luchetti was atwitter about her salad and made me promise to tell her what they said about it. I doubted they gave a shit about her salad, but I said I would do as she asked.

Remy carried the wine and a bottle of Chopin vodka. I delivered Luchetti's heart on two platters and adjusted the place settings yet again. I considered spitting on Westerfield's salad but I didn't know if I could get away with it in front of Remy.

"I'd do him," Remy said suddenly, apropos of nothing. She was struggling with the foil knife and the wine.

I thought I'd misunderstood what she said and asked her to repeat herself.

"I would do him." She jerked her head toward the living room. "Paul Westerfield. I'd fuck him."

I couldn't suppress a horrified shudder. I told her not to be ridiculous, the man was old enough to be her *great* grandpa. She shrugged, cranked the corkscrew. "Why not? He's rich, and he's sexy as hell. Like Schwarzenegger crossed with that other guy. You know that big guy who's always really funny. Miss Patten sure as shit gets around."

The cork popped loudly and, without commenting on whether Sugar "got around" or on Remy's opinion that Paul Westerfield must be a stallion in the sack, I went to announce lunch. They had put on music—Rachmaninoff, if I wasn't mistaken—and I couldn't hear much talking because he had her down on that couch with his hairy hand up her dress.

"Lunch," I announced, raising my voice over the music.

They froze, then she giggled and Westerfield hauled himself off of her while she straightened her dress. Neither one of them spared so much as a glance in my direction. He tried to grab her ass as they went out.

25

Cut to staff lunch the next day. Becker and Remy having finished and gone off to their respective tasks, Luchetti was pumping Vernon for gossip. I could have told her that nothing interesting happened. After lunch yesterday Sugar and Paul darling had retired to her suite with the bottle of Chopin (found empty this morning, stood next to her bedroom door). And Westerfield had stayed until nearly midnight.

"You don't like him," Luchetti said to Vernon.

He shrugged. "My feelings about Mr. Westerfield don't matter."

Luchetti turned to me. "Poor Miss Patten," she said.

I asked her why she would say that, and Vernon said, "We've seen it all before, Danvers," and I said, "Seen what?"

Luchetti exchanged an uneasy glance with Vernon, who shook his head slightly. "Miss Patten doesn't have a good track record," she said. "That's all."

"His reputation is worrisome," Vernon said. "He usually dates much younger women."

I suggested that perhaps Miss Patten's age made her even more attractive to somebody like Westerfield, and Luchetti patted my hand in a patronizing way, "You're a nice girl, Danvers." She sent Vernon a sly glance. "But you haven't been here long. Miss Patten is—"

"Fragile," Vernon interrupted, his expression a warning.

"Right," Luchetti said. "She's … what do you call it … vulnerable to certain kinds of men."

"It's highly unprofessional," Vernon said. "On his part."

"Highly unprofessional," Luchetti repeated.

When I came into the dressing room Sugar was wearing Westerfield's sweat-stained shirt with the sleeves pushed up, half-heartedly slapping a black leather cat-o'-nine-tails feebly against a defenseless window seat. She flicked the whip toward me. "What's that look about?" she demanded. "I'm the one who should be mad at *you* for stabbing me. You deserve a punishment."

I said I was fairly certain that the bench wasn't going to fight back, but she shouldn't be so sure about me.

"I'm never sure about you," Sugar said, dropping the whip onto the window seat. From the bureau she snatched up the girdle that still bore traces of blood on the waistband, bunched it into a ball, and tossed it at me.

"I don't think the stain will come out," I said. "Sorry about that."

She stuck out her tongue at me. "Throw it away," she said. "Paul doesn't like it."

I didn't ask why he didn't like it. I knew why. I took the girdle into the bathroom. A used condom lay at the bottom of the wastebasket. I dropped the girdle on top of it.

"Now Danny," Sugar said when I came out, "Paul and I had a talk, and we decided you're coming with us on location. We're shooting in Vancouver."

I laughed. Ha ha, good joke.

"I told Paul I need you," Sugar said. "He's already approved it on the line-item budget. You're going to be my very own personal assistant. I feel like that's a step up, don't you? A little more pay. So much more fun than what you do now. You'll probably even get your name in the credits. Assistant to Bebe Patten."

I said that sounded wonderful and all, and I was flattered of course, but what about my job here at Patten House?

Sugar waved that away. "Verny'll find us somebody to do your job here while we're gone. I made Paul see how perfect you would be, and he's super excited about you."

Some people sniff oranges to relieve stress. It sounds weird, but it's true. I read it somewhere. Some like to pet puppies or do goat yoga or wear a rubber band on their wrist and snap it when they're obsessing over a problem with multiple potential resolutions. For me, there is nothing more clarifying than cleaning something. So I decided to wash the floor in the second-floor half bath after I found a trio of dead ants behind the bidet. Becker probably didn't leave their carcasses there on purpose, but I wouldn't have been surprised if she had.

"Hey Cinderella, I need your help with something."

Sugar stood in the doorway. I dropped my scrubber in the bucket and followed her to her bedroom, where she locked the door behind us.

"You need to do me a favor, okay?"

I asked if I was allowed to know what the favor was before I agreed, and she said okay, picking up a hand-shaped paddle and slapping it against the side of her leg. A Mickey Mouse hand, all fat, stubby fingers. It would sting if applied to bare skin.

"Paul says I have to know what it feels like to *receive* a spanking, or else I won't be able to make it real on camera." Sugar stepped closer and offered me the paddle.

I asked her if she had picked that paddle because frankly it was pretty silly, and she was all *no, of course not!* but her denial was so unconvincing I was sure she had. I found it endearing that Sugar Callahan wasn't as bulletproof as she pretended. At least she hadn't asked me to wear a ball gag or a gimp suit. What was a little spanking between friends?

I took the paddle from her. "So I guess this means I get to touch you, but you don't get to touch me?"

She smiled. "You're my favorite, you know."

I said, "We should have a safe word," and she said, "Oh yeah, what should it be?" So I said, How about Hollywood? and she said, "Okay, Hollywood it is." Then she dropped her pants and bent over the end of the bed, lifting her naked bum into the air.

Sometimes you do what you're told even if it seems wrong.

26

Sugar left in a swirl of bold perfume and bolder yellow chiffon. She was meeting Paul darling and an actor whose name she wouldn't divulge (in case it jinxed it) at the Sunset Tower Hotel for drinks and dinner. If this actor signed on, it could make or break the project. She said Paul was as nervous as she was. They both really wanted this guy, so she needed to look sexy but also accessible.

The halter dress plunged to just above her navel, and we'd had to tape the edge of the neckline to her bare flesh in the front so that everything would stay in place. "We wouldn't want my titties falling out before we get to the main course, now would we?" Sugar said, making final adjustments and watching herself in the mirror.

She had been talking nonstop about Westerfield's *genius*. How he knew everything there was to know about everything. Apparently. It was tiresome in the extreme. And Paul darling was going to take her shopping because nothing in either of her two dressing rooms or the walk-in closet in her bedroom was quite right for the split-personality character she was playing. Wearing the character's clothes was key to her process.

It's my moment, she repeated over and over. Nobody would be able to write her off, not anymore. They'd have to see her as a *real* actor, not just Artie Patten's kid. She held her hair away from her neck so I could attach the diamond solitaire necklace around her neck.

"It's all about psychosexual *repression*," she said. "Paul says I've got that in spades." She giggled in a way that set my teeth on edge. "I'm basically playing Jekyll and Hyde but with a lot of kinky sex and a pinch of twisted stuff."

How original.

"Paul's so *brilliant* to make this film. At this cultural moment. Nobody's done anything like it. They're all too afraid to explore female sexual empowerment in exactly this way."

So, which was it? Repression or empowerment? Those two concepts seemed to exist in opposition. Besides, I could think of quite a few films I'd seen that explored those kinds of themes, films I was sure were better than whatever Paul darling could cook up.

"We're all winning *awards* for this picture, you'll see," Sugar said. "And Vernon will see how wrong he is about this project. About Paul too."

I didn't like to caution her about counting her awards before they're bestowed, or counting on Vernon wanting anything other than to see Westerfield gone.

"Wouldn't that be a kick in the teeth for dear old Mummy and Daddy? If I won an Oscar and they never did? They'd roll over in their graves." Sugar's laugh was brittle. "Except I had them both cremated, so I guess they wouldn't be able to roll over."

After her reaction the last time I'd mentioned her parents, I almost didn't ask what she thought her father would make of Westerfield's film, but in the end I couldn't resist the temptation, and surprisingly, Sugar was unperturbed. She adjusted the egg-shaped diamond where it nestled in her cleavage. "I'm sure Daddy would love Paul's movie. He adored naughty stories." She turned to me. "They knew each other, I told you that. Paul's a lot younger, of course. He was a kid when they were in their heyday. I was a menopause baby, you know."

She bent over to stuff her feet into a pair of canary yellow silk slingback pumps, putting a hand on my shoulder for balance, the diamond egg swinging, dazzling the light. I didn't know much about diamonds, but when she'd pulled it from the safe and opened the velvet box, I'd felt compelled to ask if it was real. It wasn't Hope Diamond big, but I'd never seen a gemstone that size except under glass in a museum.

"If Mommy hadn't made all those shit movies, I'd be trying to live on what Daddy left me," Sugar said, pausing for dramatic effect. "Which was nothing, in case you're wondering." She dangled the necklace toward me. "I should probably have a security guard with me when I wear it. It's insured for two million." She turned back to her own reflection with that look on her face like she had after I'd spanked her, the eyes half-mast, that slow burn of a smile with her tongue pressed between that gap. "By the way," she said. "I think some of Daddy's old pornos on VHS are still around here somewhere. I'll get Verny to dig them up for movie night. That would be a turn-on. The four of us?"

I could only imagine what Vernon would say if she suggested it. And the thought of cozying up with her and Paul darling—with or without Vernon—to get turned on by creepy, old-school porn on a big screen was enough to give me hives. There were some lines worth drawing.

Luchetti had left hours earlier and Vernon was watching television in his room, so I was on my own, bored and chafing at the thick silence in the house, the weight of all its possessions pressing down on my head, so many tasks to be performed until they had to be done all over again.

After eating a lonely cheese and pickle sandwich standing at the kitchen counter, I went back upstairs to Sugar's bedroom. I rationalized my snooping by performing turndown service but without the bulk-bought chocolate wafer left on her pillow.

A manuscript with a blue paper cover lay on her bedside table. Above the author's name—Paul Westerfield—was the title: *The Songbird and the Lioness.* I hesitated for half a second before snatching it up. I'd heard only fragments of the dialogue when she was memorizing her lines. She'd left a yellow highlighter between its pages to mark her place.

This scene was between her character—Catherine/Crystelle—and a guy called Seth. They were arguing overdramatically, indicated by way too many exclamation points (!!), the gist of which was Crystelle proclaiming herself free to do as she pleases, that Seth had no right to judge her. From my perspective the Seth character demonstrated a limited imagination and a lot of judgment. But, predictably, at the end of the scene she is jumping into bed with the judgy guy. The sex was described explicitly and went on for another page of densely packed paragraphs of who did what to whom. It read more like masturbation material for Mr. Paul Westerfield than a script you'd turn into a good movie. Even a half-decent porno, for that matter.

At the end of the scene, I laid the script on my lap and sat down on the bed, stroking the silky coverlet and thinking about Westerfield pawing Sugar, perhaps right then, the way Seth does Crystelle in his stupid screenplay. And now no girdle to get in his way.

I figured Vernon was right about the overall quality of the script based on even that little bit I'd just read. Once upon a time, Paul Westerfield had been ubiquitous. He was the store-brand cereal, always in stock. But his filmography was overly populated with thin plots and busty female characters that were only there to prance around in scanty clothing while portraying a crack assassin or a prostitute on crack. Oh sure, sometimes the female character was the faithful wife left at home with the kids who had no clue what her husband was up to when he left the house. The way Sugar saw it, this new film was going to shock Westerfield's critics by proving them wrong, all while courting controversy and an NC-17 rating that would appeal to a younger, presumably kink-interested audience.

I picked up the script again and went to the last scene. Seth is weeping over the grave of Catherine/Crystelle, who has apparently died at some point in the last act. The final lines of voiceover dialogue read: *I forgive you, my lioness, for everything you were. As for you, my sweet songbird, I forgive you too, for everything you never had the chance to become.*

No hesitation. I yanked that page out, folding it into a tight little rectangle so it would fit perfectly in my apron pocket. I put the script back on the table, exactly as I had found it. I turned down the bed, plumped the pillows and arranged her slippers, laying her favorite negligee, a sheer number with a lace bodice, across the end of the bed.

She didn't come home that night.

27

I watched Sugar from the doorway as she came tripping barefooted across the cobblestone driveway. She wore an oversized white shirt—*Paul's* shirt. The big diamond around her neck threw sparks in the early morning sunlight. She had the yellow dress in her fist.

I said, "What happened to your shoes?"

"Oh, hello," she said when I stood back to let her in.

She moved past me toward the kitchen, trailing the dress across the floor. The way she treated it pained me. I asked her again where her shoes were, and she said, "Probably somewhere on Sunset," which didn't make any sense.

Tossing the dress carelessly over the back of one of the chairs at the breakfast bar, she said, "Is there any coffee?" She slid onto a chair and put her chin on her hands, watching while I made the coffee. "Where is everybody?"

I reminded her it was Mrs. Luchetti's day off and handed her the espresso, a spoon, and two sugar cubes in a little crystal dish. She plopped the cubes into the cup and stirred it with a little too much force, scraping the spoon against the ceramic. "Where's Verny?" she asked.

He could be in his office, I told her. She bellowed his name, and we waited for him to shout an answer or appear. When he didn't do either, she said, "Are you sure he's here?"

To change the subject, I picked up the dress and asked her what happened, and she said to throw it away. "I never want to see it again," she said. "Paul hates the color. He thinks it's too young for me and I'm too sophisticated for it."

I asked her how the meeting had gone the night before, and she said, "We got him," and I said that was good news, and she shrugged then got up to look in the refrigerator, pulling out an airtight container of homemade eclairs.

"Verny!" she hollered into the void. We both waited a few seconds, listening to the silence, then she said, "God, that man is shiftless. I don't think he's ever put in a full day of work." She grinned, showing that gap, and took a greedy bite of eclair, smearing chocolate and pastry cream across her cheek.

Her eyes were raccooned with melted mascara, and there was a reddened area on the lower part of her neck, presumably from the rubbing of Paul darling's unshaven cheeks against her delicate skin.

"Stop looking at me like that," Sugar said with a belligerent tone in her voice.

I said I wasn't looking at her in any kind of way, and she sneered as though I'd insulted her. "Go find Verny," she said, dismissing me.

I left her licking her fingers and drinking her espresso.

Vernon was not in his room. He wasn't poolside, where he normally took his morning coffee under the umbrella. But I had evidently wasted my time looking, because when I went back inside ready to acknowledge defeat, Vernon and Sugar were both there, talking in hushed tones. I debated waiting. It was a unique opportunity to eavesdrop. On the other hand I did not want to be labeled a creep if they caught me. I went into the kitchen.

"I told you already," Vernon was saying in this quiet voice I interpreted to be barely holding the line on rage. "I had errands," he said, "and I went out to do them."

"But I don't like it when you don't leave me a note or let me know where you're going," Sugar said. "I pay you to be *here*. And I expect you to be reachable *whenever* I need you."

They were at the breakfast bar, facing each other, knees touching. I might as well have been invisible. They were focused only on each other.

"I'm not your lapdog, sweetie, no matter how much you pay me." The wide smile was in direct contradiction to the murder in Vernon's eyes.

"But you are!" Sugar said. "You are *my* big, furry lapdog and I'm your little kitten." She took his hand and made him pet her shoulder.

Vernon pulled his hand away, not bothering to disguise his disgust. "What about you, dearest?" he said. "You stayed out all night and not a word. I was worried. So was Danvers. Sleeping with your director is a cliche, isn't it."

She shot back. "You get busy with every fag who walks into this house. Don't think I don't know."

That word as jarring as a slap across the face.

Vernon cleared his throat. I pictured him picking up that container of eclairs and smashing them into her face. He shot his cuffs. "Then I guess it's a good thing that I can supply you with condoms and pick up your prescriptions when you get careless with some Tom's *dick*."

I could feel my adrenaline ramping up. Like those times Patty would get into it with whatever dick she was riding and wind up with a broken arm or a split lip. But, as the joke goes, you should've seen the other guy. My mother always played for keeps, even when she ultimately lost the fight. In that way, we are very much alike.

"I don't care who you fuck, Verny, you know that." Sugar's voice trembled. "But you really aren't allowed to be mad that I'm riding *Paul's* dick. Okay?"

"I'm not mad," Vernon said.

He sounded so extremely mad.

"We're creating real magic together," Sugar said. "Pure cinema. You'll see."

"I know, sweetie … It's just … I worry about your safety."

They both looked over at me. I stayed very still and averted my gaze until they went back to their staring contest.

"You know I care about you as much as I would my own sister," Vernon said. "This role is not right for you. You're better than this."

But Sugar put her hand in front of his face. "Stop! I *want* this. And if you don't like it …" She made an impatient sound, and scraped her chair back. "I'm going up to shower. You should do the same. And brush your teeth. Your breath stinks."

She looked at me, hating me as much as Vernon. Hatred by association.

"I'm not to be disturbed today," she announced to the room and walked out, leaving the yellow dress behind.

I slid over to pick it up off the chair. Vernon had this unnerving, thousand-yard stare. I told him she didn't mean it. She was just upset. But I wasn't convincing either of us.

"We're in trouble, Danvers," he said.

I left him brooding in the kitchen and took the dress to my room. *He* was in trouble. I was in like Flynn and I was going to hold on tight. If Vernon was going to screw up and get himself fired, that didn't have to affect my standing. I wasn't going to let Vernon's agenda around this movie, whatever it was, stand in my way.

In front of the full-length bathroom mirror, I held Sugar's dress against me, smoothing the chiffon skirt. That canary yellow was not my color and the style didn't flatter me, but there was something thrilling in imagining myself wearing it. I lifted the hem of the skirt to my nose. A familiar melange of odors. Smoke and perspiration. Restaurant food. Sugar's perfume.

I left the dress draped over the shower rod. I would air it out. And I would take good care of it in case she ever changed her mind.

28

To say my day-to-day job was unpredictable is an understatement. I worshiped order, schedules, routine. This was chaos in every sense of the word. I had arrived with an expectation of what I'd be doing once I was Bebe Patten's housekeeper, had formed a picture of what that kind of life would be like during the month before I met her, but I was rapidly learning that picture didn't—it couldn't—match my reality.

Well, okay. Adjust. I had already seen it all, hadn't I? I was sophisticated. Sugar's hot-cold attitudes were not going to get to me. My seat belt was fastened and I was braced for whatever was going to come at me. And I certainly didn't intend to second-guess Sugar's decisions the way Vernon did.

After their dustup, Sugar announced that Vernon and I were always to be within immediate reach, her demands overriding what she deemed our less important contractual obligations or tasks. Ever since, Vernon's phone pinged constantly with requests and errands. I had to be available whenever to do whatever. If whatever regularly included some light bondage and additional spanking sessions, I didn't see anything to gain by balking. Sugar and I understood each other. I would know when it went too far and I would stop it. Until then, I would fulfill any brief I was given and with maximum efficiency and minimum fuss.

That day I woke to the steady whoosh of wind, dust devils dancing and chasing each other along the stone pathways. Everybody agreed that it was highly unusual for the winds to blow this strong so late in the season.

Sugar was in a dark mood when I brought her coffee. She had her nose buried in her script. "I hate the wind, don't you?" she said. "Such a bore."

The weather reports were cagey about the fire danger, and I seemed to be the only one concerned about it. People in Los Angeles were equally nonchalant about earthquakes and the massive headache, and terror, that generally accompanied driving on the freeways. In time I hoped to become as casual about these natural and unnatural aspects of life in California. But the wind and its effects unnerved me.

The air quality index had become so poor that nobody on the grounds crew was working that day. I hadn't glimpsed Alice for a while and guessed she was avoiding me. But even Luchetti had called to say that her son didn't want her driving. The freeways got crazier when the winds blew.

Meanwhile, Sugar remained holed up in her bedroom, still in her pajamas when I checked on her at noon, sitting up in bed writing notes in her script, face screwed up in concentration. She declined food—*Don't tempt me!*—but asked for the special bottled water she preferred and the half-empty bottle of three-hundred-dollar Swedish gin she and Vernon had been drinking the past few days.

When I returned with the drinks, she was in the shower, so I left the tray on the bureau. The door to the bathroom was closed, so I sneaked a peek at the script. *Would Catherine say this?* Sugar had scrawled next to a bit of dialogue. Then below, *Crystelle instead? Ask P.* I startled and dropped the script when the door to the bathroom suddenly opened.

Sugar's eyes went from the script on the floor to my face. "Are you snooping, Danny?"

Always best to confess when you're caught, and I accepted my punishment without complaint. I was to run lines with her, playing the part of Seth, Catherine's lover, in a scene that was giving her trouble.

My very own copy of the script arrived by courier a couple of hours later. When I took it upstairs Sugar said her plan to rehearse with me had been approved by the director himself. Because it is impossible for me to describe either the specifics or tone of the scene, I have provided the relevant pages of the screenplay here.

```
Catherine has a menu in front of her. She looks puzzled by
it.

                    CATHERINE
          I don't know what this stuff is.

                    SETH
          It's Japanese … look, I'll order
          for both of us.

                    CATHERINE
          I'm not eating raw fish, thank you
          very much.

                    SETH
          Aw, why not? I love raw fish.

Seth's glance is lewd.

                    CATHERINE
          Don't be gross.

                    SETH
          Was I? Sorry. It's just so adorable
          when you blush.

                    CATHERINE
          Raw fish?! That's worse than eating
          mystery meat!!
```

```
                    SETH
          What's wrong with mystery meat?
          It's not so bad.

                    CATHERINE
          You never ate mystery meat!

                    SETH
          I sure did. I used to love mystery
          meat.

                    CATHERINE
          I used to love it too!

Their eyes meet. Seth is already in love with this mystery
woman.
                    SETH
          Queen Catherine, you have captured
          my soul.

                    CATHERINE
          Shut up! I hate it when you call me
          that. And you're being very silly!


                    SETH
          But why is that silly? It's true.
          You are a queen among women.

                    CATHERINE
          I spend my days as a Kleenex for
          snot-nosed six year olds! Half the
          time, I feel ...

                    SETH
          You feel ... what?

Seth takes Catherine's hand, raises it to his sensual lips
and kisses the tip of each finger. When he gets to her thumb,
he takes it into his mouth and sucks it gently.

Catherine is shocked. But mostly, she's aroused. She wishes
he would fuck her right there, right then. She reins in her
basest desires, lowering her eyes so he won't see the lust,
her longing.
                    SETH
               (in a husky voice)
          And what do you feel now, Queen
          Catherine? Hmm ...?
```

We rehearsed the scene over and over again, Sugar adjusting the tone of her dialogue with each go. Her performance ranged on a scale between full-on hysterical to completely flat and inexpressive. She explained that she was trying different approaches to playing Catherine. She didn't ask for my opinion of her performance, but she did say (somewhat grudgingly) that I had some natural ability. It was clear she enjoyed me sucking her thumb.

29

The winds left the same way they came, abruptly in the night, which should have been a good omen, except then I broke a mirror so those Santa Anas had the last word.

After it happened, it was *seven years of bad luck, bad luck comes in threes* on rotation in my brain, all day. I braced myself for what was sure to come next, nostalgic for that girl behind the front desk at the Tower Arms. Before Mike and his five grand. Before Ian. Before Cal. Before.

I'd been upstairs packing some things for Sugar to take with her to Paul darling's Laguna Beach "shack," which had been featured in *Architectural Digest* in the early aughts when it was owned by an actor known for his ubiquity in 1980s horror films. I'd never heard of the actor, but I was learning that was how Hollywood was. Everything was a reference to the business. The town feasted on degrees of separation, the lower the number the better. Going to the same hairstylist as a certain A-list actor was almost as good as being repped by their agent. The rules of the business were hard to follow, but Sugar knew the threads that connected everyone. She was, after all, born to it.

So, how the mirror broke. Sugar had asked me to apply sunscreen to her back. An innocuous enough request, but she couldn't have known the visceral reaction I would have, how much I wouldn't want to do that, not at all, not ever. How immediately it took me back to that lucky-streak year. With Patty. The Sands. Those not-so-shining adolescent experimentations. All of it crowding into my consciousness, shaking me to my core.

Patty had loved the pool at the Sands, but she hated the sun. I hated (was afraid of) the pool and loved the sun. Such was the nature of our relationship.

My mother's maternal instinct was nonexistent, my birth a regrettable accident, me at any age a burden that provoked never-ending irritation. Patty's neglect was as purposeful as her gambling. She worked hard at both. But at least I was there to rub sunscreen on the places she couldn't reach so she could sit by the pool and never get a tan line. She'd give me a slap if I didn't warm the lotion first, if I didn't cover every inch of exposed skin.

The tube of lotion in Sugar's hand, some expensive French brand. I took it from her and she turned, lowered the straps of her bra. Her freckles made constellations. I wanted to do it for Sugar, not Patty—kept saying to myself *not Patty not Patty*—but in the end the overpowering scent of that lotion filled my mouth and I retched, bile rising into my throat. I spun away—too quickly—and my foot caught the leg of her dressing table.

I saw it all happen in slow motion. My hands out, instinctively grabbing for purchase, and the makeup mirror crashing to the floor, face up. A spew of sparkling glass shards skittering across the hardwood floor. The force sending a small shower of glass arrows airborne to embed themselves, glistening, in the adjacent carpeting.

Our eyes met. If it targets you, bad luck really can't be prevented. Did we both see it coming?

I carried her bag to the car with the weight of what had happened pulling at me. Defeat seemed inevitable.

Paul, darling! Sugar purred as she settled into the leather seat of the vintage convertible Porsche. Every time we saw Westerfield he was behind the wheel of a different antique car, and Vernon had explained that they were probably all rentals. *What a pompous douche* were his exact words.

Westerfield inspected me over the rim of his aviators. "My, my," he said. "You've got this one well trained, haven't you?"

Sugar gazed up at me, lips curved into a gentle smile. "Danny's in love with me."

He winked at me like he and I both knew it was true. Like we were in on the joke together. I very much wanted to slap that look off his face. As they drove off Sugar didn't so much as glance back at me.

Then Vernon was suddenly there, standing right behind me. "Westerfield must *really* like her," he said. I asked why he would say that and he laughed. "Have you ever driven from here to Laguna Beach? It's a *commitment.*"

Remy, Becker, and I were lunching on Luchetti's eggplant panini, and judging by Remy's and Becker's ecstatic reactions, it was a staff favorite. I'd noticed that Luchetti was likely to give you extra-large portions of whatever dish you complimented, so both maids said the sandwiches were *ten stars* and reaped the benefits of their brownnosing by receiving an extra sandwich for them to split.

Everything had been peaceful, everyone focusing on the food. Then, her mouth full, Becker asked why I had the boss's yellow dress hanging in my closet. "She give you that dress, or did you steal it?" Becker said.

I said she had no business looking in my closet. I was hyperaware of

Luchetti, quiet and watchful next to me.

"The boss never gave me a dress." Becker looked at Remy. "She ever give you a dress?" Remy shook her head, her eyes bouncing from me to Becker and back again. "But this one's *special.*"

I said obviously it was part of my job to look after Miss Patten's wardrobe, and I had the dress because it needed airing.

"In your closet?" Becker said.

I was calm. I took the high road. But (I thought) the message I delivered was unmistakable: mind your own fucking business or you might find yourself out of a job.

Becker gave me exaggerated big eyes and continued chewing, sharing an amused glance with Remy. "Airing it out." She laughed, and Remy wanted to laugh but registered my expression and went back to stuffing her face with sandwich. After that the two of them finished their lunch quickly and left to go back to work.

"You can't fire her," Luchetti said quietly. "That's Vernon's job." She lifted a shoulder. "But don't let her talk to you like that or she'll own you. Set some boundaries, young lady."

Boundaries. Check. I thanked Luchetti for her input and told her I'd handle Becker, don't worry about that.

30

"Danvers!" Alice called out. "Come, sit."

I had sought out the tranquility of a pristine blue-sky day, without a whisper of wind, to think. I didn't want to believe I was out of my depth. Admitting that would be impossible. Besides, who would I tell? Vernon? He'd lose faith in me, maybe even fire me. But ever since Sugar had gotten the part in Westerfield's movie, every day felt like my first day on the job. Every day brought another pop quiz in a subject I hadn't known I should be studying for. My limits—those all-important boundaries—were unknowable. I regularly frightened myself.

But here was Alice and her crew having lunch under the shade of an olive tree. So normal it hurt. As I came closer Alice said, "Everybody, this is Danvers … That's Udo and Eddy." Everybody said hello.

The younger guy had a thick neck and oversized muscles. His ears stuck out at right angles on his head. Udo was a compact man with muscular forearms and a friendly face. And if that topiary was even partly his work, the man was an artist. That made Alice one too. I looked at her with new appreciation.

I asked what was for lunch and Alice held up her sandwich. "Avocado and tomato. Want a bite?" Said with this cheeky little smile.

I said no thanks but I was friendly when I said it.

"You're good on a ladder," Udo said.

I asked how he knew that, with possibly more hostility than necessary.

"We saw you," Alice said. "Washing the balcony windows a couple weeks ago. Udo's been talking about it ever since." She laughed.

"We could use somebody like you for ladder work," Udo said. "Eddy here … he's timid on the twelve-footer, so he's no good for the high work."

"Lift works quicker," Eddy said around a mouthful of sandwich, unfazed, or maybe uninterested in Udo's assessment, I wasn't sure which. He was definitely Vernon's type. Jacked and quiet.

"How's it going so far?" Udo asked in an overly casual way. "Is she keeping you busy?"

Eddy let out a grunt, which was either agreement or mirth. Alice's eyes were watchful.

I said "Busy enough," and Udo said, "We know all about how she keeps house staff *busy*."

I bristled, said Miss Patten was an ideal employer—in fact, the easiest I'd ever worked for. Who was gossiping? Had to be Becker or Luchetti. I'd have to find out. I stood up to leave.

"You're an expert on Bebe Patten now?" Alice said mildly. "How long have you known her? Twenty-four hours?"

Udo and Eddy exchanged amused glances. Alice chewed her sandwich, watching me.

"I spend every day with her," I said.

"Do you …" Alice said with a smirk.

The little group were all silent. I was rooted, not willing to turn my back on them, as if they might rise up and attack me.

"Well, anyway …," Alice said, rolling her eyes.

I wanted to slap her mocking face, so I walked away, but pretty soon I heard footsteps behind me. I whirled around. Alice's cheeks were pink. She had the grace to look ashamed. I asked what she wanted. I had things to do.

"We were *joking*," Alice said. "I mean, we all know Miss Patten is … who she is."

"Which means what?" I said, a sharp edge in my voice. "Why work for somebody you don't respect?"

She looked at me like I had grown a second head. "Are you serious?" We stared at each other. She looked away first.

"You don't know what you're dealing with," Alice said. "Set some boundaries."

That word again. I told Alice I didn't need any advice from her and left her standing there.

Chaos had arrived in the form of Paul Westerfield and his film, and we were all swept up in it even if some of us didn't want to acknowledge or accept it.

31

One morning Sugar announced that Vernon and I were to plan and execute an exclusive party that would be a mingling of New and Old Hollywood. It was critical that everything be meticulously presented. The food and drink, the styling of the event, all had to evoke taste as well as opulence. Every guest would receive a gift bag with a small fortune's worth of giveaways, from two-thousand-dollar perfumes to thousand-dollar wristwatches. We were buying in bulk. You just knew Paul Westerfield was behind all of this reckless extravagance.

"We want flowers everywhere," Sugar said. "The environment should feel like a fantasy of scent and color."

"How about stargazer lilies?" Vernon suggested.

"It's a party, Verny, not a fucking funeral," she said. "I want over-the-top, okay? Rare orchids, extinct plants if you can get them. This needs to be all about promoting the film and impressing these fuckers. Got it?"

Later I found Vernon at his desk, stewing. He launched into a tirade about spending that kind of money for a fucking giveaway, acting like it was *his* money being thrown away. I suggested he keep his voice down, but I agreed that obtaining extinct flowers was a bit colonialist. Luchetti was always listening, and it didn't do us any good to give her news items to broadcast to every other staff member.

Vernon leaned over and pulled out a desk drawer. He plopped the bottle of tequila on the desk, pulled the stopper and tipped the bottle back. When he'd quenched his thirst, he put the stopper back in and the bottle back in the drawer. He looked at me. "Where are my manners? Would you like?"

I tried to make him feel better by suggesting that he could probably do some lucrative vendor extortion on bulk purchases of French perfume and Swiss wristwatches, so that would be some consolation, wouldn't it? Money could buy happiness if not love, right?

Vernon laughed. "Well, now Danvers … that's a damn good idea. At the very least we'll get some nice door prizes for ourselves."

I didn't say I preferred cold, hard cash, because I had managed to cheer him up at the thought of free shit. For me money in hand is the only way you kept the wolves off the doorstep. No French perfume, Swiss watch, or supposedly safe bet ever saved anyone from financial disaster.

I told him to take it easy with the tequila at this time of day, but he laughed. "Don't worry," he said. "I've got immunity."

As if the uneasy undercurrents between Vernon and Sugar weren't difficult enough to navigate, I also had to keep up with Westerfield's increasingly unpredictable demands for specific floral or food and cocktail selections, usually delivered by text message in the early morning hours. I pictured him lying in his bed, dreaming up ways to make our lives difficult. He seemed to be a strong believer in *keep them on their toes*, whether he was directing Sugar to immerse herself in the lifestyle of a dominatrix with an obedient servant (me) or telling Vernon how to do his job. Apparently, none of us were yet up to his standards.

This morning's text from Westerfield had felt ominous.

meetg L @ 12
have list for you. b there

I found him in the kitchen chatting up Luchetti. She seemed upset, sending me distress signals with her eyes when Westerfield turned to me. "Luchetti is getting sidelined for the catering, but she'll be doing all the desserts. Isn't that right?" Luchetti's nod was sullen. "And we're changing florists, Danny. Vernon's guy is a piece of shit who charges way too much. Take a note."

I told him Vernon would never agree to that.

Westerfield puffed out his chest. "Vernon's not in charge here, is he?" He held out his hand. "Give me your hand."

I put both hands behind my back. What came next happened so fast I didn't have time to react. He jumped off his chair with a snarl, yanked my arms loose, gripped my right hand, and wrote a single word on it with a Sharpie. His paw was moist and my fingers squirmed to get away. "There," he said. "That's the florist. Ask for Sidney."

Luchetti's eyes behind her glasses were dark with hostility. Westerfield sat back down, this smug look of amusement on his face, as if he hadn't just behaved like a fucking lunatic. I left the room and went immediately to scrub off the word he'd scrawled there. *Petunia.* Yeah, well, petunias stink like cat piss.

As the date of the party loomed closer, Sugar bounced between euphoria and dread, exhibiting more extreme behavior than ever, but Vernon confided that these large swings were in fact characteristic of a cycle. It was still worrisome, and he was concerned she could be headed for a fall. I asked what that meant and he wouldn't say, but he was debating whether to suggest she see her nutritionist for B-12 shots.

When Sugar was in the euphoric phase, she'd go off with Vernon shopping and come home with piles of baubles and clothes that she couldn't live without. You had to be careful when she was like this or she'd latch onto you and you couldn't get anything else done. We played a lot of dress up. Even Vernon got pulled in.

Every day for an entire week, Luchetti had to make fresh, cream-filled croissants (a specialty of the old lady's) because Sugar had a *craving*, and since we didn't keep any leftovers whatever wasn't eaten had to be thrown away. Somewhere was a stinking mountain of Bebe Patten's rotting, rejected leftovers.

Sugar knew Remy was uncomfortable with seeing her nude, so she would walk around the house without a stitch on, eat a snack by the pool, oblivious to any and all eyes, and later laugh at the maid's discomfort. "She's so uptight, isn't she, Danny?" Remy complained to me numerous times about Miss Patten's vagina hanging out and how she didn't need to see that. But I was too busy managing my own emotions to take the time to explain female anatomy to poor Remy. I was surprised nobody quit during this period.

After the high came the low, and Sugar took her frustration out on Vernon and me.

I bothered her. I was *too slow* or I moved *too fast*. I sidetracked her merely by walking into the room. The coffee didn't taste fresh, or it tasted burned, or I had simply *made it wrong*. I had allowed her to run out of her favorite after-bath moisturizer. I was trying to scorch her by making the bathwater too hot. I sensed Westerfield's presence behind every mood swing.

I wouldn't have denied, had anyone bothered to ask me, that Sugar's constantly shifting attitude toward me stung. But I was better off than Vernon. For him, Sugar saved the more viciously personal attacks. His cologne made her want to vomit. *You stink like a French fairy.* His weight was out of control. *You're really getting* fat, *Verny. Seriously, you need to go on a diet and get some exercise. Nobody wants a fatty.*

When she threw a shoe at Vernon's head and called him an idiot because he briefly interrupted a phone call with Paul darling, Vernon took off in the Land Rover and didn't come back all day. The trouble was Sugar had asked him the night before to bring her the mail the minute it arrived, as she was awaiting important documents related to the film, so he had only been doing what she wanted.

I nervously watched Sugar stew all day. For all Vernon's faults, he was solidly committed to the job and I enjoyed working with him. His admirable competence outweighed his pitch black, world-weary cynicism. I hoped he wouldn't quit or, worse, be fired. For all my internal bravado, my place in the hierarchy felt increasingly tenuous.

When Vernon got back from his day away Sugar lit into him with Mrs. Luchetti and me standing there as witnesses, frozen in place, afraid to draw her attention our way.

I ought to fire your lazy ass.

How dare you take my car without permission!

I pay you to take whatever shit I decide to throw at you. And if you don't like it, you can see yourself out.

The room held its breath, but Vernon handled the situation like a consummate professional, quietly admitting in front of everyone that he'd been derelict and he would never make that mistake again. His performance of servility was impressive and that's all Sugar heard.

32

"We have to do more," Vernon said.

His office reeked of booze and unwashed armpit, and no amount of cologne and room deodorizer could mask it. He lay on the couch, his arm over his eyes. It was a Thursday morning, unusually hot and strangely sticky. The air quality index that day was again pronounced dire on the morning local news shows. But Sugar was on a rampage about some specific errand Vernon needed to run for her. No one else would do. *Tell him to wear a goddamn gas mask if it's that bad.*

"Fuck her," he said, his voice muffled by his shirtsleeve.

I gently closed the door behind me and went over to him. I asked, with deliberate irony, if he was alright, and he cackled. "You mean am I sloshed?" Vernon said. "Yes. The fucking room is spinning and spinning, and I'm just fine and dandy."

I offered a variety of excuses for Sugar's meanness toward him. She was under intense pressure from Westerfield. She didn't mean what she said, because clearly Vernon was the one she trusted the most or she would've let me run the errand. When that got no reaction I told him to pull himself together. I said this was no time to fall apart. But I had zero experience with a situation like this and no confidence that I would be able to get Vernon back on track.

"Please, Vernon," I said. "We need you."

He peered at me through bloodshot eyes. "It's probably only because she's too embarrassed to ask you to do it," he said. "Do you realize …" He struggled to sit up, reaching out his hand, so I helped haul him to a sitting position. He sat there for a second, running a hand through his stiff hair, then shook himself like a dog.

"Do you realize," he said, "that those two idiots started cooking up this little independent film project while they were both in *rehab* up there? Rehab, Danvers …"

Pointing out that Vernon had fed her vodka on her first night home was a little too on the nose given his delicate state, so I suggested that maybe it was time to get rid of all the booze in the house, at least hide it all somewhere she wouldn't be able to access.

"Won't work. Believe me." Vernon put his head back against the couch cushion and gazed bleakly at the ceiling. "Westerfield's got her convinced she's going to be a big star after this. Where does that leave *us?*"

He suddenly clapped a hand over his mouth, mumbling about water, and rushed into his private bathroom. I couldn't *not hear* the harsh retching sounds coming from the bathroom, and I was praying Sugar wouldn't lose patience and come looking for us. If she were to see Vernon in such a state, he might not have a job by day's end.

But after only a couple of minutes Vernon came out, standing a bit more upright. He'd combed his hair and tucked in his shirt. His breath smelled minty fresh. He smoothed the front of his shirt and checked the immaculate knotting of his tie.

"Miss Patten's current attitude is not good," he said, picking up his suit jacket and inspecting it for lint. He fixed me with a serious look. "For any of us." He put his jacket on. "It's your time to shine, Danvers. You'll have to be the one who gets rid of Westerfield."

I told him I didn't see how I could be helpful in that regard. And he said, "You need to let Sugar seduce you."

It suddenly seemed so obvious that I was slightly embarrassed to have missed it. Vernon … Luchetti … Alice. They had all hinted at it. But Sugar was just a flirt who had a way of getting you to do things you wouldn't think of doing until she asked you to do them. Call it charm as manipulation. I had assumed her behavior was meaningless, definitely not serious. She wanted adoration, not sex.

I told him, without hesitation, I would never do any such thing. I was a professional. I was here to do a job, and while I understood this situation was a bit different than usual, it wasn't *so* different that something like that would ever be a consideration. Besides, what made him think Sugar would even try to take her flirtation that far?

He stared at me with pity in his eyes. "Because she's done it before," he said. "Many times. Why do you think the previous housekeeper left? I thought you understood what *this situation* was. And you crossed the line before yourself, didn't you?" Vernon said, his expression mild. "With the daughter? In Brooklyn."

Blood rushed up my neck. "I told you what they said about me wasn't true."

"But it was true," he insisted. "The girl was smitten. Ian had to pull you off the project."

So now I knew for sure what I had suspected but hadn't wanted to acknowledge. Ian had told Vernon everything. Probably couched as a friendly heads-up. Marie Danvers doesn't have *boundaries*.

I vehemently denied that Cal and I had been anything, desperately needed to make Vernon believe me. If Calista Whitaker had been smitten, it was with only one thing: escaping the yoke of her parents. She used *me*, I hadn't done anything to encourage her. Even to my own ears, I sounded like a liar.

Vernon listened. Politely. Then he said, "I know about you and *Sugar*." He smiled. "Isn't that what you call her, in private? That was a clever move, Danvers. She loves it. She talks about you all the time when I'm alone with her. How you look like a beautiful boy. How you enjoy giving her a little daytime punishment. How *open* you are."

I struggled to find a way to respond, eyeing the door. I had the strongest urge to bolt. Except where was I going to go?

"Well," Vernon drawled, "if you think you've been discreet, let me assure you that everyone is aware that Princess likes you. And it's only a matter of time before the inevitable happens."

I found my voice then, suggesting he was insane if he thought I was going to sleep with the boss. Or try to break up the relationship between her and Westerfield. Even if I wanted to—which I did not—Vernon didn't really get it.

"Get what?" Vernon looked at me as if I were stupid. "Don't you read the tabloids?"

I said, "Look, Vernon. I don't want to be crass, but what kind of pussy power do you think I have? Sugar *wants* this movie. She thinks it's her destiny. Get it through your head."

But Vernon shrugged that off. "She'll get over it."

I laughed at his refusal to understand. I had tried, but there was no convincing him of Bebe Patten's unwavering dedication to her comeback.

Vernon straightened his tie, shot his cuffs, and pronounced himself ready to face another afternoon selecting vibrators if that's what it took, because *we* were going to win this game, not Westerfield.

I told him I was uninterested in the solution he'd laid out, but I would help him if he could come up with a better scheme.

Vernon nodded. "You're stubborn, but even the stubborn ones eventually give in." As he walked out, "You're going to succeed where Russo failed. I can feel it, Danvers. And I'm never wrong about these things. Trust me."

I hated those two words. I'd heard *trust me* all my life from people who had ultimately proved utterly untrustworthy.

33

Three days before the party, the Becker problem reached a crisis point, and I may or may not have assaulted her. Even with witnesses in the room, nobody saw exactly what happened, and it was still my word against hers when it came down to it.

It had been raining for twenty-four hours straight and everyone was on edge. The news was full of images of multimillion-dollar houses—like Patten House—sliding off their precarious perches during these kinds of weather events. Massive, top-heavy palm trees fell right over and crushed your Bentley or Lamborghini. You could marvel at the human ability to believe bad things don't happen to you if you have enough money.

I woke that morning with a sense of doom, a feeling only enhanced when I opened the drapes. The sky over the hills was low and dark, the clouds shaded angry green like you see on those Weather Channel shows about tornados and supercell thunderstorms. It was a busy day ahead, and I was going to have to drag myself kicking and screaming into it when all I really wanted to do was go back to bed and hide under the covers.

As I was considering all the ways that our party preparations would be complicated by the ongoing rain, the first drops pelted the window, and by the time I was showered and dressed it was a steady downpour.

It started in the most mundane way, as you might expect. Becker and I were putting away a grocery delivery to help Luchetti, who had her hands full.

"You sure have been taking a lot of abuse lately." Becker's mocking gaze challenged me. "She doesn't need you or Vernon anymore, now that she's got herself a new boyfriend."

Apparently Becker had witnessed enough of the recent shift in dynamics between us and Sugar to make assumptions, but I laughed it off and told her she didn't know what she was talking about. I asked Becker how she thought anything would get done around here if it weren't for me, and for Vernon.

Becker smirked when I turned to face her, holding a large can of Luchetti's favorite imported Italian tomatoes in my hand. I had not directly dealt with the woman's disrespect or her snooping, but I thought we had magically come to an unspoken agreement without me having to do anything to make it happen.

Luchetti gave me a look, then bent her head and kept chop, chop, chopping chives for garnish.

Becker settled her hip against the counter, tapping her pink painted talons. "Now that she's screwing the big-shot director, she don't need you two to play sandwich. Am I right? Are you sad she doesn't love you anymore?"

"The can slipped out of my hand."

"She says you did it on purpose."

I'd been called on the carpet in Vernon's uncarpeted office.

"It was unfortunate that her hand happened to be in the way." I was clumsy, yes, at worst. But it was an accident. *Obviously.*

Vernon gazed at me, his expression bland. "Luchetti says Becker was being inappropriate, but that doesn't excuse what you did."

I wasn't admitting anything, but we both knew. I asked how she could have known about the whole sandwich thing. "I may have told her," Vernon said with a nonchalant shrug. "I had to give Becker a hefty cash severance in exchange for her signature on a release promising not to sue us, or sell her story to the tabloids. I'll probably have to throw some cash at Luchetti too. All of it will have to come out of your cut. And *Princess* is not to know anything about any of this. Or Westerfield either. Are we clear?"

Yeah. Clear as mud. I wasn't about to whine about the money. And I was actually grateful to Vernon for his ability to look past my behavior and stand up for me.

"No more assaulting the maids, okay, Danvers?" he said. Then he handed me the first-aid kit and asked me to return it to his bathroom.

I wouldn't have been tempted to snoop except he was preoccupied with the party and the problem I'd created. I had never been inside his suite alone, and I admit I was curious about his background. He guarded his rooms and kept nothing personal in sight, so what might I find in all those closed cupboards and drawers? The temptation was irresistible.

I made a face at my reflection in his bathroom mirror. *Bye, bye Becker.* Good riddance. I opened the cabinet next to the sink. Expensive skin care brands and colognes, several different types of razors, condoms in various colors and flavors. In the other was more of the same plus an interesting variety of prescription medications, only some that bore Vernon's name on the label. "Beatrice Patten" was printed on the labels for the Adderall, Xanax, and Klonopin. There were also two boxes of Plan B in that name.

Beatrice. If I had a name like that I would use it. It was sad Sugar didn't like it. As for the party drugs, I assumed that Vernon was keeping them out of her reach.

Back in the bedroom I made a quick circuit, opening drawers and closets and finding nothing except a lot of designer clothes and two dozen pairs of shoes (I counted). Then I hit the matching bedside tables. One drawer was completely empty and had dust in its corners. The other was jammed. Two Rolexes inside their boxes and one empty Breguet box (presumably the watch Vernon was wearing that day), a silk sleep mask and a litter of earplugs, a bag of mini chocolate bars, an address book that had only one entry (the phone number for Chin Chin), a pair of velvet-lined handcuffs (how had Sugar known about that?), and shoved in the back of the drawer, a bundle of papers tied together with a blue ribbon. I would have missed them if I hadn't been diligent.

The papers turned out to be letters dating back five years, when Vernon began working for Sugar. All handwritten on monogrammed stationery. The initials IStM scrawled above Ian's engraved return address on 85th Street.

34

Gaston was a short, rather slim man with silver hair and a slight French accent who had arrived with tasting samples for the party. He was a bit older than the men Vernon usually flirted with, but I caught a vibe so I made an excuse and left them chewing on shaved roast beef *en croûte de moutarde* while Luchetti looked on in judgment. Her nose had been out of joint since Westerfield sidelined her and hired outside catering.

I retrieved the letters that I'd taken from Vernon's drawer and slipped into his room to put them back. I'd read them, and even though I still had unanswered questions they had explained some things I was still processing. The fact was, the mere existence of the letters had shaken me. Ian had hidden his real self from me, probably from everyone, except Dai Vernon. That much was crystal clear. And never mind that I'd done the same. My secrecy was justified.

Some of the letters were long and filled with the mundane details of life and work. But inevitably all of the notes would slide into sentimental longing. *I miss you, Daddy bear. I'm always thinking about Bali, all those luscious hot nights. When are you coming east again? I've been naughty but … nothing compares to you, as the song says.*

Also among the letters were postcards, and even birthday cards. The postcards often had hastily scribbled one-liners that seemed coded in a secret language that only they two could interpret. *Keep your fork, my dear, there's pie.* Written on the back of a postcard depicting a creature called a Jackalope with a Texas zip code. Or, *One down, two more to go on the block—celebrate!* That, written on the back of a Polaroid of Ian standing in front of the David statue in Florence, Italy.

One or two of the letters hinted at more serious matters of money and trouble with certain people or projects. *Need advance for overtime this month. L.O. knows, will have to be paid.* ("paid" was double underlined). *Cash needed ASAP, project capital running low.*

And finally, there was one in which I had taken center stage. That had been the hardest to take. You think you know people, but it turns out you can always be wrong about everything. I put the bundle of papers back into the drawer exactly as they had been.

When I came back out into the hall Luchetti was standing in front of my bedroom door across the way, her hand poised to knock. "Did you need something?" I said. I knew I was being weird and overly casual as I pulled Vernon's door closed behind me. She stared at me, her expression opaque. Luchetti was sharp and she had the ability to rattle me, like a ghost of Patty crossed with any one of a number of people who had long ago decided I was irredeemable.

"Vernon wants you to try the desserts." The old lady strolled over to me. "What were you doing in there?"

I wound my way through an elaborate explanation involving laundry and wanting to help Vernon out since he was so busy with the party preparations.

"You're doing his laundry." Luchetti gave a little head wag of disbelief.

"That's right," I said, hoping it didn't sound as defensive to her as it did to me.

She stared at me. I gave it back. We were in a standoff. So I made the first move and motioned her to follow me inside my room. I closed the door behind us and told her to have a seat.

"That's okay," Luchetti said. "I'll stand. What do you want?"

She had her arms crossed. I decided to show her my belly. I told her I would very much appreciate it if she didn't tell Vernon I'd been in his room.

"So you weren't doing his laundry." Her tone was bone-dry.

I shook my head, and Luchetti's thin lips formed a half-smile. I said I hadn't been up to anything underhanded. I said, "Can you believe the size of his bathroom?"

She ignored my deflection. "Did you take something or put something back?"

I gave up then and asked how much it would take to keep her mouth shut. Luchetti's smile finally landed. She said, "That depends," and I told her to quit fucking around and give me a number.

"Okay, don't get huffy," she said. "I could take a generous cash payment now. Or you could convince Vernon to give me a *decent* bonus this year."

So I said how about both.

With that settled, we went back to the kitchen, where I had to taste four different desserts and offer my opinion on which we should serve. I voted for the princess cake, but they chose Black Forest mousse bombs. I did a pretty good job of pretending to care about any of it.

I love you, Ian had written numerous times in his letters. I studied Vernon with new eyes. Somehow this man had fucked his way into Ian's impenetrable heart.

When the doorbell rang, I expected some last-minute delivery, so I was unpleasantly surprised to find Paul Westerfield standing on the step, dressed in a creased white linen suit with a bright blue T-shirt tucked into his pants.

I opened the door wide to let him in, but instead of ignoring me as he usually did Westerfield said, "Danny! I was hoping it would be you."

I wanted to slap my name out of his mouth, but I smiled sweetly and invited him in. He bounded past me, then stood waiting in the middle of the foyer as if he was interested in the *ikebana* floral arrangement on the hexagonal cherrywood table.

I asked if he wanted me to call Miss Patten to the great room, and he said, "Oh no, we're going upstairs." He gestured at me. "After you." When I hesitated he got impatient. "Go, girl. She's waiting for us."

He went to take my arm, but I slapped his hand away and marched ahead. He was chuckling as we mounted the stairs. At the top I stood to the side.

"You first," he said. He was huffing and puffing like he could have a heart attack. I pictured him pitching forward onto his ugly face. Lights irrevocably out. I asked him where we were going.

"Dressing room," Westerfield said, showing his crooked teeth.

When we walked in, Sugar stood on the platform wearing a sheer, full-length bodysuit that hid nothing. "You like?" she said.

Sugar could handle being stared at, I'll give her that. A good trait for an actor.

"I like," Westerfield growled from behind me. "Totally Crystelle."

"But Catherine too. Don't you think, Paul?"

I stepped forward briskly and asked how I could help.

35

Westerfield swung the door closed. Sugar stepped down off the dais and sashayed over to the closet while he draped himself all over the chaise longue. There was a buzzing energy in the room I didn't like. Something was brewing between them and somehow it involved me, trapped like a fox surrounded by hounds bent on murder.

Sugar paged through the hangers, not looking over at me when she pulled out a single-sleeved, off-shoulder, Missoni silk caftan in a subtle geometric pattern of greens and grays. The dress had a beautiful drape. I hadn't seen her wear it. Now she waved it like a flag.

"This is the one we liked, isn't it, Paul darling?"

Watching us from under hooded eyes, he nodded. Sugar clutched my arm and I resisted the urge to shove her hand off me. She wouldn't look me in the eye. "Isn't this fun?" she said.

When she said that, it raised the hair on the back of my neck. People who'd say *isn't this fun* were usually about to perpetrate some kind of dirty trick on you.

Sugar slid the caftan off the padded hanger and held it against herself, finally facing me. I recognized the look she gave me. It was the same expression she wore in that photograph with her parents. The same one when she gazed at me across that room, Paul darling nuzzling her crotch, the camera on "record." An expression as blank as a white wall.

"I need you to hem this for me," she said. Abruptly handing me the empty hanger, Sugar stepped back up onto the platform, giving Westerfield an unobstructed view of her backside before pulling the caftan over her head. It settled around her like liquid.

"Let's go, Danny," Sugar said, snapping her fingers. "We don't have all day."

So I got my pincushion and my hem tool and knelt at her feet. The bottom flared, so it took me some time to work my way around. Westerfield sat there, silently watching, while Sugar stood over me, humming with anarchic energy. I jabbed my thumb more than once, not enough to draw blood and ruin something, but just enough to remind me to pay attention. *Isn't this fun.* Fun like putting glass in the oatmeal.

Westerfield suddenly cleared his throat. "Your girl reminds me of this nun I had in school," he said. "She had that same look. All tamped down on the outside and fire on the inside."

"Our shy little nun," Sugar put a hand on the top of my head and I looked up. "Keep pinning," she whispered.

"I used to pleasure myself, thinking about that nun," Westerfield said.

"What a naughty boy you were," Sugar said.

I kept pinning, trying to quiet my quivering insides. It wasn't like I'd never been the object of sexual harassment. I'd worked in hospitality. This was not that. This was something else. Something even more menacing.

"Forbidden things are sweeter, aren't they, baby?" Westerfield said.

I wanted to laugh. At him. At the situation. I wished for a witness to this bullshit, because this was such a perfect example of how fucked up the men of Westerfield's generation were. Wanting Sugar to put a stop to it was futile. She was playing her usual games.

Call it my trauma or whatever you want, but I have always hated when people talked about me as if I wasn't right there. I pushed another pin in the endless hem of that caftan, while I pictured a soft-bodied Paul Westerfield doll, pictured sticking him full of those long, sharp hatpins with the pearls on the end that you sometimes see in antique shops. Pins in his beady eyes, his wet mouth, his vulnerable groin. I pushed them deeper and deeper until he squirmed in agony. I pushed them far enough inside to reach all his soft, defenseless parts.

Kind, old Dr. Kristoffer. *Do you know why you're here …?*

I pushed the last pin into place and stood up. Sugar was staring at herself in the mirror, lost in her thoughts.

I told her to take off the dress and I'd get it hemmed right away. I knew I sounded clipped, anxious. The hounds were at my heels but the safety of the den was only steps away, if I could just … get there.

"Is that okay with you?" Westerfield said sharply, his eyes on Sugar. "Is she allowed to speak to you that way?"

As if on cue, Sugar abruptly pulled off the caftan and dropped it to the floor in front of her in one fluid motion. I didn't hide my annoyance when I bent to pick it up, and when her foot pushed me off balance, I went down on my knees. She kept her foot flat on my back, her weight pressing me down. "Stay," she said.

I must have lost time because I don't remember anything until the weight was lifted and I went scurrying away on all fours, jumping to my feet, that fucking caftan in my fist.

They both looked at me as if nothing had happened. Blood pounded in my ears. I couldn't unclench my teeth, my tongue had glued itself to the roof of my mouth.

"You're all set when *I* say," she said.

I said *stop it*. Or I said *fuck it*. Or maybe I said nothing.

"Put her in her place, Crystelle," Westerfield's lips were pulled back in a grin that showed all his big, ugly teeth.

I said something along the lines of "Are you (fucking) kidding me" and had retreated halfway to the door when Sugar's voice stopped me dead.

"Did I say you could go, Cinderella?"

When I turned Sugar smiled, that gap between her teeth catching the tip of her tongue. She walked over to me, leaned in, her breath tickling my ear as she whispered, "Play along, okay?" Then she turned and walked back over to the mirror to look at herself and pretend to check her makeup. "You like it when I tell you what to do," Sugar said to her reflection. "So say it. Say you like me to tell you what to do." She turned to face me. "If you say it, Danny, you can go."

So if you think this was the moment when I balked, think again. Of course I said it.

The second I spat out the words, Westerfield was on his feet like he'd placed a big bet at the Super Bowl and was watching his team win. He was clapping and acting like a freak. "Bravo, Crystelle!"

Before I could stop her Sugar pulled me into this tight hug, a blast furnace of soft flesh pressed against me. I met Westerfield's triumphant gaze over her shoulder telling me: *I can make her do anything. I can make her hurt you in ways you haven't even imagined yet.*

Sugar let me go and threw herself at Westerfield. "See, Paul? I told you I could improv."

36

I went (fled) to my room, dodging other people like I was moving through enemy territory. When Vernon came looking for me a bit later, I told him I had cramps. He went away quickly.

Improv. That's what Sugar had called it. With my humiliation as the goal.

Obviously Westerfield had planned it. But they'd executed it together. Accepting that Sugar was so willing to use me that way was going to take time. But it was my hatred for Westerfield, and everything he represented, that kept me from walking out that day. I saw myself packing my bags, imagining Vernon's face when I quit. But after that the screen went blank. Where was I going to go? Not back to New York. Not back to Ian.

I will credit good old Patty for inspiring my keen thirst for revenge. The last words she ever spoke to me could be stitched on a throw pillow. *Life isn't a walk in the park. You have to go along to get along.* Well, if I had to go along, I intended to give Westerfield what he deserved.

After I made the decision to stay I was still buzzing with adrenaline, so I went outside to walk it off. I wasn't expecting to find Alice and Udo in the topiary garden, still at it this late in the day, and I would have sneaked away except Udo looked up and called a greeting. He was standing next to a wheelbarrow full of twigs and cuttings. Alice was on a short stepladder hand clipping the back of a crouched hedgehog composed of boxwood and yew.

"Where'd you come from?" She looked semi-happy to see me. What harm would it do to be, even for a short while, the person she thought I was. I called on those skills one uses in any bar with any girl: I smiled and told her she was exactly the person I was hoping to run into. It made her blush in a pretty adorable way. Alice was sunlight and fresh air. Sugar was a stormy vortex of triggers and confusion. And Cal? We'd had that palm-to-palm insight into each other's natures. Until she threw it all away.

Alice glanced around at me, held my gaze for an extra second, this half-smile on her face, then went back to her task. Snip snip. It didn't always have to be so serious. What Alice wanted from me was simple. Easy.

Udo had gone back to stacking and piling plant material in the wheelbarrow. There were still more clippings, so I picked up a handful of branches and laid them on top of the pile. Udo protested, but I waved that off and we finished loading up the barrow. Alice climbed down and collapsed the ladder, that same half-smile quirking her lips. What would it be like to kiss her?

Alice handed Udo the ladder to hold down the pile of brush and off he went. "Meet you at the truck," he called over his shoulder. "Bye, Danvers. Thanks for your help."

I told Alice her topiary was looking very good, and that *she* looked very good, and I reached out and rubbed a bit of dirt off her chin. She got bashful and went back to loading the other wheelbarrow. I pitched in, and she said, "I doubt anybody at their party will care, but it does look good around here, doesn't it? Thanks for noticing."

She raked up the last bits while I watched her. She had grace and efficiency in her motions, the strong muscles of her arms bunching with every pull of the rake. Her scent was a pungent, not unpleasant odor of well-earned sweat and pine bark mulch.

I didn't think about the consequences. I walked over, took the rake out of her hands, and kissed her. We staggered around, gripped in a ridiculous dance, mouths glued. The kissing was more than I expected, slower, more exploratory and altogether tempting, and suddenly we were on the ground and I was rolling Alice onto her back, unzipping her jumpsuit. She heaved up to meet my hand as I touched warm skin and taut belly muscles.

Cal.

That name, unbidden, was the hiss of water putting out a fire.

Cal.

I rolled off Alice and got up, brushing nonexistent grass off my trousers. I formulated a humbling apology. I was out of line, I told her. I got caught up and I shouldn't have. Very sorry. So very sorry.

Alice still had not moved. That forgiving magic light was slipping away and she looked washed out and tired, a little sad. I was calculating what else I had to say or do in order to be able to leave her there without looking like a complete asshole.

"Is everything okay with you?" Alice asked.

That caught me completely off guard. The look on her face was thoughtful, puzzled.

"You seem … weird," she said. "I don't want you to take this the wrong way, okay?" She got up, brushing stray bits of dirt from her filthy coveralls. "I mean … I like you, Danvers, but … we're not gonna fuck right now. I mean

… no." She waited for me to say something, but I had nothing more to offer, so she picked up the wheelbarrow handles. "We can try this again sometime," she said. "But not here. I don't like what this place does to people."

$$37$$

Ever since Sugar had announced her intention to throw this party, the house had been a stream of strangers from early in the morning until quitting time at five, but now, twenty-four hours before the big day, the activity and deliveries ramped up tenfold with vans and box trucks jockeying for space in the service drive. Catering staff whose names I would forget the minute they introduced themselves rushed around, setting up staging.

The nonstop action helped me put some distance between what had happened between me and Alice. I'd been going back and forth between judging her for giving me mixed signals and hating myself for being so weak about a spoiled jerk like Cal Whitaker who was probably somewhere right now enjoying herself while she ruined somebody else's life. Alice could never understand the forces that chained me, dooming me to repeat my mistakes.

I also spent a not insignificant amount of mental effort developing grim fantasies of ways I could get back at Cal, make Paul Westerfield pay, and punish Sugar for her callous behavior. Looking back, it's easier to see where you went wrong, how you were all in for something so wrong. Like a gambling habit, revenge can backfire and blow a hole straight through your heart, but you just keep rolling the dice or spinning that wheel because you can't see any other way.

The day before the party, just before lunch, the usually unflappable Luchetti unraveled, storming off in tears because Remy allowed a pan of puff pastry to burn while Luchetti was busy, so Vernon asked me to take over deliveries while he went off to comfort the old gal and get her back on track. I reminded him to tell her about the extra staff bonus that was coming to her after we pulled off the party, hoping that would help calm her upset and be added insurance to keep her lip buttoned about my spying. One whispered word from Luchetti into Vernon's ear could cause a ripple effect of consequences for my spying.

At the back driveway, a young man was offloading buckets of flowers from a pale blue van with the name Petunia painted on its side, each letter of the word made out of cutesy leaves and petals. It was a lot of additional flowers. I estimated thousands of dollars worth of roses alone, but also giant lilies and other exotic-looking blooms. Their combined fragrances were carried on the breeze. It was a lot.

I told the guy we definitely hadn't ordered lilies, and he looked at me blankly, shrugged, and said, "I don't know. I just deliver them." When I held out my hand to sign the paperwork he hesitated.

Being taller than he was, I squared my shoulders and told him I was fully authorized, that I was the *executive* housekeeper and Mr. Vernon was busy with other important business. "Give me the paperwork," I said.

But he shook his head, consulted his clipboard. "The order is in Mr. Paul Westerfield's name, and I was told he needs to sign. Personally." He looked a bit uncomfortable, but somehow I sensed he wouldn't budge.

I told him he'd have to wait then, as I wasn't sure where Mr. Westerfield was. I didn't bother to hide my annoyance. I gestured at the buckets and told him to bring them inside so they wouldn't wilt in the heat.

I thought he would argue about that too, but he picked up a bucket in each arm and I held the door for him. On my way through the kitchen I saw that everything was at a standstill and Remy was snacking on the canapé filling.

I asked her what the hell she thought she was doing, and she took a languid lick of the spoon, daring me. "I just wanted a taste," she said.

I snatched the spoon from her hand and tossed it in the sink with a clatter, ordering her to help the flower guy get the rest of the flowers inside.

Westerfield's voice boomed from the general direction of the foyer. I found him facing off against a woman attired in a designer-label suit and Manolo Blahnik slingbacks. They both looked at me when I arrived, their expressions tense.

"What do you want?" Westerfield barked.

I was an unwelcome interruption. I smiled inside and told him sweetly that his flower delivery had arrived. "They need *your* signature, sir."

He waved me away and turned his attention back to the woman. "How dare you push your way into my house. I've told you ten times already. Your guy is dead wrong. Or he's a goddamn liar."

I was undecided whether I should back away or stay. He had definitely said *my* house. I stayed put.

"You're the *liar*," the woman said. "It's a goddamn fake, and I want my money back."

Westerfield snorted dismissively. "This is a waste of my time."

The woman lowered her voice and turned her back on me. "Do you really want to do this in front of her?"

"Her? You mean the maid?" Westerfield said loudly. He turned to me. "You're the soul of discretion, aren't you?"

I didn't answer.

The woman jabbed a finger at Westerfield's face. "I've called my attorney," she said. "So you'll be hearing from her. It's not going to go well for you."

Westerfield got puffy, and it was obvious she wasn't sure what he was prepared to do. But neither was I. It was a riveting moment.

"I sold you that painting in good faith, Elaine," Westerfield hissed, spittle flying. "Now you have buyer's remorse so you go around and lie about its authenticity and try to ruin my reputation with my friends and my backers. Do you really think that's a good idea? Do you know who I am?"

The woman named Elaine sneered. "You're broke, Paul. And you're a crook, and everybody's going to know it when I'm done with you." She delivered the line with decent bravado, but Westerfield laughed in her face.

"You're in the wrong business, darlin'," he said. Mr. Condescending. "You need brass balls to get where I am in this industry. I've got Jason and Cary on speed dial. Who do you have?"

That was when she glanced over at me and our eyes met. I wanted to give her a sign, but I couldn't afford to form on-the-spot alliances with strangers, even if their grudges aligned with mine. I gave a little shrug.

Disappointed, she turned back to Westerfield. "It's a *fake*," she spat. "You're going to give me that money back, asshole, or I tell everybody what a phony scumbag you are."

"Fuck you, you miserable *stupid* bitch." Westerfield jabbed his sausage finger in her face, and she took an involuntary step back on those heels, ankles wobbling a little. "In fact, *my* attorney loves making other people's lives miserable. He'll enjoy destroying you and your bitch lawyer in court. Now get out of my house." He turned his back on her.

If she'd had a weapon—let's say, a hammer—that would have been the time to strike. I saw him collapsed on the floor, his cracked skull oozing brains, a wide pool of blood spreading like a halo around his head.

But what happened was, Elaine turned on her heel and walked out without another word.

Westerfield swiveled on his heels and called after her, "Get ready, sweetheart. And don't spread any more lies about that Warhol, or I'll personally see to it you never work again." After she unsuccessfully tried to slam that enormous front door, he walked over and swung it closed, then turned to me. "Fucking cunt *television* producer. I'll ruin her."

I reminded him in a mild tone about the guy waiting for his signature, managing to keep my expression neutral as he pushed by me. I wanted to rub his nose in the fact that everybody in the house now knew his business. Well, everybody except his star. So far he had been able to hide his true nature from Sugar.

38

I was trying to absorb what I'd heard but I couldn't put together what it all meant. If Elaine was to be believed, Paul Westerfield was broke. And he had sold her a Warhol that might be a fake. I couldn't wait to tell Vernon about what I'd witnessed.

The kitchen was deserted, which meant Remy was probably taking yet another break to smoke one of her generic cigarettes and watch her YouTube videos. But she wasn't in her usual spot, sitting on the little cast iron bench by the door, so I went looking for her and interrupted Westerfield and flower boy in the middle of a hushed conversation through the window of the van, Westerfield's hands gripping the door frame.

The big man took his hands away when he saw me, then looked back at flower boy. "You have my number, right?"

Westerfield strode past me, muttering, "Everybody's a fucking actor," and went into the house. When I looked back at the van, flower boy was checking his look in the rearview and smoothing his hair with his hand.

Much later, over pizza and generous pours of red wine, I told Vernon about Elaine and the allegedly fake Warhol that Westerfield had sold her. We both agreed that Westerfield was a lot less rich than his stable of vintage cars and fancy real estate holdings would indicate.

"He's probably mortgaged up to his eyeballs," Vernon said. "And he's crooked. So that's interesting, Danvers." He tapped his fingers on the table. "I'll see what else I can find out. Good job."

I was this close to telling Vernon about the "improv" in Sugar's dressing room, but it felt like tattling rather than adding ammunition to any campaign to rid ourselves of Westerfield. Besides, I sensed that Vernon would interpret that scene as yet another indication that Sugar had a real thing for me.

But Westerfield in the mix had changed everything between her and me. I had my guard up now. And I would have to find a way to manage Paul darling on my own.

The day of the party I was up at five.

I dressed carefully for the work day, and to my surprise Vernon complimented my appearance when I walked into the kitchen at six. Even more surprising was that he was sober, fully dressed, shaved, and carefully groomed at that hour.

"I made you coffee." He slid a cup across the counter. "I was up late last night, making calls on your behalf. The caterer is sending two extras to help Mrs. L. so you're off the hook for kitchen police."

I wanted to know how I would be utilized, and he said, "Can't you guess?"

So I said, "Emptying ashtrays?"

"Nobody smokes *inside* these days," Vernon laughed. "Try again."

"I get the night off?"

"Very funny, Danvers." He shook his head. "You're it. Princess wants you to help her get ready." He chuckled. "If she tries to get cozy tonight, let her. But make sure you imply that the role in this shitty film isn't right for her. Hit her insecurities. Tell her she's overreaching. You feel me?"

When I brought coffee, Westerfield was lounging beneath the painting in Sugar's little sitting room. He was dressed sloppily, as usual, in rumpled khaki pants and one of his ubiquitous pit-stained white polo shirts.

"Good morning," he said, putting aside the Christie's auction catalog he was reading. His upper arms were old-man slack, but he had the look of a brawler, somebody you'd bet on in a bar fight.

I put the coffee tray down, and he said, "What, no cappuccino for me?"

I said I didn't know he wanted a cappuccino and asked if I should go immediately and make him one.

"You'd do that?" he said.

Of course, sir. I'll be happy to poison it too.

"Sit down," he said, making the two words into one.

I was all, *gee whiz, sorry about that, can't stay, wanted downstairs.*

"And I want you upstairs," he said. "Who's gonna win this one?"

So I sat, folding my hands primly on my lap. If he wanted a nun he was going to get one.

"Where are you from?" he said, starting right in on the interrogation.

"New York, sir."

"The city?"

I told him here, there, and everywhere, and he squinted at me with suspicion. I said, "What is this, an inquisition?" and he snorted a laugh.

"Get you alone and your Irish comes out, is that it, Danny?"

I shrugged.

"What's your background?" he said. "Who are your people?"

I said orphans didn't have people.

His eyes bored into me. "Great story. But you're lying."

I said it was true, every word, and if he didn't believe it that was a *you* problem.

He tapped his forehead with a fat forefinger. "How does a smart cookie like you wind up wearing an apron and cleaning up after people? What do you get out of it?"

I stood up to leave.

"Okay, okay," he held up his hands in mocking surrender. "I'm getting the message. You can go, Sister Danny."

I called that interaction a draw.

39

Sugar sat on the dressing room couch in front of the large window overlooking the pool, backlit by the rising sun, so I didn't properly register what she'd done. But then she stood up and turned to face me. I guess my shock was evident because she giggled and fluffed her newly platinum blonde hair. The stylist had trimmed it into a severe bob and ironed it straight.

"Say hello to Catherine," she said. "Or is it Crystelle?"

Her brows had been thinned, darkened, and reshaped as well. The overall effect was strange to say the least, since with that hair and those eyebrows, she looked very much like the photos of young Rose Patten.

"Do you like it?" she said.

"Whose idea was that?" I said. "Or is it a wig?"

"A wig?" She snorted. "It took Sheena hours to get it this shade," she said. "I'm probably poisoned from all the chemicals. But wait till you see the makeup Paul has designed. It's *wild*. I get to wear fake eyelashes and everything!"

Like this little kid. I told her she looked like a completely different person. I thought I was hiding my true feelings, but she narrowed her eyes at me as if she wasn't sure if I was mocking her. Then she decided I was right, saying that's exactly what she was. She had *transformed* into Catherine/Crystelle.

Sugar went over to the dresser and started pulling out bra and panty sets and tossing them on top of the marble. I couldn't let her make a mess of things, so I went to assist and she stepped aside, leaning her hip against the bureau. "Let's pick something white and modest. Like a school teacher would wear."

I raised an eyebrow at her. There was nothing like that in her lingerie collection and we both knew it.

"Something white." Sugar waved her hand. "I'll work on that other part. I guess I need to go shopping for granny panties."

I pulled out four different sets that were closest to white.

"Things are coming together, Danny," she said. "*Finally*. Isn't it exciting? Aren't you excited about the party? You're going to meet Joey Alter."

I said I was *super* excited, and she was oblivious to my sarcasm, which was kind of funny.

"Verny should try to be more like you," she said. "You get it."

I told her absolutely, I got it. For sure. You want this part so much, there might be no end to the lengths you'll go to *get it*.

She dropped her kimono, and while she looked through the options I'd pulled from the drawer, I noticed that she had gotten a Brazilian wax and the freshly denuded skin looked angry and raw.

"Yeah, I got my lawn mowed." Sugar laughed. "It's okay, Danny … you're allowed to look. It itches like crazy." She scratched at herself gingerly using just the tips of her pointed nails.

Choosing a pair of white lace bikinis, she used my arm to steady herself while she pulled them on.

In the mirror she inspected the choice of undergarments critically. "You're not upset with me, are you? That thing with me and Paul the other day?"

I shook my head. Oh no. It's all good. I *get it*.

"It was Paul's idea," she eyed me defensively. "He likes to provoke people. He's like a teenager that way." She shrugged, looked away. "I know he's weird sometimes. But brilliant people often are, aren't they?"

Yeah, brilliant people were often allowed to be jerky assholes.

She came and stood next to me, watching while I folded and put away the items strewn across the bureau.

"Paul's jealous of Verny," she said casually, apropos of nothing. The reason was that Paul simply couldn't imagine anybody sleeping in the same bed and not fucking. "I keep telling him Verny's a queer. We're not *fucking*. But he's so old-school sometimes."

I yanked the drawer open again and aimlessly rearranged the arranged undergarments.

"You'll get used to Paul," Sugar said. "We're all going to be spending massive amounts of time together once we start shooting."

I closed the drawer again, opened my mouth, then shut it again. Sugar most certainly didn't *get it*, so what was the point.

"You look pretty tonight," she said and put her hand on my waist. "We're in this together … aren't we? Girls against boys?" She booped the end of my nose as if I were a sad puppy she'd found abandoned by the side of the road. Her voice got husky. "Besides, we both know you like it when I boss you around."

Her performance was sexy psychopath from a cheesy nineties thriller.

But she wasn't wrong. I had shown only a ready willingness to let her manipulate me. I said her bossing me around was my job description after all, and she said, "Exactly, that's what I mean! You get it."

And that was how I wound up wearing Rose Patten's top, and her gold necklace, to the big party.

Sugar told me she didn't want me looking like the housekeeper. Instead, I was to wear the turquoise tank she'd chosen because it was perfect for my body type, so like Mommy's. And if anybody asked about it, I was to tell them that Rose Patten had worn the tank in *Carol in the Cage*, a Patten collaboration from the late eighties about a go-go dancer who tragically dies of a heroin overdose. As for the necklace, it had been a twentieth-anniversary gift from Artie to Rose so it had sentimental value. It would be a secret symbol of our special bond, and if Westerfield asked me about it I was instructed to tell him that.

Sugar was truly delighted with herself but I tried to back out. I respectfully declined. Look! I was already dressed. And I *was* in fact the housekeeper, so I should probably look like I was. I didn't add that I had zero interest in telling Westerfield anything about our supposed special bond or anything else.

I could have predicted her response: "Don't be such a *puritan*, Danny! Come on! Live a little!" I should have come up with better excuses. Before I could stop her Sugar's fingers were in my hair, setting it free of the hairband I'd used to keep it off my face. She fluffed it this way and that. I cringed away from our repeated reflections in the big mirrors.

"Take off your clothes," she said.

I let annoyance creep into my refusal. I said I'd change in my own room if she was really going to insist on this change of outfits, but she said, "Do it. And don't question me," and I guess she was practicing her improv again.

I didn't want to be prudish about it, so I took off my apron and shirt quickly. I reached for the top but she snatched it away. "Not so fast," she said. "The bra. It's gotta go. It'll show." She held up the thin straps of the tank top and gave me this impatient look. "It's not like I haven't seen them before."

I ripped the bra off like a Band-Aid and dropped it ceremoniously on top of my pile of clothing. I told her to stop staring but I didn't put any bite into the request. She handed me the top and I pulled it over my head, tucking it in.

"Oh, see?" Sugar said. "That looks so good. Look—" and she spun me around.

I said, "What the fuck did you do to my hair?" and she said, "I fixed it," and I said, "You're taking this role pretty seriously, huh?"

But Sugar wasn't finished. "Don't move," she said and went over to the safe, consulting this little piece of paper she took from her belt drawer.

Her hands were hot when she put the choker around my neck. A chunk of coiled gold rested in the hollow of my throat. A yoke binding us. But my reflection egged me on. *Get it.*

"This is our debut," Sugar said, watching my face.

Before she released me to go downstairs and begin receiving her guests, she insisted on one last touch, dabbing some lip color on me from a palette of rosy shades on her dressing table.

"Kisses are the best way to set lipstick," she said. "Mummy taught me that."

40

Our debut. What a joke. I was a glorified cater waiter standing by to refresh drinks while Sugar played the gracious hostess with all the tanned and wrinkled old men who grabbed her ass. The overdressed girls were obvious in their envy. They smiled at Sugar's face then turned around and talked shit about her. The room buzzed with honey-dipped, venomous whispering about whether she'd had plastic surgery or was fucking Westerfield to get the part. I hated their smug superiority.

Red-faced from drink, Westerfield's booming, self-important voice ricocheted around the room, his gaze occasionally landing on me, speculative and ironic. Had he chosen my attire?

I spent a lot of time on the fringes watching the play of one-upmanship unfolding. Meanwhile Vernon looked like he was having fun circulating and acting like he was somebody. I could tell he was taking credit for the success that the party was turning out to be.

I kept willing Sugar to give me a smile or a wink. *We're in this together. Girls against boys, right?* But I could never catch her eye.

I tried not to see Westerfield gesturing at me with his empty glass until everyone he was holding court with turned to stare expectantly in my direction and I couldn't ignore him without raising a fuss.

I made my way over to the group, where Sugar was chatting up a fashionably shave-headed man in Armani standing next to Westerfield. The man had an artificially tight-faced blonde dripping in ostentatious diamonds hanging on his arm like she was at the Oscars. Whoever she was, she seemed completely uninterested in everything, her wide blue eyes blank and glassy. Maybe she was high or already drunk.

Westerfield growled and shoved his glass at me. "You're supposed to be looking after us."

A drunken voice rose above the noise, "But you have to admit, at least Artie was a great director. Can you name *one* goddamn Paul Westerfield film that didn't suck balls?"

It was weird how the whole room got suddenly quiet.

Then Westerfield said, loudly, "I can." And the room erupted into laughter, some of it not even forced. Score one for Paul darling's self-awareness.

I delivered Westerfield's drink and then Sugar needed another so I ran back and forth for a while. I realized none of these people were different from anybody else at any party anywhere. There were the ones who never shut up about themselves and the ones who made you work to get a conversation going. The difference was that everybody was here to get noticed or make a deal. This wasn't socializing. It was business.

During a lull I fetched up next to Armani Suit and Blondie, his bored date. Armani looked drunk by then. Blondie stood with her elbows bent, clutching an absurdly tiny beaded bag with bright yellow-painted talons, the other hand wrapped around the stem of her crystal champagne glass. She was elegant and weary as hell of Armani suit. If she'd worn a sign, it couldn't have been more obvious that she wasn't in it because of a deep love for her date. It was funny to me that he couldn't see that. Maybe he didn't care.

"I'm not investing in this ridiculous movie," Armani Suit said in a bitter undertone. "It's a scam. These schmucks always fall for a guy like him."

I couldn't disagree with that. People fell for Westerfield's glib bullshit all day long. I'd seen it with my own eyes.

"Look at you," Vernon said, sidling up to me. "I knew that necklace would suit you better than it does her fat neck. Not sure about the—" He waved a hand toward the turquoise tank. "I tried to get her to loan you the vintage Vivienne Westwood dinner jacket that Rose wore to the Oscars in ninety-seven. That would have been a statement, but she insisted on whatever that is you're wearing." He put a hand over his mouth to hide his grin.

So her dressing me up in Mommy's clothes had been Vernon's idea.

He chuckled. "When she gets fixated on someone she likes to remake them. I didn't use a tailor until she suggested it." He squared his shoulders. "No regrets here. I don't think I've ever seen you wear lipstick either …"

Vernon fancied himself the puppet master, fine. But that didn't mean it was true. The fact was, Sugar was listening to Westerfield now. If he wanted her to shave her head she would do it. And if Westerfield ever decided he wanted Vernon out of the picture, I wasn't sure she'd step in to save him. Or me.

"What do you think of her hair?" Vernon whispered. "Awful, isn't it? With her complexion?"

Across the room, Westerfield had his back to his date and was chatting up a twenty-something wannabe in a red sequined catsuit. He kept glancing at his cellphone and seemed distracted. Sugar had that gap between her front teeth on full display, laughing at everything. She looked sensational in the caftan, the side slit showing a lot of mesh-covered thigh, glossy black painted toenails peeking out from under that expertly shortened hem.

Vernon said, "I don't suppose you speak German." When I shook my head he said, "A shame. You'd be popular."

I laughed. "What the fuck does that even mean?"

And he said, "Berlin has lots of rich old lesbians looking for love …" I told him to shut up and stop talking shit. He shrugged, unoffended. "I'm just sayin' …"

We both heard Westerfield's booming laugh and winced at the same time. Vernon said, "What a prick." Then his cell phone buzzed. He looked up at me with uncharacteristic excitement. "Oh my god," he breathed. "It's Joey Alter … he's here. Go let him in."

I left Vernon checking his look in the mirror. He was wearing a very nice, custom Tom Ford suit that he told me Sugar had given him for his last birthday. He looked slick, but I doubted Joey Alter would notice or care about Vernon or his very nice suit.

When I opened the door and was actually face-to-face with The Voice of a Generation, Joey Alter, pop star turned serious actor, I immediately registered that he was better-looking and a hell of a lot shorter than he looked on-screen. This was the stud stallion they had all been waiting for? People say stars never quite look like themselves when you meet them in person because photographs tell lies that can go either way. That was certainly the case with Joey Alter. He had a beautiful face with a square jaw the camera loved, heavy black brows over absurdly thick-lashed, almost black eyes. But, no shade intended, the man couldn't have been taller than five-seven and he looked decidedly anorexic.

"Welcome to Patten House, Mr. Alter," I said with exaggerated joy, pulling the heavy door wide. "Please come through. May I take your jacket, sir?"

He strolled in and handed me his artistically worn leather bomber jacket with a smile that didn't quite reach his eyes. He was wearing tight black jeans and a well-fitted cashmere V-neck sweater. The visible part of his chest was smooth and hair-free.

Joey Alter smiled emptily, rubbing his palms together. "Where am I going?"

I told him to follow me and waved him into the great room, where an uproar ensued and he was immediately mobbed. I left him there to go back and drop his jacket in the room we had set aside as a coat check, ironically called the Library because it had one shelf of old hardcover bestsellers by various pulp authors that nobody cared to read.

We had set up a rented chrome rack behind a white-draped folding table, where a bored-looking girl, one of Gaston's crew, leafed listlessly through an old copy of *Women's Wear Daily*.

I handed over the coat. "Mr. Alter's jacket," I said.

Her eyes went wide, but she obediently wrote his name on a numbered tag and tore off the bottom half, handing it back to me without saying anything. Then she clasped her hands together and, chewing her bottom lip, said, "Oh my god … what's he like?"

I told her how should I know? All I did was show him where the party was.

"Is he as handsome in person?" she said hopefully. "I *love* him."

So I told her Joey Alter had a big zit on his cheek and stank like old piss.

"Har, har," the girl said.

I asked her what her name was and she said Lexus, like the car. And I had to hand it to her, I didn't have a clever comeback for that.

"Any idea how late this thing's going to go?" Lexus-like-the-car asked.

I said I had no idea but I offered to bring her something to drink if she was thirsty, which she declined, holding up a can of Red Bull. "What's Bebe Patten like?" Lexus said. "I *loved* her in *Evil Girls*. Have you seen it?"

I said of course, who hasn't? I asked her what she *loved* about it, since she seemed to *love* so many things, and she said, "Bebe Patten played a bad bitch and I *love* bad bitches, don't you?" I had to try hard not to roll my eyes.

"I'd *love* to be Bebe's personal assistant," Lexus said, again with that note of hope, like she thought maybe I'd throw in a good word for her, like she thought she would have a chance at a job like that.

"Sorry," I said coolly. "She already has one of those."

41

Sometime around midnight, Westerfield gathered everyone around him, bellowing about an important announcement he had to make. He stood in front of the wall of glass that looked out on the lighted pool behind him. Sugar and Joey Alter stood off to the side, both showing the awkward body language of people who are impressed with each other but don't want to show it. Luchetti, who had finished up in the kitchen, came over to where I was observing the action from the back of the room.

"What now?" she hissed in my ear.

Westerfield held up his script, the one with the blue paper cover. "I've been working on this project for ten years," he said. "Ten years of fuckers like *you*"—finger stab—"and *you*"—finger stab—"and *you* slamming the door in my face. But let's not focus on that. I finally got my yes." He looked over at Sugar and she shot him an encouraging smile. So did Joey Alter. There was some rustling, a few coughs. I half expected music to play him offstage. *Get to the point, Paul darling. We're aging here.*

"Thanks to this incredible little lady," Westerfield held out his hand and Sugar glanced quickly at Joey Alter then stepped forward to take it. "Thanks to this visionary, a girl who knows show business inside and out, we're gonna make this motherfucker, aren't we, baby?" He leaned over and nuzzled her ear. Sugar cleared her throat. She was nervous. Her mouth twitched and she licked her lips. "Do you want me to …?"

"Yes, baby girl," Westerfield said smoothly, "I want you to say something! Now go on. You can do it." He looked to us for the laugh at her expense—Big Man having to soothe Baby Girl's nerves at having to speak to the big, scary crowd. He was rewarded with a few titters and a surprising dark look from her that she masked with a sarcastic smile.

Westerfield put his hand in the small of Sugar's back and pushed her forward a little. She clasped her hands together and said, "Well, I … Well, thank you, Paul, first of all. I'm excited to be part of this amazing project, obviously. And Joey, thank you for believing in us." He nodded at her and cast his eyes down in a perfect show of bashful pride.

"This script …" Sugar said. "It's just so brilliant, and Paul is going to direct the hell out of this picture." She put her hands over her heart as she looked out at us. "And I believe in it …"—she flashed Westerfield a sly glance over her shoulder—"I believe in it so much, I'm investing *ten million dollars* of my own money to make *The Songbird and the Lioness*." She turned to Westerfield and started to clap, alone at first, then Joey Alter joined in and then everybody was clapping to celebrate the big man's incredible luck in finding a baby girl like thirty-eight-year-old Bebe Patten to lavish him with a small fortune to make his shitty project.

The applause wound down quickly, and the guests, released, started milling around again, ready to gossip about this latest juicy turn of events, looking for another drink or diving into the mini-eclairs, profiteroles, and napoleons from the dessert tray. A few men went over to Westerfield and Sugar to clap him on the back and hug and kiss her. Joey Alter watched it all, a small ironic smile on his face.

Luchetti raised her eyebrows at me and shrugged. I shrugged back. Our silent communication was in perfect agreement. Rich people gonna rich people.

Two supermodel types walked by us on their way to the powder room.

"Now I get it," said the blonde with an up-do, her eyes passing over me and Luchetti as if we were furniture.

"I know, right?" her friend, the blonde with beach waves, said. "I wish I had ten mil lying around so my boyfriend could make a movie with me in the starring role." She tossed her shiny mane. "And I've had better champagne at parties in Sherman Oaks."

As the crowd thinned, I watched Vernon separate himself from those gathered around Sugar and Westerfield and wander out onto the patio. He was smiling with his teeth showing the way he did when he was really angry with somebody.

Luchetti turned to me and said, "Where'd you get that necklace?"

My hand went to my throat and I said, "It's Miss Patten's … um, Rose's …" My voice trailed off.

"Oh, is it now." Luchetti looked me up and down. "You look different. You aren't wearing a bra."

I threw her an exasperated look and she made a clicking sound with her tongue. "Vernon tells me we're getting bonuses after this. Will I have you to thank if mine is … extra large?"

I said I thought she'd be pleased. Luchetti looked around at the milling party guests with a sour expression. "Well, it looks like that was the big finale and not a minute too soon. I hate driving at night."

"Get Armen to drive you," I said to her retreating back.

She waved a hand. "No, thanks. I don't trust foreigners."

I went outside, but Vernon had already left poolside. I wouldn't have found him except that I spotted the glowing end of a cigarette in the kitchen garden. He was sitting on the stone wall, smoking and scowling at the sky.

I said I didn't know he smoked and he said, "I don't." Then he said he'd bummed one from Joey Alter. I guess I sounded like I didn't believe him because he got all haughty and told me he'd bummed cigarettes from dukes and a few baronesses. Joey Alter wasn't that special.

"That little prick is *too* pretty, don't you think?" Vernon said, to which I replied, "Well, he's certainly little," and that made him laugh.

I waited while he smoked the cigarette down to the filter. We watched people mingling outside on the pool deck, clutching their gift bag giveaways, their raised, excited voices those of people who've had too much to drink and a feast of scandalous speculation.

With a sigh Vernon flicked the butt, sparks flying, into the raised bed where it landed among the tomato plants. He said, "I didn't get you any perfume, but I did save you a Longines. If you want to pawn it, you could probably get seven-fifty for it. Just so you know, I did get bulk pricing in the end."

I got up to retrieve his cigarette butt, squashed it, and put it on the wall between us, Vernon's baleful gaze following my every move. I said, "You wouldn't want to start a fire, would you?"

"I don't know … Maybe I would," Vernon said. "I would've loved to see the look on the trust manager's face when she told that pompous bastard what the money was for. Larry likes to act like it's his money."

"So do you," I pointed out.

"Well, I've worked a helluva lot harder to earn it than he has," Vernon said without any sense of irony. He tutted. "Larry must be shitting bricks that she's spending it on a fucking pipe dream movie project."

42

If Vernon and I had already understood that Westerfield was going to be a bigger problem than anybody anticipated, the next day our worst fears were realized when I heard a commotion and discovered Westerfield and Armen carrying boxes and suitcases into the house.

"Sister Danny!" Westerfield thrust a large suitcase at me. "This goes upstairs." He glanced at the stacked half dozen or so boxes and turned to Armen. "These will have to go into the sitting room off Miss Patten's bedroom," he said. "We'll be using that space as a preproduction office."

"*Upstairs*, Mr. Westerfield?" I couldn't process what was happening. The suitcase was heavy. I put it down.

"I'm moving in," he said, all sly smile and wink. "Chop-chop, people." He clapped his hands, grabbed an overstuffed leather satchel, and strode past us.

I exchanged alarmed glances with Armen and told him I'd find out what was going on, but in the meantime we needed to do what Westerfield said. I hefted the suitcase and Armen grabbed two boxes.

Upstairs, the bomb exploded on impact.

Armen and I pulled up short outside the door of the morning room where Sugar was sitting on Vernon's lap, his arm laid across her thighs, her head nestled into his neck.

"Bebe, baby!" Westerfield bellowed. "Am I too late for some of that excellent coffee?" He put his suitcase down and said with great good humor, "What do we have here? Can I join the cuddle puddle?"

Sugar immediately jumped up and threw herself at Westerfield. I couldn't see what passed unspoken between Westerfield and Vernon because their backs were turned, but it must have catalyzed Vernon because he stood up abruptly. Then he caught sight of the suitcase in my hand and behind me, the boxes in Armen's arms.

"What's all this?" Vernon said through clenched teeth.

"Bring those boxes in here," Westerfield said briskly to Armen and, turning to Vernon, "Surprise! This is now the temporary production office for TSATL."

It took me less time than Vernon to translate the acronym as the title of Westerfield's film, but when I caught the imperceptible widening of Vernon's eyes in disbelief I had to suppress a bark of inappropriate laughter. The big man snuggled Sugar against his side with a paw that wandered down her back to grip a handful of her ass. She squealed and swatted him away.

"Now, where's my damn coffee?" Westerfield growled.

"What is he talking about?" A half-smile quirked Vernon's lips, giving the lie to the murderous look in his eyes.

"I was going to tell you," Sugar said.

We all knew she was lying when she said it.

Westerfield tried to hand Vernon his leather bag but Vernon wasn't having it, so Westerfield turned to me and Armen. "What are you two doing just standing there? Get moving!"

"Where am I taking this, Mr. Westerfield?" I asked, though honestly I didn't want to know.

"The bedroom across the hall," he said. "That's right, people. Call the tabloids. We're shacking up."

From the first day of Paul darling's unwelcome arrival in our midst, various things needed to be changed according to his liking and tastes.

He didn't like the sofa in the great room because it wasn't comfortable and he preferred Scandinavian. A new sectional arrived and the old one was carried out.

The guest room bed wasn't comfortable enough. A new, custom bed was exchanged.

He hated the lighting in the foyer, and the dining table chandelier. New lights were chosen and a team of electricians arrived to install them.

His bathroom wasn't up to snuff. He wanted a more modern vanity and a new, extra-deep tub large enough to accommodate two, or three, people. The plumbers had been in the house for days.

He thought the pool company wasn't doing a good job. A new pool company was hired.

He criticized Luchetti's use of garlic, bemoaned Remy's lack of attention to detail, whined about Armen's driving and Vernon's management of the staff. I was constantly told I was doing it wrong, from the way I folded his towels to the way I tucked in his bedsheets. One day he instructed me to go buy a decent pair of shoes so I couldn't sneak up on him. "What are you, some kind of ninja?" he growled. "Gonna slit my throat when I least expect it?" It was almost like he could read my mind.

The outside crews fared worse. Paul darling decided Sugar was spending too much money on groundskeeping, especially the topiary garden, which should be turned into a tennis court for resale value. When Sugar pointed out that she didn't even play tennis, he scoffed, "Well, I fucking play tennis. Don't my needs count?"

The end result was that Alice and her crew were part of the cuts. Luchetti was lamenting the loss of her good buddy Udo, while I had a confusing, mixed reaction to the knowledge that I would likely never see Alice again. Meanwhile, the topiary began to sprout untidy protrusions and nobody was there to snip them away.

He even interfered with Luchetti's menu planning, saying the food was too high in carbs and fat, and then, spurred by his claim, Sugar accused Luchetti of trying to make her gain the weight she'd lost at "the spa," which in turn caused Luchetti to threaten to quit. Vernon had to talk her off the ledge.

The stupid thing was that Westerfield was the one constantly asking the cook to create desserts and baked goods that he would eat in front of Sugar, saying she needed to keep extra weight off "for the camera," needed to be more self-disciplined, learn how to feel hunger.

It was downright abusive. But Sugar was molding herself in the image he projected onto her. She watched us scurry around to keep up with his demands, no matter how outrageous, accepting everything as justifiable.

Paul knows how to run a set, and this is no different.

Paul thinks I let you guys have too much freedom to do what you want instead of what we want. He thinks that dynamic needs to change.

Paul Westerfield probably brought the staff together as little else would have. We were in a siege situation, united in our hatred, as it became more apparent that he was here to stay and there was nothing we could do to get rid of him.

43

When I first saw the men, I decided they looked like FBI agents. Well-groomed and dressed in black suits, they wore their dark sunglasses into the house.

"Hi, there," said the younger one pleasantly. He had a square head with sandy hair brushing his expensive suit collar. "We're here to see Paul?"

The other, with his lined face, dark hair and beard, smiled with his lips. "He's expecting us," he said.

I was hoping they had come to arrest the Big Man for some crime. He was probably guilty of many. I pictured him, hands cuffed, being put into the SUV and driven away, never to return.

I brought them to Westerfield, who was in the middle of a phone call. "That's right," he was saying. "Half a mil gets you exec producer credit. Hold on—" He put his hand over the phone receiver and frowned at the three of us. "You guys are early."

The two men looked at each other, expressionless, and he went back to his call. "Gotta wrap this up, Hal. Don't think about it too long. You want to get in on this, I promise you." He put the phone down and sprang to his feet, glad-handing and backslapping the two guys.

"You said two o'clock, Paul," dark hair said, looking pointedly at his watch.

"Did I? Okay, well, that's fine. Danny, have Luchetti put some refreshments together. What will you have, gentlemen? I'm drinking Artie Patten's forty-year-old scotch."

So, not policemen.

I reminded Westerfield that Mrs. Luchetti had called in sick that day and that I was on my own with Vernon out on errands, and he said, "Well, Jesus Christ, sister. You do it then. Maybe that aged cheddar and those crackers with the seeds, some olives. You know the drill. And bring it up to the office. We're having a production meeting."

As they walked through the downstairs, Westerfield loudly valued the paintings displayed on the walls. A Sheets watercolor here, a Man Ray photograph there. I gathered the refreshments and asked Remy to carry one tray while I took the other. She'd been extra crabby that day, complaining that the noise of the various construction projects around the house was giving her a migraine. I said she could go home early if she wanted and got a rare, sincere thank-you in response.

When we went in with the trays the three men were gathered in front of Sugar's painting above the chaise longue.

Sandy hair was saying, "… certainly a market for this kind of stuff now."

I laid the drinks tray on the table next to them and started to open the bottle to pour the drinks, but Westerfield's sharp *No, no, leave it* made me think he realized he and his buddies weren't being discreet with the help.

So we left them to it, and in the hallway Remy said she was going home. Since no one else was around, I slipped into Sugar's dressing room. I could hear them clearly enough from my hiding place. They were still talking about the painting. Westerfield wanted to know how fast "it" could happen, and one of the guys—I guessed sandy hair—asked if this painting was "all there was." Westerfield hemmed and hawed, but then he said, "There's a diamond, but what about the painting, guys? Is it a go?" After an elongated pause, glasses clinked and Westerfield said, "Good, good. Drink up, fellas. We're about to make some money!"

When they left the two men thanked me politely for the refreshments, but as soon as the door closed Westerfield said, "This is between us, sister. You got that?"

I half-shrugged, half-nodded.

"I mean it," he said. "No telling," and he pressed a grubby forefinger to my lips. It took every ounce of self-control not to grab that finger and bend it back until it snapped. Then he smirked as if he knew what I was thinking and stepped away. "You're a gem," he said. "I might have to steal you away from her."

Happy scenarios of bloody mayhem involving a lead pipe making repeated contact with his face made short work of the clearing up. He and his friends had hit the scotch hard enough, but they hadn't touched much of the food. It would all have to be thrown away regardless. Wasteful people.

Then I saw a business card lying on the carpet, half-hidden by the table leg. *Barguet and Associates, Fine Art Purveyors.* With an address in Beverly Hills.

"Who are they?" I asked.

"Never heard of them." Vernon tapped the desk with the card. "But I'll find out."

I suggested that maybe Westerfield was getting desperate about rising costs on the movie, and Vernon said if that was so we'd need to be prepared for anything to happen.

Just then the door opened and the man himself stood in the doorway. Vernon rose to his feet, snapped, "Have you ever heard of knocking? Danvers and I are in a meeting."

Westerfield grinned. "Afraid I might catch you two up to no good?"

"It's common courtesy in this house," Vernon said.

"I have a job for you, *Verny*," he said. And then he was gone.

"No respect." Vernon heaved a sigh and picked up his jacket, shrugging it on and adjusting his shirt cuffs. "Let's see what this fucker has in mind, shall we?"

Later he told me that Westerfield had instructed him to call a certain art dealer in Beverly Hills by the name of Roland Barguet and arrange to have his shipper crate and transport Sugar's painting as well as the Man Ray photograph. They were both to be *assessed by experts* for insurance purposes as it was clear they were currently undervalued.

The message was unmistakable. Vernon was being outmaneuvered.

44

"This way, right?"

Joey Alter had arrived in his black Porsche convertible at exactly 11 a.m., waltzing in on the balls of his little feet.

I trailed along behind him, waited while he nosed around, particularly enraptured by the shelf of awards bestowed on the elder Pattens. Most of them were just cheesy statues won for Arthur Patten's direction from obscure European film festivals nobody has ever heard of, and behind that row, as if hiding, Rose Patten's SAG award statuette.

"Pretty cool, huh?" Joey Alter said. "Hollywood history, right there." He turned his trademark thousand-megawatt smile on me and I asked if I could get him anything.

"Oh, no. I'm fine," he said. "Aren't they coming down soon?"

I had no idea, because nobody had seen either one of them yet that morning. They had been Do Not Disturb status in her rooms and Westerfield had already sent me away twice. I told Joey Alter I would check with Miss Patten and went upstairs, this time knocking quite firmly on the door to Sugar's bedroom.

"What do you want?" Westerfield growled when he swung the door open.

His fly gaped open. He followed my gaze and laughed. "Oops. Want to give me a hand with that?" Then he made an ostentatious show of tucking and zipping while I told him through gritted teeth that Joey Alter had arrived and was waiting.

Beyond his shoulder, Sugar sat on the velvet loveseat at the end of her bed. Melted mascara raccooned her eyes. She was dressed in a shiny pink latex dress. Across her lap lay the cat-o'-nine-tails.

I said good morning to her, but she wouldn't look at me and didn't respond.

"Don't mind her," Westerfield said. "She's *menstruating*. Tell Joey we'll be down in a minute." He lowered his voice, "Stay close by. I have a job for you."

Sugar stood up then and turned her back to us.

"Go away now," he said. "Crystelle and I need to get ready."

Downstairs, Joey Alter was languidly turning the pages of the script draped across his lap. I relayed Westerfield's message and he flashed that smile again and said, "Call me Joey."

I left him there, but soon enough the three of them came trooping into the kitchen.

"Company's on the move," Westerfield announced in his resonant voice.

Sugar had repaired the exaggerated clown makeup he designed for her, the thickly furred lashes, the black eyeliner that extended into an exaggerated cat eye along her temple, a shade of red on her lips called the Passion of Christ.

When her gaze passed over me I saw she was *in character*, her gaze cold and inward.

"I want you to put together a nice basket of nibbles for us," Westerfield said to me. "We must have sustenance for our labors."

I was about to tell him, politely, that food preparation wasn't in my job description, but he snapped his fingers in my face and said, "Pay attention when I'm speaking to you. A nice red, one good champagne, and make sure Artie's scotch is tucked in there. No paper napkins or plastic shit, okay?"

"Crystal and china, sir?"

He narrowed his eyes like he knew I was making fun of him. Then he turned to address Sugar and Joey Alter.

"We are embarking on an epic metaphysical journey, dear ones," Westerfield said. "We must treat it with the gravity it deserves." They each smiled politely in response and he turned back to me, eyes full of spite and superiority. "Are we good? We'll wait for you by the pool."

I asked how long we would be, since I had tasks I needed to complete, and he got real snappy. "You're going for however long I want you," he said. "Is that clear?"

When Sugar led us to the service path I knew immediately where we were headed for rehearsal. I was in the rear with one picnic basket in my left hand and the sectioned bottle carrier in my right, with Joey in front of me carrying the second picnic basket with more food. She was barefooted and seemingly unfazed by the sharp gravel, the strappy heels she was to wear as Crystelle dangling from her fingertips. Westerfield lugged a heavy-looking camera case and kept up a running commentary on the *spirituality* of the dominant–submissive relationship between the characters and how Artie Patten believed every director and actor were locked into a power struggle, how Patten had made it a point of honor to get every actor to cry. In fact, one time, during one of the theatrical evenings, Artie had absolutely *wrecked* this young actress by making her tell the audience about her bed wetting, a problem that had lasted well into her teens, getting her to describe in excruciating detail how her parents punished her for it. It was, Westerfield said with obvious relish, *very disturbing shit*.

"That's not disturbing, that's *abuse*," Joey Alter said, surprising all of us by stating the obvious. Then he laughed. "Is that the kind of director you are, Paul?"

"Maybe it made that girl a better actress," Westerfield snapped, obviously irritated that Joey Alter had stolen his thunder. When he said that Sugar threw him a deadly look.

While Westerfield set up the video camera he instructed me about how to use it. I was to be the camera operator, so when he said "roll camera" I would hit the red button to start taping. Once I saw the red light blinking, I had to say the word "speed" and then wait until he said "cut" before touching it again to stop taping. "Idiot proof," he said and clapped me on the back.

The camera tripod was set next to a portable fixture on a stand to light the two folding chairs set on that rotten stage. After he finished instructing me, he and Joey Alter attacked the food, but Sugar couldn't be persuaded to eat anything. Westerfield tried force feeding her a cracker loaded with caviar and sour cream, but she shoved his hand away and the cracker splatted on the dirt floor. He grumbled about her being clumsy and childish. The two men drank their Perrier right out of the bottles. The wine and spirits would be a reward for a successful rehearsal.

I perched on the periphery, watching Sugar/Crystelle watching the two men stuff their faces. It wasn't possible to tell what she's thinking, but I hoped she was having second thoughts about Paul darling and his movie. I believed Vernon's campaign to undermine her confidence was the wrong approach. What we ought to be doing is planting doubt about *him*.

I turned to look at the two men. They were talking in undertones and I didn't catch the words, but I caught a vibe that made me wonder about their connection. Westerfield swallowed a scoop of caviar and swigged his water, then he winked at Joey Alter, who blushed all kinds of red—if I hadn't seen it with my own eyes, I wouldn't have believed it.

Westerfield rubbed his hands together like some villain in a silent movie. "Let's get this fetish party started."

I got ready to push a button while Westerfield made indiscernible adjustments to the single light source. I could smell the caviar on his breath every time he leaned over my shoulder to look into the viewfinder. *Keep it steady, sister.* His big paw kept finding its way to land on my shoulder and I had to resist the urge to jerk away when he let it linger a little too long.

"Positions, please!" Westerfield shouted unnecessarily.

45

Crystelle and Seth faced each other on the stage. The bizarre makeup emphasized the feral, wolf-like quality of her pale eyes, but the smile she gave to Joey Alter was pure Sugar when she leaned toward him, whispering something. Her scene partner nodded, smiled back. I heard her say "Break a leg," and he said, "You too."

This whole time, as Westerfield was framing up his shot, he was breathing down my neck and touching me when he didn't need to. Finally he was finished and retreated to the director's chair with his name embroidered on the back.

Westerfield flipped open the script on his lap. "Now, children, we begin," he said. "First, let's set the scene." He flapped pages back and forth. His self-importance was comical.

"Scene forty-five is Seth's first encounter with Crystelle," he announced. "Seth has followed Catherine to the Dungeon where, as her alter ego Crystelle, she plies her trade as the city's most infamous dominatrix. Seth gets into a violent argument with another patron twice his size and gives the guy a beatdown, so we now know that this mild, loving man, the gentle lover of sweet Catherine, can be a badass motherfucker." Westerfield looked over at me. "Sorry for the language, sister."

I glared at him but he was too impressed with himself to notice.

"So, we're with Seth," he went on, "as he pushes his way to the front to see Crystelle with a cat-o'-nine-tails whipping a naked girl wearing a blindfold. Seth is disgusted by the audience cheering her on but it also gets him really hot"—Westerfield chuckled—"so he follows Crystelle to her dressing room. Let's take it from the top, shall we?"

Sugar and Joey settled themselves, making intense eye contact. Westerfield looked at me. My finger hovered over the red button.

"Roll camera …"

I pressed the button. The red light blinked. "Speed."

"And … action!"

"Wait!" Sugar held up her hand. "Paul … I was thinking. Instead of her being so cold, what if she tries to provoke him. She loves him. She wants to make him react to her. She wants to fuck his brains out."

"Cut!" Westerfield bared his teeth in barely suppressed aggravation. "Baby girl, we already talked about this. That's not Crystelle."

"I know," she said firmly. "But I don't agree." She flicked a glance at Joey.

Joey cut in, "We could try it two different ways, couldn't we, Paul? Let Bebe try something on the second take?"

Westerfield shook his head. "Just stick to the script, Beatrice. Thank you for the input, Joey. Let's go again. Roll camera!"

I pressed the red button again.

And that was how it went all afternoon. She would try to change something and he would talk over her or put down her ideas. Joey gave up interjecting and sat quietly through their arguments, consulting his watch every now and then, looking bored. Finally, Westerfield lost it, throwing his script down and storming out. I wanted to applaud. *Bravo, Sugar.* You finally pushed the right button.

Sugar and Joey put their heads together but I couldn't hear what they were saying. She was giving him licked lips and that tongue peeking out between the gap in her front teeth. He was trying to make her think he was interested in whatever was on offer, but I saw through his act. I had pegged Joey Alter as someone you could think you knew but later find out you had him all wrong.

After a few minutes Westerfield came back all red in the face and announced they were going to keep doing it until *she* got it right.

That was when Sugar stood up and said, "I have to pee."

"So, go," Westerfield said. "We won't look."

Joey tilted his chin up and pretended to be intrigued by the wires hanging from the roof of the tent.

"I need to go back to the house, Paul," Sugar said.

I started to get up and Westerfield made a chopping motion at me with his hand. "Stay put." He glared at Sugar. "Be brave, baby girl. Go take a piss in the great outdoors because you aren't going back to the house until you get this scene."

Sugar narrowed her eyes. "Maybe you'd like me to *take a piss* right here in front of everybody. Is that what it would take to get you hard?"

Westerfield looked like he wanted to throw something at her, but instead he threw up his hands and said, "Okay, so I guess Princess Patten is too afraid she'll get urine on her shoes. Let's call this a wrap. I need a fucking drink."

Sugar held out her hand to Joey and said, "You were really great."

"So were you," he said, bringing her hand to his lips for a kiss.

"I'm not a *princess*," she said. "I'm on my *period*."

That Joey Alter smile didn't falter. "I understand," he said. "Go take care of yourself. I'll see you soon." Then he kissed her on both cheeks and helped her off the stage while Westerfield glowered at them both from his special chair.

I followed along behind her and she turned and said, "No, no, Danny," waving me off.

"Oooh, somebody's angry," Westerfield said. "Do you want to be great? You better learn how to take direction."

Sugar smiled to herself and walked out with a wave. I scrambled to put away the lunch things and pull out the libations. I was anxious to get back to the safety of the house, away from the tension Westerfield had wrought with his "direction."

"Pour us two double hits of scotch, sister," Westerfield said. "Joey and I need something stronger than wine after this bullshit."

Joey wanted to know the story behind Westerfield calling me sister, but caught on quickly that neither one of us was going to explain that one when Westerfield changed the subject, asking Joey if he'd ever drunk scotch that had been aged longer than he'd been alive.

I handed them their double shots in the crystal tumblers I'd brought, and Joey raised his glass. "To the lion, himself," Joey said.

"Here's mud in your eye," Westerfield growled.

Their glasses clinked. Westerfield put the glass to his lips and immediately let out a shrill yelp, clapping his hand to his mouth. Blood oozed between his fingers. "Son of a bitch," he said and held the glass out, squinting at the edge. "It's chipped."

46

To say I was sorry that Paul darling got an extra helping of karma that day would be lying, but the incident was hardly my fault. Of course I apologized anyway, but it was difficult to sound truly contrite since I wasn't guilty of anything. Shit happens, but I was not to blame even though he made out like I was. As if I would deliberately chip an expensive crystal glass like that. It was all quite unfair.

Vernon's reaction was equally unconcerned when he saw Westerfield holding that bloody napkin to his face upon our hasty return. He calmly inquired if the big man would like Armen to drive him to his doctor but, like the brown nose he was proving to be, Joey said he'd take Westerfield in his car. After they left Vernon offered to help me bring things back from the tent.

When Vernon asked me what happened I told him everything except how Westerfield behaved toward me when he thought nobody was paying attention. As soon as Vernon saw the setup in the tent, he said, "What's this guy up to? I'm surprised she went along with this. She hates this place."

I handed over the offending glass for his inspection. His mouth quirked into a half-smile as he tipped the damaged glass, pouring out bloody scotch onto the ground. He wrapped the glass in a dirty napkin, shoving it in the bottom of one of the baskets.

"I suggested she could make a bundle on a subdivide with these views, but no," Vernon sighed. "She says she wants to watch all of it rot." He picked up the bottle of scotch. "Over four hundred dollars a sip, this is. There are only four bottles left in the cellar, and it looks like that bastard is going to succeed in finishing them all before we're rid of him."

I suggested that Artie's ghost had chipped the glass, and that made us both chuckle.

It was getting dark when we got back to the house, and I offered to clean up by myself but Vernon pitched in and soon we had everything put away. Then he poured us each a four-hundred-dollar shot of scotch. Neither of us needed to check the rim for chips.

"To Arthur Patten," Vernon said. "And to Paul Westerfield getting exactly what he deserves."

We had barely taken a sip when the security panel chimed, indicating the front gate had opened. I put down my glass and told him I'd take care of it.

I watched through the glass wall of the foyer as Westerfield got out of Joey's car. He gave a little wave when the Porsche took off. I had the door open before he could even extend his hand to touch it and offered a reasonable quotient of faux concern.

Westerfield's swollen, purpled bottom lip bore four spidery black stitches, Frankenstein-style, and they had evidently given him some good drugs because he smiled cheerily, his distorted lip pulling oddly at his cheek. "What do you think?" he said. "Should I forget the plastic surgeon and keep the scar?" He gave a hyena laugh. "Scars are a good way to identify your corpse." Now he plucked at the blood-stained front of his shirt. "How about this blood? Can you get it out?"

I said I'd be happy to see what I could do to remove the stain, while knowing full well it was hopeless.

Westerfield suddenly stripped the shirt off and dropped it on the floor between us. His barrel chest was a mat of salt and pepper curls. He had steel rings piercing both nipples. I felt such a strong revulsion that I had to avert my eyes.

He laughed. "I expect you to do more than try, *sister*. Otherwise you'll have to replace the shirt. That was a Lorenzo Uomo. Vintage. One of my favorites."

I said why would I have to replace his shirt, none of this was my fault, and he just said, "Uh-huh," like he didn't believe me. After leaving me with instructions to bring him food and more scotch, he took himself upstairs and I bent to pick up the shirt. The dried blood had soaked through and stiffened the fabric. It was definitely a loss. Anybody could see that.

I brought the tray up to his room, but it was Sugar's voice saying *come in* when I tapped on the door. She was sitting up in his bed, rumpled and undressed. Westerfield was in the shower and had left the bathroom door half open, so I crossed the room and pulled it closed before fussing with the arrangement of sliced meats and cheeses on the plate, the garlic-stuffed olives Westerfield favored, and a plate of freshly baked brownies that Vernon had surprised me by suggesting I offer them to satisfy the old man's sweet tooth. Finally, I asked Sugar how she was doing.

"Come here a minute," she said and patted the bed.

I perched on the edge. She looked a little ragged—skin pale, with dark circles under her eyes—but somehow that made her face more attractive. I was getting used to the bleached hair and I could already see roots.

"I know you didn't do that on purpose," she said. "You wouldn't *hurt* him."

I started to offer a well-rehearsed defense and denial, but she said, "Shh … don't worry. It's okay. He deserved to feel some pain today." She leaned toward me and lowered her voice, "What do you think of Joey Alter? Isn't he gorgeous?"

Westerfield threw open the door of the bathroom, a towel wrapped high around his waist, and I sprang to my feet. The last thing I wanted to see was half-naked Paul Westerfield again.

"Who's gorgeous? Are you two talking about me?" The big man crawled onto the bed next to Sugar, wincing as if his lip hurt him.

If only that glass had cut an artery.

Sugar cooed over him for a minute, poking the stitches with her pointed nails, and he said, "Ouch," and "That hurts, do it again," which made her giggle. He looked at me. "Just because the field is muddy doesn't mean you have to call off the game." Westerfield put his paw on Sugar's exposed breast and caressed her roughly, nuzzling her neck, all the while saying "Ow ow ow."

I turned to leave, but he barked that he wasn't done with me and then he got up off the bed, adjusted the towel, and walked over to the tray of food and drink. He picked up the crystal glass and ran his finger over the entire edge before pouring himself a full glass. He popped an olive into his mouth, chewing with his mouth open.

"Where's my camera?" he said. Picking up the entire wedge of cheese, he used those raggedy teeth to bite off a chunk and chased it with a big swallow of scotch.

I said I had returned the camera to the "production office."

"Good girl," he said, nudging aside a piece of salami with a finger. "I need you on camera again tomorrow." He chose a brownie, inspecting it critically. "Are these fresh?" he said. "They look dry." He ate the thing in two bites, then brushed crumbs off his chest, rubbing one of the nipple rings absently. "See what you can do about my shirt, okay." He looked up at me, his gaze a challenge, and took a humongous bite of a second brownie.

47

The next morning when I came into the kitchen Vernon was feeding leftover brownies into the disposal.

I told Vernon about Westerfield parading around without his clothes on and how he'd made sure I saw his pierced nipples, how he was demanding that I somehow get the blood out of his precious shirt.

"You know how he is," Vernon said, unconcerned. "We're not real people to him. Besides, he likes getting a rise out of you because of her. It turns him on, the son of a bitch."

"Good morning!"

We were both stunned into silence when Sugar swanned into the kitchen dressed as herself in bum-hugging, low-slung blue jeans and one of Westerfield's oversized shirts.

"Who's a son of a bitch?" she said, sliding onto the chair next to me.

"What's got you in such a good mood this morning?" Vernon said smoothly.

She shrugged. "Paul's not feeling well so I have the day off. Is there coffee for me too, Danny?"

"What's wrong with him?" Vernon asked.

I handed her the coffee.

"Tummy trouble, I guess." She made a face. "It started last night. It's probably the pain medication. His lip looks even worse than it did yesterday." She sipped the coffee. "I had to sleep alone because Verny wasn't available."

"How sad," Vernon said, while sounding happy about her sleeping arrangement.

She suppressed a giggle. "Oh, Verny, give it a rest." To me she said, "Could you bring Paul some dry toast? He really is suffering."

Vernon and I exchanged glances that weren't entirely sympathetic to Westerfield's "suffering," but I got up and set about fixing the toast while she bent our ears about how uncomfortable it was to wear latex in this heat *for rehearsals*. How she'd probably already lost several pounds *from sweating*. How she had decided to quit sugar for good, now that she was totally detoxed from its effects, so much so that it wasn't hard at all to resist those brownies Vernon had made.

"Well, good for you," Vernon said.

"Paul wouldn't share anyway, the greedy little monster." She shrugged. "He wanted them all for himself." Vernon's laughter in response was giddy.

I took the toast and a bottle of Perrier alongside a glass of ice upstairs, but there was no answer when I knocked, so I opened the door thinking he'd be sleeping but he wasn't in bed, and the bathroom door was closed. The room smelled of shit and body odor and I held my breath while I was in there. When I was leaving, a terrible groan issued from the bathroom. Then he called out, "Is that you, baby?" so I quickly ducked out of there, quietly closing the door behind me.

Back downstairs, Luchetti had arrived and was moving about the kitchen opening and closing cupboards.

Sugar and Vernon had taken themselves outside and were sitting by the pool. I watched them for a minute, talking animatedly and laughing, their heads together over some magazine. Meanwhile, Luchetti was going from one cupboard to the next as if she couldn't find something. She went to the refrigerator and looked inside, moving things around.

"What are you looking for?" I asked.

"Those brownies Vernon baked. I wanted to try one and see if they're as good as mine. He used my recipe," she said with a bit of pride.

"Oh, he threw them out."

"He said he'd save me one." She was irritated.

"It's the rule, isn't it?" I said.

But then it hit me: Why had Vernon thrown those brownies away when he'd promised to let Luchetti have one? I didn't have time to ponder that, because just then the doorbell pealed and the screen showed Alice waiting at the front door.

She was wearing the same grubby overalls as usual but with her hair down. Alice had nice hair.

"How are you?" I asked.

"Can we walk? I don't have a lot of time. We're on a job over by Canyon Creek but I wanted to come by and—" She stopped. "I just want to talk to you."

I stepped outside and followed her across the croquet court where there were shaded benches. I had never seen anyone playing croquet since I'd arrived.

"I wanted to call you so many times but I didn't have your number," she said after we sat down.

I told her I understood and that it was okay.

"I know it's *okay*, Danvers." She made an impatient sound. "I don't even know your first name."

"It's Marie," I said. I could tell she was trying to build up to something, so I prompted her. "What did you want to talk about?"

Alice turned to face me, her mouth drawn into a serious line. "Listen to me, okay? That woman is no good. She's spoiled and manipulative and … Well, you probably don't know this, but people talk about how unprofessional she is. With her staff. Like totally crossing lines. Getting *involved* with people and making them sign NDAs. It's so inappropriate. And Vernon's nasty and a control freak. I've heard things about him too. Like he's not … well, he's not ethical. Did you know that he gets the good-looking delivery guys to do him sexual favors in exchange for stuff? I mean, it's gross. Eddy said Vernon tried it on with him a few times, but Eddy's got a boyfriend so he said no thanks. And I don't know about Paul Westerfield either, because Udo said he's the one that got us fired so he must be a real dick too."

Finally she ran out of steam, looked away. I wasn't sure how to respond. "Why are you telling me all this?" I said. "What's the point?"

"You could do better than this," Alice said. "You really could."

"Is that why you came here today?" I kept my voice low, but I didn't try to hide what I was feeling, the anger bubbling just under the surface. "You show up here just to criticize Miss Patten—my employer? To talk trash about my immediate superior? To tell me I could get a better job? Do you expect me to agree with you? To quit my job because you say so? Because you listen to stupid, unfounded rumors?"

"I don't think you're like them," Alice said flatly. "But I think she's got her hooks in you." She had this defeated look on her face. "I guess it was inevitable. After Russo."

I asked her what about Russo, so she told me how Bebe Patten had, in her words, basically sexually assaulted her last housekeeper. How Russo had been fired for putting her foot down and saying no. How this was no different from any of those other #MeToo situations except that Bebe Patten got away with it because she was a woman.

I stood up. I told Alice I didn't believe any of it, that it sounded like bullshit to me. I said she didn't know anything about anything and she especially didn't know *me*.

She looked up. "Okay, so I don't know you and you aren't interested in the truth, but for some reason I care about you."

I told her I didn't want her to care. I didn't need anything from her.

Alice stood up. "This isn't your home, Danvers," she said. "You don't mean anything to her. She'll throw you away when she's finished with you. That's how she operates."

We faced each other. Combatants.

Alice sighed, fished around in her pocket, and handed me a slip of paper. "This is my address and my cell number," she said. "If you get in a jam all you have to do is call. I mean that."

I snatched that paper from her fingers and tore it in half right in front of her nose. We parted without saying goodbye.

48

I didn't need Alice, and now she was out of my life. Good riddance.

I didn't trust myself to be around anyone after that, so I set out for the Aerie, where I knew I would have all the privacy I needed to eventually calm myself. I was sweating by the time I pushed through the gate. That crouching house drew me to it, and I went straight to the un-boarded-up side door and slipped inside.

The house seemed to be listening, daring me to disrupt the silence with the unnerving sound of my shoes scraping through grit on the kitchen linoleum when I emerged from the stairwell.

Don't wake it up, whatever it *is.*

I decided to inspect the kitchen cupboards. In one were row upon row of dusty VHS tapes, some with labels and protective plastic boxes, most of them unlabeled. The ones that were labeled bore dates and lettered notations that didn't make sense to me.

Moth-eaten telephone books going back many years were piled in another cupboard. The next contained stacks of manuscript boxes. I found old telephone and utility bills from twenty years earlier. In another was a faded yellow, bound script. The front page read, *To Each Their Own by Arthur Patten* with a copyright date of 1971. In the last cupboard was a cookbook entirely in French, and some dented, botulism-laden canned vegetables and tuna circa who-knew-when since they didn't even bear expiration dates.

I wandered into the dining room, where the encroaching bougainvillea continued to pump out those weird flowers, seemingly in more profusion than before. I was determined to make it upstairs this time. Hadn't Alice said that was the creepiest part? But what was there to be afraid of, aside from a few mouse corpses and some spiders?

In the high-ceilinged living room, a large wagon wheel lighting fixture fashioned out of wood dangled overhead. Had this ever been a place where people lived such supposedly successful lives? It didn't seem possible.

Cat's curiosity pulled me up those turning stairs. When I passed, the wagon wheel swayed as if pushed by an unseen hand. This house was full of ghost drafts. Ahead of me was a long hallway. I had the strangest feeling that

I was going to find something I didn't want to see, but that didn't stop me.

The first doorway revealed a large bathroom with walls painted sickly green and cracked black and white herringbone tile on the floor. The outdated jacuzzi tub had a wide crack down the center. A chipped porcelain sink rested on the floor. The most incongruous thing was a urinal on the far wall.

The next two rooms were piled with junk. In the first, old moldy mattresses, several broken wooden chairs, a hideous white and gilt bureau with a spidered bad-luck mirror above it, all the drawers missing. The second room was empty save for four recliners set in a circle with a rickety tray table in the center, presumably so the ghosts could play cards or discuss their problems over TV dinners.

There was a roomy linen closet behind another door, shelves filled with sheets smelling of mildew in a variety of patterns popular probably forty years ago. A plastic ruffled shower cap lay abandoned on the floor.

The end of the hall took a sharp right turn and so did I. Along the left wall were windows looking out over the steep canyon, the glass long gone. A big, lazy fly buzzed around one of the frames and I automatically shooed it out of there. *Don't get stuck in here. You'll die.*

I wanted to laugh at such dramatic thoughts, but I didn't fancy hearing the sound of my own laughter echoing back at me.

At the end of the hall was a closed door and, since I hadn't seen any room large enough to rightfully be called a main, I assumed that bedroom must lie on the other side, but as I walked toward it I was eerily conscious of the rhythm of my steps, half-remembered lyrics of a children's song marking the beats.

If you go down in the woods today, you're sure of a big surprise.
If you go down in the woods today, you'd better go in disguise.

I was being ridiculous. There was nothing to be afraid of. It was only an unhappy, empty house. I turned the knob and pushed the door open.

"Danny! Thank god it's *you!*"

The remainder of that day I walked around and responded as if I were present, but I was numb. In shock. Somehow Ian St. Martin was *here*, and he was camping out in the Aerie. I couldn't wrap my head around it.

Sugar and Vernon spent the entire day by the pool, and I was glad neither required anything of me. Westerfield remained sequestered in his room. I was convinced my inadvertent discovery would show on my face if anybody cared to notice, so I hid behind myriad inconsequential tasks.

At Vernon's request Luchetti served up turkey club sandwiches with homemade french fries for lunch, plus more fresh-baked brownies, which I delivered as they lay cuddled under the cabana. Vernon sent me a knowing look and joked that Westerfield must have gotten sick from eating too many brownies the previous night, and Sugar laughed and said it served Paul right for being such a hog.

I retired to my room before dinner by lying that I wasn't feeling well.

49

Ian was here because he had nowhere else to go. What shocked me more than his sudden reappearance was that he had been sleeping on top of an old, sagging mattress on that filthy floor. At least the sleeping bag and pillow looked new, as did the battery lantern he said he only used "as necessary" in order to avoid detection by stray gardeners and nosey parkers. He might have been referring to Alice but he never said so.

His Globe-Trotter suitcase was set on top of an old chest with tarnished brass detailing, the things inside neatly folded. When I'd asked how he ate, he said Vernon brought him some food every day. I didn't want to know what he used for a bathroom, but I assumed it was primitive and probably unsanitary. Yet Ian seemed strangely proud of his willingness to sleep rough.

Something had happened in New York, but he was unwilling to talk about the circumstances that had led to him being "cast out on the street," as he put it. But where were all the rest of his belongings? The one-of-a-kind furnishings, the crystal and Tiffany china, his extensive wardrobe. It had obviously been a dramatic fall, and I was curious. Why had he shown up here of all places?

Vernon came to my door at around eight o'clock, but I ignored his knock and he went away. At eleven it was safe to emerge from my room. When I came into the main part of the house I could hear faint television noise from upstairs, but otherwise it was quiet. I slipped out the kitchen door.

I had a flashlight but didn't need it, since most of the grounds featured either in-ground or overhead lighting that came on at dusk and went off at dawn. I only had to hope I'd evade the sprinklers that went off on a schedule I never paid attention to.

Instead of going into the ruined house by the open door on the side and navigating those terrifying stairs at night, I went around to the back, where the empty pool and the house itself crumbled toward their inevitable slide into the canyon. I called his name and he appeared at the row of windows above, waved, and then disappeared from sight.

As I waited, I cycled through a range of emotions, the buzz of seeing him again, his being in California and what it meant. This was not random. He'd obviously shown up here because of Vernon. Those letters he'd written over the years proved their relationship was longstanding and seemingly romantic. There was more to the story he was telling about his hasty departure from New York.

Ian emerged from the shadows around the side of the house, approaching me cautiously as if I were a dangerous wild animal he had to be wary of. He was dressed in jeans and a clean, loose white shirt, untucked, his streaky hair flopping onto his forehead. We sat down on the stone wall above a steep drop.

"Are you sure this is safe?" he said, looking over his shoulder.

"Not if there's an earthquake," I said.

"Oh Danny. Why'd you have to bring that up?" He sighed. "God, I miss New York. All we have to worry about are terrorists and corrupt politicians." He slipped his arm around my waist and pulled me close. I pushed him away, but gently, and he blew hot breath into my ear, teasing it with his tongue. "Why not?"

I disentangled myself and moved a couple of feet away.

"Aren't you glad to see me?" he said with this sad look. "Can't you be kind? Just once?"

That stung mostly because I hadn't considered that he might actually be in real trouble. I said I was sorry and asked again what had happened. I told him he could tell me the truth. I wouldn't judge.

"I don't *blame* you," he said, "but it all went to shit after you left." His hair fell across his eyes when he bent his head. His hands clenched and unclenched. When he looked up he had tears in his eyes. "It was close, Danny … really, really close. I don't know if I can ever go back. Not now."

I slid back over to him and put my arm around his shoulders. He leaned into me, snuck his hand around my waist again. But I let him. It was like I had Ian back. The Ian who had shown me more kindness than I'd ever shown him because I could be a suspicious bitch sometimes.

After a minute he sat up, blew his nose on a pristine handkerchief he pulled from his pocket, and apologized for being so emo. In a casual voice he said, "So what's going on between you and Bebe Patten?" The way he said it, I knew without any doubt that was what he'd been wanting to ask me all along. My skin prickled with apprehension.

I said, "What's going on between you and Dai Vernon?"

He pulled his chin back, "Where the fuck does that come from? Don't be ridiculous. There's nothing going on with me and Dai Vernon other than he's an old friend and he's offered me a place to crash till I get back on my feet."

Why was he lying? I was suddenly cold and pulled my sweater closer around me.

"Yes … Vernon and I had a thing," Ian said. "Years ago. And we're still close." He stared at me. "You're jealous?"

Was I? I wouldn't admit it even if it was true.

"I'm flattered," he said, running his thumb across my bottom lip. "I didn't know you cared. But let's get back to you and Bebe Patten."

I asked if that was the real reason he'd come all the way from New York to camp out in an abandoned house. "Look around, Ian. This isn't safe."

"What do you mean?"

"What if you get caught?"

He laughed.

I decided to go with a direct approach. "Are you and Vernon running a project on Bebe? Is it the diamond?"

Ian chuckled. "You are too smart for your own good, Danny. But let's not get ahead of ourselves. This is a delicate moment."

What was so delicate about it, I wanted to know.

"There is an … obstacle that needs to be removed."

Westerfield.

"Let's talk about him," he said.

What about him? He was making a movie and she was the star of the movie. It was her dream come true. There wasn't much else to tell.

"She's dumped a lot of money into Westerfield's pocket," Ian said, a thoughtful expression on his face. "So he *has* to be taken out of the equation before he takes it all."

I asked him what the hell he thought any of us could do. Sugar was unstoppable. And Westerfield was vicious and sly. The man knew exactly how to keep his star dangling while he dug around in her psyche. And picked her pockets.

"Don't be naive, Danny," Ian said. "Why do you think you're here?"

I had been so focused on the pain of Cal's humiliating betrayal that I hadn't questioned Ian's too-easy solution to my screwing up the Whitaker job. Ian had always been able to read my every thought, and now he smiled, took my hand, raised it to his lips, kissed the palm. A shiver went through me.

"Don't worry," he said, "from everything I hear, you've made quite an impression on Bebe *and* Westerfield. If you got them both in bed, you could do some serious damage to their relationship, whatever it is. I have faith in your abilities, Danny. I always have."

Then he got to his feet, matter-of-factly brushing grit off the seat of his pants. The plan was twisted and I could see the logic of it, imagine all too easily how they had come up with it. Too bad the very thought of manipulating Sugar that way, or bedding Westerfield, made me sick.

"It won't work," I told him, keeping my voice calm and even. "But even if I succeeded, then what?"

"We pick up where we left off," he said. "Everybody gets their nest feathered."

"You and Vernon rutting around on a pile of money. Isn't that how you put it in your letter?"

He looked genuinely surprised. "Well, bravo. Resourceful kitten, you are. It doesn't pay to underestimate you, does it?"

And yet they always did.

Vernon was lurking in the shadow of the cabana when I was coming across the pool deck, and I almost leaped out of my own skin when he said my name.

"Couldn't sleep, huh?" he said, emerging into the half-light. "Me either."

He was dressed in pajamas and a handsome red velvet robe with a gold rope belt.

"It's a beautiful night," I said.

He laughed. "It's almost one in the morning."

"It's a beautiful morning, then."

"I was about to pour myself a nightcap," he said. "Are you interested?"

I wasn't, but we went to his room and drank straight tequila from a two-hundred-dollar bottle he said he'd gotten on his last vacation to San Miguel, Mexico. He was in the middle of a long-winded and explicit story about being in bed with two German guys at once when I started to feel the tequila and abruptly excused myself to go back to my room.

Tequila had a tendency to make me unpredictable and combative, and even though Vernon was acting as if he didn't suspect anything I was almost certain he knew where I'd been, who I'd been talking to, and what we'd discussed. I didn't feel up to playing games with Vernon when I was under the influence.

I fell onto my bed in my clothes, pulled the comforter over myself, and passed out.

50

I'm on the set of a movie, but I don't recognize any of the people around me. They're all rushing around and talking to each other but I can't understand what they're saying. I need to get out before they find out I don't belong there. I realize that we're all gathered in that big living room in the Aerie, and suddenly everybody stops and looks upward and there's Sugar in that transparent bodysuit, spinning around and around on that wooden wagon wheel chandelier, performing an acrobatic routine. Paul darling stands on the landing, towel-wrapped torso, bare chested. He's using a long wand-like thing to prod her. To keep her spinning. I worry, *Where is Ian? They're going to catch him.* The next thing I know I'm in that basement room and I'm upset because now I have to go up those dark stairs alone, to warn him. But maybe he heard all the commotion and got away and hid somehow. "He's in the refrigerator," Vernon says. "Go ahead, open it. You'll see." "But he can't breathe in there," I say. "That's right," Vernon says, "It's okay." But I know it's not okay. That it's never going to be okay. Ever again.

I made it to the bathroom. Just. But that was what I got for drinking tequila.

I kept an eye on Vernon's whereabouts. But, if he was delivering sustenance and himself to Ian's hideaway, I couldn't catch him doing it. He was always where I expected him to be, a magician able to distract your eye while he performed his tricks.

Westerfield was still recovering two days later, forced to eat a so-called bland diet after his bout with "intestinal flu," looking like a prize jackass eating his oatmeal and sipping Arthur's whiskey with a straw because of the injured lip.

But he was subdued too. We all noted a subtle change in his personality. A shrinking in on himself, as if in recognition of his own vulnerability. I think Westerfield's weakness made Sugar bolder, and now I often overheard them disputing this line or that action as they continued "rehearsing" in his bedroom—without me or Joey Alter to witness their arguments. One time she yelled that *his* movie wouldn't be possible without *her* and he shouldn't forget that. It was quiet after that.

During this forced lull in preproduction as Westerfield healed his wounds, I avoided getting into prolonged discussions with Vernon or Sugar and I stayed well away from the Aerie and Ian, but I couldn't escape Westerfield, who insisted I bring him coffee in bed and watched me with this heavy-lidded, lick-lipping leer while I changed his bedsheets and cleaned his bathroom. He'd sit on the settee by the window to keep an eye on me while he pretended to work on his script or made loud, cryptic phone calls about percentages and back-end money. He certainly enjoyed watching other people labor.

By day three of attending to his every need, I was reaching the end of my patience. As if sensing my shortening fuse he chose that day to bring up his ruined shirt again. He asked me if I'd been able to remove the blood stain. I told him I had not been successful and affected remorse.

"You don't seem anxious to make this situation right," he said.

I said I was not a miracle worker. Blood was virtually impossible to remove entirely. I said, "Haven't you seen your own movies?"

"Very funny," he said.

I told him I hadn't been trying to be funny.

"Are you going to buy me a new shirt?"

Nope.

"You think I don't know you did that on purpose? Chipped that glass? I know you did it."

I denied it with conviction. He sat back and contemplated me in silence. "You dykes are all alike. You just hate men."

I didn't bother to hide my laughter.

"Do you think this is as bad as it could get?" he said. "I say the word and you're gone."

I smiled. "Will there be anything else, *sir?*"

"Don't fuck with me, little nun. You don't want me as an enemy."

My campaign to fuck with Paul Westerfield began in earnest the next day, on the heels of his demand that I press his dinner jacket for an important meeting with potential investors. He would be tied up all day in Los Angeles, then be home to change around four and back to it, with more meetings planned for dinner at the Polo Lounge in Beverly Hills. He recited all this like I cared about his schedule.

I watched him leave that morning, surprised Sugar trusted him with Cherry Baby.

When I took the jacket from his closet it reeked of stale body odor, and there was a sprinkling of old dandruff embedded in the material across the shoulders. I carried it at arm's length to the laundry room and dropped it on the floor, kicking it with the toe of my shoe. I couldn't help myself. I stomped on that thing as if he were in it, writhing in pain, and as I did a plan formed.

I didn't expect Sugar to be in her dressing room when I went to fetch some essential tools, but there she was, contemplating a rainbow row of dresses. A halo of auburn roots showed a stark contrast to the flat platinum color of her hair.

She glanced over her shoulder at me. "Have you seen Paul? He's not in his room."

I told her he'd gone. She asked where and I told her what he'd told me, that he had all-day meetings in Los Angeles. "He didn't say anything to me about it," she said, annoyed.

That's when I mentioned my surprise that he'd taken Cherry Baby.

She slowly turned to face me. "But … how did he get the key?"

So she hadn't known.

"Well, where in the fuck was Verny?" she said, her voice rising. "He should've *stopped* Paul. Nobody drives that car but me. It was a gift from Daddy."

I said Vernon wasn't around when Westerfield left, that he'd gone out with Armen in the Mercedes.

"Oh god," she said impatiently. "Are those two still fucking? Verny told me that was over. I swear he gets more dick without leaving the house than a West Hollywood rent boy." She went back to the closet, roughly pushing the hangers back and forth along the rack in a twitchy, aggravated way.

"What do you think?" She pulled out a candy pink Oscar de la Renta sleeveless dress with a square neck and held it up. "This one? Or …" then she pulled out a black and white belted Gucci shirt dress, "… this one?"

I considered both garments. "The Gucci," I told her. "For the fit."

She put the pink frock back in the closet. "I think you're right," she said. "And it's a little more Catherine. Because of the *fit*."

I asked if she was rehearsing today and she said Joey Alter was coming over. "*Paul* arranged it," she said. "So it's stupid that he just takes off, but fuck him. Maybe Joey and I will finally get somewhere without his interference. Paul's an absolute tyrant when he gets an idea in his head."

As if I didn't know that.

She pulled the dress over her head and I helped her zip it up. She cinched the belt tight and regarded herself in the mirror. "You're really brilliant at this, you know that?" She smiled at her reflection. "This dress is *exactly* Catherine." Her gaze slid toward me. "Paul's got a big dinner meeting tonight. Another five million at stake. Pray he doesn't blow it by talking too much, because then he'll come home and take it out on all of us. He's such a *baby* when things don't go his way."

She walked over to me. "You've been avoiding me lately. Even Verny says it."

I made excuses about how busy Mr. Westerfield had been keeping me since he'd been sick, and she laughed like I'd told her a joke. "Wasn't that *horrible*? And he wanted *me* to play nursemaid. But I was, like, no thank you and good luck."

Sugar put her hand up to toy with my hair. "Why do you torture it like that? I thought we decided you look better untamed." She pushed her fingers through my hair, mussing it, arranging it, her face close enough to kiss. She leaned toward me as if she was going to go for it, then pulled back. "There," she said. "That's better. I don't think you know how attractive you are." She turned away, back to her reflection. "I don't like it when you punish me. But you shouldn't be jealous I'm with Paul. He doesn't change this."

Maybe I wanted to see if what Ian and Vernon believed was true. I came up behind her, leaned in, and lightly kissed her bare shoulder. Sugar turned immediately, melting against me, but I went slow. Explored her with the lightest touch of my fingers, tasting her skin with just the tip of my tongue. Suddenly she was nibbling my neck, taking the skin between her teeth. I pulled away as if she'd burned me. That was taking it too far. The echo of lying in the grass with Cal as she marked me hers was too much. I asked Sugar if she was being herself or Crystelle when we kissed.

"What do you think?" she said, straightening her dress where my hands had wrinkled it. "Go away now and stop distracting me ... I have to study lines for Joey."

51

Back in the laundry room, I leaned against the closed door to slow my galloping heart rate. What was I doing to myself? Was I really considering Ian and Vernon's plan? I pushed the thought away and, locking the door, knelt in front of Westerfield's jacket, lying unloved on the floor where I'd left it. It would have had a beautiful drape worn by the right person, but I couldn't picture it ever looking anything but ill-fitting on the big man.

I reached into my pocket and pulled out the fabric scissors I'd retrieved from my sewing basket. They had razor sharp, needle-nosed blades. Holding the scissors by the closed handles, I stabbed Paul Westerfield's body over and over and over again. He could scream all he wanted. He was helpless to stop me. Blood welled up, darkening the fabric. His eyes went blank. He was dead.

After that I snipped a series of tiny x-shaped cuts in a random pattern over the front of the jacket and along both sleeves. Unless you were looking for them, the nap of the fabric hid the cuts.

Flipping the jacket open I turned it inside out. The silk lining was nicely sewn. I didn't recognize the French label, but I knew the jacket had to be expensive. The scissor blades snicked as I filleted the jacket's inner flesh. I cut the entire lining out of both front flaps, folding the silken pieces into small squares that fit into my apron pocket. Then I turned the jacket right side out again, put away my scissors and pressed its carcass with great care.

At precisely four-thirty, Westerfield appeared in the kitchen where I was keeping Luchetti company while she made a sriracha cream sauce to go with the sea bass she was preparing for Joey Alter and Miss Patten's dinner.

Those two had been gone all afternoon, back to rehearsing in the Theater of All Potential, and Luchetti told me that Westerfield hadn't been home ten minutes before she saw him walking in that direction. We were both surprised to see him return so soon.

"Hello, Mr. Paul," Luchetti said. "Did you find them?"

He seemed off. Without acknowledging her he asked me where I'd left his jacket. I told him I hadn't been able to find it. Sorry.

"For fuck's sake, what do you mean you couldn't find it?" he said. "It's right in my fucking closet."

Luchetti tutted at his language but he glared her into silence.

"Are you fucking around? Because I'm not in the mood for bullshit from a glorified *maid*."

Luchetti's gaze bounced from me to him and back again.

I said again I was sorry, but I had searched and it wasn't there.

"Fuck that." He stormed out of the room. After he left Luchetti said, "What'd you do to it?" I repeated that I hadn't been able to find it but I don't think she believed me.

Less than five minutes later he was back, his face mottled red with anger. "It's not there," he said. "Go look for it."

I asked where exactly he'd like me to look and he heaved a dramatic sigh. "Every-fucking-where. I'm going to take a shower. Then I'm going to get dressed. And *you* are going to find my jacket and make sure it's pressed and ready. I'm in a hurry."

His exit was over-the-top, like he was an actor in a soap opera, and Luchetti let out a long, low whistle.

"I guess I better get started looking every-fucking-where," I said and we both laughed.

He found me as I was "searching" the downstairs coat closet. He was all shiny-cheeked from a shave, his hair wet and slicked back behind his furry ears. He was wearing well-cut slacks and a tight black turtleneck that showed the bumps of those nipple rings.

I told him I hadn't yet located his jacket, and he said, "Are you fucking kidding me?"

I could smell the whiskey on his breath as I backed out of the closet. "I'm sorry, but it isn't here, *sir*. I've looked everywhere, like you asked. Perhaps you left it somewhere else and then forgot."

He wanted to throttle me, which was delightful. "Could it be at your house?" I went on. "Or in your car?"

"It's not at my goddamn house," he said. "And it's not in my goddamn car."

"Well, those are the only places I haven't looked yet." I started toward the door to the garage and he was right on my heels, breathing down my neck.

I opened the door and gestured for him to go in ahead of me, but he held back. "After you," he said.

Behind me he raised the key fob and beeped the locks open on his

Mercedes. I started on the passenger side, while he stood there watching me with folded arms. There was a crumpled Bob's Big Boy burger wrapper, a couple of empty cigarette packs on the passenger side floorboard and a pile of his ubiquitous blue-bound scripts on the seat. No jacket.

I closed the door, then went to open the back door. We both saw it at the same time. "Oh my gosh," I said, with an Academy Award–worthy impression of surprise. I picked up the jacket and laid it over my arm. Westerfield snatched it away from me and I stepped back. "You must have forgotten it was in your car, sir."

"I did *not* forget anything of the kind." He leaned in and hissed, "You're a useless cunt."

He went to slide his arm into the sleeve but was having trouble. He pulled his arm out and took a close look at the jacket, holding it up to the light. It was kind of a cool effect, the light shining through those tiny x's in the fabric where the lining had been cut away. He peered at the shredded lining on the back of the jacket, then down into the sleeve, as if he couldn't understand what he was seeing.

I waited quietly, my hands folded demurely in front of me, an inquiring look on my face.

The color had drained from his cheeks and his jaw muscle jumped. Without any warning he threw the jacket at me. I caught it with one hand before it hit the floor.

"You must have had some kind of critter invasion in your car," I said mildly. "They probably got in when the garage door was left open. They'll hide in cars, you know. And make little nests? I've heard they'll even store nuts in the door and roof panels. You'd better have the car inspected to see where they're getting in."

I thought he might strike me, but instead he slammed the door to his Merc, walked over to Cherry Baby, and threw himself into the driver's seat, attempting to back over me when he pulled out. Luckily, I saw that coming and got out of the way.

When I went inside, I took that jacket upstairs and hung it in his closet.

52

Paul Westerfield vanished from our lives the night he drove off with Cherry Baby in a huff over his ruined jacket. Unfortunately, he could not be reached for explanation no matter how many times Sugar called his service and left messages that escalated from worry to outrage to tearful pleas to return her call.

She finally sent Vernon to his house but he wasn't there, or wasn't answering the door. She called Joey Alter every day, crying because she thought either Westerfield was lying dead in a ditch somewhere or had absconded to Tahiti with her money. Vernon's money was on the Tahiti connection. I hoped he was dead in the ditch.

But then, a week after he drove away for his dinner meeting at the Polo Lounge, Paul Westerfield returned.

He gave me a start when he waltzed into the kitchen and threw the car key on the counter. "Where is she?" he snarled.

I told him she was in the screening room watching a movie with Vernon and didn't want to be disturbed. The last part was untrue. She'd made it crystal clear to all of us: if we even so much as got a whiff of his aftershave we were to report to her immediately, but experience had taught me that it was sometimes important to withhold certain information.

As he was accustomed to doing, he hollered her name. I noted that the swelling of his injured lip was greatly reduced and the stitches had loosened. He fingered them, glaring at me.

I asked him if he would like to go through, and he snapped, "No, I would not like to *go through*," and shouted for her again.

We both heard the slap of bare feet running. Sugar pulled up short when she saw him, tears in her eyes. She was actually glad to see him. That was a blow I didn't see coming.

"Hello, Bebe."

"You're … all right."

"Were you worried about me, baby?"

He gave her a brief hug and winked at me. He took her arm, roughly steering her away and out of earshot. I didn't follow, not because he clearly didn't want me to but because I didn't want to witness their reunion. It wasn't like there was anything I could do to stop it.

Then Sugar's voice, raised to a screech. "Motherfucker! How dare you!"

When I peered around the corner she was pacing at the foot of the stairs. Westerfield stood there, arms folded, looking impatient.

"It's *mine*! You have *no right* to it. Where the *fuck* have you been, and why haven't you returned my calls? Tell me the truth, Paul."

He got in her face, acting the gangster, the dialogue as predictable and dismissive as you'd expect. "I'm not your *servant*," he spat. "And you're not my *wife*. I don't answer to you and I don't owe you shit. I've been making deals, okay?"

Vernon appeared, drawn by curiosity same as me.

"Driving *my* car?" she yelled. "*Selling* my painting?"

"You sound like a screeching harpy, babe." Westerfield drew an exaggerated breath, as if she had danced upon his last nerve. "As a matter of fact, darling Beatrice, yes, I sold your painting. And you should be grateful. My guys got us enough money for it to hire the production designer I wanted."

"I don't give a *shit* about the production designer," she screamed. "I want my painting."

His expression was pained. "Stop being a child. You need to think bigger. *My* film is more important than *your* goddamn painting."

"It's *my* film as much as it is yours, asshole."

"You don't really understand how anything works, do you?" Westerfield registered my and Vernon's presence. "The help lurking around as usual, eh?" he sneered. "I need something to eat and Arthur's finest. My room. And make it snappy. I'm beat."

He turned to go and Sugar swung a roundhouse punch at his upper arm. He flinched from surprise more than the force of the blow and grabbed her wrist. They wrestled for a few seconds and Vernon took a step toward him, but Westerfield held up a fist. "Don't try it," he warned. To her he said, "You never said I couldn't borrow your fucking precious car. It's a gas guzzler anyway. I spent a small fortune on fuel. And here's a little reminder. You gave me sole discretion to do whatever I wanted with that painting. It's in our contract."

"I most certainly did *not*!" she shrieked. "You sold something that isn't yours!"

Westerfield winced at the decibel level. "Read the contract before you sign, darling. Rule number one," he said in a mocking tone. "Look, sweetheart, I'm tired. I've been driving for nineteen hours and I need a fucking drink, not you *nagging* me because I got you a ten percent markup on what you paid for some *minor* painting. It's for the good of the movie. That's all you need to know."

Then he literally lifted Sugar out of his way and marched up the stairs.

She stood where he'd put her, body rigid, hands clenched. "Do something," she whispered, those silver eyes dark with emotion, and Vernon rushed over and put his arm around her waist. She collapsed into his arms, wailing.

I prepared Westerfield's snack tray while Sugar alternated between fury and tears. It took significant cajoling to understand exactly what had happened, but we found out it was all too true: Westerfield had sold her painting. He'd needed more money for his budget, simple as that. And he had taken Cherry Baby to scout locations across the border in Vancouver because his first choice (Toronto) turned out to be too expensive.

None of which explained how he could sell something that wasn't his, contract or not. Or take her car and not show even minimal courtesy to let her know where he was.

Vernon didn't hesitate to point out that Westerfield's actions were not only terribly inconsiderate, they were also possibly criminal. And those art dealers? They hadn't acted in good faith either. They ought to be investigated.

I thought he was nervy to suggest investigating anybody. Those sorts of things go both ways, and if you can't afford to be scrutinized best not to scrutinize others.

But every unscrupulous act Vernon pointed out only served to rile her more. And maybe that was Vernon's end game in this scene. Fanning the flames benefited him.

Westerfield was throwing clothes into his leather satchel when I entered his room with the dinner tray.

"Oh good," he said. "I'm starving."

I put the tray down and he attacked the sandwich I'd made, still careful to bite with the uninjured side of his mouth. I poured him a slug of scotch and held it out to him.

"Are you going away again?" I asked.

He inspected the glass, then shot me a look. "You'd like that, wouldn't you?" He washed down the bite of sandwich with a healthy swallow, then said, "Things are moving fast now. Gotta be ready for the next phase, am I right?" He was clearly amused by the mayhem he'd caused. "You should come work for me." He took a step closer to me but I held my ground. "I can think of all kinds of ways to have fun with you."

I told him I was perfectly happy exactly where I was.

"With Bebe Patten's foot on your back?"

I shrugged. *Better than* your *foot.*

"I know you like it that way," he said, "but I could do so much more for you."

He was clearly warming to his fantasy, so I said he sounded like a character in one of his crappy films. He took me by the arm, pulling me in close. I struggled but he had me in an iron grip. "Don't play with me unless you mean it, sister." He shoved his hand between my legs and I wrenched away from him.

He laughed. "Get out of my room."

At the doorway I turned. "If you ever touch me again, I'll make sure you need more than stitches."

"Promises, promises," he said.

I slammed the door on his dreadful, evil face.

Sugar was waiting in the doorway of the morning room when I came out and motioned for me to come in, locking the door behind me. Vernon came in through her bedroom.

"What did he say to you?" Sugar demanded. "You look upset."

I told her Westerfield wanted me to work for him.

"What!" Vernon scowled. "As what?"

I said as a housekeeper, of course.

"And what did you say?" Vernon demanded.

Obviously I declined.

"Of course she did!" Sugar looked at Vernon. "Can you believe that!"

"I'm not surprised," Vernon said. "He's a crook, darling. You have to face it."

"No … NO! I'm going to beat him at his own game," she said. "I'm the star. And if I hadn't backed him …" Her jaw worked. "Without me, he doesn't have a movie." Then she turned to me and said, "Run me a bath, Danny. I'm about to jump out of my own skin."

53

Vernon and I sat in the kitchen, drinking coffee and trying to figure out Westerfield's angle. The priority, according to Vernon, was to continue to sow doubt with Sugar about the man's ultimate intentions. "It's the only way to finish this charade of a movie project," he said.

In that we were united. I looked at Vernon. "Wait. Are you saying Westerfield isn't really making this movie?"

"I told you," he said with exaggerated patience. "This is a scam and she's the mark." Vernon shook his head. "That fucker has enough of a sense of self-preservation to not actually go through with it. His script is crap. She's a crap actor. He saw an opportunity to fleece her, and took it." I opened my mouth to protest, to say *Isn't that what you're doing?* but he went on. "Besides, Westerfield's got her money now, and there are all kinds of ways to leave a project in permanent development. Happens a lot. Well, not the part about swindling a gullible narcissist out of millions by promising her stardom." He watched me, gauging my reaction to what he was saying.

"What will happen to Sugar?"

"Oh, she'll be fine," Vernon said breezily. "I'll be here to pick up the pieces."

The way he said it sounded like I was not part of that future, but I was afraid to pursue that line of inquiry. I suddenly had the sensation that I was balancing on a mighty thin wire.

"She sure as shit isn't going to sail off into the sunset with Joey Alter if Westerfield goes AWOL," Vernon said. "Joey might be fucking her, but it's not serious. You know as well as I do that she makes it hard to say no."

I didn't answer. The news that Sugar and Joey Alter were an item had escaped my attention. I wasn't sure whether to believe Vernon or not.

"Anyway," he said, "Bebe is way too old for him. He'll lose interest the minute this project goes belly up." He laughed at the expression on my face. "You didn't know, did you? I'm surprised she didn't share all the dirty details with you too. Don't worry, Danvers, you still have a chance with her if you put your mind to it." He folded his arms across his chest.

I told him I didn't believe any of it. How did he know all this? Was he there? But even as I said those things, doubt made my denial sound pathetic. And then Vernon said, "Ask Ian. He'll tell you. He saw them going at it during their *rehearsal* the other day."

I should have guessed Ian would be curious about that haunted theater, so I wasn't surprised to see him sitting in Paul Westerfield's director's chair, juggling two oranges with one hand.

"It's harder than it looks," Ian said, effortlessly catching and throwing, catching and throwing. Over and over. It was hypnotic.

"When did you pick up juggling?" I said.

"I watched some YouTube videos." He glanced over at me. "I have a lot of time on my hands right now."

Like that was somehow my fault.

"I think I'd make a great director," he mused, those oranges going up and down, up and down. "Such a power trip telling people how to say their lines, moving them around like pawns, telling them when they should laugh or cry …"

I said I didn't think that was how it worked.

"Oh, I suppose you've learned everything there is to know about the art of directing from polishing Paul Westerfield's brass dick."

I told him he was being an ass.

He sighed. "I'm sick of it, Danny. Hiding. Waiting backstage. It's … awful. I can't sleep on that filthy fucking floor any longer. My back is killing me. And I hear things in that house at night. Scurrying little rodent feet. I think I'm losing my mind."

I said it was probably coyotes, not mice.

He stopped juggling, catching both oranges in his palm. "Oh, see? There you go again. Pretending to make me feel better while making me feel worse." He got to his feet, put the oranges on the chair, and came over to me, pulling me into his arms. "C'mon, don't you wanna fuck?"

I had thought he was the prettiest man I'd ever seen, and now I only saw corruption in that beauty. "Are you lying? About seeing her with Joey Alter?"

"Why do you care?" Ian made a face. "Poor Danny. You always want what you can't have, is that it?"

I told him to *shut up* and he laughed. "If you're so curious, yes," he said. "I saw her doing it with Joey with my own two eyes." He pointed at the tent wall. "Made a peephole right over there so I could keep watch and take notes. They were so involved in their *acting*, I had to wonder if that's all it was. I guess Pauly boy did too when he showed up." He shrugged. I hoped he would stop talking so I could digest this unwelcome information, but he kept going. "The old man didn't say a word. I'm guessing his dick shriveled up seeing the girth of that stud's cock—"

He gazed at me with something like pity, which made me want to hurt him. I accused him. *He was a bad friend. He'd set me up. They wanted me to do things that were more than criminal, they were just* wrong. "You should have warned me what I was getting into," I scolded him.

"What are you getting into? Money? A great place to live?" He squinted at me. "Right and wrong don't enter into this, darling Danny. And if it wasn't for me befriending you, teaching you everything you know, you'd still be working for twenty bucks an hour and living in a hovel in the outer boroughs. How about some gratitude for getting you out of your shitty life?" He stood up. Impatient. Jittery. "Are we gonna fuck or not? I'm bored."

When I replied *definitely not*, he complained I was giving him blue balls. Score one for me.

Westerfield staged Sugar's humiliation the morning after he returned, over breakfast in the dining room, and made sure we were all witnesses to it. She was out as Dr. Jekyll and Ms. Hyde and was being replaced by a younger, *more talented* actress. She was instead offered a small role as Veronica, Catherine/Crystelle's mother, a broken-down alcoholic and drug addict. It was a real showcase role. Perfect for her.

Yes, Sugar could try suing him but, in case she had forgotten, he had that "special insurance," and he was willing to use it if she didn't accept his creative decision-making.

Then he walked out with the leather bag he'd packed, and without a single thank-you for her or any of the rest of us, assigning me one final task: to pack the remainder of his belongings and bring them to his house by the end of the day.

She had taken his entire speech without outward emotion but, when the door closed on his departure, she fled upstairs and locked herself in her bedroom. I went up and down all day, knocking and calling to her to let me in, but when she didn't come out by the evening some of us were concerned that she might do herself harm.

"She is *not* going to do any harm to *herself*," Vernon reassured me. "No, we're the ones she's going to suck the life out of." He was on guard duty, insisting she only needed some "rest," whispering that he'd given her a strong sedative because she'd been so upset and she was *really out of it.*

Within a couple of hours of his departure, Westerfield's belongings were all packed and stacked at the front door. I was sent with his things and a handwritten letter from her on rose-scented, monogrammed stationery. The envelope was sealed and I desperately wanted to see what she'd said, but there wasn't time to figure out how to accomplish that. Armen and I drove into the hills in heavy silence.

When we got there, I was surprised that the big man's house was so unassuming. Stark white stucco box with a deeply set, ornately carved front door and an oversized garage.

We unloaded boxes and luggage and Armen rang the doorbell. Finally, a shriveled little man wearing dark slacks and a neat short-sleeved white shirt opened the door, rubbing his eyes like he'd just woken up.

"We have Mr. Westerfield's things," I announced. "Is he home?"

The man shook his head mutely, and we began carrying the stuff inside. When we had everything transferred, I asked if I could leave an important letter for his boss from Miss Bebe Patten, and he showed me to the "study," which was more like an office and screening room combined.

Built-in shelves were filled with books, those ubiquitous paper-bound screenplays covered every surface, and a low-slung leather sectional faced a large entertainment cabinet with oversized projection television. The cabinet doors were left open, showing rows of video tapes. I laid her letter on his desk and followed the little man back through the house.

When I got back, I sneaked upstairs, and when I heard Vernon's voice overlaid with Sugar's I hid in Westerfield's abandoned room until he came out of her bedroom and went back downstairs. Westerfield had left the dinner jacket hanging in the closet. The scent of his sweat hung in the room. Remy and I would have to do a thorough cleaning to get rid of every microbe he'd left behind.

When I was sure Vernon was gone, I went across the hall. Sugar was lying on top of the bed with a blanket tucked around her. She stared listlessly at the ceiling, her eyes glassy from crying, but she sat up when I came in, this sad, hopeful look on her face.

"Did you see him?" She didn't seem completely in control of her limbs, and I thought about those medications with her name on them that I'd seen in Vernon's bathroom. Was he dosing her for her benefit, or to control her?

I told her Westerfield had not been at home when we arrived.

"But you left the letter?" she said anxiously. When I nodded, she fell back, closing her eyes. I took her hand, and she squeezed my fingers so hard it hurt, but I didn't dare take my hand away until she'd fallen asleep.

I woke with a start to loud knocking on my bedroom door and Vernon's muffled voice. "Danvers, it's me. Get up!"

I opened the door and he pushed past me. "Hurry up. She wants you to ride shotgun."

I was blurry with sleep, but he was in a lather of impatience, grabbing my shoes, pressing them into my hands. "Move!" He took in my sweatpants and T-shirt. "You're fine. Let's *go*. I don't want her to leave without you."

Leave? I grabbed an old blue hoodie from the hook in my bathroom and stumbled after Vernon's retreating figure.

In the garage, the rumble of Cherry Baby's motor vibrated in my chest. Vernon pushed me toward the passenger side and went over to the driver's side, leaning his elbows on the window and speaking in a low tone so I couldn't hear what he was saying to her.

When I got in her face was turned toward him. "I'll be fine."

"You be careful, you hear me? Don't kill yourself."

"Yes, daddy," she said.

Vernon frowned, then waved a hand at me. "Good luck!"

She turned to look at me. "Danny's not afraid, are you?"

I shook my head, and Sugar whooped and slammed the car into reverse, burning rubber, before slamming it back into drive. I would have given money to see Vernon's face when she peeled out of there.

Once we were on Patten Lane, she moderated her speed. "Verny's such a killjoy," she said. "Get something on the radio." She pointed to the right-hand knob.

I fiddled with it, her saying, "Not that song!" or "Ew, no!" until we landed on an all-night rock station, and then she said, "Turn it up! It's my song."

55

We drove through sleeping Brentwood while Sugar sang along with a woman singing about honey and pie. I asked where we were going and she jabbed her finger at a passing sign: SANTA MONICA 4 MI.

She slid me a look. "I talked to Joey and he pretended to be surprised about me being fired. But I could tell he was lying. They always cover for each other." She pressed down on the accelerator.

"People lie all the time," I said, holding onto the door handle, and she said, "Especially men," a remark for which I had no argument.

We turned onto Coldwater Canyon Drive and my blood ran cold. I knew immediately where we were going when she made the turn.

"I should have put arsenic in his precious scotch," Sugar said. "That would have been a piece of cake. Why didn't I think of it? We should have brought him a bottle of Daddy's scotch with an extra surprise in it. We could watch him dying, slowly and painfully, for hours. Wouldn't that be fun?"

It wasn't anything worse than thoughts I'd already had, but I said, "They would catch you. Poison is usually a woman's method. And, you have a motive."

"Right." She thought about it. "Okay, what about draining the brake fluid in his car? That could work."

"Do you know how to do that?"

"No. Do you?" She eyed me sidelong, her gaze speculative.

I told her no. Besides, that was risky since he could hurt somebody else in a crash, and it wouldn't be right to cause collateral damage, would it?

"That depends," she said. "How about the old-fashioned way?" She held up her right hand with her pistol finger pointed toward me. "Pow! One shot to the back of the head, execution-style."

"A bloody mess," I said.

"But you could help me clean it up."

I laughed out loud at the image that conjured up. The two of us on our hands and knees covered in blood spray, scrub, scrub, scrubbing away.

"Do you even have a gun?" I said.

"No, but I could get one."

"Forget the gun," I said decisively.

"In the dining room with a candlestick?" she said.

"Too much potential to leave physical evidence. I've seen those shows. Half a fingerprint or one skin cell and you're done for."

"Okay … I've got it!" She took a sharp hairpin turn a little too fast. She glanced over at me. "Scared?"

I admitted I was … a little.

"Good," she said. "A little fear will keep us on our toes."

I asked her what her intention was, once we got to our destination.

"Wait … Here's the perfect plan," she said. "Dissolve a few Ambien tabs in his drink, and when he passes out, drag him into the pool and hold him under till he drowns."

Everybody's seen that movie, I told her. They got caught. She would get caught.

"What movie?" she asked.

She genuinely didn't know, so I told her. "*Diabolique*," I said.

"Ohhh …" She had this puzzled look on her face. "That was Sharon Stone, right?"

That made me smile. I said Simone Signoret was in the original, much better version of the film.

"Who?"

I told her she shouldn't talk this way around anybody other than me, because we both knew we were only kidding around but other people might not.

She waved her hand, dismissing my concern. "Whatever. Whoa …" She slowed the car. "Look for Cordel Trail. That's our turn."

We crept forward now, looking from side to side to spot the turn. "There!" she cried, all malevolent excitement.

I asked again what she was planning. Her smile was chilling. "I'm going to tell him to his face what a scumbag he is," she said. "And we're going to make him give me that tape."

"Tape? What tape?"

"The video of us fucking," she said. "It was supposed to be only that one time. But then he kept doing it because he said watching us doing it helped him … you know, get it up. And I don't know … it was kind of a turn on at first. But now he's got that tape. And he's holding it over my head so he can make his fucking movie with *my* money and some other girl in *my* role." She rolled her neck and gripped the wheel. "If he doesn't give it back, I swear I really will kill him."

56

The right turn off Cordel Trail said *Private Drive*. She took the right and turned off the headlights. At the top of Paul Westerfield's long driveway was the semicircular parking area where I'd been only hours earlier. Two other cars were parked there now: Joey Alter's black Porsche and a tan vintage Volkswagen "bug."

Sugar pulled in and turned off the car. We both looked at the house and listened to Cherry Baby's engine ticking.

"The house doesn't look like much from here, does it?" Sugar said. "But in the back, it's got jetliner views." She got out of the car and slammed the door. "Come on. Now I can tell both of them they aren't making this movie without me."

I was busy wondering how I was going to get her out of there if things turned ugly.

We took a path that led around the side yard of the house. She'd been here enough times to be familiar with the layout. We passed an outdoor kitchen under a modern steel pergola, and as we approached the corner of the house she kept me behind her, taking my hand as we walked together into enemy territory.

But no enemies were in sight. The pool gave off an eerie, wavering green light. Steam rose off the heated water. Without warning, the robot pool cleaner whirred and began its rhythmic circuit. We both registered at the same time a different, and unmistakable, rhythmic moaning coming from inside the cabana on the opposite side of the pool patio.

"Holy shit," Sugar said, her wide silver eyes gleaming.

"Shhh …" I dragged her into the shadow created by the overhang of the roof. "Let's leave now. Before they catch us."

She shook me off. "But I wanna see," she said.

I thought about stopping her, but then I followed her over there.

Westerfield. Joey Alter. A leggy blonde. Three nude bodies dimly illuminated by fairy lights strung above, splayed across a king-size platform bed, busy with each other, oblivious to us watching. A video camera with red "record" light blinking was set up at the end of the bed, capturing the action.

226

I took her arm, pulled her away, and then we ran.

We cruised into Santa Monica along the beachfront promenade with the radio playing a variety of disco hits. Turning into the parking lot of Luigi's Italian restaurant, she slipped the waiting valet her car key wrapped with a hundred-dollar bill. When he told her the kitchen was closed and only the bar was open, she said, "That's fine. We're not hungry."

First, we walked down to the beach and kicked off our shoes to go ankle deep in the receding surf. We didn't say anything, because there was nothing left to say. After a while my feet went numb, so I went and sat down on the sand, watching the water advance and retreat until she joined me a few minutes later.

"I don't know why I'm surprised." Sugar dug her toes into the sand. "He tried to get me to do that … with you and him." She registered my look of horror. "I told him no, obviously. That's when he came up with that whole … improv thing. He wanted to see what you'd do. And I should've said no to that too. I see that now."

It wasn't exactly an apology, but I accepted it as if it were.

She shook her head. "But I never suspected Joey went that way."

I didn't like that she sounded so disappointed.

"I gave that fucker everything," she said bitterly. "I really believed his bullshit promises. He said if I gave him that money he'd give me the chance to show what I could do." She wiped her nose on her sleeve. "I want him to fucking die for what he's done to us."

I had been waiting for Sugar, sitting at that restaurant bar, for twenty-six minutes and roughly eighteen seconds and counting. The bartender and a group of three middle-aged women on the other side of the bar had to be wondering the same thing, given my state of dishevelment: can this loser afford to pay the bill? With drinks starting at twenty bucks a pop, and my wallet left behind, the answer was no, but surely Sugar hadn't just … left me.

The large dining room was deserted and they would soon be closing the bar. I nervously sipped the margarita she'd ordered for me. I had told her tequila was not my friend but she wouldn't believe me. The drink tasted like lemon-flavored gasoline.

I finally made up my mind that I had to figure out where she'd gone off to. As I slid off the barstool Sugar waltzed in from the veranda on the far side of the empty dining room, leaning on the arm of an elegant older man dressed in a well-tailored suit.

I watched her dance up onto her toes to kiss him. The kiss lingered. He was smiling, nodding at what she whispered in his ear.

She hurried over to me then. "Listen, I'm sorry to have to do this, but can you drive Cherry Baby home? You know how to drive, right?"

I was about to refuse, confess that I didn't have a driver's license, but she didn't give me a chance. "Great," she said, patting my arm. "Don't worry, I know you'll be careful with her. The valet will give you directions so you don't get lost. I'll give him another hundred on the way out." Then she laid three one-hundred-dollar bills on the bar top and leaned in to whisper in my ear, "We'll figure out how to get the tape back tomorrow." Her breath tickled as she brushed lips against my cheek. Then she was gone.

57

I had not driven a car in many years, and never a vehicle like Cherry Baby. It took me a minute to get used to the power of her engine, big and muscular. The slightest pressure of my foot against the gas pedal made her leap forward, so I started talking to her out loud and she seemed to listen.

Cruising along the well-lit, middle-of-the-night streets of Santa Monica, I decided Cherry Baby and I were characters in a movie. None of this was real. Not yet. No one knew where I was, and I was going places I'd never been. Unanchored, we floated toward the edge of something, and I steered the car easily on those hairpin turns as Mulholland climbed into the hills.

When I got to the fork at Cordel Trail, I stopped the car and sat for a while. Minutes? An hour? I don't know how long I waited or even what I was waiting for. I felt in a state of suspension. But there was no turning back now. I took the road marked Private.

This time when I pulled into the driveway, the vehicles that had been there earlier were gone and the air was eerily still when I stepped out and eased the car door shut. I followed the path to the back guided by that weird ambient light that bleeds everywhere in Los Angeles. Overhead a faraway jet slid across the sky.

Westerfield stood next to the cabana. I stuck to the shadows and slipped inside the house, unseen.

It took me a couple of minutes to orient myself, since I had only previously entered at the front, but I found the study easily enough. I didn't need to turn on a light once I opened the drapes. I could see that the letter I had delivered for her remained on his desk blotter, unopened and evidently unread.

When I looked up I got quite a shock. Hanging on the wall over his wide desk were two incongruous paintings, side by side. One was a Warhol *Flowers* painting (blue flowers, bright green grass against a black background). The other was Sugar's painting, the one he'd claimed to have sold. The paintings had not been there when I had delivered Sugar's letter. For a mad moment I considered slashing both of them. But the impulse passed and I got down to business.

Using the bottom of my T-shirt as a barrier against incriminating evidence, I opened the entertainment cabinet. The top two rows were VHS tapes, well-known movies going back years, in plain white covers marked with the movie title and *For Your Consideration*. But there, half-hidden behind a stack of papers on the bottom shelf, a cardboard box loosely sealed by a strip of plastic tape with AMATEUR HOUR written across it in red marker.

The box contained smaller videotapes, each marked with letter pairs and dates, as well as a stack of Polaroids showing closeups of various body parts that gave me the impression Westerfield fancied himself an amateur Mapplethorpe. I wished I had the time to look for the Man Ray photograph he'd stolen. I had no doubt it was there, stashed somewhere in the house. But that was another distraction, and the clock was ticking.

I grabbed the only tape marked BP, with dates roughly matching the weeks of his and Sugar's ill-fated affair, and slid it into my pocket. Then I grabbed the whole box, elbowed the cabinet doors closed, snatched the letter off his desk, drew the drapes, and went out.

I remember the way Westerfield looked at me from across the lighted pool. Puzzled. Annoyed, maybe. Those beady eyes amused as well. He lacked the imagination to understand why I was there. To him I represented no threat.

"Oh, terrific," he said in a bored tone. "It's you."

I put the box of videotapes on a nearby chaise longue and walked toward him. He had a drink in his hand and he slurped the dregs as I moved toward him, keeping his eyes on me but calm, unsuspecting. The flagstones around the pool ran to a low wall at the edge of the cliff. Below lay the canyon. The quiet was unnatural. The world was holding its breath.

"What are you doing here?" he said impatiently. "It's late. Does Bebe really think sending you will get me to change my mind?"

I told him Bebe had not sent me.

"Are you here to beg?" he said. "As much as I'd like to see that, I'm immune to that kind of approach." He leered at me and walked away, toward the edge. I closed the gap between us. He turned to face me. "Jesus Christ, girl, what do you want?"

"Do you really want to know?"

He threw me a boyish grin. "Look, Danny … what can I say? Things don't always work out. You need to be tough-skinned to survive in this fucking business. You need discipline. She has none. Surely you recognize that."

He said it in that way mean people do. When they want you to take their side and agree with whatever nasty thing they're saying.

"She's a very confused woman." He shook his head, staring down into his empty glass. When he looked up, he was grinning with those ugly teeth right in my face. "Did you ever ask yourself why she surrounds herself with faggots and dykes?"

I told him he should be more careful with his words.

"Oh yeah? What are you gonna do about it?" He laughed at me. "I'm not telling you anything you don't know. You live there. You know what she's like. And Vernon, pompous little cock blocker. If you ask me, those two deserve each other." He squinted at me. "But you're smart," he said. "I saw that right away. You've got *layers.*"

He was so pleased with himself.

"So tell me I'm wrong," he said. "Bebe Patten is a closet case *drunk* who can't act her way out of a paper bag. She has no friends except for the ones she pays to clean her house." He was angry as if it was my fault he had to say these awful things. "No? Okay … I'll make it real simple so you can run back to that crazy bitch and explain it to her. She doesn't get the part in my movie because *she can't act.* But I gave her a good time and I have the evidence to prove it. Make sure you tell her that. And she still gets a single card credit, which is more than she deserves. Frankly, she needs to stop complaining about how sad her childhood was and grow the fuck up."

He stared at me. The king had spoken. "You're not as smart as you think you are," I told him.

"And neither are you, apparently, or you'd know this is pointless." His smirk was infuriating.

I said fraud was a crime and he ought to be in jail for what he did. He threw his head back and laughed for a while. When he was finished, I said, "I saw the paintings in there. You're a common thief."

His glare said he was tired of me and my shenanigans. "You don't know anything and you can't prove anything either. You're a fuckin' loser. You lick her boots."

"At least I'm not a fuckin' *poser,*" I snapped.

"Go away." He made a shooing motion. "You're boring the shit out of me."

Then he turned his back on me and took a couple steps closer to the edge, hands clasped behind his back. He put a foot up onto the stone wall and struck a pose. The king surveying his kingdom. Answerable to no one.

I cat-stepped over to stand next to him and leaned out to look down. A steep, rocky drop through chaparral and sporadic clumps of seedy lupine.

The bottom, a good forty feet down.

I smiled when I looked over at him.

"What are you doing?" His voice when he said it was sharp, almost as if he was afraid.

"You're not going to make that movie. Your script is shitty," I said. "Everybody knows it. Including you."

He narrowed his eyes. "Coming from you, I'll take that as a compliment." He was swaying, face red from drink.

When I sprang forward, the pool's robot cleaner simultaneously jolted into action, and Westerfield startled. He pivoted, throwing himself off-balance, the empty glass arcing as it flew out of his hand. Realization dawned but it was too late. His arms pinwheeled and he let out a strangled scream as he followed that glass over the edge.

Looking down into the darkness of the canyon floor, I couldn't make out his expression. He didn't make any sound. All I saw was the white of his shirt, and it looked like surrender.

PART THREE

AFTER

1

I thought I would feel something. In the many years since that night, I have wondered if it's an essential malfunction or my greatest strength, this ability to take an irrevocable action and, afterward, understand it as necessary. Even right. Certainly justified. Dr. Kristoffer had told me I should think of my mind as a computer with a chip missing, that it was my duty to learn how not to do certain things. It used to bother me when she'd say that, but I know now she had a point.

I like to think I've used my malfunction primarily in the service of others, but that night I stood at the precipice and I told Paul Westerfield the truth even if he couldn't hear me. Whether or not I'd been instrumental in his mishap, I had no regrets. I thought he should know that. And whatever he might think, I had gone there for myself. If I helped Sugar in the process that was strictly a bonus.

No one saw me when I got back to Patten House and pulled Cherry Baby into the garage. I rehearsed various speeches about how Miss Patten picked up a stranger and went off with him, but didn't have to deliver any lies. No one was in the house. I even knocked on Vernon's door (which was locked), but he didn't answer. I didn't wonder where he was because I didn't care. I went to bed and slept better than I had for weeks.

Vernon had slammed the newspaper down on the counter in front of me. A smiling picture as Westerfield had looked perhaps twenty years earlier and a headline:

PAUL WESTERFIELD FILM DIRECTOR FOUND DEAD

> *Paul Westerfield, known for his 1980s*
> *blockbuster films, has died, the victim*
> *of an apparent accident near his home*
> *today, police said. Westerfield, 67,*
> *was discovered unconscious at 4:26*

> *a.m. presenting with multiple life-*
> *threatening injuries in what appeared*
> *to be an accidental fall at his home in*
> *Los Angeles. A police spokesperson says,*
> *"Mr. Westerfield was critically injured*
> *but still alive when discovered by a*
> *dog walker who notified the police*
> *and rescue services. Although attended*
> *by quick-acting emergency medical*
> *personnel, Mr. Westerfield was then*
> *pronounced dead at the scene."*

"Isn't it convenient?" Vernon crowed.

His cheery attitude grated.

"He saved us all a lot of trouble," Vernon went on. "And dying in such a cinematic way? How perfect is that?" He laughed with delight.

The chime indicated the front gate had opened. "Now who could that be?" he said, though we both assumed it was Sugar.

Vernon went out, prepared for drama, but I stayed there reading the rest of the article, which intimated that the fall may have been due to alcohol intoxication. No mention of any particular injuries or the classic "signs of a struggle." They listed Westerfield's films and accomplishments as well as his interest in collecting modern art, his two ex-wives, and his son who was a lobbyist living in Washington, D.C.

Sugar came into the kitchen trailed by Vernon, who was shooting me looks past her shoulder. I folded the paper and turned it over.

"I saw it already," she said flatly. "I'm fine." Then she threw herself at Vernon and burst into tears.

I let Vernon take her away to lie down. I was exhausted by both of them. Vernon's happiness that Westerfield was permanently out of our lives and Sugar's dramatic outburst of emotion. She hadn't even glanced at me once. Jittery about having to deal with Luchetti and her inevitable, avid interest in Paul Westerfield's untimely death, I escaped out the front door when I saw her Ford Focus pull in at the back.

The previously manicured grounds were suffering from the neglect of the past few weeks. The kitchen garden shriveling from lack of water, the espaliered fruit trees drooping, and the croquet lawn now a spreading area of yellowing grass in spite of illegal sprinklers. Under a sun I had begun to regard as relentless and malevolent, the only plant that continued to thrive was the bougainvillea, climbing everywhere it could reach, its dusty green leaves a backdrop to brilliant vermilion, pale pink, and dead white flowers.

I stood outside the Aerie for some time, drawn there but then unwilling to go inside. He would still be asleep at this hour anyway. Ian was a night-seeking vampire and, for as long as I'd known him, he rarely rose before eleven. I don't know what I expected him to say, but I had come there wanting something like commiseration from somebody who knew me.

I had turned to leave when Vernon came through the gate. I walked over to him. "I was looking for you," he said rather sourly. I asked how Sugar was. "She now claims she was deeply in love," he said. I laughed because it seemed like a bad joke. But Vernon said, "I think playing the part of a bereaved girlfriend entertains her," and lifted an indifferent shoulder. "Ian's gone. In case you're wondering. We thought it would be best if we set him up somewhere more comfortable, with a working toilet."

So Ian had gone without saying goodbye. I didn't like that it hurt to think about that.

"Look, we need to get rid of any trace of Ian inside," Vernon jerked his head toward the crumbling house, "and Westerfield too. You can help."

First, we went upstairs and made sure Ian had left nothing behind. He had missed a single black sock, which Vernon scooped up and shoved into his pocket. Otherwise, we left the room as filthy and abandoned as it must have been before Ian briefly inhabited it.

In the Theater of All Potential, the oranges Ian had been juggling lay on the canvas seat of the director's chair, shriveled and already graying with mold. Westerfield's marked-up script lay on the ground next to the chair, where he'd thrown it in anger that day they'd rehearsed. It seemed like a long time ago.

The table where I'd laid out the drinks and snacks was strewn with animal droppings, rodents attracted by the crumbs we'd left behind. Yet no animals had touched that cracker Sugar had slapped out of Westerfield's hand. It still lay where it had landed.

Vernon swept the rat turds off the table with a handkerchief and turned the table on its side to collapse the legs. I picked up Westerfield's script, tucking it under my arm, and flicked the oranges onto the floor before I folded up the director's chair.

"She wants that script," Vernon said. "Hers is missing the last page and she wants to preserve his *genius*," in air quotes.

We argued over what to do with Westerfield's personalized chair. Why not keep it? Vernon thought it highly amusing to be in possession of that particular dead man's director's chair. It was now a novelty piece. Probably worth serious money. We could sell it on eBay to those idiots who collected Hollywood memorabilia. Over my objection, he hid the chair in the mudroom closet where Sugar would be unlikely to look.

Luchetti was in a tizzy when we came in, her face screwed up as if she were about to cry.

"Oh, thank god," she said, breathless. "Miss Patten's in a bad way. She came down a few minutes ago and she took a bottle of Mr. Paul's favorite drink from the cabinet, but when I offered her a glass for it, she told me …"—she lowered her voice—"she told me to fuck off. And now she's in the great room and she's breaking things."

As punctuation to Luchetti's statement we heard a terrible *crack* and went running toward the sound, crowding each other to see what she'd done. Sugar stood in the center of the room, chest heaving, wearing Westerfield's pit-stained polo shirt, a look of triumph and some twisted form of heartbreak distorting her face. And all around her the broken things.

When she saw us, Sugar's laughter took on an edge that gave me a shiver. She pointed and laughed. Rose Patten's SAG award statuette lay on the floor below a large, spidered fracture in one of the collapsible glass doors. The statuette gently rocked back and forth, one arm gone. We all stood there, frozen in shock, until Sugar turned and marched back toward that shelf of awards to grab something else to throw.

"Stop her!" Luchetti cried.

Vernon sprang back to life and ran to intercept her. They struggled with one of her father's awards until finally she let it go, collapsing at Vernon's feet, weeping dramatically. "None of it matters … none of it means anything … it's over." Her cries turned into piercing, inarticulate screaming.

Luchetti and I exchanged alarmed glances and I approached, though not without some dread. She was like a wild animal, injured and potentially dangerous. Vernon was crouched next to her, holding her, whispering into her two-tone hair. I sat down on her other side and she clutched at my hand and pulled it to her, squeezing my fingers painfully. She howled and howled until her voice gave out. It was an operatic, over-the-top performance but I understood. It wasn't that Westerfield was dead. It was that he'd taken her dream with him.

We finally got her quiet and onto her feet. We brought her into the kitchen, where we sat her by the window while Luchetti brewed tea and set some of her favorite eclairs on a plate. But all of our careful handling only made her start wailing again. Finally Vernon gripped her forearm and said sharply, "Beatrice, you need to calm down. This isn't helping you or anybody. You're going to make yourself ill. Let daddy put you to bed."

She allowed him to take her away.

Luchetti looked at me and said, "I'm getting too old for this shit."

2

Two weeks passed. Two weeks during which I did some soul-searching. I had to admit that I had on some level caused Sugar the extreme pain she was feeling. She had believed she was going to change Westerfield's mind, bully him legally to reinstate her in the leading role. She knew lawyers who could probably make a case that she'd signed those contracts under duress.

But I knew better. Westerfield was never going to change. He would have gone on harming people, just so he could pretend he was still somebody. I wasn't sorry because there was nothing to be sorry for.

He fell.

He died.

Sugar would overcome this and find a new way to be happy. Hadn't Vernon said so himself?

Westerfield's funeral was fairly well attended, we were told. Dressed all in black latex and against Vernon's advice, Sugar made up her face in the Crystelle makeup and went to the nondenominational service held at the Wilshire Country Club.

After the public service, she told us how she strong-armed her way into the limousine with the two ex-wives and Westerfield's son and went to the private graveside service, even though they hadn't invited her. She'd gotten her picture in *The Hollywood Reporter*, a fact that seemed to thrill her.

No matter what persuasion Vernon tried, she refused to take any steps to get her money back from Westerfield's estate, even to call the lawyer, start an inquiry, and *get the process started*. I had to wonder what had happened to the Warhol and her Fini hanging in his office. I should have destroyed those paintings when I had the chance. I was certain the exes and his son had absconded with them, that they'd disappear forever into somebody's private vault.

It drove Vernon crazy when Sugar talked about how much the film meant to her, speculating about buying the rights and producing it herself. She said she'd do it much cheaper if she was on her own. Maybe shoot it on video. People were doing that all the time now. She didn't need to follow the old rules. I encouraged her. Why not?

Finally, Vernon asked me to broach the subject of getting the money back. I told him I would, but I kept managing to put him off, saying I hadn't found the right time yet.

Meanwhile Sugar spent a lot of time in bed, drinking liters of vodka, eating Luchetti's prodigious output of baked goods, and watching junk television. Occasionally I would sit with her so she could talk through her feelings. Sometimes she hated Westerfield. Yet she could appreciate that he'd brought out the best in her performance, despite his cruel methods. He'd given her a chance because he believed in her talent. But he'd also robbed her of her big chance because he was jealous of her talent. It was karmic that he'd fallen off that cliff after what he'd done. How awful it must have been for him, lying there … dying alone. But he deserved to suffer, yes indeed. Her greatest role, the one she was born to play, had been stolen from her. She could have won an Oscar.

We didn't talk about that night when Sugar had left me to my own devices in Santa Monica with the keys to Cherry Baby. At every opportunity I reminded her, casually, not to ever mention our visit to Westerfield's house that night, especially not to Vernon. People wouldn't understand. It could be misconstrued. It wasn't clear how much got absorbed.

She took to sleeping with Westerfield's script next to her, and sometimes she'd read passages from it and analyze his notations in the margins as if she were studying the profound hieroglyphics of a god of cinema. She was still talking about producing, directing, and starring in the film and doing it all herself. She had the whole fantasy planned. She'd dedicate it to him. She'd do it so much better than he ever could have. This film was going to break barriers and prove she was the true scion of the Patten legacy.

Since it was such a touchy subject for Vernon I didn't tell him any of this, and she stopped confiding in Vernon because he was always on her back about the money, the money, the money.

It was an unintended irony that, at least for now, Paul Westerfield was as present as he'd been when he was alive.

We kept the house running. We all did our parts. Vernon rehired the gardeners, and one day soon after, Udo came to the back door for a taste of Luchetti's sweets, casually mentioning when I was in earshot that Alice had left the company to start her own business. I was happy for her. Or I had mixed feelings about it. Alice was moving forward. I wasn't so sure about myself.

Naturally, Vernon was angry about my lack of progress and I was as tired of his nagging as Sugar. One time he went too far. He was harassing her, making it impossible for her to *think*. "Do you even care about me at all? Get out! I can't stand looking at you!" After that Sugar shut Vernon down completely, and his pressure campaign on me ramped up. "Make it happen, Danvers. You're the only one who can."

He didn't know her at all. But I was starting to think I didn't either.

3

I expected to see a man in a brown or gray or blue uniform holding a package and a clipboard when I opened the door. Instead, I was looking into Ian's face. Flashing a strange, toothy smile, he held out a business card for me to take. "Good afternoon," he said.

The baritone was wholly unlike his normal tenor.

"I'm Archer Anson, of Anson and McCoy. I'm here to see Beatrice Patten."

I hesitated.

"Let me in," he said under his breath.

I turned on my heel without taking the card and "Mr. Anson" followed me to the library.

He strolled around the room, looking at the family photos and the shelf of book club bestsellers, while I noted each change in his appearance. He had made himself even taller with lifts in his mirror-shined shoes. His suit was conservatively cut, navy wool with a subtle pinstripe, the shirt snowy white, the tie gray silk, perfectly knotted. Sporting a neatly trimmed goatee and thick dark eyebrows, he'd gotten a spray tan that completely changed his complexion to match the dark brown dye job on his hair and the brown contact lenses to hide his blue eyes. His nails were unpolished and clipped in a square, masculine style and his hair was slicked back from his forehead and held down by a lot of shiny gel. Every bit of it, including the fake grill and square designer glasses, made him look like whoever he was impersonating: rich and superior and unrecognizable as himself. Overall, the disguise was Hollywood-level slick.

He turned and looked at me, amused. "The Pattens' taste in literature is questionable."

"What do you think you're doing?" I said.

In his regular voice, "You're going to tell her I'm here or I'll go upstairs and tell her myself. I know the way."

"You're crazy."

"Do you like my new look?" He straightened his sleeve cuff, unbuttoning his suit coat to adjust the diamond tie pin.

"Who are you supposed to be?"

He held out the card again, a bit impatiently, so I took it. *Archer Anson, Esq. Anson & McCoy, attorneys-at-law.* An address on Wilshire.

"My *father* owns the firm," he said in his other voice. "I'm here to speak with Ms. Patten about an important matter."

I stared at him. His expression was cold. In his real voice he said, "You've been slow-walking this project and now the professionals need to step in. It's not that hard to see, is it, Danny?"

Sugar was listlessly watching some daytime soap opera with the sound turned off. I told her she had a visitor, and when she asked me who it was I handed her the card. She sat up, alarmed.

"Why's he here?" she whispered. "What does he want?"

I wanted to tell her it would be all right, but I couldn't be sure it was going to be. I told her he hadn't told me why he'd come or what he wanted. I asked her if she needed me to help her get ready, and she threw the covers back. "Tell him I'll be down in a minute," she said.

I went back downstairs and met Luchetti waiting for me in the hallway.

"Who's that guy?" she pointed toward the great room where Ian had taken himself, lounging on Westerfield's Scandi sectional, arms outstretched, a serene expression on his face as he looked out on the pool.

I told Luchetti it was a lawyer and she raised her eyebrows. "Wonder what he wants," she said.

Everything. He wants everything.

4

I told Ian Miss Patten would be down shortly and he tried to get me to stay, pretend we were strangers and make small talk, but I left him there to entertain himself while he waited.

Forty-five minutes later, Sugar came down dressed in that black and white Gucci shirt dress, face scrubbed clean, two-tone hair scraped into a high ponytail. She was barefoot.

I came out of the kitchen to intercept her. "He's in the great room," I said and followed her in, waiting by her side as Ian jumped up and walked over, hand extended. The way he introduced himself was a parody. I willed her to see through him.

"You're Karl's son?" she said.

"Hmm. Is there some private place where we could talk?" he asked, with a glance in my direction. He towered over her. She looked at him with a strange mixture of fear and fascination in her eyes.

To me, she said, "We'll be in the library. Can you bring us some refreshments?" To him, "What would you like? Coffee?" She laughed nervously. "I suppose it's too early for cocktails."

Ian chuckled good-naturedly. "I'll have whatever you're having, Ms. Patten."

She glanced at me. "Two Bloody Marys. Thank you, Danny."

He grinned over his shoulder as he ushered her out of the room. "You must look like your mother," she was saying. "I haven't met her."

And he said, "Some people tell me I don't look like either one of my parents."

I brought the cocktails with a plate of salmon toasts Luchetti had whipped up while I mixed the drinks.

I knocked and Ian's "Archer" voice called out, "Come in."

When I opened the door, she was standing at the window behind the desk with her back turned and Ian was leaning against the bookshelf. I set the tray down in the heavy silence. She didn't turn around. I asked if everything

245

was all right.

"Beatrice has had a bit of a shock," Ian said smoothly. "Here …" He picked up her drink and handed it to her. "This should help." She raised the glass to her lips and swallowed half of it as he watched, avoiding looking at either of us. He turned to me. "Danny, is it?"

"It's Danvers," Sugar said.

"Oh, of course," he said, with an amused glance in my direction. "Well, if we need anything else, *Danvers*, we'll let you know." He raised his glass to his lips to hide a triumphant smile.

Ignoring him, I said, "Miss Patten, are you sure you're alright?"

But she didn't reply and Ian reached out and stroked her shoulder. "She'll be fine, won't you, Beatrice?"

They were in there for another hour, and when they emerged she looked shell-shocked from whatever had transpired, and half-drunk from the second Bloody I'd served her. Without a word, she went upstairs while I escorted Ian to the door.

I followed him out, pulling the big door closed behind me. I couldn't risk Luchetti hearing what I had to say. I demanded to know what he'd told her, and he said, "I'm afraid that's a confidential matter between a lawyer and his client." Then he leaned toward me and, in his real voice, whispered, "This is the part of the story where maximum pressure is placed on all the characters. Stay tuned …"

And that was when I knew Ian had been a sham inside a Russian doll of shams. Nothing real there. Nothing left to say.

5

He drove away in a flashy metallic green Audi sedan and I hurried to find her, do damage control if I could. What I didn't expect was to find her in Westerfield's renovated bathroom in the process of butchering her hair with my sewing shears.

I froze in the doorway, eyeing the sharp points of those scissors where she was hacking hanks of hair close to her left cheek. Her approach to the task was haphazard at best, and yet I was secretly pleased she was removing the last traces of Westerfield's influence—and glad I wouldn't have to look at that unnatural platinum hair any longer. She was chopping it Joan of Arc short.

"What?" She paused, looking at me resentfully in the mirror.

I took a step into the bathroom and said softly, "Let me help you."

She laughed bitterly, said, "You can't help me," and continued scissoring away the blonde, dropping the hair into the sink.

"Please. Give me the scissors." I kept my voice gentle, cajoling, the way you'd talk to a skittish wild animal. I knew nothing about hair cutting, but at this rate I worried she'd have to get her entire head shaved if somebody didn't step in to try to fix the mess she was making.

She slammed the scissors down on the counter and glared at me.

"It can't be that bad," I said. "What did he tell you?"

"Conservatorship. That's what he fucking told me," she picked up the scissors again and waved them around. "They're going to put me under a conservatorship. Do you know what that means? Do you?"

"But why?" I asked. "Did he give you a reason?"

"Because of *Paul.* Because I gave *Paul* all that money for the film. And now *Paul's* gone and the money's gone and I hate him. He's dead and I hate him."

I asked her what Westerfield had done with the money, and she snapped, "How the fuck should I know? Probably offshore somewhere since his lawyer swears he doesn't know anything about any ten million dollars. Turns out Westerfield was practically a pauper, up to his eyeballs in debt. And my lawyer is saying since I can't handle my own affairs they'll have to take the reins. That's what this asshole said. *We'll have to take the reins.* There'll be a hearing in front of a judge and they'll make out like I'm some kind of a mental case burning cash in my fire pit. It'll be a horror show. And Junior was so sweet about all of it." Her scissor hand dropped to her side. Her shoulders drooped. "What a prick."

I went over and gently took the scissors from her hand and went behind her to try to fix the back. It was terribly uneven. The blades of the shears would be ruined from cutting hair, but I could always get another pair.

Neither of us spoke while I tried to make sense of what she'd started, then I turned her around and did what I could with the front.

She stared at her reflection when I was finished, turning her head to look at the sides.

"You always surprise me, Danny," she said.

I cornered Vernon in his office before he could even remove his jacket. "What's the problem?" he said.

"You said she'd be fine," I said. "But she's just cut off all her hair. With my sewing scissors. Ian really scared her and now she's punishing herself."

"Oh for god's sake, don't be so dramatic," Vernon said. "You're as bad as she is."

I was desperately trying not to scream at him. "How do you know she won't try to check who Archer Anson is?" I said, forcibly keeping my voice even. "Is there even an Archer Anson at all?"

"She'll do nothing precisely *because* she's scared," he said. "And we need to keep her tied in knots until everything's signed. She'll be fine."

My blood ran cold.

"Listen, our plan is simple. First, we scare the shit out of her with the threat of conservatorship. Next, I offer to become her power of attorney instead. Then I can protect her assets and she'll be free to do whatever as long as she behaves. When it's all set up, we can start diverting money somewhere safe and put the diamond and other valuables into a Swiss safety deposit box. I have a … a friend all lined up to take care of the banking details."

The plan. Their plan. His and Ian's.

"What if I don't want to go along with your plan?" I asked.

He stared at me. "But why wouldn't you? You have everything to gain from it."

"You can't play with her life like that. She's a person, not some cash machine."

"God, you're a hypocrite. Was Paul Westerfield a person when you pushed him off the ledge?"

Regrettably, I had no quick comeback for that.

"I found your little hidey hole, Danvers," Vernon said. "And you didn't even know your collectibles were gone, did you?" His smile was pure spite. "I discovered so many interesting things. And I made sure to handle everything carefully. You know, to preserve any fingerprint evidence. Did you watch any of her sex tape?" He laughed at me. "I did. It was boring. Homemade porn is rarely any good."

He took a deep breath and stood up, rolling his neck. "Let's see … what else did I find? A certain threatening letter from dear demented Bebe to the dead guy. Oh, and her yellow Vera Wang, the leather pants … that lining you cut out of his dinner jacket which, by the way, I also kept. This should be a lesson to you. Don't keep mementoes."

He pulled his door open, a sign that I was being dismissed. "I do have a question, though. That page you tore out of her script. Why'd you do that?" His gaze held a sort of benevolent pity. "I have everything in a safe place. For a rainy day. You can't win, Danvers. But if you go along, at least you won't lose."

That night, while we slept unaware, she took Cherry Baby for one last ride.

But the combined substances in her bloodstream made her extra careless. She hit a guardrail on the Pacific Coast Highway and rolled the car. She emerged from the wreck miraculously unhurt except for a sprained ankle. She was reportedly stone-cold sober, at least according to the bystanders. The breathalyzer the police took at the scene said otherwise.

An officer telephoned in the predawn hours to tell Vernon to come get her. Somehow, after a closed-door meeting with somebody over there who had the clout to arrange such things, they issued her a ticket and a hefty fine as opposed to a DUI citation. I'm assuming somebody received a cash bribe from Vernon, but maybe they were fans of Arthur and Rose Patten's *oeuvre*. It didn't escape my notice that she had sent for Vernon to come get her, not me.

She arrived home limping and chastened, teeth chattering with post-trauma adrenaline and some newly sprouted painful bruising on her abdomen where the seat belt had held her down and saved her life. Despite all of our urgings, she refused to go to the hospital or call her family doctor. Given the circumstances, it was clear that wrecking Cherry Baby would kickstart Vernon's plan.

6

The day after Cherry Baby died, I told her everything, and it happened so naturally it was almost as if I'd understood, at least on a subconscious level, that I was always going to betray Vernon and Ian to save my own skin.

Sugar had risen unusually early given the previous day's events and I was surprised to find her swimming laps when I went into the kitchen to make coffee. I brought out two espressos on a tray. I sipped my coffee and watched her swim, impressed by her underwater turns and effortless stroke, despite her injuries.

While I waited for her I rehearsed possible scenes. I was still undecided whether to take an indirect approach or cut to the heart of it. *They want your money and they're willing to do whatever it takes to get it.*

After another ten minutes of swimming, she hauled herself out of the water onto the flagstone pool deck. She flexed her sore ankle, wincing.

"How does it feel?"

She shrugged. "Are you always up this early?" She got to her feet, limping only slightly. The abdominal bruise had already started to rainbow. She waved away the coffee I offered. "I'm turning over a new leaf, Danny," she said. "No caffeine, no sugar … no more anything *fun*. I'm recommitting to my sobriety, blah blah blah. It'll be good for me, don't you think?"

I told her I was sure that was true.

She put a hand on her hip. "If we're going to be *real*, you shouldn't agree with me just because I say so." She sat down on the lounger and stretched out her legs.

She wanted me to be real. Surely that was the sign I needed. I smoothed my apron over my knees.

"Anyway …" She ran her fingers through what was left of her hair.

She seemed so content that I wavered. I was about to blow up what was left of her life.

Yank the scab off, Marie.

"There's something you need to know," I said.

After I finished laying it all out, she was quiet, but I could see she was making the connections, reframing the meaning of all the signs that she'd missed.

"You should have told me before now," she said, an accusing look in her eyes.

I told her I was sorry. And I meant it.

"It's unbelievable," she said, a note of wonder in her voice. "Do you really think Vernon … I mean, did he really *kill* Paul? Push him? That isn't like him … I feel like he couldn't do something like that."

I said I didn't know for certain but that he'd told me he had her letter. And her tape. How else could he have gotten them?

She nodded. But she seemed unconvinced that Vernon had threatened me to keep me quiet. Injecting into it all the pain and betrayal I was actually feeling, I said softly, "I couldn't be sure what they were capable of. I'm not proud of myself for keeping it from you, but Vernon isn't who you think he is. He's dangerous." I looked down at my lap.

She patted my arm. "No one can ever see that tape."

7

She stayed locked in her room all day, out-waiting every attempt Vernon made to get in. No sweet-talking on his part opened that door. When he expressed worry in front of me and Luchetti, I reminded him that there was no way she would kill herself. Hadn't he said so himself?

He was in a snit after that and went into his office, slamming the door. When Luchetti took a bathroom break I sneaked a listen on the kitchen extension. I wasn't at all surprised to hear Ian's voice on the other end. Their panicked conversation told me that I was now the director of the drama. The actors were in their places and saying their lines with the correct amount of emotion.

A couple of minutes later Vernon emerged wearing his suit jacket, eyebrows knitted into a straight, angry line when he saw me.

"Is your entire job standing around? Why don't you go fucking clean something?" I gave him a cool look and was rewarded with a grunt of frustration. "I'm going out," he said. "Get her out of that goddamn room. We need to get this train rolling. It's on you, if things don't go to plan."

I saluted him, and when his back was turned I flipped him off, which, by sheer accident, Luchetti caught as she returned from her bathroom break.

Vernon slammed the door as he left.

"Wait," Luchetti said, confused. "Now you two are fighting?"

I told her I had to go clean something.

We broke the lock on Vernon's door in order to get it open, but a cashmere scarf wrapped around the business end of the tire iron mitigated some of the damage to the wood framing. The scarf was toast, but Sugar didn't care.

Once inside we worked quickly. Sugar took the closet, searching every shelf, pocket, and shoe, while I rifled through the bedside tables. We each took drawers in the large bureau. By the end we'd scored rolls of cash we didn't have time to count, her letter to Westerfield, Ian's love letters to Vernon, and an envelope containing a durable power of attorney, printed on authentic-looking Anson and McCoy stationery, authorizing Vernon to act on her behalf, completed and ready for her signature. She paused over the yellow dress and the pants he'd stuffed into a plastic bag with the scraps from Westerfield's jacket.

"What the fuck …?" she said, holding up the plastic bag.

I shrugged and told her I'd take care of getting rid of the stuff. She added it to the pile of things on his bed.

"What a creep," she said. "But where's the goddamn tape? That's what we need."

I said it had to be in the bathroom, and when we went in there Sugar was horrified to see her mother's now one-armed statuette decorating the back of the toilet. She snatched it up, holding it protectively under her arm, while I searched the medicine cabinets. When I showed her the array of pills, some of them prescribed for her, she said, "How the hell did he do that? He always told me the pills were his."

When we had looked everywhere in the bathroom and still had not found the tape, I started to wonder if maybe Ian was hiding that piece of crucial evidence. But on the other hand, everything I knew about Vernon told me he wouldn't trust it to Ian, that he'd never allow something that valuable to his plan out of his sight. I went over to the toilet and lifted the lid on the tank. Duct-taped to the porcelain next to the float was a flat, watertight container.

Voila.

I convinced her it would be best for me to be absent when Vernon returned, so when the gate chimed and I saw the Mercedes come up the drive, I walked out the front door as he drove through to the back.

Luchetti later told me the scene between them was pretty epic. She'd never seen Vernon so livid or Miss Patten so heartless.

"It got personal," Luchetti said. "They were screaming insults at each other. He called her a cunt and she called him a criminal. I don't know what the hell is going on here, and I don't like it."

But I did. I loved it. Vernon and Ian were getting everything they deserved. And I was still standing.

After Luchetti left for the day, I was in the kitchen fixing myself a cup of herbal tea when she came in, dressed in jeans and a sweater, a strangely serene look on her face.

I asked if she wanted a cup and she said we could do better than that, pulling a chilled bottle of Veuve Clicquot from the wine fridge and popping the cork. She waved me away when I tried to hand her a glass. She tipped the bottle and took a long pull, letting out a delicate burp as she handed me the bottle.

"Cheers." *Here's mud in your eye, Ian.*

We passed the bottle back and forth for a while.

"Vernon said exactly what you said he would," Sugar said. "He flat out denied having anything to do with Paul. He said you must have gone there, in Cherry Baby. You *did* drive her that night. He said you had way more of a motive to kill Paul than he did."

"None of us liked him," I said quickly.

"But you wouldn't kill somebody. Paul *fell.* He was *drunk.* What a loser."

"Exactly," I said. "The police said so."

"Vernon said it was you that took the dress and the pants, but I told him I was done believing anything he had to say about anything." She traced a pattern on the marble surface of the countertop with her finger. "He had a fit when I wouldn't let him clean out *his* office. But I was like, no way, buster, and I made him give me all of his keys. Then he wanted me to let Armen drive him somewhere." She scoffed. "I said, hell no. You're taking a cab, Verny. And I'm not paying for it."

I grabbed the champagne and took a big swallow. I asked her what Vernon had said about his accomplice.

Sugar laughed. "I told him to tell his boyfriend I never believed for a minute he was a lawyer. Or related to Karl Anson. Oh, he tried playing the victim, going on and on about how devious *you* are. He claimed you were going to say you and I planned it together and that I was the one who, you know … pushed Paul. He was only trying to stop you by taking the tape and hiding it. Insane, right?"

I couldn't get my mouth to work. My thoughts tumbled over each other. Bloody scotch and snatched embraces on the sly, the feel of her skin against my cheek … the look of pity in Alice's face and disapproval in Luchetti's … Becker's broken fingers. A man falling off a cliff. And that uncanny silence. Nothing real or true can survive in that kind of an environment.

"What a desperate little man," Sugar said.

I wanted more than champagne. I needed something to knock me all the way out.

"Are you okay?" she said.

I nodded dumbly.

And then she said, "By the way, I'll be going away for a while. I booked a vacation in the Alps. Switzerland this time. Their spas are fabulous. Doesn't that sound delicious? You'll stay here and look after things for me."

8

Dai Vernon was the last person I was expecting to see coming out of the CVS on San Vicente.

We eyed each other. He looked disheveled, like he used to on Sunday mornings after a particularly hard-drinking weekend. I was conscious of him noticing the highlights she suggested I add to my hair, the chic sweater, the "it" jeans, and my new velvet ballet flats (all going-away gifts, with love and kisses).

I said it was good to see him, proud that my voice was level, letting him know he didn't intimidate me.

But Vernon plowed past the niceties, fixed me with a hard stare. "I knew it had to be you who screwed the plan," he said. "But Ian's the one you should be afraid of. Not me."

"I'm not afraid," I smirked and stepped around him.

"Driving yourself?" he said, scurrying to keep up with me. "Where's Armen?"

I said Armen would be gone in two days' time. He'd gotten a job driving for some executive at Warner Brothers.

"Luchetti?"

I stopped, facing him. "Look, what's your point? What do you want me to say? I won."

His face got that thunderous look that used to scare me. "Let's have a chat," he said. "I'll buy you a—whatever you want. Serious offer. I just want to talk."

So I agreed to go with him to the pizza place across the street, where he requested a table in the back and a vodka, neat. I ordered an iced tea.

"Do you have any idea what you've done?" he said.

I asked if that was a rhetorical question and he said he really wanted to know if I was aware of the consequences of my actions, so I said, "I saved the princess."

He chuckled with genuine amusement. "Okay, Danvers, okay."

The drinks came and he gulped half his shot, then put the glass down and twirled it with one hand. "We're coming after you," he said softly. "And don't doubt … we're going to get what we came here for."

I considered him over the rim of my iced tea before gently setting it down. "It's over, Vernon," I said. "Give it up."

"Oh, Danvers … this is *not* over. You are *not* safe. Bebe Patten is *not* saved." He paused, making sure he had my attention. "Do you understand what I'm saying? Ian and I … we can be your best friends, generous to a fault … or we can decide you're in our way. You don't want to be in our way."

I told him he was full of shit and he gave me a look like he was sorry for me. I suggested he and Ian go find a new victim. I said he couldn't possibly think he was ever going to get back in her good graces. If he did he was delusional.

"No," he shook his head. "Delusional is thinking you can get away with murder."

I didn't even give him the satisfaction of a blink.

He smiled tightly and swallowed the rest of his drink. When he held out his hand it caught me off guard, but I shook it.

"Well, good luck to you." He stood up. "See you soon." Then he left.

I threw cash on the table to cover the drinks and followed him, but when I emerged from the restaurant the usually clear sky was spitting rain and Vernon had vanished.

There had been so much to do to get Sugar ready for her trip and I'd been overwhelmed by what needed to happen. Without Vernon everything fell to me, and I kept screwing things up, yet she was so patient those last few days.

Sugar had needed special documents because she had decided to stay for a while, take French and Italian lessons with a private tutor there. She was considering a run at the European film industry, breezily telling me she might never come back. I'd spent hours on the telephone with the secretaries at Anson and McCoy and the secretaries at the consulates and the customer service agents at the travel agency. I went to bed anxious that I'd forgotten something important and woke up anxious for the same reason.

But, the day before she left, her papers finally arrived via Karl Anson. I remember that jolt of recognition. He was the same man she had gone off with that night in Santa Monica when I was left with Cherry Baby and my fateful decision.

They sat side by side in the great room, his arm across the back of the couch, hand occasionally dropping paternally onto her shoulder. Whatever they were discussing required lowered voices, and whenever I entered the room to refill their sparkling water or ask if they needed anything, they'd go quiet, politely waiting until I left the room before resuming their conversation.

When he left they shook hands. All very formal, without a hint of the warmth they'd demonstrated on that other night, a lifetime ago.

I dreaded saying goodbye. My future was bleak. I would eventually go quietly insane.

While Armen carried her luggage out to be loaded into the car, I went upstairs to let her know the car was out front. She stood at the three-way mirror in her dressing room, putting the final touches on her makeup.

Together we had chosen the chunky-knit oatmeal cowl-neck sweater and navy slacks. She'd added the diamond solitaire necklace and an oversized pair of Versace sunglasses. With her newly styled short hair, she looked *tres chic*, and I told her she looked like Jean Seberg in *Breathless*, but she'd never seen that movie so she didn't really get the compliment.

She slipped the lipstick into the Chloe bag she'd chosen to carry on and said, "Come here," pulling me into her arms. "Kiss me goodbye, Danny."

I put into that kiss everything I couldn't say. But she was weightless. Already gone. And she drove away as she always did, without waving goodbye.

9

It was only me now, and I was a ghost. Armen had gone on to his new gig, Luchetti had been given leave with pay, and Sugar had simply let Remy go. Sometimes I heard things, at night. I slept with my door locked.

Though nothing really needed to be done, I scrubbed and vacuumed daily. It helped me banish the sickening swirl of my own thoughts, the repetitive replaying of scenes and the various ways I could have altered the trajectory of fate that had brought me to this lonely dead end.

Walking helped. Sometimes I even ventured down Patten Lane to the main road. But, even when I took that back path to the Aerie, I didn't go past the gate. I was afraid terrible things would happen to me if I did. Or maybe it was the nightmare I kept having about a spinning wagon wheel and Ian's corpse in a refrigerator.

Ian called me on the third day of my isolation. He was going back to New York. He and Vernon had gone their separate ways.

I wanted to believe him, so I agreed to meet at Beverly Gardens Park at three in the afternoon. A public place, in daylight, with other people around, seemed like the safest bet. Just in case Vernon wasn't lying.

I dressed carefully in clothes pulled from her closet, a pair of D and G pants in soft gray gabardine and a Tom Ford teal blouse with a pointed collar. Teal was our color, Sugar's and mine. At the last minute I punched in the code to retrieve that gold collar from her jewelry safe. I wore it as a shield against disaster.

We chose a bench in the shade. Ian looked me over appreciatively. "You look … *rich*, Danny," he said.

"And you look like yourself again," I said.

He shoved a hand through his Afghan-hound streaky hair. There was a new hint of gray under the streaks like he'd aged since I'd last seen him.

"So, you didn't bring Vernon along?" I said. "Or is he hiding in the bushes waiting to ambush me?"

"I told you, he's gone." He seemed sad. Sincerely sad.

I told him all the things Vernon had said. "He said you wanted to kill me."

Ian was unperturbed. "Vernon was angry after it all went down. With you and me. We had words. He blamed me. It was your fault. And her fault. Everybody's fault but his own." He sighed. "You don't have to worry."

"That is some whitewashing," I said. "You were my friend. You manipulated and used me. You don't get to play hero."

I was afraid to look at his face, afraid of what I might see there, afraid of what I might do if I saw it. I focused on his elegant hands, folded on his knees.

"I was the one who got you fired," he said.

I was struggling to catch up and I asked him what he was talking about.

He smiled. "I want you to know that I was the one. Calista Whitaker didn't have a clue. I heard she was upset that you left like that. Without even saying a tender goodbye." His tone mocked me.

I stared at his face, seeing the cruelty and ugliness that must have always been there, and yet my mind still refused to accept that he would have done that. I denied it to myself and to him. No, that can't be true.

"You always seem to fall for the wrong woman," he said. "We can't escape who we are, Danny."

I sat there for a long time after Ian left. Even when fog clears, you can still find it impossible to see.

When I got back to the house there was a black Mercedes in the driveway and Karl Anson was standing at the doorway. He turned to watch me park the Land Rover, and before I got out I took off the necklace and slid it into my pocket.

He lifted a hand in greeting. "Let's go inside, shall we?"

"Of course," I said and punched my code into the keypad, a new security precaution. I swung open the big door for him and followed him inside.

He paused in the foyer, then we went through to the great room.

"We should sit down," he said.

Something was coming. I could see it in the way he held himself, shoulders rigid when he reached into his inner jacket pocket and held out an envelope.

For Danvers was written on it in Sugar's handwriting.

"Don't open that yet," he said when I took it from him. "First, I have been instructed to thank you for your service to Patten House. Even though you haven't been here long, Miss Patten appreciates that you made significant and lasting improvements that will surely help the housekeeper who will be replacing you."

I was being let go.

"Miss Patten feels that she needs a fresh start," he said.

I fingered the envelope.

"That envelope contains your severance check. Miss Patten wanted to make sure you had a bit of a cushion to start again. Maybe you'll return to the East Coast."

It sounded like a suggestion. Karl Anson stood up then, clearly relieved and anxious to be gone.

I stayed where I was, that unopened envelope on my lap.

"You have until tomorrow morning to pack your things and vacate the premises," he said. "We'll have someone drive you wherever you'd like to go so you don't have to worry about a taxi."

He said a few more meaningless things I didn't listen to. When he was gone, I slid my finger under the flap and gave myself a vicious paper cut, which was a bit of over-the-top karma.

The check was for one month's salary.

And there was a letter.

> *Dear Danny,*
> *I've had a lot of time to think and I realize your obsession with me is unhealthy. You built up something in your mind that never existed and I should never have allowed you to take advantage of my good nature. You should also know that as far as PW is concerned, I <u>never wanted</u> <u>that outcome</u>. But I have destroyed the tape. You're welcome. Please don't ever contact me again. I won't answer.*
>
> *Good luck,*
> *B*

10

Some people don't know the meaning of the word *friend*. I try to live up to my own high expectations of what that word means, but those people simply don't have any concept of what it means to give and receive love. Ian. Sugar. Both had double-crossed me in the end.

But it wasn't Sugar's lack of gratitude. It wasn't her decision to cast me out because she couldn't face her own demons. It wasn't even her inability to acknowledge her own guilt. No. Sugar wanted to have the last word, but I wasn't going to let her have it. She didn't deserve that. So I left behind a message where I knew she'd find it, tucked into a particular pink handbag I had no more use for. Then I walked out of that cursed glass house for the last time, a little after seven-thirty the next morning.

My driver was a sixty-ish woman named Susie who wore a shapeless sundress and a lot of lip gloss below a fringe of iron gray hair. Her cheery attitude got on my nerves, so I made a point of answering monosyllabically until she gave up trying to make conversation and turned up the music.

I tried not to play reruns while I watched Los Angeles stream past the car window. This wasn't the time for that. Now was about resetting. If nothing else I had learned transferable skills and indelible lessons from my time at Patten House. I would get over Sugar Callahan as soon as possible. I would put myself first. I would rise from these ashes.

The address was located in an unfamiliar neighborhood and it took almost an hour to get there because of the inevitable L.A. traffic. When the car stopped, I gave the driver a twenty-dollar tip and she helped me get my two bags out of the car. Then she said, "Good luck, hon," like she knew I'd need it and drove off.

I was facing one of those typical apartment complexes you see all over the city, always named something like Villa Vista or Canyon View, the words spelled out in neon script, the building itself a bit worn but tidy, with balconies and a central courtyard, sometimes a fountain recycling water into a half-hearted spray. I picked up my suitcase and walked through the archway, looking for what I hoped would be lucky apartment number 7.

I confronted the door, lightheaded with fear, but finally managed to make myself raise my fist and knock. An agonizing couple of minutes, then the door opened and Alice stood there, a cup of coffee in one hand and puzzled expectation on her face. She looked at me, then at my suitcases.

I said, "Can I come in?"

Dear B,
Go on lying to yourself, but we both know you're the one who's obsessed, with <u>me</u>. I will haunt your dreams.

You'll never be able to forget me.
D

EPILOGUE

Manderley

Manderley is so much more than I could have anticipated, and when Oscar finally stops the car I am at a loss for words.

"All right, ma'am?" Oscar catches my eye and smiles encouragement in the rearview. He hops out of the car as the front door opens.

Rebecca and Maxim de Winter emerge from that grand doorway. They're holding hands. The Perfect Couple. He's wearing off-white flannel trousers, an impeccably tailored, open-throated linen shirt under a woolen argyle vest, coarse graying hair immaculately combed back off a high forehead. Older than she, but handsome in a weathered way. She's wearing well-fitted slacks and a gorgeous tweed jacket over a low-cut silk blouse. Her long hair is plaited into a careless braid that decorates one shoulder.

De Winter beats Oscar to the car door, opening it, peering in, his white-tooth smile wide and welcoming.

"Mrs. Danvers!" he says. "I've heard so much about you. How wonderful to finally meet you."

I step out of the car as Mrs. de Winter glides toward me, regal and cat-like, a coy smile playing around her lips as she holds out her hand. The touch of her fingers, the warmth of her palm against mine, is an immediate electric communication.

"Mrs. Danvers, I'm *so* pleased to meet you in person instead of on a computer screen." She gives a little delighted laugh. "Won't you come inside? You must be exhausted but hopefully not too much so. I do hope you enjoyed your journey across little old England."

She's talking fast, nervously fingering that braid. She turns to de Winter. "Darling, drinks on the terrace? Yes? Oscar, please bring Mrs. Danvers's luggage to her room." She links her arm with mine, leaning into me like we're already chums. "I'll give you the tour," she says.

After I'm shown the most important bits, as she puts it, we end in my new suite where my luggage, having been delivered, awaits unpacking. The room is furnished with style and comfort in mind and boasts lovely west-facing windows with a view of the river. It has a large, private en suite bath. The towels are embroidered with her monogram in a modern script: *CRdW.*

We stand together by the window, looking out on the river. The landscape is breathtaking. The weight is lifting. That was then, and now I'm alive again.

She looks pleased when I hand her the flat box wrapped in iridescent white paper and tied with a gold bow.

"What's this?"

I tell her it's a special gift.

"Shall I open it now?"

We look at each other—the thrilling *reality* of me being there—as she unties the bow and carefully unwraps the box. She opens it, looks down. A sharp gasp. "Ohhh," she says. "This is …" She holds up the gold choker chain, weighs it in her palm. "It's too much, Danny. This must have cost a fortune."

I like the way it looks in her hand, but I want to see it on her so I tell her how I knew it would be the perfect gift. I reach to take it so I can place it around her neck, but she holds the necklace away from me, puts it back in the box, flustered. The box goes into the pocket of her jacket and she steps away, goes over to sit on the edge of my bed.

"You really shouldn't have," she says, bouncing up and down a little. "It's a new mattress. Why don't you come try it?"

So I do. And I push her back onto that new mattress. We slide easily into each other's arms. It's what we've waited for. That first kiss is so soft and sweet. Then she rolls me onto my back, climbs onto me, her braid brushing my cheek. She looks into me and sees what I can't say. She kisses me again, and it's the first time I've ever been kissed with such ferocious need. She's ravenous. I gladly give her back everything she's hungry for.

I've already forgotten everything except the sensation that is her flesh-and-blood presence. The weight of her on top of me and the way our bodies fit together. The scent of her hair. Floral, musky. The way the hollow of her throat pulses when I press my lips to it. When she goes up on her elbow, I take the end of her braid into my mouth and she giggles. I undo the top button of her blouse, then the second … but she stops me as I'm unbuttoning the last, before I can slip my hand inside.

"Not now, Danny. I'm on a leash, remember? We need to go downstairs. He'll be expecting us."

So we sit up and I help her button the shirt back up, even while I try to tempt her to give in by kissing her while I do it. The tip of her nose, her lips, again that pulse point in her throat. But there's an undeniable shift in her attention.

"I was a brat," she says.

"And I was a coward," I say.

"We let them come between us."

"And we don't have to do that any longer," I tell her.

She tells me she wants to be the last thing I think of when I go to sleep.

I want to ask her something ... or rather, I want to ask her so many things. But I don't know where to start and that's okay because we have time. I'm here to stay.

"It feels like a dream, doesn't it?" she says.

"If so, we're dreaming it together." I stand up because I want to kiss her again, put my arms around her and pull her back to the bed ... but her phone interrupts. "It's Max. He wants to know why it's taking so long." She looks up, distracted, that nervousness returning. "Come down when you're ready, okay?"

Before she leaves, she hands me back the box with the necklace inside. I'm to keep it safe. It would be difficult explaining such an extravagant gift to Max. "I'll wear it only for you, dearest Danny," she says.

Cal. I speak her name, as if saying it will keep her with me a few precious seconds longer.

Her eyes widen and she lays her index finger against her lips before she slips away, closing the door behind her.

ACKNOWLEDGMENTS

It has taken years—and many thousands of words written and discarded, and written and discarded—for Mrs. Danvers to show herself to me. But finally, here she is in all of her queer, flawed glory. Thank you to Daphne du Maurier for creating a character so indelible that the mere mention of her name conjures mystery and strikes fear in the hearts of naive brides.

I want to thank Betsy Carson for her incredible stores of patience with a very impatient writer, and her razor-sharp ability to point with unerring accuracy where I veered off course in the characterizations. Also eternal gratitude for the many times she helped me find the scene I needed in order to bring a cohesive story to the page.

Deepest gratitude is also owed to Joan Adler for being my bestie and number one fan. Having such a close and eager reader standing by to read multiple drafts from start to finish was absolutely invaluable. And I couldn't ask for a more ardent defender of even Danny's most egregious actions.

Thank you to Danielle Winston for being with me every step of the way, cheering me on and believing in this story.

Thanks also to Jen Dupree for encouraging me to keep calm and carry on in my most discouraged moments.

My dear friend Reggie Burrows Hodges believed in me and offered financial support at a critical moment. For that support and especially for his friendship, I am forever thankful.

Thank you to my beta readers Tasha Judson, Gio Bellonci, Peter Bellonci and Kari Wagner who all encouraged me to keep going while offering perspectives I hadn't considered.

Thanks also to Sarah Holland, Leah Gage and Connie-Marie Puckett for their encouragement when this story was still an embryo being workshopped in our writing group.

Many thanks to Amy Chamberlain for proofreading the manuscript and catching important last-minute errors and omissions. And, finally, utmost gratitude to Molly McGrath and her team at Pink Eraser Press who have made the book look great.